THE CATCH

SHARI LOW & ROSS KING

Boldwood

First published in Great Britain in 2023 by Boldwood Books Ltd.

Copyright © Shari Low and Ross King, 2023

Cover Design by Alice Moore Design

Cover Photography: Shutterstock

The moral right of Shari Low and Ross King to be identified as the authors of this work has been asserted in accordance with the Copyright, Designs and Patents Act 1988.

All rights reserved. No part of this book may be reproduced in any form or by any electronic or mechanical means, including information storage and retrieval systems, without written permission from the author, except for the use of brief quotations in a book review.

This book is a work of fiction and, except in the case of historical fact, any resemblance to actual persons, living or dead, is purely coincidental.

Every effort has been made to obtain the necessary permissions with reference to copyright material, both illustrative and quoted. We apologise for any omissions in this respect and will be pleased to make the appropriate acknowledgements in any future edition.

A CIP catalogue record for this book is available from the British Library.

Paperback ISBN 978-1-80426-780-6

Large Print ISBN 978-1-80426-779-0

Hardback ISBN 978-1-80426-781-3

Ebook ISBN 978-1-80426-777-6

Kindle ISBN 978-1-80426-778-3

Audio CD ISBN 978-1-80426-786-8

MP3 CD ISBN 978-1-80426-785-1

Digital audio download ISBN 978-1-80426-782-0

Boldwood Books Ltd
23 Bowerdean Street
London SW6 3TN
www.boldwoodbooks.com

ABOUT THE AUTHORS...

When a budding radio DJ and actor, met a young nightclub manager in Glasgow in the late 1980s, little did they know that over thirty years and thousands of miles later they would still be friends.

Los Angeles-based Ross King MBE is a four-time News Emmy award-winning TV and radio host, actor, producer, writer, voice over artist and performer. King has starred in London's West End, appeared in over ten movies and hosted TV shows in the UK, Europe, USA and Australia. He has also presented countless radio shows and pens a Sunday newspaper column. In 2018 he received an MBE from the Queen for services to Broadcasting, the Arts and Charity.

Best-selling author Shari Low released her first book in 2001. Since then, she has published over thirty novels, selling over two million books world-wide, including the recent hits *One Summer Sunrise* and *One Last Day Of Summer*. Shari splits her time between Glasgow and Los Angeles, and wherever she is, she's probably writing the next chapter of a book.

Visit Ross's website at www.rossking.com
Visit Shari's website at www.sharilow.com

*From Ross – For David Johnston King and Isabel King, my heroes, my pals and my 'Pops and Wee Bella'. Forever in my heart.
And for the best sister in the world, Elaine, and the family, Jim, Hollie and Euan.*

*From Shari – For Betty Murphy, a woman whose strength, love and substance live on in the ones she left behind. We miss you every day.
And for my love, John, and our family, who are everything, always.*

INTRODUCTION

Have you read *The Rise*, the first book in the Hollywood trilogy?

If not, don't worry, we've got it all covered right here.

Here's what you need to know from *The Rise*...

Mirren McLean, Davie Johnston and Zander Leith – three Hollywood superstars who grew up together in a tough housing estate in Glasgow.

Back then, Mirren's mother, Marilyn, was the mistress of Zander's father, a violent gangster called Jono Leith.

Neglected, living in poverty, the three youngsters were inseparable, the family that they chose for themselves.

Until the unthinkable happened.

Jono Leith raped seventeen-year-old Mirren and her mother killed him. Not because Marilyn was protecting her daughter, but because she was consumed with jealousy that Jono had touched another woman.

Desperate to escape the horror of what had just happened, the three youngsters covered it up, burying Jono's body under the shed in Davie's garden.

Marilyn disappeared into the wind, and the world thought Jono had gone to ground to avoid rival gangsters. He wasn't missed.

That could have been the end of it. Case closed.

However, as a way to process the trauma, Mirren wrote the story of what happened and against all odds, it found its way to a Hollywood producer, Wes Lomax.

He turned Mirren's words into a movie, *The Brutal Circle*, a cult hit that unexpectedly became a box office smash, winning Mirren, Davie and Zander an Oscar for Best Original Screenplay.

The whole world believed it was fiction and the success brought brand new Hollywood lives for the three Scots.

But fame and fortune came at a price.

The shame and pain of finding success by capitalising on the worst moment in their lives, drove the three of them apart. They didn't speak for twenty years, until a young journalist from Scotland, Sarah McKenzie, began digging into their past.

Eventually, Sarah discovered the truth about what happened to Jono Leith, but by then it was too late. She'd fallen in love with Davie Johnston and killed the story to protect him.

Along the way, the ghosts of the past brought the hope of resolution.

Sarah's investigation forced Mirren, Davie and Zander to reconnect, twenty years after they'd walked away from each other.

It hasn't been easy. The pain is still there. Mirren's mother has been dead to her all these years. Davie's discovery that Jono Leith was his father too has been hard to digest. And Zander's demons from his childhood still push him towards a bottle.

But they're trying.

Because in the City of Angels, everyone is chasing the fairy-tale ending.

THE HOLLYWOOD CAST

Mirren's World

Mirren McLean: Born and raised in Glasgow, now a major Hollywood player, best-selling author, Oscar winning screenwriter, director and producer of the iconic Clansman movies.

Jack Gore: Mirren's ex-husband of almost two decades, movie producer turned mid-life crisis cliché.

Chloe Gore: Mirren's daughter, wild child, addict, troubled soul. Died last year from an overdose, aged 18.

Logan Gore: Mirren's son, lead guitarist and singer in South City, the band that's on the walls of teenagers across the globe.

Marilyn McLean: Mirren's mother, last seen on the day she murdered her lover, Jono Leith.

Lou Cole: Mirren's best friend of twenty years, journalist, gossip queen, and editor of the Hollywood Post.

Perry Scholl: Mirren's long-time lawyer and friend.

Brad Bernson: A trusted private investigator who doesn't ask questions, but always finds answers.

Lex Callaghan: Movie star, plays the lead role in *The Clansman* but shuns the limelight when he's off-screen.

Cara Callaghan: Lex's wife, a Native American beauty who runs an equine therapy centre at their fifteen-hundred-acre ranch in Santa Barbara.

Deeko: the manager of South City. Keeps the band members Logan, Jonell, Ringo, Lincoln and D'Arby in check.

Davie's World

Davie Johnston: multi-millionaire presenter/host and producer of some of the biggest reality hits on American television.

Jenny Rico: Davie's ex-wife, lead actress on hit TV cop show, Streets Of Power.

Darcy Jay: Jenny Rico's partner both on and off screen.

Bella and Bray: Davie and Jenny's 8 year old, red-haired twins, stars of the sitcom, *Family Three*.

Ena Johnston: Davie's mother and keeper of his secrets.

Cal Wolfe: Davie's ruthless, sharp-suited agent. A moral vacuum in a world where all that matters is power and profit.

Mark Bock: Davie's straight-shooting head of security.

Drego and Alina: Davie's loyal gardener/driver and his tempestuous housekeeper.

Mellie Santos – the mildly terrifying, caustic producer on *Here's Davie* and *American Stars*.

Lainey Anders and Princess: country legend and obnoxious pop sensation, the other judges on *American Stars*.

Lauren Finney: singer, songwriter, presenter, winner of *American Stars*. Under Davie's guidance, she's gone from being a small-town girl with a high-school sweetheart, to being one of the most popular young stars on television.

Carmella Cass and Jizzo: stars of Davie's hit show, *Beauty and the Beats*.

Zander's World

Zander Leith: icon, actor, all-action hero and star of the Dunhill movie franchise. Also loner, addict, and no stranger to uninvited violence, rehab and jail cells.

Jono Leith: Zander's father, Glasgow gangster, and one of the most evil bastards to ever walk the earth.

Maggie Leith: Zander's faithful, abused and battered mother, who believes that the answer to everything is prayer.

Hollie Callan: Zander's personal assistant, right hand woman, and unfailingly loyal, smart-mouthed friend.

Adrianna Guilloti: Founder of the eponymous luxury menswear brand, Zander's lover and latest addiction.

Carlton Farnsworth: – Adrianna's husband. New York millionaire property developer, shadier than the trees in Central Park.

Raymo Cash: reality star, pond life.

Don Michael Domas, actor, Lee Vandan, male model, Josh Wilson, script writer – Zander's surfing and poker buddies.

Wes Lomax: Legendary studio head, with a sexual appetite that's as ferocious as his temper.

John Wood: Lomax head of security.

Sarah's World

Sarah McKenzie: Journalist from Glasgow. Came to LA to investigate rumours about Davie, Zander and Mirren's past lives, but fell in love with Davie Johnston.

Ed McCallum: Sarah's former boss and editor of *The Daily Scot*.

Manny Murphy: Glasgow crime boss, now deceased, the source of the stories about Jono Leith, his disappearance and his link to Zander.

Myla Rivera: TV news reporter.

PROLOGUE

THE LOMAX OSCAR AFTER-PARTY, BEVERLY HILLS HEIGHTS HOTEL, 2014

'Hollywood' – Michael Bublé

It wasn't your typical Hollywood threesome. No one could take their eyes off them.

All night the official photographers had been firing flashes like strobes in their direction.

The managers, the PRs and the agents who'd kill to have them on their client lists would need a chiropractor to sort out the neck pain caused by keeping them within view no matter which part of the room they moved to. Even the A-list movie stars who demanded all the oxygen in the room, the ones who'd thought of nothing but themselves since their cheap Sunday-best shoes first hit Hollywood tarmac, were fascinated by the trio, who had been inseparable all evening.

Zander Leith. Mirren McLean. Davie Johnston. The actor. The writer. The producer.

Individually they were people to be reckoned with, stellar forces that were circled by lesser beings in an industry that prized profit, power, beauty and talent. In that order. But together they were Hollywood royalty

– three childhood friends from Glasgow, Scotland who had won their first Oscar when they were barely in their twenties. Two decades later, they still had the kind of three-in-a-billion careers that others would kill for. They had history, they had a unique connection, and they all shared the knowledge that the very event that created their success could one day bury them.

But not tonight.

Tonight, on the most hallowed of Hollywood occasions, the ballroom at the Beverly Hills Heights Hotel was a glittering collection of industry stars and heroes past and present, of $10,000 suits, beauty queens and billionaires, all gathered at the invitation of Wes Lomax, studio owner and – when it came to making movies – more powerful than God.

There were three other big events in town on that balmy March night in 2014: the *Vanity Fair* party, Elton John's AIDS Foundation benefit and, of course, the Governor's Ball. But it said everything about the power and status of Lomax that the tickets everyone wanted would gain them exclusive entry to his celebration, where they could breathe in the most rarefied atmosphere of all. And if they didn't get access? Better to leave the country, feign illness or find another career, because if they weren't seen here, it said they either weren't big enough or they were over – and those were the two Hollywood crimes that could never be forgiven.

The walls were solid masses of flowers, banks of ornate white roses and lilies rising from floor to ceiling. The chandeliers were glittering crowns on a room filled with jewels, haute couture and enough silicon to fill a valley.

It was manufactured perfection. And it didn't come any more perfect than the trio at the centre of the star-filled galaxy.

A hundred and ten pounds of former Miss Alabama sashayed past Zander and smiled.

'Can I get you anything, Mr Leith?' Her low purr oozed promise, an offer that replicated a million others over the course of his twenty years as the most messed-up but utterly irresistible bad boy of the movie world.

Most of the women in the room would fail a polygraph if they claimed they'd never thought about having a night of passion with Zander Leith. He was the nation's go-to action hero, the Hollywood personification of sheer down-and-dirty, give-it-to-me-now sex, his physical perfection made all the more attractive because he was totally unaware that when the gorgeous woman at the next table looked at him, all she saw was her next orgasm.

Zander acknowledged Miss Alabama's offer with a smile that said 'gentle refusal'.

Not because any of the rumours swirling about his relationship status were true. He'd been linked in the press to everyone from his PA, Hollie, to Madonna.

Tonight he was off the market because he was only here for the beautiful woman beside him in the exquisite blush Dior gown, her Titian curls swept up to emphasize her perfect bone structure, her eyes the same deep shade as the sapphires that glistened in her ears. Mirren's wide smile didn't waver as she shared the love with everyone she spoke to, paying grateful thanks to an industry that had just given her yet another small, gold, naked but genital-free statue, this time for original screenplay on the new *Clansman* box office smash. *Clansman* was Mirren McLean's baby. She'd written twelve novels featuring the Scottish hero, penned scripts for five of them, and nailed down a studio deal that now allowed her to direct and produce her own movies.

Her power in this town had grown with every dollar of the hundred million plus that each one had earned at the box office.

'Hey, don't let me stop you,' Mirren murmured, having caught both the blatant offer and the subtle refusal in her peripheral vision. Zander's green eyes crinkled at the side as he returned her smile and Mirren realised she'd never seen him looking this good. The months off booze and drugs had been good for him, as had the training regime for his next movie, the seventh in the Dunhill spy series. There was no danger of a Bond-like scenario in which the leading man was replaced every few years.

Zander still had it.

A couple of inches over six feet, he had the craggy good looks, the action-hero jawline, which contrasted with a disarming grin that made even the staunchest resolve crumble. His blond hair, naturally wavy, curled over the collar of his shirt, a captivating contrast to the formality of his Tom Ford suit.

On the other side of Mirren, Davie Johnston leaned into the centre of the triumvirate and joked in hushed, serious tones. 'She only gave you that come-on because I'd knocked her back.' They laughed, the irony not lost on any of them. On any other day, Davie Johnston was a catch. Multi-millionaire producer, a serious power player and physically cute. Yep, cute. Tom Cruise-short, Bradley Cooper curls, Michael J. Fox grin, Simon Cowell ego – all of which was elevated to 'A-list desirability' by the fact that he was Davie Johnston, the man who could turn any nobody into a star.

'Oh fuck, ex-wife at nine o'clock,' Davie muttered. 'Brace yourselves for incoming hostility.' The others immediately went to movie-star DEFCON 1 – wide smiles, utterly fake but convincing, designed to disarm the two approaching females. Jenny Rico, Davie's ex-wife, tall, dark-haired goddess, star of the crime drama *Streets of Power*, holding hands with her co-star on the show and co-recipient of the hottest woman on earth award, Darcy Jay.

Sadly for Davie, what had started off as an occasional threesome had ended in a permanent coupling for the two women. Penis not required. It was a relief when the ambush was halted by a drum roll emitting from the speakers at the front of the room. The overhead lights dimmed, allowing two spotlights to focus on Wes Lomax, a sixty-something deity, who was deigning to address the crowd, fully aware that half the room were devotees who worshipped at his temple of power and the other half despised him. Welcome to Hollywood.

A hush descended.

'Ladies and gentlemen, I'd like to say a few words.' His smug grin enhanced by the combination of attention and the growing sensation inside his Gucci trousers, caused by the Viagra he'd popped an hour before. 'I'd like to congratulate all you guys out there who were winners tonight. Even the ones who weren't in my movies.'

Cue sycophantic laughter from the audience.

'... and it was a great night for Lomax. Best Movie...' He paused to wait for the obligatory cheer. 'Best Supporting actor and actress...'

Another round of congratulatory adulation.

'And finally, the pinnacle of excellence, Best Producer...'

More applause as the flush of his face made an even stronger contrast to his thick mane of impeccably coiffed white hair.

'But tonight, another member of the Lomax family is going home with the gold. A returning member. Many years ago, Lomax Films gave this lady her first break. Over the last two decades I've tried to persuade her to come back home, but, well, she played hard to get. And you all know how well I deal with rejection.'

His faux self-deprecating grin set off another round of amused, exaggerated laughs.

'Ladies and gentlemen, I'd like to announce a new partnership. Tonight, Mirren McLean, author, director, producer and Oscar winner for the second time for Best Original Screenplay, will be rejoining Lomax Films and will make the next two *Clansman* movies here... Where she belongs.'

The vibrations from the thunderous applause made the trays of champagne glasses on the bar tremble. Mirren, smiling widely, nodded her thanks to her peers, then blew a kiss to the beaming man on the stage.

Davie Johnston's breath was hot in her ear as he whispered, 'Did you know he was gonna do that?'

Still grinning at the flashing camera bulbs, Mirren barely moved her lips. 'Not a clue,' she hissed. 'Ink's barely bloody dry.'

Zander leaned in for a congratulatory kiss. 'You OK?'

Still smiling, Mirren squeezed his arm. 'I am... But I'll love you forever if you get me out of here.'

It was all she had to say.

They knew. The three of them shared a silent language that they'd learned as children back in Glasgow. A glance. A nod. A frown. They knew each other inside out, and they knew it all: what they'd risked, what they'd shared and what they'd done to get here. Only they knew that their real story would blow their high-action thrillers and epic dramas out of the water.

It took them an hour to work their way to the exit, doing the standard shake-and-fake, pressing flesh and saying all the right things along the way – even if it was utterly insincere.

'I'll call you tomorrow, Marti. Yep, we gotta get something in the pipeline.'

'Leo, you were sensational. I'm a huge fan.'

'Will, you're too kind. Of course, it's the *Clansman* team that deserve this, not me.'

When they finally made it outside, it was nudging 2 a.m., but there was still a crowd of paparazzi and fans behind the cordons on the other side of the street. An explosion of flashes heralded their arrival. Still on show, keep smiling.

Mirren spoke to the valet. 'The McLean limo, please.'

At the same moment, one of the other valets grinned at Davie. 'Mr Johnston, your car is on the way. I radioed ahead for it.'

Davie shook his hand in thanks, leaving a hundred-dollar bill on the man's palm.

'Bunking off so soon?'

For the first time tonight, Mirren's smile was genuine as she turned to see Lex Callaghan, the handsome star of her *Clansman* movies, a protective arm slung casually around the shoulders of his wife, Cara.

Mirren embraced them both. 'Babe, you get more gorgeous every day,' she told Cara. It felt like the first real thing she'd said all night. Cara was stunning – Native American roots had given her long, dark hair that fell in soft waves to the small of her back and required no adornment other than the sprinkling of ruby flowers around her left ear. Her face was perfection, with high cheekbones and a full mouth that softened her slate-grey eyes, which held far more compassion and wisdom than anyone Mirren knew. This was a rare trip off the Santa Barbara ranch for Cara, who preferred to shun the limelight and concentrate on running her equine therapy centre for those damaged by drugs, alcohol or any of life's cruelties.

It made Mirren's heart soar to see Cara with Lex, the heart-thudding, butch leading man in both their lives. For Mirren, it was purely professional. Since the moment he'd walked into the casting office a decade before, he'd been her *Clansman*, the Highland hero who defended lands and honour in sixteenth-century Scotland in five consecutive movies.

But when he left the set, he was all Cara's. He eschewed the celebrity circuit and banalities of fame, and headed home to the wife he adored. They had a true love story. They'd been together since they were sixteen and he'd once told Mirren he had never doubted for a moment that he and Cara had mated for life.

It was more than a happy ending. It was hope for all of them. 'I'm dragging him away, Mirren, sorry.' They both knew that Cara's words were in jest. Lex hated these staged events and Mirren had to coax him into coming along to occasions that millions would give anything to attend. He'd accepted his invitation to tonight's ceremony an hour before the deadline, and only then because Mirren had threatened – jokingly – to replace him with Hugh Jackman in *Clansman 6*.

The flashes and the audible excitement on the other side of the road still permeated the air. The spectators would be dining out on this for months and the paps would already be spending the pay cheque they'd get for these shots. McLean, Johnston, Leith and Callaghan shooting the breeze – cash in the bank for the photographer who got the best image.

Davie's Bentley slid round the corner and came to a stop in front of him. Not that he'd driven here himself. Oh no. No one drove to the Oscars. He'd sent the driver away when they arrived at the Lomax ball, deciding to stick to just a couple of drinks and then chauffeur himself home. Sometimes he just liked to drive alone late at night. Clear his head. Think things through. And right now, he had a lot to think about. Immediately behind the Bentley, Mirren and Zander's car slid into position. One of the valets stopped speaking into a walkie-talkie and sighed. Shit. How come he had to be the one to deliver bad news? 'Mr Callaghan, I'm afraid your limo will be another ten minutes – it's just manoeuvring out of the gridlock at the end of the drive.'

'Told you we should have brought a horse,' Lex quipped to the group. Another pay cheque for the pap who caught the spontaneous laughter.

'Jump in with us and we'll give you a lift,' Mirren immediately offered.

Lex put his hand up to protest, but Cara stopped him. 'Callaghan, don't you dare refuse. You're not standing here in six-inch heels that have left you with no feeling in your feet for the last hour.'

'But we're heading north,' Lex stated. 'Opposite direction from you guys.'

Davie stepped forward with the obvious solution, addressing Mirren and Zander. 'Why don't you two come with me and I'll drop you home? If you behave, we'll get drive-through,' he joked.

Mirren nodded. 'Sounds like a plan.' She turned back to Lex and Cara. 'And then you guys can just take our limo. Wes Lomax is paying for it, so be sure to clock up the miles.'

'I've always wanted to go to Tijuana,' Cara shrugged, laughing. Mirren giggled, then suddenly realised that it was a long time since she'd heard that noise coming from her lips. She didn't even care that by dawn the snaps of Zander's arm around her shoulders would have the world speculating that they were a couple. By lunchtime they'd be engaged, and by supper she'd be pregnant with his twins.

Kisses, hugs and handshakes were exchanged, before Lex and Cara headed to the limo, while Mirren, Zander and Davie stepped towards the Bentley, thanking the valet, who had the doors open and waiting for them. Zander gestured to Mirren to take the front passenger seat.

The buzz across the street ramped up a notch as the paps fought to shoot off a last image and the civilian spectators screeched down their phones to their friends, describing the star-studded scene in front of them, desperately seizing a moment of reflected glory just by their proximity to a group of strangers they felt they knew intimately.

Only one stood utterly still, eyes trained forward, face impassive.

Lex and Cara entered the limo, and the doors closed. Davie joked about his new career as a chauffeur as he pulled on his seatbelt in the Bentley.

Zander sighed with relief that he'd got through a night without slipping a waiter a hundred dollars to procure him a bottle of Jack Daniel's.

Mirren gathered the hem of her blush-coloured gown as she stepped into her seat, grateful that a night that had come with immeasurable risk was over without incident. They'd done it. Made it through.

Behind them, the limo driver restarted his engine.

Davie put his foot on the gas, heard a cry, looked around. A woman running towards him, clutching a bag, pulling something from it.

He froze.

Neither car moved, yet there was an earth-trembling bang. A blinding flash. The ripping of metal. Screams.

In a split second their world exploded.

Then all that was left was a deafening silence.

In that devastating instant, one heart stopped beating.

And then another.

1

SIRENS AND SCREAMS

Live Report Breaking News – Los Angeles

'I'm Myla Rivera, live here on CXY 5, coming to you from the Lomax Academy Awards after party, as we bring you the horrific breaking news that there has been an explosion outside the Beverly Hills Heights Hotel. The incident happened as the stars celebrated the biggest night of awards season. Details are sketchy right now, but I can tell you that there are reports of casualties, and police are looking at the possibility of a terrorist attack, with claims that this could be the work of a suicide bomber.'

2

DAVIE JOHNSTON

Two Months Earlier Los Angeles, Jan 2014

'Uptown Funk' – Mark Ronson & Bruno Mars

'OK, Davie, final soundcheck and then we're ready to go.'

The voice in his ear was female, warm and professional, right up until the moment it barked, 'And stop fucking rearranging your balls. You did it twice in rehearsals. Middle America will have a stroke if you do that live on air.'

Davie grinned as he gave the camera in front of him the finger, eliciting a raucous chuckle in his earpiece.

Mellie Santos was a notorious pain in the ass, brutally honest, toe-curlingly impolite and a self-proclaimed ill-tempered bitch, but she had been his first choice for producer and director of his new talk show, *Here's Davie Johnston*, because she was the best.

This was uncharted waters for him. After years of producing reality-TV hits, he was stepping in front of the camera again, but this time without a script.

But the biggest twist? It was all going to be live.

Fuck it, if he was going to do it, he might as well do it with a risk factor that made his aforementioned balls retreat into his body in fear.

Live. It was crazy. Insane. The only other talk show that went out in real time was *The Elaine Show*, but that dealt with the risky unpredictability by sticking to the fluffy stuff: stars plugging their own movies, or spinning a good news story aimed at winning hearts.

That wasn't what Davie was after.

For the last decade he'd been the most successful producer of reality shows in the nation and now he had three in the top ten.

The Dream Machine was a sentimental slushfest that made ordinary people's wishes come true and left the viewing nation sobbing into their Saturday-night pizzas.

Then there was *Beauty and the Beats*, a fly-on-the-wall show following the lives of Carmella Cass, an eccentric, explosive supermodel and Jizzo Stacks, an ageing rock god. A monster ratings hit, it was currently sitting in the number two position in the ratings.

Of course, *American Stars* was still number-one prime-time gold, giving a smug V-sign of triumph to the runners-up, *The Voice* and *American Idol*. His production company owned the rights, so it added several zeros to his bank balance every year. For the first few seasons, he'd presented the show, but a blip of crap publicity last year had seen him dropped from the screen. Giving the network the final say on who presented it probably hadn't been his best move. At the first sign of trouble, they'd dumped him without hesitation.

Last year, his marriage had imploded, he'd faced a landslide of negative press, and he'd had more rocky career moments than Sylvester Stallone.

The fickle world of fame had given him a metaphorical kicking.

But that was then, and things could flip on a dime in Tinseltown.

After a few lucky breaks, a major public redemption campaign, and plenty of carefully pre-planned, deliberately choreographed humility for the cameras, he was on fire yet again, and, man, he deserved it.

He was back on the current series of *American Stars* as a judge, airing

Tuesday nights, and he'd be on the screen from Wednesday through to Sunday with *Here's Davie Johnston*. And the cherry on top, the confirmation that all his sins had been forgiven, was the announcement that he'd been booked to co-present the Oscars in two month's time.

World domination was just around the corner.

Mellie's voice was barking instructions in his ear again. 'OK, Davie, are you ready? Cutting to camera one. Jenny and Darcy are in the wings. People, listen up and don't fuck up. Just don't dare. We're going live in ten, nine, eight...'

A cramping sensation took hold in his stomach, while an irrepressible grin hijacked his face. This was it. The network had trailed this show to death, and the advertised guests would have viewers clicking on in their millions.

It helped that there was a bit of strategic cross-pollination.

The first half of the show was finally going to deliver the interview the TV fans of the world had been waiting for: Davie Johnston, his ex-wife, Jenny Rico, and her current lover, Darcy Jay.

The second half was switching it up, with Jizzo Stacks and Carmella Cass, the stars of *Beauty and the Beats*. With any luck, they'd have stopped on the way to do a few lines and a bottle of Jack, and they'd be as messed up and unpredictable as always. Viewers lapped that stuff up. Those two were the more outrageous versions of the Osbournes. Think love children of Oliver Reed and Joan Rivers. On steroids. After a three-day bender. Davie adjusted his shirt collar – pale blue, no tie; it was the outfit that had scored highest with the test audiences. The lights in the studio dimmed and a ripple of anticipation ran through the audience.

This was it.

Three, two, one and cue the announcer's bellow of 'Heeeeeeeeeeeere's Davie Johnston!'

The spotlights flooded the stage, then settled on Davie, standing front and centre against a midnight backdrop of stars. To his left, Cain Canning fronted his band, singing a funked-up soul hit that had been top of the Billboard chart for the last week. None of the standard, cop-out, houseband crap for this show. Davie wanted stars. Stars playing the opening, stars on the sofa, stars begging him for screen time. Whatever it took, he was going to make this the one show no one wanted to miss. And he wanted the two Jimmys, Fallon and Kimmel, to form a posse and kill for his ratings.

Cute grin, feigned modesty, gracious acceptance of applause. 'Thank you. Thank you. Thank you. Welcome to the show.'

More thunderous applause. The warm-up guy had them practically jumping off their chairs – a plus-factor in getting them up on their feet for the mandatory standing ovation. They liked those in this town. A waiter making a great job of reciting the specials could get a whole room on its feet.

Davie rolled straight into the introductions: another stipulation when they were planning the show. There were to be no self-serving, ego-stroking, bullshit opening monologue. Let's face it, nobody cared. No one wanted to listen to some overpaid host telling shit jokes his writing team had spent three days coming up with. Nope, straight into the action.

'And here tonight, my first two guests... And incidentally, the fee for this appearance will be deducted from this month's alimony cheque...'

The laughter was loud and genuine.

'Please welcome the stars of the sexiest cop show on TV, my beautiful ex-wife, Jenny Rico, and her gorgeous partner, on and off screen, Darcy Jay!'

With flair, elan and a beaming smile, he stepped to the side, right arm stretched to welcome his first guests. He could see Jenny, just off stage, smoothing down the front of her leather trousers and adjusting her cleavage to the point of voluminous perfection. Darcy was dressed in a more tailored style, in black crêpe pencil trousers and a tuxedo jacket that fastened with one button over what looked like a naked torso. He could absolutely see why this woman turned his wife on.

The roar of the audience escalated to fever pitch as the three of them met and hugged like one big happy family. Which they were. One big happy, bitchy, malicious, back-biting family.

The truth was, he wanted them on the show premiere, but they needed it as much as he did. Since they'd gone public with their relationship, the reaction had been lukewarm, and ratings had wobbled on *Streets of Power*.

Puritanical Middle America, the god-fearing lot who kept a Bible on the nightstand and a rifle under the bed, didn't approve. So tonight was about softening the backlash and letting the world see that all parties were cool with the new arrangement.

Sure, it was also for killer ratings, but in truth, he'd been equally as crap in their ten-year marriage as Jenny, so he owed her this favour. And even if he didn't, she had him by the balls over access to the kids, so right now he'd strut across the stage wearing bells dangling from the very same balls if it was part of the deal.

Darcy and Jenny waved at the audience, then settled on the cream leather sofa, close enough to suggest intimacy for the voyeurs, but conscious to ensure their body language towards Davie was open and friendly.

It was a consummate performance. An onlooker would never guess that his ex-wife thought he was a dickhead and her partner didn't disagree.

In reality, relations between them were about as taught as the faces in a Beverly Hills post-surgery recovery room. He was the first to admit he'd been a poor father to their twins, Bella and Bray, eight-year-old stars of the weekly sitcom *Family Three*. When they'd all lived under one roof, he'd made no time for them, was barely part of their lives. But he was trying to make it up to them now.

'Welcome, welcome!' he gushed, inciting another rousing cheer from the audience.

As soon as the two women sat down, he cut right to the chase. 'So shall we clear up a few of the details about the journey to this point?' He had to make a conscious effort not to roll his eyes. Why did everything have to be a bloody journey? It wasn't a two-day road trip with a stop off at a spa. The truth was that their perfect Hollywood marriage had been a sham for years.

But instead of saying any of this, he found himself nodding as Jenny and Darcy gave the world an elaborately manufactured, agreed version of events. Jenny's marriage to Davie had been wonderful, but when she found herself attracted to Darcy, her co-star on *Streets of Power*, they'd all sat down, discussed it maturely and decided to follow their hearts. No, there had never been a moment of animosity; yes, the children had fully adapted to their new life, and, of course, they were going to be co-parents and best friends forever.

That one earned more enthusiastic audience approval. 'Jesus, Davie, can you stop this Mills and Boon shit before I vomit?' Mellie said in his ear. For a split second Davie considered telling the truth. Yep, that would send tomorrow's catch-up figures into the fricking stratosphere. Here were Darcy and Jenny, flaunting their new-found devotion and carefully omitting the fact that they'd first hooked up more than seven years ago, when the three of them got wasted on the opening night of *Streets of Power* and then went on to spend the next twelve hours indulging in three-way hedonism at Chateau Marmont. Between orgasms, he thought he'd died and gone to porn heaven that night. Instead, he'd boarded the train to Splitsville.

But hey, he wasn't bitter.

He'd kept the $40-million Bel Air home, the cars, more money than he could spend in a lifetime and... His eyes drifted to the auburn-haired babe right beside camera 2. The 'journey' via Splitsville had also led him to Sarah Mckenzie. A Scottish journalist. A fierce brain. And his official 'monogamous friends with benefits' relationship.

'OK, Davie, wind it up. Two minutes to ad break, and we'll have to bring Jizzo on while we're off air. The fucker is so wasted he can barely walk straight.'

The audience took Davie's smile to be just a warm, tender reaction to Jenny and Darcy's well-rehearsed bullshit. Their benevolence might waver if they knew he was actually close to punching the air with delight. Yes! Jizzo plus wasted equalled TV sensation. Look, he'd never professed to own a space on the moral high ground.

He signalled to Jenny that it was time to go for the big ending and she caught it immediately. They may have hated each other's guts by the end of the marriage, but they could always read what the other one was thinking.

'I just want to thank Davie,' Jenny was saying now, facing the audience while gesturing in his direction. He'd specifically insisted that the front row be filled with gorgeous creatures, and two of them cooed, 'Aaaaah,' as Jenny spoke. Davie really hoped Jenny was watching them, and not noticing Sarah making retching gestures twenty feet to the left.

'He absolutely accepted my decision and my sexuality...' Oh dear god, she was turning on the tears, the movie-star sobs that made her utterly mesmerizing as a single drop ran down her ski-slope cheekbone. '... and he's just been the best friend and the best father ever.' She looked at Darcy, then back at her ex-husband. 'We love him. And we know he loves us too.'

What a pile of crap. Davie leaned over and put his hand on hers as he nodded. 'I always will, babe. We're family. All three of us. And on that happy note –' he looked straight down camera 2 '– stay with us. We'll be right back.'

Cain and his band burst into song, the lights went up, and – always aware that someone might have smuggled a phone past security – the star ex-couple kept huge grins on their faces as they hugged goodbye.

Only when Jenny was in close did she whisper in his ear, 'Your girlfriend's a bitch.' Ah, so she'd seen Sarah's nauseated verdict on proceedings.

Gently, he broke away, his smile still beaming. 'We always did have so much in common.' Then turning to Darcy, 'Bye, honey. It's been a blast.'

His mischievous gloat was cut short by a commotion in the wings. Jizzo Stacks was singing 'Delilah' as he careered off the set partition, a song that gave a better reflection of his age than his much-lifted face.

Over twenty visits to the cosmetic surgeon's table, daily gym workouts and a 1980s rock weave had left him looking slightly weird, but a good two decades younger than his sixty-year-old self. Then there were the vitamin shots, the only legal drugs in a cocktail of steroids (for his workouts), blow (to relax), amphetamines (to get his rocks off) and coke (to get high). The man was a walking pharmacy, but at least he was walking with a supermodel by his side. Carmella Cass, six feet tall, tumbling blonde waves, *Sports Illustrated* cover girl three years in a row and, according to endless polls in men's mags - the owner of the best pair of natural breasts in North America. The woman was glorious, the Elle Macpherson of the new millennium, with a beach body that somehow developed despite the fact she grew up on Cheetos in a trailer park in Detroit. Davie was never sure if their coupling was real or just a great premise for a TV show. The nation was split in its opinion on the romance-showmance debate, but millions still tuned in weekly to watch an incredibly wealthy man, who should be counting down to retirement, drink tequila shots from a glass wedged in his twenty-five-year-old girlfriend's cleavage.

'Davie baby!' Jizzo roared when he set eyes on the man who was technically his boss. Lurching forward, he was only saved from performing a Jack Daniel's touchdown by the quick reflexes of two floor managers and Mellie, who was currently holding him up by the weave.

'If this comes off, I swear to God I'll have nightmares for life,' she muttered. 'OK, get him on the sofa.'

The liquor had been removed, and the founding member of Leather Pants Anonymous had been parked, cowhide first, on the sofa, when Carmella wandered on to join him.

'Sorry – had to pee,' she announced, immediately drawing everyone within earshot's attention to the white denim daisy dukes that barely covered her butt cheeks. Making eye contact, Davie could see she was pretty wasted too, but Carmella covered it well – her speech was lucid, her eyes bright, and she was only slightly on the frenetic side of animated.

Perfect. He and Mellie had already discussed the subjects he planned to cover tonight – Jizzo and Carmella's relationship, sex and, of course, their show. He also had a dozen questions prepared in his mind if the interview dried up, but with the two of them this well-oiled, there was no chance of that happening.

He just wanted them to be their normal wild selves, and let a couple of bombshells slip, and they'd be viral on social media within the hour. #heresdaviejohnston #jizzostacks #itakemyteethoutbeforesex

The ludicrous thought made Davie smile... then peer at Jizzo's teeth.

Mellie was making her way back to the gallery now, while cueing up the second half of the show. 'OK, people, ten seconds to the kind of carnage that could end our careers. Six, five, four...'

Davie adjusted his shirt collar again, thanked the make-up girl – what was her name? Zoe? Zane? Zelda? Christ, he was fairly sure they'd hooked up a few years ago when she'd first arrived to work for him – and decided on his opening line. The key was to ask a perfectly innocent question, but one that he knew Jizzo would give an outrageous answer to.

He decided to ask Jizzo to share his favourite thing about Carmella.

Any other guy would look at his partner lovingly, before going for eyes, soul or heart. That's because any other guy would lie through his teeth. But not Jizzo. Davie knew he'd had way too many drinks from the liquor bottle of truth.

Out of the corner of his eye, Davie saw the make-up girl – Zoe, Zelda, Zane – glance at Jizzo and then root herself to the spot. The audience saw her reaction as well. Thankfully, they were too far away to realise that the reason for it was the tiny ring of white powder round Jizzo's right nostril.

Instantly, Davie was out his chair, leaning over, disguising his actions as a man-hug while using the cuff of his shirt to dust off the evidence from the guest's nasal cavity.

'Davie, what the fuck?' Mellie roared, before continuing, 'Two, one... And we're back. I think I've just aged ten fricking years.'

Davie zoned her out as he made the intros, with Jizzo leaning over to give him a high five and Carmella blowing him a kiss, before waving at the audience. Every man out there sat a little higher in his chair, puffed his chest out a little more and wished he'd stuck with that band he'd joined at school.

'Guys, you know I love you both,' Davie started, eliciting another kiss from Carmella. 'And the show is great.'

'Yeah!' yelled Jizzo, punching the air, while nodding to an invisible beat from inside his head.

'Oh my God, we, like, love doing it.' Carmella leaned forward, her breasts threatening to escape the white tank she clearly wore with no bra.

'I think the most fascinating thing for us viewers...' Davie went on, completely ignoring the fact that he was more than just a 'viewer'. As creator and producer, the royalties from this month's *Beauty and the Beats* alone would allow him to buy a new beach house in Hawaii. '... is the incredible connection and love between the two of you. Jizzo, I know it's a tough choice, but what do you adore most about the beautiful Carmella?'

Fist pump over, the rock god stared at the white crocodile cowboy boots – with disguised lifts – that protruded from the bottoms of his black leather jeans.

Davie paused to let him answer, aware that the substances coursing through his veins were probably causing the pharmaceutical equivalent of a satellite delay.

Only when the silence became uncomfortable did Davie cajole, 'So come on, Jizzo, don't be coy here.'

Still nothing.

Had he fallen asleep? Oh fuck, he had. He was actually sleeping.

In the gallery, Mellie spotted it too. 'Holy shit, what's with this guy? Cut to Carmella. Cut to Carmella! Davie, you have to pull this back!' she barked.

Davie was about to do exactly as she asked when Jizzo's head slumped to the side. Was this a wind-up? He wanted outrageous; he wanted wild; he wanted action that the whole world would be talking about the next day.

At no point did he want to see a guest pass out on the sofa. Aware that he was live and he'd be judged by the actions he took in the next moment, he ignored Mellie and instead leaned over and touched Jizzo's arm. 'Hey, man, are you OK?' That was it. Tender. Caring. Human. Real. If tomorrow's press used any of those adjectives, he'd be happy. They were definitely preferable to 'heartless bastard'.

Jizzo didn't move for a few seconds, not even a flicker; then events took a turn that Davie struggled to process.

Jizzo's whole body sagged to the side; his mouth fell open; his eyes stayed shut.

'Wake him up! wake him up,' Mellie was hissing now.

But Davie wasn't listening. He'd seen this before, knew what it looked like, even though it was so out of context he just couldn't absorb it.

For once, the consummate performer forgot where he was. His next urgent words went out to the watching world and would be repeated in articles, in videos, in conversations for hours, days, weeks and months to come.

'Get medics in here now. I think Jizzo just died.'

3

MIRREN MCLEAN

'Wish You Were Here' – Pink Floyd

Mirren McLean glanced around the antique burr-walnut board-room table and realised that all eyes were on her. It was the movie-industry equivalent of the Last Supper. Twelve suits, at least half of them playing the role of Judas, all waiting expectantly for an answer to a question that she wasn't even sure she remembered.

Focus. Come on, focus.

She pulled back into the moment. Contracts. That's what they'd been talking about. OK, contracts. Renewals.

'Ladies and gentlemen, with all due respect, I believe you people are tasked with negotiating and shaping the deal, then giving me the relevant information to make informed decisions. I don't yet feel I have that.' Direct words, spoken calmly. Tantrums and diva strops had never been her thing.

Two of the assembled started to speak over each other and she put her hand up to shush them both.

'Perry, you shoot first. Summarize it for us,' she said, nodding to Perry Scholl, the lawyer she'd recruited out of a tiny office in Santa Monica to negotiate the very first *Clansman* deal a decade before. Several movies later, the partnership had reaped unprecedented profit, and the arrangement had been a fruitful one for both sides.

Perry put down her Mont Blanc pen – a Christmas gift from Mirren after *Clansman 3* broke box-office records – and exhaled. 'OK, so the situation is this. Pictor want to do a deal for the next two *Clansman* movies, but they want to squeeze us on terms—'

'I hardly think "squeezing" is an apt description,' interjected Euan Stoker, the newly appointed chief legal suit for Pictor. There had been a top-level clear-out at the studio only a few months before and the new head guy, an all-out corporate action man called Mike Feechan, had brought in his own people to several of the top posts.

'Sorry, I was being polite,' Perry conceded sweetly. 'Do you prefer "bend us over and fuck us on terms"?'

As Stoker's eyes widened, Mirren fought to contain a smile. She'd seen Perry's innocent charm work in the past, lulling the opposition into a false sense of security before she dealt a killer blow.

Mirren shot her a look that told her to ease off. It wasn't time for hostilities yet. She still had a deep sense that she owed Pictor a measure of loyalty. The first two of Mirren's bestselling *Clansman* novels had been made into films by a Pictor team, with Mirren as writer. The epic tales of a warrior in ancient Scotland had been phenomenal hits, surpassing expectations and selling across the globe. But Mirren wanted more than a writing credit. When she'd boldly told them she wanted to direct and produce the third, they'd taken a chance on her and it had paid off. The box office had grown 20 per cent with every movie; merchandise added the cherry on top, making the studio billions and putting Mirren into the exclusive club of the very richest and most powerful producer-directors. And that was on top of the global sales she achieved with the books on which the movies were based. *Clansman* was an international phenomenon, a world-beating brand, and it was all hers, thanks to her unusual combination of skills: creativity, a razor-sharp business brain and balls of steel. Not to mention a small, hand-picked team who were unfailingly loyal.

The edge of her Aspinal of London moleskin notebook glowed, telling her that the screen was lighting up on the iPhone that was tucked underneath it. She surreptitiously checked it and saw that it was an alarm she'd set earlier to remind her when this had taken enough of her day. It was time to leave this lot to duke it out.

'Ladies and gentlemen, I'm afraid I have another appointment. In my absence, Perry has full authority to speak for me.' The dark eyes of her lawyer gave her a glance that was a mixture of pride, thanks and conspiracy, with just a hint of surprise.

Mirren had never bailed out on a business meeting as important as this one before. Of course, they all understood. That was the thing about grief. About the need to be alone. About the feeling that time was too precious to waste it where you didn't want to be. Eventually, life was supposed to get back to normal after a piece of your heart was crushed, but she knew now that it never would. All she could do was to spend as much time as possible in places she wanted to be, with people she wanted to be with, and that wasn't here, in fraught negotiations about her future. Especially not today.

Mirren grabbed her jacket, a pale cream Giorgio Armani blazer that dressed up black tailored trousers and a matching cashmere vest. The standard uniform of black was particularly striking against her pale complexion and the waves of red hair that a side plait was struggling to contain. Newspaper articles often referred to her as a classic beauty. Her straight nose, wide-set eyes and beautifully carved cheekbones gave her a striking profile that had seen her compared to everyone from Nicole Kidman to Grace Kelly to Meryl Streep. Mirren was happy to take the compliments.

It took twenty minutes in light, mid-afternoon traffic to reach the Pacific Coast Highway, the sound of the country-music channel drowning out the soft purr of her silver Mercedes-AMG. The rasping tones of Blake Shelton faded out, and the DJ announced a retro track was up next. The opening bars of Martina McBride's 'A Broken Wing' blasted from the speakers. It used to be one of her favourite songs, but that was before. Before her heart was broken, before she learned to cry.

Mirren flicked a button on the steering wheel, changing the channel to a pop station, and despite the tightness that was crushing her chest, she smiled as she recognized the tune.

'Not Giving You Back' by South City, a five-piece boy band that had sold more records in the US than any other act last year, a five-piece that was now rivalling the worldwide success of One Direction.

The lead singer's voice was as smooth and soulful as it got, a testimony – Mirren knew – to a mother who had been a Motown backing singer for two decades. But it was the second voice on the harmonies that invoked a swell of something good in her heart.

She had no idea where her son, Logan Gore, got his voice from, since she couldn't hold a note and neither could his father.

She slowed behind a vintage Ferrari as she approached the gates to Malibu Colony, then sped up again as the security guard waved her on, aware that several CCTV cameras had tracked her arrival. She hated the intrusion of the surveillance, but it did provide a certain level of comfort. Living in the Colony, one of the most expensive areas in the country, on a beachfront street that was populated by movie stars, producers, IT legends and a couple of big-spending rappers, it was inevitable that security would sit somewhere between 'overcautious' and 'paranoid'.

Some had moved here for the ego trip. Some for the investment. But Mirren had arrived more than a decade before looking for solitude, peace, a safe haven for the children and direct access to golden sands so private that she often felt like she was the only person on earth.

In a time of intrusive social media, compulsory networking and pervasive press scrutiny, that was, for her, the best feeling in the world.

Of course, back then, they'd been a family. Jack and Mirren, and Chloe and Logan. True, Jack had spent most of their years together out on location, producing and directing some of the biggest movies of the last couple of decades, but when he was home, her whole world was under that roof. Chloe and Logan were great kids: fun, crazy company. They'd always thought that Chloe's insatiable thirst for adventure and excitement would take her into the business or onto the stage, while Logan's shy, self-effacing charm would sit well behind the scenes. How wrong they had been. Logan found a passion for singing, and what began with jamming sessions in the garage with some friends had led to South City and posters on the walls of teenage girls all over America. And Chloe? That thirst for adventure took her to toilet floors, crack dens, rehab and the mortuary. Dead at eighteen. Gone. A loss that had changed Mirren so irrevocably, in so many ways. The thought made another piece of Mirren's heart shatter, but she couldn't indulge her pain now. Later. But not now.

Pulling into the drive of her white California contemporary home, she took a deep breath. And another. OK, smile on, head up. Strong. Logan was sitting at the dining table in the kitchen, a semi-circular booth that looked like it belonged in a 1950s diner. Every detail of the room had been designed by Mirren with a family in mind. A perfect family. The one she'd dreamed of having since she was a little girl, bringing herself up on a tough Glasgow housing estate.

A movie reel on fast forward played through her mind. Arriving in LA in the eighties, with Davie and Zander, inseparable friends since the night they saw her, twelve years old, sitting in the street late at night. Back then, they were the only two people she loved in the world. They had nothing but each other, and for a while that seemed like it was enough.

The images skipped through time.

A few years later, picking up the Oscar for the movie that had brought them to LA, the moment that pain and betrayal had forced them to walk away from each other.

Fast-forward to a few years later still.

Logan and his big sister, Chloe, only a year between them, making potato prints at the table. The two of them doing home-work there. The pubescent years when the only communication was a sneer and an irritated sigh. Then the laughs came back and the three of them, four if Jack was home, would have home-made burgers on a Friday night and sit there for hours, just being the family that belonged there.

'Hey, Mom. You OK?' Her boy. Logan Gore. Eighteen now and six feet tall, and, according to the fan sites, 170 pounds of blond, ripped, six-pack muscular perfection. Mirren didn't care if it showed bias for her to agree.

She tossed her jacket onto a chair and kicked off her heels, before leaning down to hug him. Arms around him, she lingered just a couple of seconds. Sometimes the human contact made it just a little bit more bearable.

'I am, honey. How about you? Dad not here yet?' she asked, already knowing the answer. There had been no sign of a midlife-crisis vehicle in the drive. God knows what it would be this month. So far, Jack had gone through a Ferrari, a Maserati, a Mclaren P1 and – ugh, make it stop – a pimped-up Escalade.

And to think, for nineteen years of marriage, she'd been under the illusion that uber-producer Jack Gore was the coolest man on the planet. It had only taken about five minutes to realise that he was far from it, right around the time she discovered he had been sharing his penis with a twenty-two-year-old starlet and then followed his raging hard-on out the door.

Clichéd as it sounded, it was for the best. The relationship with the actress, Mercedes Dance, had only lasted as long as it took for the paternity test to confirm that the baby she was carrying wasn't Jack's. Bizarrely, Mirren felt sorry for him. Back in cliché-land, there was no fool like a rich guy who was heading for fifty and who was stupid enough to believe for a second that a hot twenty-something babe was attracted to his personality. According to the tabloids, Mercedes and her baby were now shacked up with the true father of the child, a buff, fledgling actor who'd had one line in the movie Jack had directed Mercedes in.

Logan jumped up when the doorbell rang, high-fiving her as he passed on the way to open the door for his father. It had been one of the boundaries she'd set when her relationship with Jack had returned to civil ground. He could come over anytime, but no keys, and there had to be an arrangement or a call first. He lost the right to wander in and out of this house in the divorce settlement. She'd taken nothing else. Didn't need his cash, his pensions or their other home in Aspen. The Colony house was all she wanted, and it was a fair price to pay for almost twenty years of devotion and two incredible kids. One incredible kid now. She'd never get used to thinking about her children in the singular. She was a mother of two. Even if only one was still with her.

The noise of Jack's cowboy boots resonated with every step across the marble tiles. Dear Lord, cowboy boots. Black. Silver tips. With dark jeans and a grey retro Guns n' Roses T-shirt. And... No. It couldn't be. But yet... Yes, that was some kind of tattoo that appeared to be protruding from the bottom of one of his sleeves. Well, hello, rock phase, we've been expecting you.

The urge to laugh was almost irresistible, but Mirren fought to keep her face straight, knowing that the least sign of amusement, the tiniest morsel of disparagement, would incur a reaction of indignant petulance, and God knows, she didn't need that today.

'Hey, babe. You look good,' he said as he dipped his head to kiss her on the cheek.

'You too,' she managed, not trusting herself to say any more. The truth was, he did actually look pretty good; he just didn't look like Jack. Sure, he still had the whole Liam Neeson, ruggedly handsome thing going on. A couple of inches taller than Logan's six feet, he had the athletic body of a guy who was vain enough to make fitness a priority in his work-life balance. But then, that was easy when your wife was taking care of every detail in your family, so that you could spend your life going from film-set location to film-set location, where you trained daily with a personal fitness expert and had the caterers prepare every meal to the exact specifications of your personal nutritionist.

Did she sound bitter? She knew she truly wasn't. Losing Jack had been a drop in the ocean of incidentals compared to the tsunami of pain that still ebbed and flowed every day without Chloe, engulfing her and then retreating, then returning, until she felt unable to take her next breath.

Having Logan home from his endless touring for a few weeks helped. Especially today.

Pulling open the rich oak Meneghini Arredamenti fridge, Mirren stacked three loaded cake plates along one arm like the professional waitress she once was. Twenty-three years later, she still had the skills.

Turning, she handed one to Logan and one to Jack, before adding the forks she'd already left out on the sparkling white marble countertop. Everything had been prepared this morning at 3 a.m., when sleep had eluded her.

'Come on, let's go.' The forced cheeriness in her voice would have been almost believable if it hadn't been for the tears in her eyes. She blinked them away. Enough. She had to hold it together, for her, for Logan, for Chloe. Hell, even for Jack.

Mirren led the way out through the back door, down the path and past the white wooden fence at the end of the yard that led directly to the beach.

Due to environmental damage, the coastline was eroding. Just like her family.

The hot sand collected between her bare toes, but she didn't register the discomfort, only stopping when they were twenty or so feet from the water's edge. Mirren hitched up her black trousers as she sat down, automatically crossing her legs, one man on either side, gazing out at the glistening waves.

Her girl was out there. Her beautiful girl. Wild, irrepressible, defiant, wonderful Chloe was in every wave that rushed towards her, every spot where the sun bounced off the water.

Throat tightening, she barely managed to swallow a tiny piece of Chloe's favourite chocolate cake. Mirren had baked it for her every year, on every birthday, and had baked it again for today, Chloe's first birthday since her ashes had been scattered on the seabed, safe, near her mother, so Mirren could protect her in the way she hadn't been able to when she was alive.

Reaching across, her hand found Logan's, and only then did she find the strength to look back out to the ocean and speak. 'Happy birthday, my darling girl. We'll never stop missing you.'

Logan's arm came around her and she rested her head on his shoulder, her other hand automatically seeking out Jack's when she heard him choke back a sob.

There were no words, no stories, no reflections on what might have been. Just three people, staring at the water, holding on to each other to survive the pain that didn't ever diminish, immersed in their memories.

Only when she shivered did Mirren realise the sun was coming down.

'Let's go in,' she said softly, standing first, then holding Logan's hand while he pulled himself up. 'Jack, you're welcome to stay.' The flush of embarrassment that crossed his face told her that he had other plans. Hadn't he always had somewhere else to be? For all those years, she'd bought the myth about the pressure of spending months of every year away on location. Only when it was over did she realise that she had no idea who he was or what his life had been.

'Or not.' She attempted to make it light-hearted, determined to ensure Logan felt comfortable when his parents were both with him.

Jack's eyes were red-rimmed as he answered. 'Thanks, but I've got a meeting. Another time.'

It was tempting to rage. Who scheduled any kind of event for their daughter's birthday? Especially since that daughter was no longer here?

There was no point waging war. Jack was Jack. He'd go out, screw a twenty-one-year-old supermodel and make himself feel better. Instant gratification. That's what she'd discovered drove him. Ego. Power. Vanity. Good luck to him. She'd spend the night with her boy, and Zander said he'd drop by later too. Her son and the man who was now, once again, like a brother to her. That was all she needed.

They were almost at the white picket gate that led back onto her property when she caught sight of the figure standing fifty yards down the sand in her peripheral vision.

At first, she thought it was a paparazzo. They occasionally came down here in the hope of catching Jennifer Aniston walking her dog. Or Pam Anderson hanging out with her boys in the water.

Perhaps one of them had been smart enough to realise that today was Chloe's birthday.

Slowing down and shielding her eyes from the glare of the setting sun, Mirren peered across. Nope, no camera. It was a woman. And there was a curve to her back, a profile to her face that jarred Mirren's soul. She squinted again, trying to get a clearer view, but the woman was on her feet now, walking in the other direction.

'You OK, Mom?' Logan asked, concerned.

Mirren shook off the insidious chill that was working its way through the marrow of her bones.

'Yeah, I'm... Sorry, it's just for a second there I thought... That woman reminded me of someone.'

'Who?' Logan was peering after the retreating form now. 'Erm... My mum.' The second it was out, she cursed herself for not thinking quickly enough to come up with a fabrication that would disguise the truth. Logan was going to be completely freaked out if she carried on like this, especially as he'd think she was clearly losing her mind. They said grief sometimes did that to people, and right now she wouldn't argue.

It was Jack who was first to point out the obvious. 'But, Mirren, honey, you know that can't be.'

It was enough to pull her out of her paralysed stare.

'I know that, Jack. Of course it isn't.' Mirren snapped back to the present and immediately went into recovery mode, preparing to trot out the same lie she'd spun since she arrived in LA. Her parents were dead. No surviving family. No DNA connection to her homeland, so no need to go back there. It was a better story than saying that she'd last spoken to her mother two decades ago, when she'd buggered off to live with some drug dealing gangster in Liverpool. Acting had never been Mirren's talent, but this performance came from years of practise.

'It's just me being... Overwhelmed. How could someone be sitting over there when they've been dead for over twenty years?'

4

ZANDER LEITH

'Rehab' – Amy Winehouse

He was peeing in a plastic cup.

He earned in excess of $30 million per movie, topping Hanks, Cruise and Downey Jr, and in a recent survey of sixteen to twenty-one-year-olds, he was more recognizable than Jesus.

Yet Zander Leith was peeing in a cup. Yup, this was living the dream.

Job done, he exited the cubicle and handed the sample over to a rotund nurse, who eyed him with deep suspicion. Cynical hostility was probably a requirement of the job. The lengths that people in the industry would go to in order to deliver clean samples was legendary. Hadn't Tom Sizemore rigged up a fake penis? There was rock bottom, and then there was attempting to pervert the truth with a manufactured knob.

The nurse gave him the minimum smile required by her last round of client relations training, accompanied by a curt 'goodbye' as he headed for the door.

It wasn't the reaction he was used to, but in all honesty, he preferred it. If someone was thoroughly unimpressed with him right from the off, then in his extensive experience, there was less chance of him letting them down when he royally fucked up.

And when it came to fuck-ups, there had been many. The magazines charted his career by the number of years in the business – twenty and counting. He charted his life by the number of times in rehab and jail. The combined total was disturbingly similar. Six or seven clinics, and at least a dozen nights in the cells after alcohol or drug-fuelled brawls. The last one came after he'd punched the face off a particularly annoying reality-TV star, but sadly that didn't buy him any leniency from the judge. The result was three months in a stunning Malibu haven of gruesome withdrawals.

That was when everything changed. It was where he'd met a spaced-out, angry and bitter teenager and they'd struck up an unlikely friendship. He was the messed-up, macho movie star; she was Chloe, the teenage daughter of Mirren McLean, the childhood friend he'd grown up with, but hadn't seen since they picked up their first Oscar in 1986.

Two broken souls, kindred spirits who were drowning in an ocean of booze and drugs.

He'd tried to help her, but this wasn't the movies. He didn't come charging in at the end and save the day. Chloe was dead. And since the day the drugs claimed her, he'd been clean.

Promises weren't enough for the insurance company, though. They were filming the seventh Seb Dunhill movie, the franchise that whipped Bond, Bourne and Indiana Jones, and the studio could only get him covered if he subjected to weekly testing. Another week, another piss in a plastic cup.

'I hope you washed your hands,' Hollie remarked as he climbed into the passenger seat of her Dodge Durango. He'd bought it for her as a Christmas present, sending her right to the top of the list of 'PAs with Fuck-off Brilliant Presents'. She deserved it. Ten years of bailing his ass out and she still stuck with him. Zander hoped it was devotion – she claimed it was masochistic tendencies that required the aid of a therapist. They both knew it was love. Not rip-your-clothes-off lust. Just the true, forgiving, platonic love of two people bound together by friendship, care and their equal ability to fuck up every romantic relationship they ever had. In Zander's case, addiction, dysfunction, demons and the serial avoidance of commitment could be blamed for his solitary status. Hollie's barrier to coupledom was a different one. During his lost years of excess, she'd regularly reminded him that she had no time to date because looking after a screwed-up movie star was an all-consuming vocation. 'I'm like a nun who devotes herself to God, except Mother Teresa never had to drag her main man out of a crack den.'

Hollie flicked her highlighted brunette waves back from her face and pulled her seatbelt over a white tailored shirt that was very slightly straining at the buttons. In any other world, her naturally large breasts and hourglass curves would put her in the 'normal size and gorgeous' category. In LA, she would undoubtedly be classed as obese. Not that she cared. She may have forty-inch hips, but she also had a completely secure body image and more confidence than a therapist's office full of size zero starlets.

Zander popped a Marlboro in his mouth but didn't light it. It was the only vice he had left, but he knew better than to spark up in Hollie's pride and joy. They pulled out of the clinic and in five minutes were on the 405 and leaving Van Nuys, heading towards West Hollywood. Hollie checked her mirrors compulsively, not for traffic situations but for paps. The testing clinic was one of six they used in rotation, so the camera-toting vultures didn't get a sniff of the visits. The Lomax Films publicity team would bring down a shit-storm of fury if their hero, Seb Dunhill, the super-spy who had the ear of every government, who had foiled several terrorist plots and even, in one movie, brought a space shuttle down safely, was filmed looking like shit after leaving a clinic in which his urine had been subjected to a dip-test. It wasn't the image they were going for.

The rest of this afternoon's activities were more in line with the desired public perception.

Hollie steered through the thirty-foot-high mahogany doors that guarded the entrance to the Combrian Hotel and jumped out. The concierge was instantly by her side.

'I'll keep it up top for you,' he said, nodding to the few exclusive spaces by the door. There were definitely some perks that came with riding with Zander Leith.

Unfortunately, Zander Leith didn't notice. He left the vehicle with an enthusiasm that sat somewhere between going to a funeral and marching down death row.

Hollie tolerated his lethargy until they walked into the 1,500-square-foot penthouse, to be greeted by a fashion mob, which burst into action as soon as he crossed the threshold. 'Cheer up,' she quipped. 'It's better than peeing in a cup.'

An hour later, as a dedicated stylist rearranged the position of his tackle so that it gave the Adrianna Guilloti trousers the most flattering drape, he decided that Hollie was wrong. What the hell was he doing here? Other than hating every second of fulfilling the requirement for a twice-a-year photo shoot that his contract with Adrianna Guilloti menswear stipulated.

Over the years he'd been offered hundreds of high-end endorsement deals, but he'd refused almost all of them. This one had come with an extra enticement in the form of the company boss, Adrianna Guilloti. Their first meeting had been drinks at Shutters on the Beach in Santa Monica. He'd thought it was to be a casual chat with the marketing chief of Guilloti and planned to blow him off and be out of there in minutes. Instead, he got the boss herself. An intoxicating blend of Spanish and Italian heritage, Adrianna had started her company from scratch, used her beauty and class to promote it, and her brains to acquire the investment needed to take it from a small, aspirational tailoring company to a design house that was uttered in the same breath as Prada and Dolce & Gabbana.

That night, semi-wasted, he'd agreed to a million-dollar deal to represent the brand. Hours later, he'd followed her to New York, taken her to a room in the Carlyle and had the most incredible weekend of sexual pleasure he'd ever known – right up until he discovered she was married to one of the shadiest but most successful property moguls in the country. Neither current affairs nor illicit affairs had ever been his strong point, so he'd cut and run. Since then, he'd seen her at business meetings and promotional functions, but never alone. For a man with addiction and compulsion issues, it was torture. Booze. Coke. Adrianna Guilloti. He craved them all, but knew that a relationship with any one of those vices could end with him on a cold slab wearing a toe tag. The very thought gave him an excruciating desire for a Jack Daniel's on the rocks. Double. He almost smiled given the irony of his current location. After three hours of photographs in the penthouse, the shoot had moved to the achingly hip bar on the roof of the hotel. It was the perfect setting for the European marketing campaign because it was the ultimate Hollywood cliché – the glorious rooftop pool area, bordered by cream seats and candle-topped tables, with a city view that was breathtakingly spectacular.

He was on the top of the world, wearing a $5,000 suit, Jack Daniel's was within reach, he was surrounded by people whose job for the day was to make him happy, and yet he couldn't ask them to bring him the only things he wanted. Really wanted. A sigh escaped him and he caught himself and shook off the melancholy. What the fuck did he have to complain about? Get a grip. Focus on the positives. Stop being a conceited arse. The legendary photographer went by just one name, Terrano. Which sure sounded more appealing than Terence Pratt, the name he was born with in Clacton, Essex. The new moniker and a French accent were developed at the same time as his first roll of film back in the 1970s. 'Ooh, j'adore. Très bon. Oui, that works. OK, Zander, ze final pose. Mid-shot.'

The image screamed '1950s movie icon' as Zander leaned his back against one of the ivy-clad pillars, hands in pockets, tie loose, top button of the shirt open, and stared into the sky, his expression a cross between pensive and brooding. Terrano was an 'Oh oui, oui, oui!' away from a climax by the time he'd shot off fifty frames and called it a wrap.

Zander shrugged off the jacket and opened the rest of the buttons on his shirt, letting the early evening breeze cool him down.

As always, Hollie appeared at his side within seconds. In her jeans and white shirt, she was a healthy contrast to the skeletal, black-clad fashionistas who had worked on the shoot. 'Man, that lot need to go eat pie,' she murmured at the retreating crowd, before continuing, 'OK, I'm off the clock and I finally have a date with a real, live man tonight. But if there's any possibility whatsoever that you're going to go sample anything stronger than coffee at the bar, I'll stick around.' She went misty-eyed. 'Ah, the good old days – gutters and groupies. I miss the old fuck-up you sometimes.'

Zander threw an arm around her. 'Me too. Who's the date?' Her eyebrows shot up. It was the reason she'd never overdose on Botox – she required some upper facial movement because her raised brows were an early warning system for acute irritation. 'What are you, my dad? The morning I pulled a stripper called Stardust out of your bed, you lost the authority to judge my relationships.'

She held out a key card. 'OK, here you go – go down one floor, and head for the suite next door to the penthouse you shot in earlier. I've put your clothes in there so you can get a shower without the risk of the photographer attempting to jump your bones. The room is booked for the night – it was on your rider – so you can hang here if you want.'

Zander shook his head. 'Nah, I'd rather get home. There's a nine p.m. meeting in Venice.'

Three AA meetings a week. That was the price of keeping the weight down on the sober side of the seesaw of addiction.

'I'm humbled by your commitment, oh, master. So, tomorrow you have fight training at ten. I'll swing by around nine thirty and pick you up.'

In the lift down from the roof, Zander held up his fist and she bumped it, before he disembarked at his floor and left her to descend to a date night. For a moment, the melancholy returned.

When was the last time he'd had a night out that didn't involve a room full of strangers with a story of addiction?

But that was the rub. After a lifetime of wasted nights, he'd had to make drastic changes when he kicked the booze. No more bars. No more clubs. No more strip joints. And if he avoided all of those, there were no more rehabs or jail cells. Most of the time, it seemed like a fair deal.

But tonight? He could swing by and see Davie, but he'd just get in the way at the studio. And he didn't want to crowd Mirren. Last night – Chloe's birthday – he'd headed over to her house early evening and ended up eating hot dogs on the beach with her and Logan. He didn't want to infringe on their space two nights in a row.

Maybe he'd call the guys and see if they were up for poker. Always a loner, he didn't have an intimate group of friends, but the closest it got – other than Mirren and Davie – were the guys he hung out with at the beach. They'd catch some waves. Sometimes rack up the poker set and pass the night betting with dimes. Don Michael Domas, star of *Call Me*, the sitcom that was pulling in the highest ratings since *Friends*. Lee Vandan, male model, who worked catwalks and photo shoots a few times a month so that he could spend the rest of his life catching waves in front of his beach shack near Zuma. Josh Wilson, a writer who'd polished the scripts of half the best action movies of the last year, earning him cheques, instead of credit. He didn't care. Zander was fairly sure he'd found the only three guys in Hollywood who would rather hang at the beach than on a film set. Suited him just fine.

The door beeped as he used the key card to enter and he headed straight for the shower, peeling his clothes off as he went. He set the temperature to the midway point and climbed in, glad of the warm jets hitting his skin from the rainfall showerhead.

For a few moments, he stood there, letting the chaos of the day wash over him, a tight knot of anxiety gradually unfurling. If he made it quick, he could be home in less than an hour, an hour out on the board, food and then meeting.

The sensation of a movement near him made him flick open his eyes, every muscle in his impeccably toned torso and arms tensing straight into defence mode.

As soon as he realised who'd come to the party, a very different muscle sprang into action.

Adrianna Guilloti had opened the glass shower door and stood there, utterly naked, except for eight-inch stiletto sandals and a gold chain that dipped between her high, generous breasts. A long, glossy plait of sleek black hair, parted in the middle, fell down her back. Her rosebud nipples were erect and a thin line of dark pubic hair was a tantalizing reminder of a weekend of highs that no drugs or booze had ever given him.

The dark red of her lips broke into a languid, irresistibly beautiful smile.

'I heard you were here today. Thought I'd see how my investment was doing.'

As she stepped out of the heels and into the shower, Zander reached one hand round her neck and pulled her face to him, the hot jets of the water no barrier as he kissed her hard, his tongue searching, tasting.

'I think you've missed me, no?' she murmured, her tone almost threatening.

He showed her just how much, until the two of them came shuddering under the jets, then slumped against the tile wall.

'I missed you,' he confirmed, smiling as he leaned over to brush the long, black strands of wet hair back from her stunning face. It was as close as they'd ever got to emotional intimacy. Their brief time together a few months before had been about nothing but pure, raw, incredible sex.

Reaching up, Adrianna slammed off the shower lever, stopping the water, then pushed herself up onto her feet, before holding out her hand in invitation.

Zander got the message. Still wet, he followed her out of the shower and into the suite, where he saw the trail of clothes she'd left on the way to the bathroom. After leading him to the bed, she pushed him downwards. There was no resistance. Only when he was flat on his back did she climb on, and instinctively his arms came to either side of her neck as he kissed her again, feeling like an alcoholic who had just opened a bottle of bourbon and couldn't stop tasting. This was such a bad idea. She was dangerous. She was wild. She was married to a guy who could have his balls for breakfast. But she was absolutely fucking incredible.

Eyes glinting with sheer sexiness, she pushed his hands away, in charge now, a very fixed idea of what she wanted. With every bite, suck and shudder, she showed him.

For a bad idea, this felt oh so fucking good.

He surrendered, ever aware that most of his favourite moments in life had started with really, really bad ideas.

5

SARAH

'You Give Me Something' – James Morrison

The paps' flashes momentarily blinded her as Sarah drove through the gates of Davie's Bel Air mansion. They'd been in permanent residence there since Jizzo Stacks had popped his cowboy boots live on air during Davie's first show. What. A. Nightmare.

The studio had descended into chaos; paramedics had been summoned, all to the soundtrack of Carmella Cass screaming at Jizzo to wake up. At the beginning of the show, the ratings were good. By the end, there wasn't a late-night viewer in the country who wasn't watching, alerted by a social-media buzz so loud it could have woken the dead. Except – oh, the heavenly irony – Jizzo. He remained very firmly on the other side.

It was one of the things that Sarah found hard to stomach about living here. Every wail of human pain and tragedy was a story, played out in the media as if it were the Lifetime movie of the week instead of someone's actual life.

And yes, she realised that was hypocritical, having spent five years on a

UK tabloid crime desk, working for the *Daily Scot*, door-stepping victims and reporting carnage in all its bloody grime and glory.

But somehow, that was OK there. That was reporting the facts. Here, everything was so wrapped up in drama and ulterior motive that it was difficult to separate the real from the performance. And that was never more obvious than in Davie's life.

What were they now? Lovers? Yes. Exclusive? Absolutely. But they weren't in an open, official, publicly acknowledged relationship. The reticence was all on her side, but she suspected that was largely to do with the fact that Davie was used to getting everything at the snap of his TV-mogul fingers. He was definitely a live-in-the-moment, go-for-it, why-wait-for-anything kind of guy who needed the world to be his and he needed it now. And he had the cash to pay for it.

She'd never be comfortable with that level of fame and power, and she wasn't sure she wanted to be. It was only six months ago that she'd moved here from Glasgow, after coming over initially to chase down a story on the relationship between Mirren, Davie and Zander. She'd had a conversation with a dying Glasgow gangster that had led her to believe that there was some kind of hidden, dark, secret in the past of Scotland's three most famous entertainment exports. She'd been right. But by the time she'd learned the truth, she'd already fallen for Davie Johnston. When the time came to choose between running the story or starting a new life with Davie, she'd quit her job and shifted her life to LA. It would have been the easiest thing in the world to move in with Davie and live the Hollywood dream of fame and fortune – it was certainly what he wanted – but in truth, the thought made her skin bristle.

She wanted to make it on her own. On her terms. And whether he liked it or not, that had to happen before she became nothing more than Davie Johnston's other half.

Her freelance work, mostly for UK tabloids and celebrity mags paid her bills, fluff pieces on the size of Kim Kardashian's arse or Charlie Sheen's legal bills (both of which appeared to be comparatively generous). It was selling her serious journalist soul, but it allowed her to concentrate on the stuff she really wanted to write. Beneath the glitter and the glitz, there was a darkness, a downward spiral of a city that survived on drugs, spin, hype and manipulation. Nothing was real here. Nothing. And it fascinated her. There had been hundreds of Hollywood bios done before, but Sarah was writing hers from an outsider's perspective, one that wasn't swayed by personal experience or lust for fame or power. She just wanted to tell the story, to look behind the Hollywood curtain and explain why a beautiful girl like Chloe Gore, born to wealth and privilege, could end up dead at eighteen. She wanted to explore why the industry supported twenty-one-year-old brats who thought their music success gave them an unlimited platform of entitlement and invincibility. And why fame-seekers in a reality TV world that was based on zero talent were prepared to – literally – exploit and risk their own lives for another million 'likes' on Instagram or Twitter.

It was a warped world, and the biggest irony of all?

In loving Davie Johnston, she was dancing with the devil. He had been the biggest manipulator of all, the king of reality TV and the Pied Piper to legions of wannabes who would do anything to achieve the fame they craved.

Last year, Davie had been accused of plotting with one of his young reality stars, Sky Nixon, to stage an overdose to push up ratings for their show. He was guilty as charged, and it had backfired spectacularly when Sky had almost died and her publicity-desperate mother overlooked the fact that she'd been in on the plan from the start, and threw Davie under a very public bus by revealing the sordid manipulation in the media. The justifiable outrage almost cost Davie his career. Only the fact that Sky and her mother were later found to have been equally culpable in the deception had, ironically, thrown him a lifeline, and allowed him to crawl back up the Hollywood ladder. There were a lot of short memories in this town, especially when it came to loveable rogues who begged for forgiveness. And Davie's knees had been raw.

Sky and her mother had sworn revenge on Davie in every publication and celebrity news show that would cover them, but no-one took them seriously. They were probably on the bus back to Nowhere Town by now.

Sarah believed he'd learned his lesson, that he'd grown and rediscovered the inherent decency at his core, but who knew? And who could ever have predicted that she'd fall in love with a guy who stood for everything she despised? Her only defence was that underneath the hustle, the deceptions, the bravado, the skewed morals and his eye-rolling tendency to be a shallow, egotistical asshole, he was just a street kid from Glasgow who'd adopted a whole load of bad habits to survive. Since he'd reunited with Mirren and Zander and laid their ghosts to rest the year before, she'd seen a different man, a loyal, loving, decent one who desperately wanted to be better. And she was absolutely there for that.

The sprinklers on Davie's manicured lawns did an elaborate dance as she wove up the twisting drive to his $40-million baroque mansion.

As she parked on the beautiful forecourt, next to a fountain that shot jets of water five feet in the air, she spotted him leaning against the open door frame, coffee in hand.

It was an appealing visual. He had no top on – always a winner, especially when he had a body that had been pummelled and shaped by a former US Olympic-team boxing champ who took his job very seriously.

This was a nightly ritual when she was heading out downtown. She'd swing by, grab a coffee and touch-base. It grounded her. Made her smile. It also ensured that – should she be massacred on the streets by some lowlife during the night – someone would report her missing. Every cloud.

A knot of tension evaporated from her shoulders as he flashed her an easy smile. 'Hey, babe, come take me away from all this.' On TV, his accent was softly Scottish, but speaking to her now, he'd slipped back into the broad Glasgow burr of his childhood. 'Sure,' she replied, grinning as she strolled towards him. 'I can offer you a night watching lowlife drug dealers off Sunset, a visit to a fast-food joint or an afternoon at my Marina del Rey apartment. But please don't bring a cat, because there's no room to swing it.'

As soon as she made the joke, she regretted it. 'And no, don't use that as another opener to a "move in here" conversation.'

He adopted an innocent expression and put his hands up in surrender. Good. Heavy conversation averted. For now.

She sat down on the doorstep, recognizing that the man lived in 30,000 square feet of Bel Air ostentation, had shitloads of drama and hassle going on thanks to the untimely death of an aging rock star, a dozen calls to return to people who were much further up the importance chain than her and at least one room in the house behind him undoubtedly contained a dozen suits mapping out strategies, yet he was here, sitting on a step with his girlfriend.

'So how's it going?' she asked.

'Crazy. The network lawyers are shitting a brick in case there's any measure of liability. The producers are secretly loving it because we ended up with the highest ratings of any debut talk show in living history. And the *Beauty and the Beats* team are freaking out because we just lost half the act. It's a whole big, incestuous cluster-fuck. But hey, did you hear the bit about the ratings?'

It was impossible not to laugh. He may be partially reformed, but he'd still concede that he was arrogant, ambitious, ruthless and shallower than an espresso. Thankfully, when he wasn't being any of the above, he was also caring and sweet and so funny he made her sides hurt. Not that she'd admit that to him.

'God, you're vile. And you're needy. And a prima donna. And high maintenance. Shall I go on?'

'Horny,' he offered, snaking his hand up the back of her vest top.

'Well, horny will have to wait. Besides, don't you have the legal team here? Aren't you supposed to be in there putting out fires?' she asked, gesturing into the house.

'Yep, but we'll only keep them waiting for ten minutes.'

Sarah leaned over and kissed him teasingly. 'Why? Are we gonna do it twice?'

'Yep, and have a cigarette in between,' Davie added, gently tugging her towards him.

She shouldn't. He had places to be. Things to be doing. Yet she was somehow sitting on top of him, legs wrapped round his waist, with hands unclipping her bra with the expertise of the oversexed. Lips locked, he used the quads that had been honed by a million squats to raise them up to a standing position; then he stepped backwards into the house, moved a couple of feet to the left and pulled open the door to the cloakroom. This wasn't their first rodeo in there. Without looking, Sarah knew that one wall was lined with oak shelving, from floor to ceiling, supporting dozens of shoes, hats, sneakers. The opposite wall had rows of coats and, underneath, myriad play things: skate-boards, two Segways, a bike and, at the back, a table used for storing hats, gloves, scarves. Or rather, it used to be. As Davie cleared it with one hand, Sarah tore her lips from his for long enough to whip her vest top over her head. The bra went with it. Davie sat her on the table and immediately dropped to take her nipple in his mouth, her head thrown back, panting, while her hands released the button on his jeans and freed him. As they moved together, it still felt new to them, even as they fell into their familiar touches, strokes, gasps, groans.

'Fuck, you're beautiful,' he whispered, moments later, watching every movement, a sheen of sweat appearing now on a torso that was as ripped as any model on a Calvin Klein billboard.

The moment he said it, she felt the tingles of an orgasm start at her pelvis and grow, spreading across her stomach, working north, a sensation of utter bliss exploding inside her, as he held her tighter, tighter, tighter...

'Sarah, Sarah, Sarah, oh fu-u-u-u-ck,' he spat through teeth that were clenched shut, his head thrown back, his eyes closed until he flopped forward, resting his chin in the space gravity had made on her chest when her breasts had slid to the side. He'd told her many times that it was his favourite part of her body, mostly because it was rarely seen in LA. You couldn't toss a silicon implant down any street without it landing on a woman whose surgically enhanced boobs stayed upright and immobile when she lay, like Sarah now, on her back.

'I bloody love you,' he said, never more handsome than when he was happy, post-coital and they were still – quite literally – joined at the hip.

Laughing, she ran one finger down the centre of his forehead, over his nose, to his mouth. He clenched his teeth round it, making her yelp.

'Ouch! No rough stuff. There are clubs you can go to for that.'

'Yeah, but I've lost my gimp mask. I think my girlfriend burned it,' he told her sorrowfully, making her giggle.

Actually giggle.

And Sarah Mckenzie, hard-assed journalist, didn't – in any other part of her life – do giggling.

That was the effect Davie Johnston had on her. He was funny, crazy, wild and she adored him.

Cupping a finger under his chin, she raised his head so that she could push back up onto her elbows. 'OK, much as that made the earth move, I need to get to work, and I believe you're supposed to be handling a dead-rock-star crisis situation. May he rest in peace.'

'I think Jizzo would approve of this interruption to proceedings,' he told her solemnly.

She slid to her feet, grinning. 'Look, if it's quiet out tonight, I'll come back over. Maybe around three. Don't wait up, though – I'll just slide in beside you and you can do all that to me again when you wake up.'

His hand slipped round her neck and he leaned in to kiss her again, lingering this time. 'I like that idea.'

Eventually, she broke off, laughing. 'OK, I have to go before I take you up on the doing-it-twice thing.' Sarah reached out for the nearest coat, giggling again when she realised that it was Davie's old Lakers jacket. She slipped it on, showing support for one of Los Angeles's two basketball teams. While utterly naked underneath.

Davie loved the image. 'I swear you're giving me another hard-on. When you're done with that, leave it out. I'm taking it upstairs, and when you come back, I'm going to teach you some serious ball control.'

If it had been uttered by any other guy, it would have come off as cheesy, but Davie was in on the joke, blatantly hamming it up, so from him, it was just funny.

When he'd pulled up and fastened his jeans, Sarah went up on her tiptoes and kissed him. 'I know everything about balls that I'll ever need to know, thanks. Now go back to work. I'm going to go wash up and then I'm out of here. Go. Shoo. See you later.'

She followed him out of the cloakroom, praying that Alina, his overwhelmingly intimidating housekeeper, wasn't around, then slipped into the foyer washroom directly next to the door. It was a wet room with a built-in shower, designed by Davie so that he didn't have to traipse to a shower room on a higher floor if he came in the door wet, muddy or cold from any form of exercise or sport.

After a quick hose-down, Sarah was dressed and back in the car.

The pap flash explosion was even more relentless on exit than it had been on entry, no photographer prepared to miss a car that might have Davie Johnston in it.

She was ten minutes away, her little red Chrysler convertible pointed in the direction of Studio City, before the spots in her eyes dissipated.

This was a strange life. In what normal world do you watch a rock star dying on air, get mobbed by paps when you drop in to see your boyfriend, shag said boyfriend in a cloakroom on his $40 million estate and then spend your nights solo, on Sunset Strip, hanging out in bars, watching the action and cultivating relationships with bar staff and security guys who could give you the heads-up on who was doing what to whom?

The lights changed and she turned onto North Beverly Glen Boulevard.

The truth was that for all the insanity and craziness of life here, she was happy. After a lifetime of Scottish rain and bluster, she adored the sunshine and the laid-back lifestyle. There was still a part of her that missed the grit of Glasgow and the intense, down-and-dirty world of the crime desk. There, it was all about the facts. Being objective. Impartial. Here, even the news reporters were allowed to make a drama out of a crisis.

Covering trite stuff as a freelancer just didn't give her the same kind of challenge or fulfilment as her old job.

Her cell phone rang through the car's Bluetooth. The screen flashed up a +44 number that was so familiar she immediately flicked a switch to answer it. 'Hello?'

'Are you missing me?' came the raspy, guttural reply. Sarah's smile was instant. Ed McCallum, editor of the *Daily Scot*, the newspaper she'd left behind.

'Madly. I pine for you every day,' she replied, realizing he'd never guess just how much truth was in that statement. Ed had been her mentor, an old-school, whisky-in-the-filing-cabinet, tough editor who bled newspaper ink. There were very few left like him.

'I can understand that. I'd miss me too.' His laugh descended into a hacking cough courtesy of twenty Benson & Hedges a day.

Sarah waited a moment. 'Did you die?' she checked when he finally stopped.

'Almost, but no.'

'Excellent. Didn't want to be hanging on here all day.'

This time, his laugh was more of a snort than a life-threatening convulsion.

'Right, ma darling, I'm phoning to see if yer up for a bit of freelance.'

'Does it pay huge amounts of cash, and will it put me in the running for some kind of career-enhancing award?'

'Neither.'

'Neither?'

'But I'll leave you my entire worldly goods when I shuffle off this mortal coil.'

'By the sound of you, that'll be soon, so keep talking.'

They both knew she'd agree, no matter what it was. She just hoped it would be something meaty that might lead to a big story, one that could give her some kind of profile here in the US.

Ed paused to dislodge phlegm from his airways yet again before he went on.

'It kinda follows on from the whole McLean, Leith, Johnston thing you looked at last year.'

The hairs on the back of her neck stood to attention. She could count on the fingers of one hand the number of people who knew the truth about them. What she'd discovered when she came over to the US to investigate the relationship between the three friends had been so shocking, so utterly horrific that she'd killed the story to protect them.

'Carry on – I'm curious,' she urged him, careful to sound casual and nonplussed so she didn't alert him to her interest. Ed McCallum could spot a story in a dark room, in a blackout, while wearing a balaclava.

'Big-time organized-crime guy Razor Ritchie has been arrested in Liverpool, his worldly goods seized, his operation wiped out. Couple of his crew are squealing like pigs. One of the things that came up is that the female who's been shacked up with the crook since anyone can remember has been shouting her mouth off that she's Mirren McLean's mother. I sent someone down to check it out, but the woman's disappeared. It's probably crap. Pretty sure we'd have heard if a Hollywood big shot's maw was shacked up with a gangster.'

Deafening claxons were reverberating in Sarah's head. 'Yeah, I'm sure we'd know that.' She tried to sound convincing as she lied. 'Let me look into it and I'll see what I can find. Be good to cover something a bit more interesting than who Gerry Butler is allegedly shagging this week.'

'Brilliant. And I wasn't kidding about the dosh. It's normal union rates, so the money's pish,' he added.

'I wouldn't expect anything else. I'm doing it for the love of you.'

'Magic. Let me know if you dig anything up. If there's anything there, I know you'll find it. Thanks, love.'

As soon as he was gone, Sarah realised her fingers were trembling on the steering wheel. Yep, if there was a story here, she had no doubt she'd find it. But as she'd already established, there was some things that were better left unfound.

6

It's my secret. I think that's what gives me the biggest kick.
This morning, I woke up and realised that I know what I'm going to do.
I know that I'm going to right the wrong. But I'm the only one who knows.
What does that make me?
It makes me the one with the power.
I have the power to take back what's mine, to destroy the person who took it away.
I can make them burn in hell. And I will.
When I'm ready. Because I know.
I know everything.

7

DAVIE

'Rock 'n' Roll Star' – Oasis

'OK, so, people, listen up – can we please, please try not to kill anyone tonight? One celebrity death is a freak event. Two is just carelessness,' Mellie warned them through their earpieces from her position in the gallery.

The world of *American Stars* was very different from the vibe on *Here's Davie Johnston*. Now on series fourteen, *American Stars* was the highest-rated talent show in the country and had spawned a galaxy of music stars, a gutter of washed-up wannabes, several drug scandals, three sex tapes and an unsubstantiated rumour of sexual encounters with at least one of the judges.

Here's Davie Johnston was shot in an intimate studio setting, designed to get the best out of the guests without them switching to performance mode at the sight of a large audience.

American Stars was at the other end of the shooting scale. Filmed in a huge sound stage, with 1,000 screaming spectators, full lights and pyro facilities at Television Centre. But the biggest difference was the noise. Like a wall of sound from the minute Davie entered the set until the curtain came down on the hysterical contestant who had just been despatched back to his old life in Arkansas.

Mellie was still chattering in their ears. 'Lainey, honey, you look gorgeous tonight.'

To Davie's immediate right, Lainey Ander's voluptuous cleavage trembled as she giggled. Yep, giggled. The woman had been the Queen of Country for four decades, thanks to a stiletto-sharp business brain that was as impressive as her ability to stay beautiful, remain current and come off as so damn sweet that the nation adored her.

'I know I do, but keep talking, sweetheart,' Lainey replied, the cute wink spreading the laughter to everyone privy to the conversation, Davie included.

Easy, generous and utterly professional, Lainey was everything that the woman on his left was not.

Princess. Just one name. Like Madonna, Cher and Britney. Princess had been a Disney star since she was delivered to a casting call for *The Mickey Mouse Club* by a mother who had absolutely no doubt in her mind that her little girl was destined for the kind of stardom that would transport them from a rented studio apartment in Compton to a gated complex in Calabasas. She'd been absolutely right.

At twenty-one, Princess had four platinum-selling albums and two critically acclaimed movies under her diamanté thong. Unfortunately, that left no room for trifling personality traits like humility, authenticity and civility; thus she was also known by just one name on the set of *American Stars* – Bitch.

Demanding, unreasonable, irrational, shrill, self-obsessed and prone to blatant rudeness, she was an absolute nightmare to deal with – and Davie loved every minute of it because those were also the reasons that she made this show compulsive viewing for the under-twenty-five demographic.

With Lainey bringing in the thirty-five-plus market, Davie scoring high in twenty to forty, and Princess on the youngsters, it was the perfect ratings balance. Six weeks in to the current season and they were killing the opposition. If Cowell or Seacrest ever retained the services of a good hitman, Davie knew he'd have to invest in a Kevlar vest.

Tonight, in a last-minute tribute/token exploitation, they'd decided to dedicate the show to the music of the late, great Jizzo Stacks, whose five-day-old corpse was still lying in a refrigerated drawer in the Los Angeles County Coroner's building. The autopsy was scheduled for the following day and the thought of it made Davie's buttocks clench, despite the fact that the suits had assured him he was not liable for Jizzo's demise. None of the blame could be laid at his door. Last time he checked, silently hoping someone would be wasted enough to give great TV wasn't a criminal offence.

Neither was making sure that his interests were fully covered and maximized. It had been a crazy few days. He'd pretty much worked round the clock, but it had all paid off. As a result of everything he'd put in place, reruns of *Beauty and the Beats* had been playing on half a dozen networks, Carmella and Jizzo's very own video channel had been reaching millions with daily updates, and the *American Stars* theme for tonight's show had been changed from 'retro disco' to 'Celebrating Jizzo'.

On top of all that, at the end of the first week, *Here's Davie Johnston* had achieved the kind of ratings that beat even the most optimistic predictions.

Win. Win. Win.

'Davie!' Mellie's voice blasted in his ear this time, so she'd obviously returned to the gallery in preparation for the count-down. 'Get the grin off your face – we're one minute to air and you have to deliver the condolences. Lainey, are you rubbing his thigh again?'

Lainey nodded, her face a picture of mischief. 'Of course, my darlin'. You know it relaxes me.'

Mellie sighed. 'It's what it's doing for Davie I'm more concerned about.'

The answer, he knew, was absolutely nothing.

He wasn't sure if he was delighted or horrified that for the first time in his life, something in his psyche had blocked him from sexual attraction to other women now that he'd met someone he'd truly fallen in love with.

Still, he went with the joke, enjoying the banter with Lainey. 'That's the kind of relaxation that beats yoga.'

'Urgh, you two are, like, so gross,' Princess spat, without even breaking her focus on the cell phone in front of her. Davie wondered for a moment if he'd ever had a conversation with her in which she'd actually put that damn phone down long enough to look him in the eye. Nope, not as far as he could remember. But then, this Bitch, with a capital 'B', knew her stuff. She'd no doubt uploaded a dozen selfies in the last ten minutes, gained a few hundred more followers from around the globe and boosted her record sales by thousands.

Who was the loser here, then?

'OK, people, here we go. Floor, get some energy in the audience. Titles roll. Panel, stand by. And three, two, one... Lauren, we're on you.'

On stage, just a spotlight, illuminating the porcelain skin and tumbling red waves of Lauren Finney, winner the year before last and this season's host. It had been Davie's idea to give her the gig this year. It made perfect sense. The girl was talented, beautiful and, unlike the snide, obnoxious Princess beside him, she had a personality that the country had fallen in love with. On themed shows like tonight, she opened with a song, before digging into the three months of intense training she'd undergone to give her the skills she needed to steer the *American Stars* juggernaut. Davie had been by her side, mentoring her every step of the way. He had a soft spot for this kid and he wanted to make it happen for her.

In previous years, with different female stars, he'd no doubt contravened several rules regarding sex in the workplace. Not now. Lauren wasn't that girl, and his relationship with Sarah had made him no longer that guy.

Giving Lauren the gig had definitely been a gamble, but one that paid off. It gave the show credibility. Lauren's debut album had just gone platinum, proving that *American Stars* lived up to its name. What better way to remind everyone of that than to have Lauren here every week? Sure, it helped that what she lacked in presentation polish she made up for in overwhelming likeability. Although, as expected, Princess didn't necessarily agree or appreciate the competition, as evidenced by the moans of 'Fuck this shit' beside him.

Mellie heard it too.

'Pipe down there, Princess. Keep your evil for the contestants,' she warned.

Davie wasn't paying attention, too focused on the stage.

Lauren looked up, blue eyes wide and oozing pain as she picked out an A-minor chord on her guitar and then almost whispered the first line of

'Cut You', Jizzo Stacks's biggest hit. Back in the 1980s, in Jizzo's heavy-metal hands, it had been a furious, demonic threat to a lover. The ethereal beauty of Lauren's incomparable voice transformed it, making it a haunting lament to lost love, the breaking of a heart that was now oozing blood, captivating a viewing audience of over 15 million.

For the first time ever, there wasn't a sound in the audience. Not a murmur. Even Princess had hushed. The idea of having Carmella make a guest appearance tonight had been floated, but Davie had blocked it for two reasons. He wanted Carmella's first public appearance to be back on his talk show. And tonight, he wanted all the focus to be on the young woman who was killing it on the stage right now.

Only when she sang the last line, one perfect tear dropping down her cheek, did the audience react. And what a reaction. Every single person was on their feet, crying, cheering, emotions raw and laid out for all to see.

Davie knew three things for sure. Tonight was going to be an incredible show.

Mellie would have captured every second of this performance and audience reaction so well that viewers across the nation would be weeping into their pizza.

And his people would have this on iTunes by midnight, where it would rise to number one within twenty-four hours. No doubt Jizzo was up there somewhere calling Davie all the fuckers under the sun for profiting from his death. But at the same time, he wouldn't expect anything less.

The rest of the show was flawless.

There were eight acts left in the competition, and any one of them had the potential to make it. Tonight, each of them raised their game in an attempt to match Lauren's impact. No one did, but their brilliant interpretations of Jizzo's hits, interspersed with VTs of other stars paying tribute to the fallen rocker, made it the perfect blend of entertainment and emotion.

That was showbiz. A year ago, Jizzo was washed up, almost a joke, a has-been with a bad weave who was desperately holding on to a fanbase that had long ago swapped their leather trousers for pension plans and brochures for assisted-living facilities. Throw in a supermodel girlfriend, a hit reality show and behaviour that would get him arrested anywhere else in the world, and the result was the kind of homage that used to be reserved for state leaders and royalty.

As the closing titles rolled with the telephone numbers that gave the viewers the opportunity to play God and vote an act off (10 cents per call, standard network rates may apply), Davie exhaled, relaxing for the first time in almost a week.

He'd done it. They'd pulled it off.

Tonight had been a good night.

In the old days, he'd want to pick up a few girls and go indulge in some serious self-congratulation in a hotel suite that came with hot and cold running excess.

But not now. Tonight, he just wanted to head home, hook up with Sarah and then wake up tomorrow morning to the ratings figures and a top iTunes position for Lauren's opening number.

It was all about the dollar, baby.

It took a couple of hours to debrief, wrap everything up, schmooze everyone who needed schmoozing and arrange a planning session for the next day.

It was almost midnight by the time he pushed through the studio doors onto the boardwalk. They'd made the decision to host the show in a lot that was accessible to the public, so that they could use the footage of the stars arriving and leaving as teasers for the shows. Only a few burly security guards and a stretch of yellow tape were restraining the small crowd, all of them holding out iPhones. God, he missed the simple days of relative obscurity and autograph books.

Nevertheless, he slipped straight into Tom Cruise mode, shaking hands, taking selfies and working his way along the line, lest someone put his refusal on Instagram and within five minutes the whole world thinks he's a dick. Again.

'Davie, we love you!'

'Can you say, "Hi, Betty!"? My mom loves you.'

Yep, he still had it. His fans still adored him. Last year was a blip, but he was headed back to the top. No more crap, no more disasters, and one day – in a ghost-written memoir – he'd claim it made him a better person. He'd say it was a turning point – had to reach rock bottom to appreciate what mattered or similar shit. Meanwhile, life was getting real good again.

'Davie...'

The voice. Male. Teenage.

His head raised to check it out and just before the point of eye contact with the young man, he saw a cloud of red coming towards him.

The recoil was automatic, as was the tight clench of his eyes as the scarlet liquid reached his face. He staggered backwards, waiting for the pain, but as the wet sticky substance ran down his hair, his face, his neck, there was only an intoxicating, metallic smell that seeped into his pores.

Davie recognised it immediately.

It was the smell of someone else's blood.

8

MIRREN

'Every Breath You Take' – Sting

The Centurion Suite at the Staples Centre wasn't their usual venue for Thursday-night dinner, but given this was the first South City concert in a three-night run, there was no way the two women, sitting anonymously at a corner table, would be anywhere else.

Lou Cole paused, a bread roll midway to her mouth. She prided herself on being the last person in Los Angeles who still consumed carbs on anything other than birthdays, Christmas or the discovery that your partner was cheating on you with a twenty-two-year-old waitress.

'Honey, you really need to get laid. Seriously. It's the only thing that will help at this point.'

Mirren tilted her head to one side, caught somewhere between amusement and outrage. 'Then I think we can give thanks that you're not a bereavement counsellor or there'd be a whole lot of shagging going on.'

'You're right. I think I missed my calling.'

Mirren couldn't resist the urge to smile. Only friends who had been together for a lifetime could spark off each other like this.

She'd first met Lou Cole when she came to Hollywood in 1992. Back then, the only three people she knew in the whole of the US were Davie and Zander, who'd come over from Scotland with her, and Wes Lomax, who had 'discovered' them. Lomax had been on a golfing trip to St Andrews when Davie had persuaded the room-service waitress to let him take an order to Lomax's room, allowing him to sneak Mirren's first attempt at writing into the legendary producer's room. Lomax had loved it, made the movie, called it *The Brutal Circle* and, goddammit, had it not won them an Oscar.

Welcome to the American dream. Come right on in.

Back then, Lou had been a feisty young journalist on the LA Times, a go-getting African American rebelling against the establishment and ambitious to the point of ruthless. It had paid off. Now she was the editor of the industry newspaper the *Hollywood Post*, a weekly publication that contained every industry move, play and piece of gossip. The stars came to her with exclusives, chose her centre pages to break stories or get ahead of scandals. In a time when the press were viewed as somewhere between rodents and serial killers on the Hollywood scale, Lou Cole still commended respect, largely because she was a force of nature with integrity, brains and the ear of every important player within a fifty mile radius of the Walk of Fame. Back in the early days, the two women would share tubs of ice cream sitting on Santa Monica Beach late at night. Lou would dream of a Pulitzer and Mirren would dream of writing bestselling novels. The Pulitzer hadn't materialized, but sheer graft had taken Lou to the top, while Mirren's *Clansman* novels had delivered stellar success that led to movie-world glory. Now, they had the money and sway to get them the best tables in Craig's and Spago, but although the locations had changed, their friendship had not. They'd been together through every crazy twist and turn that life had thrown at them.

Lou had never married, but there had been a couple of long-term relationships that perished because they always came second place to her career. She had been Chloe's godmother, was a second mom to Logan and came close to punching out Jack Gore when he'd betrayed Mirren. She was the secret-keeper in Mirren's life, the person who knew everything. Almost everything. Mirren had never told her the real reason that she, Davie and

Zander had come off that stage at the Oscars over twenty years ago and gone their separate ways, with no contact until events of recent months brought them back together. She'd never told her the truth about her life back in Scotland.

One day, she'd tell her everything. But not yet.

As if she'd tuned into Mirren's thoughts, Lou wiped hot mustard from her bottom lip and asked, 'So how's the big childhood-friends reunion thing working out?'

'It's...' Mirren paused, searching for the words. 'It's... Weird. Davie and I have had dinner a couple of times, it feels easy and familiar and then I remember that we're not sixteen any more and he's not Davie Johnston from two houses away. It's like I don't know him, yet there's a love there. It's like having a piece of me back and trying to work out where it fits.' Lou nodded as she bit down on another fry. 'Very poetic, my friend. And what about my favourite sex god? Tell me you've got naked with him. You'll go right up in my estimations.'

'Sorry.' Mirren shook her head, grinning. 'I know you don't get this, because you have no emotional depth and you're sex-obsessed...'

'All true,' Lou agreed.

'But Zander and I grew up with a brother-sister vibe and that's exactly how it still feels.'

'What a waste.'

'See previous comment about shallow and sex-driven. Anyway, he came over on Chloe's birthday and hung out with Logan and me.'

'Where was Fucker Gore?'

Mirren raised an eyebrow in mock rebuke. While she'd lost all her animosity against her arrogant asshole of an ex-husband, put all her negative feelings to one side for Logan's sake, Lou fully intended to bear the grudge on her friend's behalf until the end of time.

'Who knows?' Mirren shrugged. 'He came over for an hour or so, then bailed out.'

Lou pursed her lips, an expression Mirren had seen a million times before. There wasn't a Hollywood innuendo, flirtation or an attraction that Lou didn't know about – ergo, it made perfect sense that she'd have the details on what Jack was up to. Usually, Mirren didn't want to know, but something in Lou's wide-eyed expression made her curious.

'OK, spill. Who is it?'

'I heard he's sending large bouquets to Carmella Cass. Daily.' It took Mirren a moment to process. 'The model from Davie's show? Whose boyfriend... What's his name?'

'Jizzo,' Lou added.

'Yeah, Jizzo. He passed away last week?'

It was phrased as a question because it just seemed too bizarre to comprehend.

Lou took a sip of beer – another rebellious throwback to her uncouth youth – as she nodded. 'Yup. Seems like Fucker Gore is lining himself up as a replacement already. Although, in the scumbag's defence, apparently he's been hitting on her for a while. Didn't take him long to move on once he found out he wasn't Mercedes Dance's baby daddy, right?'

'Ah, suddenly, the rock T-shirts and tattoos make sense,' Mirren nodded, laughing at the ridiculousness of it.

'A tattoo? No. Fricking. Way,' Lou shrieked, finding it equally hilarious.

'Way,' Mirren added, the giggles contagious. Both women were wiping tears away, when, like an ascending ringtone, the volume of the buzz in the room got louder. Mirren soon spotted why.

Tonight there was a very different crowd to the one that usually congregated in the Staples Centre for Lakers and Clippers games. At this moment, there were almost 20,000 in the stadium, taking it to full capacity, and the majority were teenage girls, most of whom had pleaded, badgered or blackmailed their parents into buying them tickets and bringing them to see the boys whose posters adorned their walls.

Located on level B, the Centurion Suite was available to those with American Express Centurion cards, the world-renowned, invitation-only black card that opened a world of spending and came with no credit limit. It was reported that the average income of a black-card holder was $1.3 million, with assets of over $16 million. And small change.

In the lounge, the black-card holders mingled with the fans who owned premier seating tickets, usually corporate big shots and those who liked to pay a premium to enjoy dinner and seats with the best view in the house.

But right now, none of the young girls in their designer clothes were looking at the buffet or at the parents who'd forked out $500 a head to get them here. Every single one of them was watching the tall guy striding across the room, tailed by two black-suited security guards, both former Navy Seals. A hundred smart phones were raised in unison and video buttons hurriedly pressed by trembling fingers. Logan Gore kissed both women on the cheek before slipping in beside his mother.

'This is so typical of you two,' he grumbled, feigning irritation. 'I give you backstage passes and where are you? Up here, having food and ignoring your poor, neglected, insecure son.'

Mirren laughed, gesturing around the room, marvelling at how grounded he was despite living in this overbearing bubble of adoration. 'Yes, I can see why you feel that you're lacking in attention.'

Chairs started creaking as girls rose to their feet. Logan and Mirren both knew what that meant. In about ten seconds they'd start circling him, asking for autographs and selfies while promising a lifetime of devotion.

One of the security guys cleared his throat and Logan sighed. 'Gotta go. Just wanted to say hello. Are you gonna watch from your booth?'

Mirren nodded. 'We'd only get in the way backstage. And this way I get to see what everyone else does. I kind of like that.'

Lou leaned over. 'And you'd better dedicate a song to me, as we both know I'm your favourite woman on God's earth.'

'I will, Aunt Lou,' Logan agreed. 'But only 'cause I'm scared of you.'

'Excellent,' Lou beamed. 'I like it when I instil dread and fear.'

Mirren smiled. These two had always had a special camaraderie and she loved that Logan had someone else who cared for him almost as much as she did.

Watching him leave, a swell of pride caught in her throat, and right behind it a wave of sadness. It was just the two of them now. This time last year, they'd been a family. Now they were a duo.

Spotting the emotional ricochet on her face, Lou reached over and put her hand on Mirren's, saying softly, 'No, no, no, no, don't, baby. Don't let it take this moment.'

Mirren nodded, grateful, and shook off the melancholy. That's how it worked. The wave of sadness ambushed you when you were down, but also when you were happy and least expecting it, taking the brief moments of joy and turning them into moments of regret and longing for the girl who was no longer here and the family unit that was long gone.

'Mirren? Hey.'

As if sent by the gods of distraction, both women looked up to see a familiar face. Mike Feechan, president of Pictor, was standing looking slightly awkward, not a stance that was familiar for a man who made deals worth millions of dollars on a daily basis. But that was in the boardroom, where he was Master of the Movie Universe. This was way out of his comfort zone. The young girl standing next to him wearing a South City T-shirt and a gold necklace that spelled out the word 'Logan' was eyeing him with undisguised scepticism.

'Mike, hi!' Mirren greeted him, raising to kiss him on both cheeks. Lou did the same, then gestured for him to join them.

'Thanks, but we already have a table.' He put his arm around the young girl who was still standing silently beside him. 'This is my daughter, Jade.'

'Hi. Lovely to meet you,' Mirren said warmly. 'Like the T-shirt.'

Jade responded with a shy, 'Thanks.'

'OK, so after spending my whole life trying – and failing – to impress her, I think I've finally managed it by telling her I work with Logan Gore's mom. So we just wanted to say hi.'

'Ahhh, I understand completely,' Mirren said. 'How about I arrange something with your dad so you can meet Logan properly?'

'That... W-would... Be... Awesome,' Jade stuttered, her excitement obvious. 'Like, totally awesome.'

Mike laughed. 'Mirren, thank you. I fear everything else life brings her will be an anti-climax after this.'

'No problem at all.'

'And now that I've resorted to emotional blackmail to coerce you into impressing my child, I'll leave you to it. I'll call you tomorrow. I think we're due to sit down and have a chat.'

'I think we are,' Mirren answered smoothly, giving no hint of her irritation over the latest *Clansman* negotiations.

Kissing both women, he mouthed another 'Thank you' and retreated to a table on the other side of the room.

'Stop it,' Mirren warned Lou.

Her friend feigned confusion. 'Stop what?'

'You're already mentally setting me up with him.'

'Yeah, and I can see why you'd hate that. I mean, I happen to know he's single. He's also successful, powerful, looks like Liev Schreiber's equally attractive brother and seems to be a caring dad who's here with his daughter instead of off trying to fuck a supermodel whose boyfriend just died. I can see why you'd hate his guts.'

'Sarcasm. Really?' Mirren retorted, enjoying playing around. Lou had a point. If she was looking for any kind of relationship, she could see that Mike would tick boxes. But the truth was, it had been twenty years since she'd had any form of physical contact with any man other than Jack Gore, and that wasn't something she was ready to change just yet.

They signed off the check and made their way out to their private viewing booth. Located right in the middle of the stadium, it had a semi-circular black leather sofa, a black high-gloss table and an eager waiter ready to take their drinks order.

He'd just hurried off to the bar when the lights went down and the contagious cheer rose to a deafening crescendo.

Spotlights roamed over the stage, the first notes of 'Not Giving You Back' were twanged on an electric guitar, and the roar got even louder.

Mirren stood, leaning against the balcony, immersed in a sea of thousands, goosebumps covering her body, completely unaware that while 20,000 people in that stadium were focused on the stage, one head in the crowd was turned the other way, looking upwards, watching her.

9

ZANDER

'I Knew You Were Trouble' – Taylor Swift

Zander held the Marlboro loosely between his lips, the tip falling dangerously close to his chest as he inhaled.

'You should give that up,' Adrianna informed him as she rose from the scrunched sheets, the flawless contours of her ass shaded by the stream of light that forced its way through the gap in the heavy chenille curtains.

'I should,' Zander agreed. 'But sometimes I kinda like things that are bad for me.'

In the last week, he'd liked the beautiful thing that was bad for him on several occasions. They'd met most days, snatched moments, usually at their favourite hotel, Shutters on the Beach, a resplendent colonial beauty on the sands at Santa Monica.

Adrianna's perfect red lips widened as she leaned back down to kiss him. 'So that's what we have in common.'

Yes, it was.

She disappeared into the shower. Zander was only dissuaded from joining her when his cell phone rang and Hollie's name flashed up. He knew better than to reject the call. Ignoring his right-hand woman was a dangerous move. It wouldn't be the first time she tracked him down and then coerced room service into opening a hotel room door for her.

'Hi,' he said, attempting to pull on his jeans with one hand.

She immediately let loose. 'Urgh, you're naked. I can tell. And you're smoking. Did we not talk about that?'

Zander's laughter made him drop the phone and he had to scramble to reclaim it. 'Your superpowers freak me right out,' he told her.

'As they should. Listen, where are you? I'm in Venice to collect you and the newsflash is that you're not here. You've got an event in four hours and I'm holding your suit. So unless you intend to go butt naked, I need to know where you are.'

'Shutters on the Beach.'

Silence. Then, 'Tell me you're having a coffee in a picturesque setting and not doing anything you shouldn't be doing... Fuck it, I don't want to know. I'll be there in fifteen.'

He hung up just as Adrianna emerged from the bathroom, already dressed in a plain white shift dress, accessorized with red stiletto heels and reapplied scarlet lipstick. The information went straight from Zander's eyes to his brain to his instant erection.

There was no doubt about it, this was a physical craving just like the one he felt for a bottle of Jack and a line of coke.

She blew him a kiss, murmured a 'Ciao' and was out the door. Ten minutes and a quick shower later, he was sitting downstairs in the restaurant, which looked out onto the famous Santa Monica boardwalk and pier. It was 5 p.m., late for the lunch crowd but too early for the evening diners.

As he sat at a window seat, he eyed the array of drinks behind the bar, feeling that familiar urge creeping through his veins. It would never leave him. That need, the absolute desperation for a shot of bourbon. But it was never just one. The first time he'd knocked back a slug of alcohol at the age of fourteen, right after he'd battered his father with a baseball bat for beating his mother one too many times, he was hooked. This was more than the West of Scotland affinity with a good drink. This was addiction, pure and simple. And he knew it was never going away, no matter how many meetings he attended. Today, he wasn't giving in to it. And hopefully not tomorrow.

When Hollie burst in, he held up his coffee cup. 'See? Coffee.'

'Which would really impress me if I didn't just see Adrianna Guilloti parked outside talking on her cell phone,' she countered dryly. 'Here's your suit – which I'm guessing is the second Adrianna Guilloti you'll have been in today.'

Zander stayed silent, but Hollie, as always, read his face. 'Urgh, you are depressingly predictable. Can I just check that you are in full knowledge of her husband's reputation? It's just that when you show up with your testicles in your mouth, I want to reassure myself that I didn't fail you by neglecting to ensure you were in full possession of the facts.'

'You can sleep easy,' Zander replied, signalling the waitress to request a coffee for Hollie. He knew exactly who Carlton Farnsworth was – a self-made billionaire who had his fingers in many pies, from nightclubs to hotels, but specialized in property. The fact that he had evaded every accusation of dodgy dealing ever levied at him spoke volumes. He owned many assets in Queens, Brooklyn and Manhattan, including – it was rumoured – hundreds of properties, a couple of iconic landmarks, several commissioners, senators, a few judges and a couple of former mayors. Not that he'd ever been charged or indicted. He was way too clever for that. But as the rumours drifted along in the gutter, he continued to expand his empire.

Of all the labels Farnsworth was credited with – mogul, investor, capitalist, criminal, fraudster, entrepreneur – the one that bothered Zander most was 'husband'. He'd had no idea Adrianna was married when he met her, but as soon as he'd found out, he'd backed off. Married women weren't his thing. He didn't have many morals, but that was one of them.

It had ended when he'd learned the truth, leaving their blistering but brief coupling in the past tense. In the months since their first encounter, he had never chased her, never attempted to disrupt her life or marriage, but when she'd shown up last week at the Combrian, he'd relapsed like an addict who'd just found himself face down on a pile of cocaine after a six-month abstention. The compulsion was just too hard to resist. This one was going to take more than a twelve-step programme to conquer.

Heading outside, there was a familiar, 'Zander, over here!' It went unacknowledged, but Hollie immediately tensed at the paparazzo's call.

As soon as they'd locked the car doors, she exhaled. 'I didn't see him when I came in, and I can usually sniff them out at a hundred yards.' She immediately pressed a button and put a call in to a contact at Zander's management team. 'Cindy, hi. It's Hollie. Listen – just in case we get any interest about Zander's movements today, I wanted to give you the heads-up that he met with Adrianna Guilloti at Shutters to discuss their next campaign. Give me a shout if any enquiries come in and I'll let you have you more details. Thanks, my darling.'

She hung up and slouched back in her seat. 'Either I've got PMT or I've got a bad feeling about this.'

'PMT,' Zander replied casually. 'Chill out, Holls. It'll be cool.'

'I'm going to get that put on your gravestone. "Here lies Zander Leith, actor and Hollywood heart-throb, who died after leaving all his worldly goods, including his Aston Martin, to his trusty assistant, Hollie. His final words before Carlton Farnsworth had him whacked were, 'Chill out, Holls. It'll be cool."'

'If you carry on with this insubordination, I'll give you the night off tonight,' Zander threatened playfully, crossing his ankles on the dashboard and earning a thigh-slap of rebuke.

'Hah! Nice try. But I only stay for the perks, and if those dry up, I'm off.'

They both knew she didn't mean it. He couldn't live without her, and she loved him enough to put up with him. Besides, he hated formal functions with a passion, so there was no way he was going to Lomax's annual pre-Golden Globes dinner without her. It was a standard fixture in the Hollywood calendar. Held one week before the ceremony, Lomax brought all the nominees together with his own stable of talent in a shameless networking event dressed up as a glitzy exercise in congratulation.

If his attendance wasn't compulsory, Zander would have blown it off years ago.

He was going, but – to Hollie's irritation – his reticence forced him to stall so much they were late in arriving, just making it to the end of the convoy of limos dropping their bejewelled cargo at the doors of the Beverly Hills Hotel.

Zander alighted first, holding the door open and taking Hollie's hand as she joined him. There was no arguing with the fact that when she was around, he felt... What was the word? Safer? Better? Less likely to completely fuck up, get wrecked on booze and coke, and punch out some irritating dickhead?

All of the above. Not to mention totally aware that if he stepped out of line, she'd soon nudge him right back into place again.

The sounds of conversation and laughter rose above the string quartet playing Handel's Water Music on the terrace, as they reached the poolside for pre-dinner drinks. Zander immediately scanned the crowd, ready to switch into 'movie-star networking mode', kicking off an hour of superficiality and inanity that he would never get back.

'OK, smile on, shoulders back, pretend you're delighted to be here,' Hollie murmured teasingly, her smile genuine as she took two glasses of OJ from a passing waitress. Zander appreciated the gesture of non-alcoholic solidarity.

The white lights surrounding the poolside and patio restaurant twinkled in the dusk, catching the diamonds around their owners' graceful and, in some cases, surgically tightened necks.

Chanel, Dior, Gucci and Halston were just some of the designer wares in attendance, parading alongside Tom Ford, Armani and the resurging cool of Burberry.

Hollie spotted Mirren chatting to Mike Feechan, head of Pictor, and nudged Zander. 'Wow, they make a stunning couple. Are they together?'

Zander shrugged and Hollie rolled her eyes. He honestly had no idea, but looking at them now, he could see what Hollie meant. Mirren was beautiful, her navy gown a stark contrast to her pale-skinned perfection and her loose red curls.

For a moment he saw her as a fifteen-year-old-girl who would bemoan her red hair while threatening retribution on anyone who teased her. That had always been Mirren – strong, independent, defiant, with the strength to endure and fight back even when her heart was hurt.

Back then, Zander had felt a brotherly affection for her, and now that they were back in each other's lives, those feelings were just as strong. The things that had happened to her would have broken most people, him included, but there she was, surviving, moving forward.

'Let's go over and say hello,' Zander suggested.

'Correct response,' Hollie replied. 'I'll know in five seconds if they're sleeping together.'

'If you could market that talent, you'd make a fortune,' Zander told her, placing a gentle hand on her back as she steered through the crowd.

'Excuse me, I—' He stopped.

In front of him, an absolute vision of gorgeousness. The red one-shouldered silk creation flattering her dark complexion, enhanced by the large ruby drop earrings. Her brown eyes smoky, her lashes accentuating their perfect shape. Her black hair parted in the middle and gathered in a loose clasp that allowed it to fall down her naked back.

'Zander Leith, a pleasure to see you here,' she declared, holding out her hand in greeting. The gesture spurred him into action and he took her hand, leaning over to kiss the familiar cheek.

'Lovely to see you too. You've met Hollie?'

'Of course.'

The two women smiled at each other, Hollie making the first move to shake hands. Zander had a feeling she'd be loving every dramatic moment of this meeting almost as much as he was hating it.

The woman turned to her companion. 'Darling, I don't think you've met, although obviously you know his movies.' She turned back to include Zander in the conversation. 'Zander, this is my husband, Carlton Farnsworth.'

Zander took the hand that was offered to him and shook it, noticing that the other man's grip was just a little tighter than necessary.

What was that about?

An affirmation of the other man's strength?

An alpha male attempting to show dominance?

An overenthusiastic welcome with no underlying meaning?

Or did Carlton Farnsworth know that just a few hours before, Zander had been in a Santa Monica hotel screwing his wife?

And if so, what was he going to do about it?

10

SARAH

'Stairway to Heaven' – Led Zeppelin

Were they really playing Zeppelin's 'Stairway to Heaven'? If they ever made a movie called *Spinal Tap: Where Are They Now?* this would be the opening scene.

Sarah had chosen to sit in the middle row of the bank of chairs laid out beside the grave at Forest Lawn. Davie stood in the front row, only a few feet away from Jizzo's imminent resting place. In front of them, a coffin shaped like a keyboard. Yep, a keyboard. Or to be more accurate, a keyboard surrounded by a dozen wreaths in the shape of musical notes.

On the other side of Davie, Sarah could see Carmella Cass, her head flopping as if supported by elastic, her wails loud.

Sarah scanned the congregation, intrigued to see who else had come to pay their respects.

Dong, Zeek and Caz, the three remaining members of Jizzo's 1980s heavy-metal band, Stone Jiz, were there, adverts for – from left to right – cosmetic surgery, hair-plugs and Zimmer frames. The latter, Caz, had almost lost the use of his legs after injecting so much heroin into his groin that his veins collapsed.

Sarah knew that Davie wanted to be anywhere but here. He wasn't great at dealing with stuff like this. Davie did optimism, superficiality and positivity – he didn't do death. That wasn't an unusual sentiment in LA. Funerals were too much of a reminder of the ageing process and mortality, which half the population spent their lives trying to deny.

For Sarah, however, this was fascinating from a journalistic perspective. Jizzo's death was – not to sound too cold or unfeeling – another chapter in her book, one that focused on celebrity departures and the illicit substances that caused their premature departures.

Michael Jackson. Overdose of Propofol. Heath Ledger. Prescription drugs. Cory Monteith. Heroin.

Jizzo Stacks. Almost every illicit drug known to man. The final toxicology results were yet to be released, but Davie had learned that initial tests indicated a veritable pharmacy of substances that were either keeping him alive or killing him. Or both.

A saxophone led the introduction to Jizzo's hit 'Cut You', and once again Lauren Finney stepped forward and sang the haunting version she'd performed on *American Stars*. The funeral was being recorded for a one-off episode of *Beauty and the Beats*, so there was a guarantee of another million or so downloads of Lauren's track on iTunes. And thanks to his production deal on both shows, there was another kerching on Davie's bank account.

Cynical? Absolutely. There was no doubt that Sarah struggled to deal with the morality of a world in which everything was for sale, including dignity and death – even more so when it was her boyfriend who was profiting from the transactions.

The truth was, if Davie didn't do it, someone else would. He was just the guy who got there first.

And he wouldn't make a cent if there wasn't a long line of willing volunteers waiting to sell out for the cameras.

Wasn't she just as bad, turning up here not to mourn the passing of a man, but to gather material for a book? That skidding noise was her rapid descent from the moral high ground. She could tell herself she was exposing truths, unearthing scandals and writing wrongs. And she was. But she also had one eye on a career path that she wanted to switch from newspapers to books.

A tortured wail snapped her attention back to the front. Lauren had finished singing, and the pallbearers were preparing to lower the casket, a process that was halted by Carmella Cass charging towards the coffin, screaming Jizzo's name, before throwing herself across the ebony and ivory of Jizzo's entombment.

Sarah knew that at least half the congregation were thinking something along the lines of 'And the Oscar for Best Dramatic Performance at the Funeral of a Reality-TV Star goes to...', but that thought was lost as she became fixated on the scene playing out in front of her.

Davie had moved towards Carmella, but he was stopped by a man in dark shades wearing a suit over a black T-shirt. It took Sarah a moment, given that he was out of context in this setting. His hair was different. Longer. And the shades were partially obscuring his face. But that was... Yep, that was Mirren McLean's ex-husband, Jack Gore. What the hell was he doing here, and why was he acting in such a proprietary way towards Carmella Cass? Gore was up there with Bruckheimer and Grazer, serious producers with incredible films to their names, and yet here he was showing up at what was, in effect, the set of a reality-TV show. One with a dearly departed rock star taking centre stage. Bizarre didn't even begin to cover it.

This was like watching a soap opera playing out right in front of you.

It did, however, bring her back to the subject of Mirren McLean. Or rather Mirren McLean's mother. After Ed Callaghan's call, asking her to do some digging on Marilyn, she'd pulled in a favour from an old friend at the *Daily Scot* and had her check the Births, Deaths and Marriages register.

Marilyn McLean. The birth was there. 1950. London Road. Glasgow. The daughter of a 'businessman' and a 'housewife'. No marriage certificate, so it looked like she'd remained single. No death certificate, so she was still alive. But then, Sarah already knew that because about eighteen months ago, when she was still a crime reporter on *The Daily Scot*, she'd seen Marilyn at the funeral of Glasgow gangster, Manny Murphy. Marilyn had been with a bloke with a scarred face that Sarah now knew was Liverpool gangster, Razor Ritchie. Which meant the story Ed told her about someone from the Liverpool gang saying Mirren's mother was making a noise down there was almost certainly true. Razor had been arrested, forcing Marilyn to crawl out from under his stone of protection and financial support. Sarah was intrigued. She'd never actually met Marilyn McLean and so far, her own research had turned up nothing more substantial: no social-network profiles, no newspaper cuttings, no criminal record, no credit rating, no known address, nothing.

Marilyn was a ghost. In the wind.

Sarah knew Marilyn had left Glasgow immediately after the horrific event that changed Mirren, Davie and Zander's lives, back in the eighties. Sarah had never asked if any of them knew where Marilyn was now. It was a scab that was there for all of them, but not one at which she felt she could pick. One day she might decide that was a mistake, but not now.

The world wasn't going to hear their secrets from her.

Sarah watched Davie now, so dignified, solemn. In the days since the phone call from Ed, she'd toyed with telling him that her former editor wanted her to look into Mirren's mother, but hadn't. He had enough on his plate. A new talk show. A top reality show. A divorce. A recent scandal. A dead rock star. Some lunatic chucking blood at him after his show.

Anyone could be behind that. Davie reckoned it was a teenage male who'd approached him, but that wouldn't be hard for anyone, even a stranger in town, to arrange. The streets of Hollywood were awash with young guys who'd come here with stars in their eyes and ended up with cardboard boxes and aspirations that no longer went any higher than renting themselves out for a few hours to earn enough money to eat. Everything was for sale here, no questions asked. Throw a bucket of blood at a celebrity? A hundred dollars and name the location.

Davie's security team hadn't been quick enough to catch the guy, and the security footage was useless because the culprit kept his hood up and his face down. Thankfully, though, his people had bought up the video coverage from the fans who'd been there that night, so they had control of what made it to the press. Davie's tech guys had analysed every tape, but not one of them caught the face of the idiot behind the stunt. All they knew so far was that it was pig's blood and some maniac had decided to make some kind of fucked-up statement by splattering Davie with it. Bizarre.

Insane. Davie had completely shrugged it off and, to her at least, was saying that he wasn't worried about it. That it was just some idiot playing a prank.

Sarah wasn't so sure. Davie had pissed off a lot of people in his past, going right back to the horrors of Davie, Zander and Mirren's years in Scotland over two decades ago. Back then, one of those people he'd crossed – perhaps more than any other - was Marilyn McLean. Was it a coincidence that Marilyn's name was resurfacing, just as someone was pulling threatening stunts on Davie?

Sarah thought it probably was. Probably. Not definitely. Her guard was up. If Marilyn was about to come out of the woodwork, then Sarah had to be the one there waiting for her.

The year before, when she'd learned about the horrific event that had made Davie, Mirren and Zander leave Scotland, she'd killed the story to protect them.

Nothing would stop her doing it again.

11

DAVIE

'Forever Young' – Rod Stewart

The assembled cast in Davie's dressing room wore the faces of the seriously irked.

Cal Wolfe, uber-agent extraordinaire. Small but wiry, impeccably tailored in suits he had made by a third-generation Savile row tailor, a man with a ruthless streak that was legendary for both its cruelty and success. Davie and Cal had been together for two decades, through the ups, downs and irritations. The year before, when Davie's career had been almost destroyed by the Sky Nixon scandal, Cal had been loyal at first but then he'd been the proverbial rat high diving off the sinking ship. However, he'd come back grovelling as Davie began to rise from the seabed and Davie had forgiven him. Almost. A few factors came into play in his decision. Their careers were too intertwined to unravel and, well, better the devil you know. Cal was a killer agent and made more money for him than anyone else would or could, so Davie had screwed him out of a couple of commission percentage points as a punishment and they were a formidable force again. And if they both dressed it up as loyalty and friendship, that was fine too.

Mark Bock, head of security for the studio was also there. An ex-cop who'd made a name for himself when he'd brought down a trafficking ring that was shipping eastern European girls into the city and pimping them out for top dollar.

Mellie, his director-producer, wore her standard look of someone who had better places to be and more urgent things to be doing. With an hour until airtime, both of those were accurate sentiments.

And in the corner, purely in an observational capacity, Sarah sat focused on her iPad. Davie had no idea what she was doing. She seemed to spend every waking hour doing research and writing her book. In the last week, she'd been particularly distracted, and if he were honest, he wished she'd let it go and chill out for a few days.

Which, yes, was like the workaholic pot calling the workaholic kettle black.

He reclined back in one of the six black leather Eames chairs that sat round the onyx coffee table. To call it a dressing room was like saying the Getty was just a house. It was 1,400 square feet of designer living-workspace, designed to accommodate his every whim, need and indulgence. From the white gloss kitchen to the mirrored bar, to the California-king bedroom in case he got cranky and needed a nap, this was the kind of room that befitted the guy who had entered a pissing contest with the other late-night talk-show hosts and was clearly winning.

Oh, and he was pissing in a jet-black marble urinal, imported from Tokyo at the cost of an average-size SUV.

Davie's attention was brought back from the Clippers game running on silent on the TV by Cal's grating irritation.

'So you have nothing? Not a fucking thing?' Cal asked, for the second or third time, his tone escalating through several stages of annoyance.

Mark Bock shook his head. 'The wacko had a hood up and some kind of covering over his face. But we've put four extra security guys on the door, stationed two out at the house and we have another two ready to be posted on close protection...'

'I'm not doing that. Forget it,' Davie said casually. He'd deliberately never employed any kind of bodyguard for his day-to-day existence, mostly because he didn't want anyone to have intimate details of his life. Secrets led to knowledge; knowledge led to blackmail; blackmail led to a hole in your bank balance or your private life being splattered across the *National Enquirer*. His marriage to Jenny had been on the rocks for a long time and he was only human. There had been several affairs, multiple one-night stands and a particularly heated sexual relationship with Vala Diaz, a Mexican goddess and actress who worked on the same show as his children, the eight year old child stars Bray and Bella Johnston.

On the roadmap of his personal life, there were many potholes – none of which he wanted anyone else to know about. Now, things were far more settled. He and Sarah were making it work and for the first time he was being faithful. But scrutiny and intrusion still made him uncomfortable, so he'd pass on having two human mountains walking three feet behind him at all times.

Anyway, this whole situation wasn't particularly fazing him. Come on, it was just some freak trying to pull a stunt that would get him a bit of notoriety and a YouTube following. Sure, it was strange that the weirdo didn't appear to have put any images online yet, but no doubt that would be his next move. In the meantime, the studio had released one photograph, with Davie looking like he was roaring with rage at his attacker. All the entertainment shows and tabloids had covered it. The result? The kind of publicity that would have cost him a sum with at least five zeros. Hi ho, silver lining. Twenty minutes of discomfort had equalled maximum exposure for the show. And with a bit of luck, the freak would now move on to his next target.

Mellie unfurled her legs from under her and stood, her spiked heels and black leather trousers giving her a look that sat somewhere between Robocop and an occupation that demanded the use of a safe word. 'Look, gents, much as this is fun, we have a show to put out in less than an hour.'

Heading for the door, clipboard in hand, she didn't wait for a reply before adding, 'If I could just ask we keep our main man in one piece, that would be lovely. He's not much, but he's all we've got.'

Davie winked as she passed him and took the break as his cue to get up too.

'Cal, I'm gonna leave this to you. Just have to go meet tonight's guests.' He didn't wait for a reply, trusting Cal to have his back on the security from now on. There was no way Cal Wolfe was going to let anything happen to the guy who made him a couple of million a year.

Heading down the corridor, he pretended to be fixated on checking his phone as he walked. Much easier than having to greet everyone who passed by, trying to catch his eye, looking for the validation of an acknowledgement from the boss. The only exception was when he passed Lauren Finney's dressing room, where he knocked on the door, popped his head in and said hi. Lauren was surrounded by make-up artists working on her hair and face, but she still grinned and blew him a kiss.

Outside the door of dressing room 2, he paused, something niggling.

It took Davie a few moments to recognize the sensation. Anxiety? No. Fear? Nope. It was… nerves. He was actually nervous. Not a full-scale, shaking, want-to-throw-up kind of deal, just a mild tremor of apprehension.

He knocked, making the 'South City' sign on the door tremble. A chorus of invitations beckoned him in.

Of course, his eyes went to Mirren first, making the tingling sensation creep a little further up the intensity scale. In blue jeans and a white skinny polo-neck sweater, her hair tied back in a messy ponytail, she looked a decade younger than her forty-one years.

Forty-one. That made him forty-two. Nearly thirty years they'd known each other.

Cliché, maybe, but who would have thought this was where they'd end up?

Their childhood homes were over five thousand miles, and light years, away from here. Smack in the middle of a rough council estate in the east end of Glasgow, they'd grown up in the same pebble-dashed terrace of five houses.

Davie lived on one end of the terrace with his mum, Ena, a grafter who'd worked three jobs to support them. Zander lived on the other end, with his dad, Jono, and his mum, Maggie. Jono Leith was the local hard man, a heavy-drinking, vicious bastard who attacked first, asked questions later.

Davie's teeth clenched at the memory of the man and the knowledge of the effect he would have on their lives. But that was later, many years after he first saw Mirren, aged twelve, sitting outside her house in the middle of the terrace, smoking a cigarette, trying to block out the noise of her mother, Marilyn, having sex with Jono inside, only two houses away from where the bastard's wife sat waiting for him. There was barely a woman on their estate that Jono hadn't shagged, but Marilyn didn't care. She saw him as a meal ticket, and was prepared to ignore her dignity, the rumours and her daughter to get him.

Every night, from the bedroom window of his house two doors away, Davie would see Mirren there, until he finally plucked up the courage to speak to her.

They soon became inseparable. Zander. Mirren. Davie. The three of them against the world. They had no money, no prospects, nowhere to go and nowhere to be, but it didn't matter.

Zander, his best mate, was the one who got the girls, while Davie was the one they all wanted as a cute, funny friend. Except Mirren.

When they were sixteen, he discovered that for some inexplicable, fan-fucking-tastic reason, she'd fallen in love with him. That would have been enough for him. Life complete. Davie and Mirren. They could have got a house on the estate and had kids, and he'd have been happy just to have her, just to breathe the same air every day and sleep beside her at night.

But it didn't play out that way.

Jono Leith, Zander's dad, had fucked up their lives, changing everything, destroying what they all had. They were forced to find new lives, here in LA, and while success had come to all three of them, their friendships and relationships with each other were collateral damage.

For twenty years, Mirren, Zander and Davie had no contact, their ties too much of a reminder of what it had cost them to get there. They lived in the same city, moved in the same circles, but always managed to avoid being in the same company, mutually understanding that their relationships belonged in another place and time. It was only when Sarah started digging into their past last year that the three of them had been forced to re-establish contact, brutally aware that what happened back then, before they left Scotland, could destroy everything they had now.

They'd stopped that happening. Only just. Now that they were back in touch, they hadn't quite figured out the new rules. They were friends again, but they had a history that could never be told. Like a family that had been ripped apart and were slowly rebuilding the bricks in their wall, laying foundations, testing for weaknesses, finding strengths, taking it slow, easing into each other again. Zander and Davie had discovered that they were half-brothers, both of them spawned by Jono, a man they both despised, so it was a tough development to process. They should have known. It was in both their DNA's to bury uncomfortable truths and harsh realities, so it made sense that they were related.

As for him and Mirren?

He wasn't the same person as that little curly-haired guy with a cheeky grin, and Mirren was no longer the angry, neglected teenager desperate to escape her life.

They were no longer in love. There was no 'Davie and Mirren'.

And he wasn't sure where that left them.

'Hi,' she smiled, rising to greet him. As she hugged him tightly, every trace of the apprehension he'd felt earlier dissipated. Behind her, an obscenely good-looking guy rose to his feet and held out his hand. 'Hey, Davie. Thanks so much for having us on the show.'

'Yeah, right,' he said, grinning at Logan Gore. 'I think the thanks should be going in the opposite direction. Really appreciate you doing this. I mean, clearly you need to get your band some more publicity,' he joked. 'I saw those sales figures today.'

Logan's smile was tempered with some humility. 'Yeah, well, you know... We try.'

From the right side of Davie's vision he saw a flying object approach and ducked out of the way just in time.

South City's lead singer, Jonell, put his hands up in surrender. 'Hey, man, sorry. Just sending my boy some vit-C,' he said, gesturing to the can of OJ that Logan had somehow caught.

'No worries. I'm just a bit jumpy about things flying in my direction,' Davie said, only half kidding.

'Shit, sorry. Heard about that whole blood thing. Scary vibe, man.' Jonell was the son of a Motown backing singer and could flip from the sweetness of Smokey to the depths of Marvin.

Logan was on bass guitar and harmonies, male-model good-looking and the all-American jock. Ringo, on drums, was delighting his parents, who saw his success as a fitting tribute to the fact that he was conceived to the soundtrack of *Sergeant Pepper*. They'd felt the names John, Paul and George were just too mainstream.

Lincoln on lead guitar and D'Arby on keyboard were two school mates who looked great and had the moves and the voices to complete the line-up.

America's teen generation had adored South City since they'd exploded onto the charts four years before, thanks to a talent show not unlike the one Davie produced. They'd long passed the talk-show circuit now that they regularly put 50,000 jean-covered teenage buttocks on seats in arenas, (they'd sold out the 20,000 capacity Staples centre five nights in a row), but over dinner at Mirren's a few weeks before, Davie had cheekily asked Logan to come on the show and was stunned and delighted when he agreed.

'You look great,' he told Mirren, realizing his arm was still around her shoulders. How did that feel? Odd. But strangely comfortable. In his life, he'd loved three people. Perhaps four. His mum and Mirren were definites. He'd thought he was in love with Jenny Rico when they first got married, but looking back, there was every possibility that was lust, with a bit of 'Can't believe I landed her' thrown in. And now Sarah. There was definitely love there. He just wasn't sure yet how deep it went or how far it would take them.

A shout from South City's stylist summoned Logan, leaving Mirren and Davie alone.

'So how's things going?' Mirren asked. 'Is all OK?'

He immediately flipped into automatic superficial mode. 'Yeah, everything's great. Ratings on both shows are blowing everyone else out the water, so we're riding high.'

A flicker of something crossed Mirren's face. What? Disappointment? Annoyance?

'I meant, is all OK with you? Have you seen Zander? Have you guys talked?'

Davie sighed. Typical Mirren. No time for bullshit or spin; just fire right to the heart.

'No, not really. Just both been too busy to hang out.'

Mirren looked thoughtful. 'You know, you really should, Davie,' she said softly. 'We've all got a lot of stuff to work through, and avoiding it won't help. You're brothers. Weird as that is.'

'I don't think that bit will ever seem real,' Davie shrugged, 'but I hear you. It's just been a bit chaotic lately.' Even to him it sounded lame, but Mirren knew him well enough not to press the point. Mirren and Zander had come back into his life and he was grateful for it, but that brought with it a whole load of stuff he'd rather leave buried. Avoidance. Spin. Superficiality. Those were far easier to deal with than probing a hornets' nest of past horrors with a stick.

'Can we have coffee later?' he asked. 'After the show?'

'I'd love to, but I've promised to head out with the guys. I'm way too old and uncool, but I think they've invited me out of sympathy. You're very welcome to join us?' Mirren's self-deprecation was accompanied by a rueful smile.

Davie immediately did the analysis in his head. Hitting the town with South City guaranteed column inches, and millions of Twitter and Instagram hits. Fantastic publicity for the show and therefore a no-brainer. 'Sure, sounds great. I'd better get back before Mellie goes on the warpath.'

Yet he was still standing there. He didn't want to leave. He didn't want to take his hand away. There was something in just being with her that was almost magnetic. Fuck, this was bizarre.

He wasn't twelve again. He was an adult. A player. A success. And his girlfriend was sitting down the corridor.

Mirren stretched up onto her toes and kissed his cheek. 'Cool. Catch you later. I'll give you a shout when I know where they're dragging me to.'

The walk back to his dressing room passed in a blur. As he opened the door, he was so distracted that it took him a moment to realise the others were still there.

Sarah was now over at the coffee table with Mark and Al, all of them huddled round her iPad, and all of them turned to stare at him, the tension palpable.

'What? What's up? You lot look like someone has died...' A pause. 'Oh fuck, don't tell me we've killed another guest.'

He was only half joking.

Sarah was the first to speak. 'Think you need to have a look at this.'

'No, he doesn't,' Cal countered blithely.

'Don't be bloody ridiculous. Of course he does,' Sarah argued. It was an incongruous sight – a twenty-six-year-old woman, in LA less than six months, taking on a guy who terrified almost everyone around him. And winning.

Davie crossed the room. 'OK, shoot. What is it?'

Sarah tilted the iPad so he could see it, then pressed 'play' on a YouTube video.

The next thirty seconds weren't a huge surprise.

Davie, coming out of the studio last week, smiling at the waiting crowd. Signing autographs. Posing for photos. Working his way towards the car that was waiting at the kerb. The camera moving closer now, the person behind it obviously heading in Davie's direction. Twenty feet away. Fifteen. Now ten. The sound of breathing providing a steady beat of a soundtrack.

Five feet. Davie starts to turn to face the camera, but before his full face comes into focus, a cloud of red crosses the image, splatters across him; he recoils; his hands fly to his face, mouth open in a twisted scream and… Freeze.

The image holds right there. Davie, covered in blood, looking like a modern-day interpretation of Edvard Munch's *Scream*.

Then the letters appear, one by one on the screen, like they are being typed by a two-fingered harbinger of foreboding.

d.a.V.i.e. J.o.H.n.S.T.o.n. W.i.l.l. D.i.e.

12

MIRREN

'Calling All Hearts' – DJ Cassidy, Featuring Jessie J and Robin Thicke

The reaction that South City got wherever they went was almost biblical, with adoring crowds amassing, then parting like the Red Sea as security cleared a path for the present-day prophets. Tonight, on Davie's show, the audience had gone wild as soon as South City took to the stage. Now, as they made their way through the tribe of fans to LiX, the trendiest nightclub on Sunset, Mirren kept her head down and went with the flow, conscious of the hands of one of the security staff on her shoulders. This was a zoo. Crazy. Chaos. She had no idea how these boys – sorry, young men – coped with this on a daily basis.

As soon as they were inside, Logan turned to check she was OK. 'I'm fine,' she shouted over the noise of the club. 'Just way too old for this.'

Logan winked, then moved with the mass as they were herded to the VIP area. As soon as the thud of the techno bass permeated her body, making it seem like it was vibrating from the inside out, she realised this was a mistake. What was she doing here? She hated clubs, hated the vibe and hated the reminder that she'd spent way too much time in them searching for Chloe, pulling her out of toilets and dragging her to the nearest ER to have her stomach pumped or her airways cleared of vomit.

She'd only come tonight because her boy asked her to, and it was an excuse to spend more time with him. And yes, there was a part of her that wanted, *needed* to watch over him, despite the fact that she told herself a hundred times a day that he wasn't Chloe. He was a different person, a stronger personality, more grounded, balanced, too smart to go down the road that killed his sister.

Yet she felt better just being here, seeing that he was OK. Somehow, in LA it was harder than when he was on the road, travelling across the globe, playing gigs. Chloe had died right here in LA, only minutes from Mirren's home, and yet she hadn't been able to protect her.

She pulled out a phone and sent a text to the only person who would understand.

Hey, are you around? I'm in LiX with Logan. Music loud. Skirts short. Too old for this. Come save me.

While she waited on an answer, she texted Davie.

Hey, hope everything is OK. Call me if you need me.

He'd agreed to come with them, then bailed after the show – something to do with a security thing, he'd said. Nothing serious. No biggie. But he just had to stay behind and sort it out. Mirren understood. She'd heard about the whole weird blood throwing incident and it gave her the creeps. There were a whole lot of crazies in this town.

She glanced around her. The VIP area already had a few people in it. Mirren recognized a couple of Clippers sitting with a Laker and several stunning women. Obviously sporting rivalry was left at the club door.

At another table, a female rapper Mirren had seen on one of the video channels was oiled up and twerking her naked ass at the camera. Mirren didn't judge. As long as these girls were doing it on their own terms, then she had no right to criticize. Silver champagne buckets loaded with Cristal and trays of tequila shooters appeared on the table, along with trays of soft drinks, a nod to the fact that none of the band was yet twenty-one. Technically, they were allowed to be here, but just couldn't drink alcohol, a situation that seemed so strange to Mirren, who came from a country where kids could drink at eighteen. Somehow it seemed more honest. The South City guys would make a pretence of sticking to soft drinks while a few of them were downing shots slipped into their Red Bulls. As long as the appearances of compliance with the law were upheld, no one would question them.

Their security team peeled off into the background, seeking out corners in which to watch their charges, never too far away to intervene if a situation got out of hand.

The LiX employees on the VIP door would make sure it didn't. This was the reason the biggest names came here. Unlike some of the other clubs, where the VIP section was just a roped-off area, here it was a separate room, one floor higher than the rest of the club. With its mirrored walls, glossy steel tables and huge white leather sofas, it was classy and spacious, but the real draw was the huge balcony that looked over the body of the club, complete with a spiral staircase that led directly down to one of the four dance floors. At the bottom, three guards made sure no one attempted to rise to a level to which they weren't entitled.

There was the irony. The guys on the dance floor wanted to experience the giddy entitlement of the VIP area. The guys in the VIP area wanted to be on the dance floor. The self-satisfaction of being given access to the top level soon wore off when they realised there was no one up there to impress.

Mirren happily found herself in a corner with Deeko, the band's manager. His track record spoke for itself. He'd turned this young group of kids into international superstars, created the icons of a generation. Yet Mirren found it difficult to take him seriously given that he was pushing thirty and still wore a baseball cap backwards. It was the small things.

Deeko's assistant, Ashika, apologetically pulled him away to speak to him, and Mirren scanned the room looking to pinpoint Logan. Then stopped. Held her breath. Over at their table, Logan was deep in conversation with a stunning girl with alabaster skin, her hair a mass of long red waves, her doe eyes huge and her lips wide in smile. It was like any one of a million memories of her children deep in discussion. Of course, it wasn't Chloe, and as she studied her for a few more seconds, she could see that despite the same long red hair, they looked very different. This girl was rounder in the face, her expression open and warm. Chloe's features had been sharper, more classic. Why wasn't she here? Chloe should be standing with her brother now, loving this, enjoying the lives they'd built. When she'd watched her children interacting, fighting, arguing, playing, chatting, she'd never realised those moments would have a finite number. If she had, she would have stopped what she was doing and savoured every second, captured every nuance and word. If only.

Released by Ashika, Deeko turned back to Mirren. 'I need to go check on security with the management downstairs. Good talking to you.'

Still rattled by the flashback, Mirren had to make a conscious effort to smile. 'You too. Deeko, who is that Logan is talking to?'

Deeko's eyes followed her gaze. 'Lauren Finney. Man, that girl is talented. Woulda signed her in a heartbeat, but she's all wrapped up.'

'She's a singer?'

'Yeah. Won *American Stars* year before last. Presenting it this year. Gonna be huge. Joni Mitchell, man. Next Joni Mitchell.'

Mirren should probably have known all that, but the months since Chloe's death had been a fog and she'd barely watched TV, rarely listened to music, kept her world small, trying to narrow the possibility of an unexpected reminder that would sear her soul. Maybe she should start pushing out those boundaries a little.

Rihanna's new track blasted through the speakers and several of the people at South City's huge table jumped to their feet and made their way out onto the balcony and down the glass staircase, Logan included. Mirren slipped onto the balcony to watch the reaction. Down below, a thousand kids were dancing, but in an incredible wave of synchronicity, their heads turned upwards, they spotted the South City boys making their way down to the dance floor, and the volume of their cheers almost drowned out the music.

An hour later, her texts unanswered, she decided to head off. It was sweet that Logan had wanted her to come along, but it was time to let him be.

'If you're asking, I'll dance with you, but it won't be pretty.' A voice from behind her but close to her ear doled out the generous offer. At the same time, a nucleus of the revellers down below spotted the new arrival up on the balcony next to Mirren, and the attention switched from the South City boys on the dance floor to the superspy above them.

It was testimony to great marketing and a fucked-up reputation that the under-thirty audience still thought Zander Leith was one of the coolest men on the planet.

Mirren didn't disagree. Especially tonight. He was tanned, and the stubble suited him. You could count the layers of his six-pack under his plain black V-neck T-shirt, and biceps the size of half-melons protruded from the sleeves. This was the kind of shape he got into every time he was filming, and it's what kept the twenty to fifty-year-old women, normally a low demographic on thrillers, flocking to the cinema to see the latest in the Seb Dunhill franchise.

'Are you, like, the nightclub superhero, riding to the rescue?' she asked, laughing, voice raised to be heard over the music rising from below. 'I didn't think you'd be around. Just texted you in hope.'

'I was heading back from a late-night shoot up at the Bowl. Apparently, some evil villain didn't like the act there tonight. Ninety ninja terrorists invaded it on the orders of a crazed dictator.'

'Did you save the day?'

'Of course. California and several other states are only still here thanks to my heroism,' Zander replied, enjoying the joke. She knew he felt it was the eternal juxtaposition – in the movie world, he was the all-encompassing hero who could disarm a terrorist group of their nuclear weapons, while in real life he wouldn't be trusted to disarm a defunct smoke alarm.

'Thanks for coming. Just felt like some company. Are you OK being here?'

Zander nodded, smiling. 'Yeah. But if you see me storming the bar, you might want to intervene.'

Mirren knew that being around alcohol was tough for him, but he'd told her many times that the only way to get over that was to face it. Tonight, he could consider it faced.

'Will do, but I might need to call Hollie for reinforcements. She not around tonight?' Mirren asked, then went on without waiting for an answer. 'You know, I really like that girl, Zander. Really like her…' Her grin and the accompanying wink made her message clear, but she clarified it just to be sure. 'I think you two would be great together.'

Zander's slow smile and shake of the head made it clear he thought differently. 'I'm way too much of a fuck-up for her. Have you seen how untogether I am?'

'I think she could handle it,' Mirren countered, enjoying playing Cupid.

Zander was still shaking his head. 'Maybe. But I love her way too much to saddle her with a guy like me.' His discomfort led to a swift deflection and change of subject. 'Anyway, how come a respected professional like Mirren McLean is hanging out in this den of debauchery?' he teased.

Mirren gestured down to the dance floor. 'Logan dragged me. I think it was out of sympathy. I've become the sad old lady following her kid around.'

Zander removed the soda from her hand and took a sip. 'On your own? That is pretty sad.'

She took her glass back off him. 'Close to desperate,' she deadpanned, realizing that she was actually starting to enjoy herself. She and Zander had slipped back into the whole brother-sister vibe they'd had when they were teenagers. It wasn't far from the truth. Zander's dad, Jono, had been shagging Mirren's mother for most of their adolescence. It could have driven them apart, but instead, their mutual contempt for their parents had welded them together. It felt a bit like that again now. Easy. Comfortable. That hadn't happened with Davie yet, but maybe it would come with time. They couldn't expect to undo twenty years of estrangement in a few months.

'Logan was on Davie's show tonight, so we headed here afterwards. Davie was supposed to come with us but he bailed. Said something had come up.'

The phone in her pocket buzzed. Probably Davie, saying he was on his way.

Excellent. Perhaps seeing Zander would help them begin to get their relationship sorted. It was time to put everything that happened behind them and move on, figure out a new basis for being back in each other's lives.

For her own sanity, Mirren knew it was the only way. She'd paid her dues, had her drama, endured more heartache than most people dealt with in a lifetime.

From now on, she wanted a smooth, pain-free road. Mirren squinted at the screen. Nope, not Davie. Sarah. She opened the text.

Hi. Something's come up that I need to speak to you about. Can we meet?

A sinking feeling made Mirren's thumb tremble very slightly as she replied.

Sure. When and where?

13

ZANDER

'Human' – The Killers

He'd thought about making an excuse. Ignoring the text. Claiming a prior engagement. But the truth was, he didn't want to go home. Sobriety he could just about handle, but it was the boredom of sticking to non-threatening environments that was eating away at his soul.

No clubs. No bars. No hitting a hotel party and seeing where the night ended up. It was a foregone conclusion. If he hit any of his usual haunts, he'd end up wasted and horizontal in a $1,000-a-night hotel suite with a stripper called Starburst. Or Destiny. Or Bubbles. Instead, he'd been heading back to an empty apartment in Venice, alone. For an addict who craved distraction and excitement, that was hard. Almost unbearable. It was the same story every night. He'd make a protein shake, then take the edge off the silence by opening the windows so he could hear the sounds of life, of music, of people walking along the Venice boardwalk below the apartment that he'd lived in since his early days in LA. There wasn't a day went by that he didn't want a drink. Or a line. Or something that gave him a high. In the old days, he'd kept a bobblehead on the dashboard, a caricature of his own image, available in the cheap souvenir stores along the Walk of Fame. His was the custom version – filled with coke and always ready to party.

Driving home, that thought had given way to a craving so strong he had reached for his cell phone – not to call a bar or a dealer. He'd flicked to his speed dial; his finger had hovered over the number attached to the contact simply listed as 'AG'. Over the years, he'd blocked out the cost of his drug addiction, and the gutters that alcohol had landed him in. In the same way, the memory of her husband's crushing handshake, and the thought that it could have a deeper meaning had long been wiped from his mind by the need for a fix of Adrianna. At that exact moment the text from Mirren had arrived. It was like a cosmic intervention and it had forced him to detour off his one way street to a bad decision.

He'd done a 180-degree turn on Melrose and headed to LiX. As he'd pulled up to the door in his Aston Martin, the valet stepped forward to greet him. At LiX, the valets were all female, all stunning and all dressed like extras in a Beyoncé video.

As he'd jumped out, the paparazzi bulbs had flashed and the crowd waiting in line had given him an enthusiastic welcome. The irony didn't escape him. On the surface, he looked like the luckiest guy in the world. In reality? He was just an addict who was grateful for the distraction.

Now, standing on the balcony, looking down on a thousand heaving, gyrating clubbers, the urge to drink, snort or shag had been pushed to one side by relief. Relief he'd managed to go another day sober. Relief that he was still standing there when statistics would probably have him in jail or dead.

Once upon a time, this would have been his idea of heaven. Now it was only bearable because Mirren was here.

It seemed she could read his mind. After hanging out on the balcony for another hour or so, Mirren said. 'Listen, I hope you don't mind, but after dragging you here, I'm ready to split. Is that OK?'

Zander nodded. The boys in the band were starting to pair off with girls, the entourage were getting drunker, and the security guys were beginning to get twitchy. Definitely time to bail out.

'Sure. I can drop you home. Could do with the drive.' He wasn't lying.

Mirren lived in Malibu and there was no better feeling than driving the PCH late at night, when the traffic was so quiet you could hear the waves of the Pacific crashing against the shore. He'd take Mirren home, maybe stay for a coffee, talk a while. He had a 7 a.m. call the next day, only six hours from now, but he was nowhere near sleep.

With a wave to Logan, they headed downstairs towards the door. Just inside, the notoriously flamboyant, cross-dressing owner, Allan Stewart, spotted them and stepped forward to bid them goodnight. He never missed an opportunity to press flesh with the great and the good, but was ultimately incredibly discreet. He knew when to shout it out and when to cover it up. The husband of a globally famous reality star who joined him every week dressed in his wife's clothes? All hushed up. The TV evangelist who claimed he was saving souls while screwing three of his twenty-something disciples in the gents' toilets. Not a word. The teen heart-throb who still wore his purity ring, despite regular threesomes with his driver and his paunchy, middle-aged manager? Hushed.

Platitudes over, Mirren and Zander headed to the door.

There, they stood to one side, to let an incoming crowd of miniskirt-clad girls and guys in Versace and Rocawear pass them.

'Well, fuck me, if it isn't the big shot with the big drug habit.'

Beside him, Zander felt Mirren tense. She hated confrontations, especially ones with an edge of menace. There were way too many memories waiting to be dredged up from that pool. The rest of the crowd moved on past, but the one who was mouthing off stood his ground at the entrance, only feet away from Zander and Mirren.

Zander recognized him. Definitely did. Absolutely. He just wasn't sure where it was from. He was lean but built, like he did more cardio than weights, and his hair was shaved into a short buzz cut. He wore an Armani T-shirt, tight across the pecs and delts, jeans that could have been painted on and black leather boots, Italian style. His voice was pure east Coast and nasal, making everything sound like the sneer it was meant to be.

Zander reached for Mirren's hand, then pulled her behind him as he stepped forward. His voice was low and measured but there was no mistaking the edge of warning. 'Mate, I don't know what your problem is, but move on.'

He of the offensive gob was having way too much fun goading them. 'But where would the fun in that be?'

The guy was so close to his face Zander could smell the halitosis. Moving forward, Zander's body language hinted at the rage that was building inside him.

Before the fumes from the dude's breath knocked him out, Zander issued another calm but deadly serious warning. 'Mate, don't do this. It won't end well.'

'Let's go,' Mirren begged, pulling him towards the door despite the fact that their new best friend was blocking their exit.

The guy's attention switched to Mirren. He stepped towards her, face only inches from hers, but Mirren didn't move, didn't flinch backwards. Zander could have called that one. He'd always thought Mirren was stronger than him and Davie combined. Zander saw that the security team from the door had spotted the situation and were making their way towards them.

'Ah, Mirren McLean. Good company you're keeping. I knew your daughter. Passing on the tips from your junkie girl to your junkie friend?'

Red mist. Brain disengaged. Zander didn't even pause for breath. He launched himself across the hallway, his force pushing the guy back past the security team and had three jabs in before the guy fell backwards through the door, hitting the deck to the soundtrack of screams from the waiting crowd. The guy with the mouth was on the street, Zander was on top of him, and he wasn't stopping. It took three of the muscle-bound door guys to pull him off and even then he managed to get in one last kick to the ribs of the bloodied punk.

That's when déjà vu kicked in.

He'd seen that red-smeared face before. Another flashback.

Around a year ago. He'd been wasted. Coming out of a club. A reality-TV guy. What was his name? Nope, he couldn't remember. Although, he should. Because back then he'd punched that guy out and he'd ended up spending the night in prison and the next three months in rehab.

It had almost cost him everything. Now he'd done it again.

But right now, right there, standing with five bruised knuckles and blood smeared on both his hands, it felt like it was worth it.

14

SARAH

'Only Women Bleed' – Julie Covington

When Mirren opened the door of her Malibu beach house, Sarah's first thought was that she looked tired.

'Good morning. Come on in,' she said, giving her a hug when she stepped forward.

Sarah liked the fact that there was none of that Hollywood air-kissing bullshit with Mirren. They'd met a few times over the last few months. On the first occasion, Mirren had thanked her for burying the story that told the truth about their lives back in Scotland two decades ago. It hadn't been mentioned since. It was almost as if it hadn't happened. But then, that was the way the three of them – Mirren, Zander and Davie – had dealt with it for all these years. Total amnesia. It had been working for them so far, so she could see why they preferred to keep it that way.

As she followed Mirren through to the kitchen, Sarah's natural reporter's scrutiny took in every detail. The house was magnificent. Gloss ebony floor, white walls, with a double hand-carved oak staircase rising to an upper interior balcony. In the middle of the room at ground level, a huge mirrored console table supported a small garden of white flowers. Simple but beautiful, classy and serene. It said more about Mirren than any industry bio. Sarah suddenly felt very underdressed in her cut-off jean shorts and white cotton tank.

For a moment, she wondered if there should be a little tug of jealousy here. Not for Mirren's fame, or her wealth, or her success – because Sarah was only too aware of the price she'd paid for it all – but because this was her boyfriend's first love, the woman he'd adored since he was a kid. No matter how hard Sarah tried, she couldn't picture Mirren and Davie together now. They'd both grown and changed. Maybe back in Glasgow, twenty, thirty years ago, they'd been compatible, but that time had passed. There was still love there, but Sarah was sure it was entirely platonic on both sides. Wasn't it?

'Coffee?'

'Please,' Sarah replied, sliding into the semi-circular dining booth and watching as Mirren pressed a few buttons on a machine that would have looked at home at NASA.

Thirty seconds later, a hot, frothy cappuccino was in front of her and Mirren slipped into the leather seat.

'How's Zander doing?' Sarah asked, and watched as Mirren winced.

'Not great. It was a total mess. The police held him for twelve hours but the Lomax lawyers got him out the next morning. Wes was not happy.'

That wasn't exactly a surprise. Even after such a short time in LA, Sarah was familiar with the omnipotent Wes Lomax's reputation. Sharp. Fierce. Brilliant. But not a man to be crossed.

'It honestly wasn't Zander's fault. The guy... What's his name?'

'Raymo Cash.'

'Seriously?'

'I'm afraid so. Apparently he changed it from something completely ordinary when he moved here. Then he got the gig on *Making It* and it stuck.'

Sarah had been unable to resist researching the guy. The ultimate fame-seeker, he'd managed to score a part in a fly-on-the-wall series about waiters in West Hollywood trying to make it as actors and used it to get face time on several other trashy reality gigs, his notoriety fuelled by a multitude of off-camera stunts, including, of course, being punched out by Zander Leith. Twice now.

'Zander had no gripe with the guy. To be honest, I don't even think he recognized him. But Ray...' She looked at Sarah quizzically.

'Raymo,' Sarah confirmed.

'He just kept spouting all this crap, determined to provoke a reaction. And then he said stuff about Chloe and Zander lost it. Reaction achieved.'

'Understandable.'

Mirren smiled sadly. 'Tell that to Wes Lomax and the cops. Anyway...' Mirren shook the subject off. 'I was a bit intrigued by your text. What's come up? Is Davie OK?'

Sarah took a deep breath, her stomach clenching with dread. Hadn't this woman been through enough, and now she was about to land a whole big pile of crazy at her door?

'Davie's fine. OK, I'm not sure how to say this, so I'm just going to blurt it out and I'm sorry.'

Two vertical lines of worry appeared in the space between Mirren's eyebrows.

'It's your mother.'

'Marilyn?' Mirren replied, stating the obvious.

Sarah nodded. 'My old editor called me from the *Daily Scot*. Said he'd heard from a couple of scumballs touting a story that the moll of some shady character in Liverpool was saying she was your mother. The guy was arrested on major organized-crime charges and now the woman has disappeared. My editor wants me to look into it and do some digging at this end, find out if there's any truth to it. They've got someone on it in the UK too, but they haven't found her yet. They want to dig up a story, do the whole 'famous writer has a gangster mother' angle. They're just looking for headlines to sell some papers, but he came to me with it and now I'm coming to you to give you a heads up and give you a chance to get ahead of it if it's true.'

Mirren sighed as she closed her eyes and rested her head back against the cream leather.

Sarah let the silence sit. There was nothing else to add. That was all she had. Better to let Mirren process it first before they could move on.

When Mirren finally spoke, the venom in her words was diluted by the sheer weariness of her tone. 'I fucking hate that bitch.'

'I can understand why,' Sarah said softly. 'So what do you want me to do? If I don't take this on, they'll put someone else on it.'

Mirren, eyes open now, took a sip of green tea from her oversized mug, while she stared straight ahead, thinking.

'You're right.' Calm. Matter-of-fact. 'Thank you.'

'When was the last time you had any contact with her?'

Mirren replaced her mug on the table and Sarah noticed that her hands were steady. There was a strength in this woman that came from somewhere deep in her core.

'The last time I saw her was that night. She was sitting there, in her kitchen, splattered in Jono Leith's blood.' Mirren paused, still staring straight ahead, her voice low and calm as if she was reciting a story that had no emotional connection to her whatsoever. 'Do you know what I remember so vividly? Her face had black mascara tracks down her cheeks. She was wearing a ridiculous baby-doll nightdress, pink, smeared with blood. But one of the straps had broken and her tit was hanging out. She didn't even realise.'

Sarah wanted to reach over, to put her hand on Mirren's, but she didn't want to overstep the boundaries, didn't know if the physical touch would be welcome.

Instead, she stayed silent. Just listened.

'She left that night and I never saw her again. I heard she went down to Liverpool, hooked up with some dealer who was importing drugs and shipping them north, but that was it.'

'You haven't heard from her since?'

'She wrote to me years ago. Sent the letter to my production office. I'm guessing she got the address online.'

Sarah's eyes widened with surprise.

Mirren carried on without prompting. 'She was demanding I send money to a PO box in Liverpool. Said I owed her that. That Davie, Zander and I had done well and she wanted a piece of it. I sealed the letter back up and returned it. There were a few phone calls to my office around then too, but they were all blocked by the switchboard. I told them Marilyn was dead and it was just some crazed fan. Didn't hear anything else.'

'Nothing?'

'No. To be honest, I hoped she really was dead. That's the story I'd been telling everyone here for the last twenty years. Even my family. Granny died before you were born. Somehow it seemed better than "granny was a ruthless, self-centred slut who neglected her child for years because all she cared about was the monster she was sleeping with".'

Mirren's words were not new to Sarah. It was a story she'd learned a year ago, when she'd first come to LA in the hope of tracking down some scandal surrounding the back story of Scotland's most famous Hollywood exports. Now she was adding a post-script to the tale. 'She isn't dead. I checked. I'm sorry. I actually saw her when I first started investigating your story. She was at the funeral of some big time hood in Glasgow. I only realised later who she was when I saw an old photo of Jono Leith with her, his wife and Davie's mother. Davie told me who the three women were.'

Mirren's jaw tightened, then she reached over, placed her hand on Sarah's, initiating the physical contact Sarah had so badly wanted to offer.

'Sarah, you know what my mother is capable of. She is an evil bitch who has no conscience, no values, no loyalty to anyone but herself. Her only obsessions are money and the men she loves. You say her husband—'

'Boyfriend.' Sarah interjected. 'I don't think they were married. Although, from what I've learned they've been together for many years.'

'So you say he was arrested?'

Sarah's talent for storing facts flipped the relevant details to the forefront of her mind.

'Yes. He's on remand, but the charges are comprehensive and the cops are pretty sure they'll stick. Apparently he was caught in a massive cross-agency sting operation that was trailing the drugs from Algiers. They'd been after him for years and they've got no doubt he'll go down.'

Mirren listened, absorbed. 'Then she'll have lost her source of income, her love and her obsession. That's how it works. It's all she cares about. When she was fucking Jono Leith, she thought about him from the minute she woke, pined for him when he wasn't there, came alive when he was – all this despite the fact he was an evil bastard whose wife lived two houses along from us.'

Sarah couldn't even begin to imagine what that had been like. Mirren's mother and Zander's dad, an affair that lasted more than a decade, one that came close to destroying them all.

'Have you told Davie?' Mirren asked.

'No. I wanted to speak to you first. And to be honest, he's got his own stuff going on just now – I didn't want to freak him out.'

Mirren's expression softened from steel to understanding. 'I think that was the wise thing to do. This wouldn't be good for him right now. For Zander either.'

'I get it,' Sarah assured her.

'So is it OK with you if we keep this between us for now? I'm not asking you to lie, and obviously if you feel you have to tell Davie at some point...'

'Then I will. But not yet. I don't want to worry him when this could all turn out to be just rumour and nonsense.'

'Thank you. I've got a private investigator that I trust. He's worked for me before. He used to go find Chloe when she went AWOL and bring her home, and then I used him again when Jack was off screwing around. I'll bring him in on this and see if he can track Marilyn down.'

'You want him to go to the UK?' Sarah asked, confused, before continuing, 'Because I've got some people over there I worked with who would be far more familiar with that world. They'd have a better chance of finding her.'

Mirren shook her head. 'I think it's too late for that. Something happened lately that made me uneasy. I thought I was imagining things, just still a bit off balance. But now it all makes perfect sense.'

'It does?'

Mirren exhaled slowly. 'My mother would do anything for money. And I have plenty of it. If her partner has been arrested, she'll come for it. In a way I always expected it. Not just for money, but for revenge too.'

'Against you?' Sarah didn't understand. 'But it was Jono who attacked you that day.'

Mirren sighed. 'She never blamed him. Even after she'd killed him, she still thought it was my fault.'

'So you think she'll come here?'

Mirren cut her off. 'Maybe. A couple of weeks ago I saw someone on the beach, someone who reminded me so much of her. I tried to tell myself I was wrong. Now, I don't think I was. I think my mother is already here.'

15

No one understands how it feels when everything is taken away. Everything.

It's like a blade has ripped through your flesh, gouged it wide open, then reached in and torn out the very part of you that makes you who you are.

I know.

I'm still bleeding from that open wound and there's no way to stop it. It'll kill me. I know that too.

But not yet.

I have to make it right first. Isn't that what love is? A promise that you'll never let go, never give up, will right the wrongs that have been committed against you and the person you're bound to forever? Even when you can no longer touch them, feel them next to you, hold them at night.

Even when that person is gone, the love is still there, and so is that obligation.

So I'm not ready to die yet.

Not until I've made them understand what they took from me. Not until I've made them see how it feels to be me.

Not until I've made them bleed.

16

DAVIE

'Man in the Mirror' – Michael Jackson

'Daddy, she's got my phone,' Bray raged, his face red with fury as he pointed at the device in his sister's hands. 'Give it back, you little shit.'

'Hey, hey, hey... That's enough,' Davie warned him. 'And stop with the language. Don't speak to your sister like that.'

Bray rounded on him. 'No wonder Darcy says she'll kick your ass.'

And there it was. It had been a whole, oh, ten minutes or so since the kids had tried to play one parenting set off against another. Not that it bothered Davie. Water off a daddy duck's back. But then, it could be worse. There was a legendary story about the child star whose mother sent him to his room for misbehaving.

'My room?' he sneered. 'They're all my rooms.'

For now, it was all about pacifying and keeping it real in a world that couldn't be more surreal.

'I'm sure one day she will. But for now, watch your language, son.'

'Or what?' Bray fronted up to him, while his twin sister, Bella, watched with amusement.

'Or I'll give your courtside ticket to the Clippers game to Justin Bieber. Don't make me do it.'

As if by magic, Bray clamped his mouth shut, and Davie fought down the urge to laugh. It was hard being eight. Especially when you were already a household name across the country, thanks to lead roles in *Family Three*, the sitcom his children, red-haired twins Bella and Bray, had starred in since they were three.

These two were fast becoming the Mary-Kate and Ashley of their generation. They lived in an adult world, were schooled on set, recognized everywhere they went. They had a manager and an agent, a publicist and – no shit – a brand manager. Yep, his kids were a brand. A brand that came with a USP – they'd made gingers cool.

How had that happened? How had he taken his eye off the ball for so long he didn't notice that his kids had become brands?

The truth was, his eye had never been on the parental ball in the first place. It had seemed like a great idea at the time. The showbiz family. He was Mr TV. Jenny was an A-list actor. And their kids were stars of one of the top rated sitcoms on network television. From the outside, it had been the perfect Hollywood family. Now it was the perfect Hollywood divorce, with two precocious eight year olds with mouths like sailors.

It mortified him now to admit it, but the kids had always been Jenny's department. He'd been too busy out there, making a buck, building his own brand, to build a relationship with them. He was trying to make up for it now. Since the divorce, and since Jenny had gone off to shack up with the woman who was apparently threatening to kick his ass, he'd been trying to make up for lost time. It wasn't easy, but at least the kids knew he was making an effort. That had to count for something, right?

There was a knock at the door; then their male nanny appeared. Yep, a male nanny. Another statement in the world of Jenny and Darcy, another attempt to squeeze his balls until he squealed. Shallow as it was, it worked. Davie tried not to mind that it was pretty obvious the kids preferred Zac to him. Zac was twenty-four, he was cool, he hung out with them all day, played football with Bray, had mani-pedis with Bella, and according to them both, he just knew 'stuff'. Jenny and Darcy had employed him four months ago after interviewing a dozen candidates from the childcare agency. It was Zac's job to get the kids where they were supposed to be, organize their schedule, oversee their schooling, mediate with the on-set studio rep and make sure all their needs were catered for. So far it was working out great. Davie wasn't sure whether that pleased him or irritated him.

'Right, guys, time to get going. Got all your stuff?' Zac asked, looking around for anything that had been left behind. 'Davie, see you later, bud.' OK, it was official – Zac irritated him. Bud? This guy didn't lack confidence, that was for sure.

'Dad, promise you won't give my ticket to Justin Bieber?' Bray asked, suitably chastised.

'I promise. See you Monday night for the game, OK?'

'OK.' He put his hand up for a knuckle-bump and Davie matched it, before hugging Bella. At least that bit came naturally now. He didn't have the answers to all this fatherhood stuff and he was pretty sure he was fucking up on a regular basis, but at least he was trying and spending time with them. It was progress.

He waved as he watched them head down the driveway, then wandered into the kitchen, where Alina was singing along to Carrie Underwood while she sliced fruit on the granite worktop. He considered it a blessing that he'd got custody of Alina in the divorce. The Russian housekeeper, 38-23-38, peroxide-blonde hair, lived in tiny skirts and six-inch mules, loved country music, cleaning, cooking and her Ukrainian husband and Davie's gardener, Drago. They'd both been with Davie for over a decade and they ran his home like clockwork. If only he could have someone to do that for the other areas in his life.

'Alina, I'm off. Get me on my cell if you need me.' She barely looked up. What she lacked in warmth and conversation, she made up for in loyalty and domestic skills. It was a fair trade.

Traffic was light, so it took him twenty minutes in the Bugatti Veyron to reach the studio. He parked in one half of his double space – the other half being reserved for the portable canopy that kept the Bugatti shielded from the sun. It wouldn't do to burn one's arse on one's monogrammed leather seats.

It was Tuesday, so that meant a solid twelve hours at the studio in rehearsals for tonight's *American Stars*. Last week's ratings had been the highest ever, and baby, it felt good. It made the ridiculous hours and the stresses of juggling two primetime shows, plus production on another three worthwhile. *Beauty and the Beats* was off air at the moment but he was making a financial killing on the reruns. He was going to have to make a decision on that show's future pretty soon, but it wasn't looking great now that the Beats himself was only playing for an audience in the rock stadium in the sky.

In the office, Mellie was waiting for him, expression thunderous. 'Where the fuck have you been? Everyone is waiting and Princess is about to throw a diva strop that will take out everyone within spitting distance.'

'Morning, darling,' he replied in a sing-song voice. 'Lovely to see you.'

'You are such an asshole,' Mellie replied, rolling her eyes, unable to mask completely the smile that was playing at the corners of her mouth.

'So what's up with the problem Princess today?' Davie asked, taking the double-shot latte that had materialized right next to him in the hand of Debs, the latest in his long line of assistants, with a quick 'thanks'.

'Mr Johnston, Carmella Cass has called four times for you.'

'No problem. I'll get back to her.'

He returned his attention to Mellie and waited for the update.

She led with, 'I'll give you three guesses.'

'Lauren?'

'And that cutting insight is why you're the boss,' Mellie teased. 'She says she's had enough of Lauren getting all the attention when she is – and I quote – "a two-bit slut with a voice like shit going down a drain". She's refusing to go on set if Lauren sings the opening number again tonight.'

Davie didn't even realise that he was running his hand through his hair. It was his automatic reaction in times of stress, irritation and unreasonable megastars. Especially ones he had no intention of humouring. Lauren was his biggest find, a girl who'd wandered into auditions a couple of years ago with only a guitar to her name. His show had made her a star and there was no limit to what she could and would achieve now. She was sweet, talented and – a fucking miracle in this industry – still completely unaffected by the tsunami of fame that had crashed over her. Princess was a stage-school brat, from wealthy parents who'd bought her way through every stage of the music industry, creating a spoilt monster on the way. She was only here because she was big right now, but it was a stardom that wouldn't last because she was a performer, not an artist. When it came to which side Davie was going to back here, there was no contest.

'Where is she?'

'In her dressing room, but she's refusing to come out until she's spoken to you. I hope you're feeling bulletproof.'

'Always,' Davie replied, before heading off down the corridor. This shouldn't be his battle to fight. Princess had managers, agents, lackeys for everything from putting on her shoes to carrying her gum. Surely her people should just call his people and sort it out?

But that wasn't how she operated. This was the third time she'd refused to go on set. There wasn't going to be a fourth.

Besides, if she played hardball, he still had the ultimate revenge – he could put her on stage and cut the auto-tune halfway through her performance. The whole world would then see that she couldn't hold a note in one of her blinged-up boots. At the door of Princess's dressing room, his brain was assaulted by the volume of the track blasting from inside. He recognized it immediately. Princess's latest song, 'Take Me Now, Boy'. Nothing like a bit of unsubtle product placement. She'd been bugging him to give her a performance slot for the last three weeks, but he just wasn't sure the explicit lyrics and the pelvic thrusts from the song's video were primetime family viewing. If he'd learned anything last year, it was that there were limits to how far he could go with the viewing public before their backlash whipped you like a twenty-foot tail on a pissed-off alligator. He didn't feel like being a casualty this week.

Nevertheless, he was aware of what she brought to the show.

The unpredictability and sheer viciousness that enticed the viewers and gave him something to play off. For once, he could be the good guy.

He knocked on the door. No answer. Hardly a surprise. There was no way anything could be heard over the music. Irritation rose to the top of his emotional pile. He had a show to run and no time for this shit. He pushed open the door and marched inside, then immediately wished that he hadn't.

Princess's dressing room had been designed to her exact specifications.

All four walls were mirrored and in the middle was a circular sofa, purple leather, surrounding a low glass table that was littered with cigarettes and bottles of Grey Goose.

Along one wall, a dressing area that Pop Bitch Barbie would be proud of, given that it contained every cosmetic, accessory and hair device currently available in the free world.

At the back of the room was a sound system with a mixing desk, and to the right, a day bed, with huge leather arms and purple silk upholstery.

That's where Princess was now, sitting cross-legged, eyes closed. Davie's first thought would have been meditation. Then yoga. Perhaps even some other kind of spiritual ritual. Yep, that would have been his first thought, if she hadn't been completely naked, except for two chains, which travelled from hoops pierced through her nipples down to a third hoop in her belly button.

Thus Davie's first thought was that he wished he could rewind time and leave this for Mellie to sort out.

In an unusual occurrence, words failed him. Her eyes were still closed, so he realised he had two choices: retreat and pretend he'd never been there or—

He didn't get to number two. The track ended and she opened her eyes, showing no surprise at all that he was standing there. She unfurled her legs and then slipped her feet into the ten-inch steel-spike-heeled stilettos on the floor in front of her, rose up and wordlessly crossed the room to the bar in the corner. There, she poured two shots of Jack Daniel's, before strutting towards him and handing half of her contraband to him. Davie took the drink, still saying nothing, transfixed by the sight of her. Standing in heels, her thighs were rock hard, her legs beautifully toned. Her hips were wide, her waist whip thin, her breasts high and full. This girl was all curves and generous proportions – not the ultra-thin model types of his past, or a naturally slender frame like Sarah. Her peroxide-blonde hair didn't match her olive skin tone, her hairless body looked odd on such a voluptuous shape and yet it all somehow worked to make her about as sexy as it got. And he had absolutely no doubt that she knew it.

Eyeing him with a look that sat somewhere between defiance and supreme confidence, Princess knocked back her drink and then dropped the glass onto the deep pile of the cream carpet. Still silent, their gazes locked, her hand went to his groin and she traced one long glitter-pink nail up the zip of his trousers. Davie didn't know if he was feeling fear, pleasure or pain, but he knew it was excruciating. Her nail was tracing its way back down when she finally spoke.

'I thought that maybe you needed to see the full range of my talents.'

Oh fuck. Oh fuck. This wasn't good.

Klaxons sounded in Davie's head. This was a bad move.

Repeat: Bad move. Yet the button of his trousers appeared suddenly to be undone.

Evacuate the building. Time to go. Do not stop to collect valuables, friends or morals.

Now his zipper had somehow slid to the bottom. Emergency situation. Risk to life. Evacuate immediately. An electric shock as a hand slipped inside his crotch. Evacuate. Evacuate immediately. Get out now, people. Davie!

Somehow, by some fucked-up osmosis or conscience, he heard that last mental scream in Sarah's voice.

He took a step backwards, desperate for breathing space. It was far enough to remove the fingers from his nethers.

Move forward. Move back. Move forward knowing that she was the ultimate manipulator who was doing this only for her own professional advancement and to play with his head. Move back knowing that he was in a relationship with a woman he truly wanted to be with. Move back. Definitely back. Preferably with his tackle intact.

'Am I interrupting something?'

Man, who sent the cavalry? He spun round to see Mellie, in the doorway, one hand on her hip, looking like she'd just walked in on them doing nothing more startling than chatting about library books.

'Nice chains,' she told Princess. 'Remind me to yank them one day. Davie, can I have a word?'

'Erm, yeah, sure.'

'Excellent. Princess, they need you on set. Much as I like the look you're going for, I'm not sure it'll work with our core audience.'

'Shame,' Princess jibed back dryly. 'I think I'm rocking it.'

'As you would,' Mellie countered. 'Davie?'

Turning on her heel, she left the room and Davie followed her, ignoring Princess's satisfied grin. His thought processes immediately went to juvenile self-defence. He hadn't actually done anything wrong. He hadn't touched her. There had been no sexual contact on his part. I did not have sexual relations with that woman.

Would he have?

Fuck, did he almost totally betray Sarah? Cue self-flagellation and condemnation.

How could he have done that? He'd been faithful to her every moment since they'd met, and OK, so they hadn't had much time for each other lately, but did that really mean he couldn't keep it in his pants when a naked twenty-one- year-old hot babe was trying to drag it out?

He was pathetic. Pathetic.

But he hadn't actually done anything, so did it count? He was definitely backing away when Mellie came in. He wouldn't have crossed that line. Didn't do it. Innocent of all charges.

He waited until they were back in the office before he spoke. 'Mellie, I—'

'Save it! I don't want to know. But you might want to do up your pants before Mark Bock gets here. He's on his way in.'

Davie had just buttoned up the waistband of his custom 501s when his head of security knocked and entered.

Bock's face was a mask of gravity as he strode over to the desk and fired up the laptop he'd carried in with him. 'You need to see this new video on YouTube.'

'Tell me it's kittens. Or suicidal goats. Or my ex-wife making out with her girlfriend,' Davie said, deploying his usual tactic of resorting to humour when things got tense.

'I wish it was.'

Bock pressed 'play' and then stood back to give Mellie and Davie full view of the screen.

'Those are my gates,' Davie announced to no one in particular.

The image was of the outside of his home, the six-foot-tall perimeter wall punctuated by two huge, solid wooden gates, decorated at the top with black iron spikes to dissuade enthusiastic fans or paparazzi from entering. He could also see the two cameras, mounted on the gate posts, both trained on the area immediately in front of the gates so they could see any caller who pressed the buzzer.

Davie already knew that whoever was turning the tables and filming the gates would be too far back for their image to be caught on his security system and made a note to address that pronto.

'So someone's got an image of the perimeter of my house. No biggie.' Davie shrugged. It was barely out of his mouth when the gates began to open. All three of them watched in silence, transfixed by the movement of the huge wooden barriers, until they were at their widest point, where they stopped to let a car exit the property.

'Oh fuck,' Davie murmured, truly chilled for the first time since this whole fiasco began.

As the black GMC came closer to the camera, he could clearly see the driver. He watched as it turned right, then headed down the street. Only when it disappeared out of sight and the focus of the camera returned to the gates did Davie realise that he'd been holding his breath since the vehicle driven by Zac and carrying his kids appeared on the screen.

A tornado of rage started to form inside him. This was crossing the line. Whatever sad fuck was filming his kids would be tracked down and he'd kill the asshole.

'Mark, get every man you've got on this. I want security on Bella and Bray, I want—'

Mark raised his hand to stop him. 'There's more, Davie.'

'What do you mean?' He watched as Mark pressed a button on the keyboard that made the image fast-forward. In almost cartoon style, the gates closed, and then the image stayed the same for a few seconds before the gates started to open again and his Bugatti took centre position on the screen. Davie wracked his memory. Yep, he'd gone out straight after the kids. Had he noticed anything? Anyone strange hanging around? nope. He'd been too busy thinking about the day ahead to notice some fucked-up freak filming from the other side of the road.

The Bugatti came closer before turning in the same direction as the

GMC and heading into the distance. The focus returned to the gates and held the shot as they slowly closed.

'Christ,' Mellie said softly. 'This ain't good.'

'It's still not done,' Mark warned, just as a cracking noise from the screen made both Mellie and Davie jolt.

If you looked closely, you could just see the end of the barrel from where the noise had originated.

Mark pressed 'rewind' and then played it again. 'Look here. You can see where the bullet hit.'

They watched closely as the barrel came just into shot, then recoiled slightly as the bullet left the chamber. Their eyes immediately went to the spot Mark was pointing at. Small chips of wood flew off the gate.

'Some bastard just shot at my house?' It was phrased as a question thanks to Davie's tone of stunned disbelief.

Mark nodded solemnly. 'I think you're going to have to start taking this seriously, Davie.'

'Fucking hell. Mellie, what do you think?' he asked, realizing that Mellie was uncharacteristically quiet.

'I think you need to catch this prick. Because despite what you said earlier, you ain't bulletproof.'

17

MIRREN

'Killer Queen' – Queen

'So where are we with the terms?' Mirren asked calmly. The current situation didn't faze her. The studio had attempted to make changes to their standard contract terms before, but they'd always managed to iron out their differences and come to a resolution that both sides could live with.

Sitting in the seat at the other side of Mirren's desk, Perry didn't even need to look down at her notes. 'We finally reached agreement on everything except the books and merchandising, but they're refusing to budge.'

'What do they want?'

'Twenty-five per cent. Right now, they're on ten.'

'What would the net effect be?'

'About ten million a year based on this year's projections.'

Mirren ran the figures through her head. She knew the studio was hurting. Cinema figures were down, and thanks to a seemingly uncontrollable pirating industry, so were DVD and online sales. Her box office had been unaffected, rising by 20 per cent last year, but the studio had taken a couple of big hits on action movies that hadn't even recouped their costs.

But just because they were hurting in other areas didn't mean they were going to take the cream off her pot. Absolutely no way. That wasn't the way they did business.

Mirren had the entire franchise to safeguard. Sure, it was riding high at the moment, but who knew what would happen in a year, two years, five years? If the *Clansman* income dipped for any reason, she still had wages to pay, jobs to protect. But it was more than that. Twenty per cent of all McLean Productions' profits were now being diverted to build Chloe's Care, a drop-in centre currently under construction in east Hollywood for young people with addiction issues. Sometimes it was her only reason for getting out of bed in the morning, the only thing that made any sense of what had happened. This was Chloe's legacy – a safe refuge where a messed-up teen could find food, shelter or someone to talk to, no matter what state they were in, no matter what they'd done to get there.

The centre was going to take over $1 million a year to run – split between Mirren's personal contribution and a portion of the profits from McLean Productions, so if she let a major studio like Pictor eat into her earnings, it eroded her ability to ride out any future downturns and therefore jeopardized the centre. That wasn't going to happen.

'Don't budge, Perry. How long have we got until contract deadline?'

'Two weeks.'

'OK. Put a call in to Wes Lomax and set up a lunch meeting. Somewhere highly visible. The Ivy. Tell them to put us up front. It'll be better than a thirty-second slot on Entertainment Tonight.'

Perry nodded, grinning, immediately understanding the strategy. 'I like your style.'

The intercom on Mirren's desk beeped and she responded to the interruption. 'Yes?'

'Your next appointment is here,' announced her secretary, Devlin, a six-foot import from NYC, who'd been with her since a few months after he'd stepped off the red-eye in search of a job behind the scenes in the industry. Mirren knew he had aspirations to move into production, but right now he was happy to learn everything he could from being the constant presence at her side.

Perry got up and headed for the door, with a parting, 'I'll keep you updated.'

'Thanks, Perry,' Mirren replied, then held out a hand to greet the replacement.

Brad Bernson had worked for her many times over the years, doing everything from tracking down the scumbags who were supplying Chloe with her drugs to doing background checks on potential employees. An ex-marine, he'd gone into the military police, rising to lieutenant colonel before retiring and setting up on his own. Mirren trusted him as much as she trusted anyone. She had to hope that, especially in this case, it wouldn't be misplaced.

Greetings over, he took the seat recently vacated by Perry. 'What can I do for you, Mirren?'

It was one of the things that Mirren liked about him – he was straight to the point. No screwing around, no unnecessary pleasantries.

'I need you to find out anything you can about this woman. Her name's Marilyn McLean. I've written down all her details.

She won't be on any US databases, but she may have entered the country in the last few weeks.'

Brad lifted the file with the photograph on the front. It had clearly been taken many years before. Mirren wasn't sure that Marilyn even resembled that image now, but Sarah had said that she'd recognised her from an old picture so the likeness must still be there. Her mother had always been supremely vain, dyeing her hair, fixating on her appearance, desperate to halt the clock of the ageing process. The blonde hair would be piled on her head, full face make-up applied before she'd leave the house, lots of pink clothes and indecently short skirts, which were excruciatingly, embarrassingly inappropriate to her teenage daughter. Marilyn didn't care. She was Jono Leith's mistress, and as long as he was happy, that was all that mattered.

The memories forced a wave of bile to rise from Mirren's stomach. There was no one she despised more than Marilyn McLean.

'Same name. Is she a family member?' Brad's right eyebrow was raised in question.

'My mother.'

'And do you want her to be approached if we find her?'

'Absolutely not. Just let me know straight away.'

'OK, will do. I'll be in touch if I have any questions after reading the file.' Brad rose and was out of there with no further discussion, leaving Mirren's teeth clenched with fear and fury. For once, she wanted Brad to fail, to discover that Marilyn was nowhere to be found.

Because if her mother was back from the dead, she wouldn't be coming for a happy family reunion.

18

ZANDER

'Closest Thing to Crazy' – Katie Melua

'What the fuck were you thinking?' Wes Lomax screamed. Yep, actually screamed. Zander was pretty sure that his hair fluttered in the blowback. No one in this town spoke to a star of Zander's calibre like that. No one. But Wes was more than just a studio head. He'd discovered Zander, Mirren and Davie twenty-two years before and made them stars, but only Zander had stayed with him since that first movie. Wes had tolerated years of negative press, defended him against all oncoming attacks, helped him through his addictions and coped with every shred of drama Zander had brought to his door. And right now, Zander knew that gave Wes the right to vent his frustrations with a baseball bat if he had one handy.

Around the boardroom table, the Lomax lawyers, publicity chiefs, exec producers, bean counters and Hollie, staring downwards in the hope of escaping the wrath. Only Zander kept his head up, although he couldn't stop a sigh. There was no getting away from the fact that he didn't come out of this well. The only ray of consolation was that Raymo Cash had refused to press charges, largely due to the fact that Mirren had told cops he made the first move.

'It was self-defence,' Zander said calmly, and not for the first time. 'The guy came at Mirren. I pushed him back.'

'Then fell on him and felt the repeated inclination to punch him in the face?' Wes didn't hide his cynicism. 'And it just had to be the same prick you punched out last time?'

'I'm just lucky like that,' Zander agreed wearily.

It was a fuck-up. There was no arguing with that. But Cash had deserved it, and given the same situation, he'd do it again. 'Where are we with this diabolical fucking disaster?' Wes was pacing now, flexing his forearms with dumbbells as he went. In his mid-sixties, he was still as trim as he'd been in his thirties. There were many facets of his character that were the stuff of legend. His voracious sexual appetite, especially for women less than half his age and preferably more than two at the same time. His instinct for making great movies, which had ensured the success of the Dunhill franchise and steered Lomax Films through a global financial crisis that had buried many bigger companies. His absolutely manic, bordering-on-psychotic temper, as illustrated right at this moment.

Paula Leno, the vice-president of publicity, a twenty-two-year veteran with the company, spoke up. 'Raymo Cash isn't pressing charges. Why go through the tiresome ignominy of a trial when he can sell his story to the tabloids instead? Of course, he's spinning a different tale to Zander, saying that he was attacked for no reason. We've put an opposing line out there via anonymous sources and all the papers have picked it up. It weighs in our favour that he's not going down the legal route, as it makes it look like he has something to hide. It also goes in our favour that the majority of the television-viewing public think he's an arrogant asshole who is utterly delusional about his talent and popularity. In short, our polling figures are showing that this hasn't dented your popularity. In fact, the opposite is true. But that's only the case because LAPD have backed up our confirmation that you were tested and shown to have no alcohol or drugs in your system. And also the fact that – to quote Lou Cole's column in the *Hollywood Post* – you looked "damn hot" while you were rolling about on the ground. You really need to send her flowers. She has been the lead voice in your media defence, probably thanks to the fact that you were defending her best friend. Gotta love press impartiality.'

Right now, Zander did. He made a mental note to thank Mirren for getting the truth out there, while Hollie made a physical note on her tablet calendar to send Lou Cole the entire contents of the most expensive flower shop she could find.

Wes looked slightly mollified by Paula's analysis of the situation, but he wasn't ready to let Zander off the hook just yet. He turned to the row of three men in suits that clearly came with a price tag including several zeros. He was obviously paying these guys way too much. 'Where are we legally?'

Brian Thompson, VP of Legal, did the talking. 'No charges, so nothing official. But it wouldn't surprise me if Cash came at Zander for financial damages. We'll set up a contingency for that. The big problem for us is insurance. At the moment, they're citing the incident as breach of Zander's behaviour clause, so we have to suspend shooting with him. Hopefully, we can get it lifted, but there are no guarantees on it. They're playing hard ball.'

'Give me a revised schedule and a cost on that,' Lomax ordered the VP of Finance, sitting at the opposite end of the table.

Zander wanted to put his head on the desk and let the cool surface of the marble ease the splitting pain in his forehead. A shooting suspension could cripple production, cost millions and – if it continued indefinitely – derail the whole movie. This was as bad as it got without the death of a star. Which right now would be a more favourable option.

Wes headed for the door. 'And Zander, son, I'm taking every dollar this costs from your obscenely bloated pay cheque.'

With that, he was off, leaving a trail of spit and fire behind him.

'That went well,' Paula noted as she rose from the table.

Zander gave her a grateful smile. They'd worked together for a long time and they had a real bond of affection, despite the fact that he'd cost her more work hours than any other Lomax talent. 'Thanks for having my back there.'

'It's my reason for being,' she told him with a smile. It was the only love in the room. The lawyers were furious, the bean counters were panicking, and Hollie was giving him the silent treatment. It lasted all the way across the car park into the car.

Zander was the first one to break the ice.

'Is this when you tell me you're going to work for Matt Damon?' he asked, repeating her much-promised threat, the one that was repeated every time he royally fucked up. Now being a case in point.

'OK, so do you want the truth, or do you want me to kiss your ass?' she finally said, rounding in the seat to face him.

'I think I'd prefer it if you would kiss my ass.'

She ignored the suggestion. 'You have got to stop doing this. I'm fucking furious, Zander. It has to stop. I was just starting to think that things were going to be OK again, that you'd kicked the booze and the coke, and I wasn't going to wake up to the headline that you were dead in some alley.' Her voice was rising with every sentence. 'I'd finally stopped worrying that some rancid woman was gonna infect you because you were too whacked out to use protection. I'd finally started trusting that I could leave you alone for a whole night without checking my phone every five minutes in case you'd gone off the rails, or got wasted or fucked up in any one of a thousand other ways. Or fricking died. I was finally getting a life. I was dating. I even had sex! And then you go and get yourself arrested.'

'But the charge didn't stick…'

'I don't care!' she was shouting now. 'And don't give me the fricking puppy-dog eyes, because they don't work on me.'

'Not at all?'

He could see by her body language that his last reply had dented the wall of her irritation. She no longer looked like she wanted to dole out the same treatment delivered to Raymo Cash. 'Zander, I love you. I do. But I swear to God…'

'Matt Damon?'

She punched him on the arm, as hard as she could.

'Matt Damon. I'll be the best fricking thing that ever happened to him.' She started up the engine and screeched out of the car park.

'I could be your assistant if you fancy a career in stunts,' Zander offered.

She ignored him, switching directly to PA mode. 'OK, so I've doubled up your training schedule for the next week to keep you busy while you're on suspension.'

'So where are we going right now?' he asked. The irony didn't escape him. He was an A-list star, recognized all over the world, barring recent events he was at the pinnacle of his career, and yet he wouldn't know where he was meant to be from one hour until the next if he didn't have Hollie there to direct him. Right now, all he wanted to do was go hang at the beach with Hollie. They could head up to Malibu, pick up coffee on the way, watch the sunset and forget the world for a few hours. Peace. Tranquillity.

'Shutters. Adrianna Guilloti has requested a meeting. I think she flew in this afternoon and the trip was unscheduled, so you might want to brace yourself for turbulence. And not the good kind.'

Zander's headache made a sudden reappearance, as, for the first time, he recognized the other consequence of the altercation. He had a strict standards clause in his Guilloti contract and he had no doubt that his recent actions breached it. He could still remember exactly what she'd said when they'd made the initial deal: Red carpets, editorials, publicity shots – all good. Fights and anything that could lead to his clothes being accessorized with handcuffs – all bad.

His nerves felt like they were on the outside of his skin as he contemplated seeing her. Of course, she'd come to terminate his endorsement contract. And sure, that wasn't ideal. But the truth was, advertisements weren't his thing, and he'd only agreed to do it in the first place because he'd wanted her so badly he'd have agreed to anything. That hadn't changed. He still thought about her constantly, craved her touch, longed to be with her. Adrianna Guilloti was his crack cocaine, only this time there was no rehab.

If she was going to terminate his contract, fair enough. At least then he'd be forced to shut that longing down. He'd beat the booze and the powder. Maybe it was time to get over this one too.

The sun was setting by the time Hollie dropped him in front of the hotel's glass doors for the meeting. 'Are you OK getting a cab home? I want to head back and get to dealing with the mountain of crap your latest stunt has unleashed upon us.'

'Sure. I'll walk home.'

'Great. Zander Leith, on the beach, walking from Santa Monica to Venice in front of several hundred tourists having an evening stroll along the boardwalk. What could go wrong?'

He put his hands up. 'OK, OK! I'll take a cab. I'll call you later.'

'Preferably not from a ten-by-twelve cell with a request for bail money,' she warned, before adding a cheeky 'love you!', then slipping the gearstick into drive and pulling away.

Inside, he scanned the foyer, but there was no sign of Adrianna. Reception had the answer, directing him to the Beach House Suite, 1,350 square feet of pale blue and white luxury situated on the third floor overlooking the sands. It was her favourite room. Overstuffed sofa, big comfortable chairs, a fire-place and shutters that could be opened to allow the breeze from the Pacific to fill the room.

It only took one knock for the door to open, and she beckoned him in. She was obviously in work mode. Her black suit was tailored to give it a masculine edge, a stark contrast to the hint of lace that protruded from the cami underneath. Her hair was tied back in a long, sleek ponytail, her feet supported by the red soles of her Louboutin ankle boots. In his jeans and white T-shirt, Zander felt decidedly underdressed.

He walked past her and felt her tense as he headed straight for the minibar, then breathe again when he pulled out a soda. 'Here to fire me?' he asked casually. He wanted this part over now, so that he could move past it and get to the bit where she told him they could have no more contact. It made perfect sense and he was in no doubt that would be the case. Adrianna Guilloti valued her time, her company and her brand. She wouldn't waste a heartbeat on a guy who had been rolling about in the street, brawling with a nobody only a few nights before. The only positive in the whole situation was that he hadn't been wearing the latest look from her spring–summer collection at the time.

'That was the purpose of my visit.' The arch of her back curved into her perfect ass as she walked to the window.

Zander didn't move. Safer over by the wall. He'd yet to manage more than a few minutes alone in a room with her without nudity being involved, so he felt it prudent to remain at a distance for now.

'But it seems that you've earned a reprieve. Our marketing team have reported that since you were apparently defending another woman from attack, your approval rating has climbed several points.'

'I thought it was only presidents who had approval ratings.'

'Presidents and you,' she spat sharply.

He wasn't sure he was getting this. She'd come here to fire him, decided not to and yet she was still giving off very distinct vibes of fury. In Zander's life, he'd had no long-term relationships. Every romance lasted a couple of months, sometimes three at the outside, all ended by him. Through choice, he'd never lived with anyone, always preferring freedom to claustrophobia. Sometimes, like now, he knew he wasn't getting the message she was delivering. When that kind of miscommunication happened, he'd invariably decide it was too much work and call it a day. Yet somehow this time the furious pout of her lips and the flash of irritation in her eyes made it impossible to leave, but impossible to stand there any longer.

Walking towards her, she folded her arms, a barrier between them, compelling him to establish the facts.

'Look, you're going to have to help me out here. So our working relationship is to continue. And our non-working relationship?'

'What is Mirren McLean to you?'

To his surprise, there was real anger in her voice. 'She's a friend,' he answered honestly.

'A friend?' Scepticism now. 'A friend that you will fight with another man for?'

'Yes, a friend, more like a sister. Ever since we were kids.'

'Like a sister? So no...' she let that one drift off and Zander laughed, finally getting it – a reaction that riled her even more. 'Hey, baby, are you jealous?' he teased, reaching out to touch her face. She slapped his hand away and he was just about to back off and give her time to cool down when she was on him, her mouth hard on his, her hands in his hair, locking his face to hers.

His blood immediately thundered to every extremity as she fiercely broke off from the kiss and sank to her knees, deftly opening his jeans and tearing down the zipper as she went. By the time her face was level with his groin, he was hard, ready for her, but she didn't do the expected. Instead, she slipped her tongue along the length of his shaft and then back down again, this time going lower, taking one of his balls in her mouth and sucking, while her hand came up to massage his erection. The pain was exquisite, extraordinary, sending tremors shooting around his body. The other ball now, sucking, teasing, gentle, hard, rough, soft, constantly changing pressure and tempo.

His hard, perfect butt cheeks clenched as he felt the stirrings of an orgasm. No, not yet. Pulling back, he leaned down, slipped his hands under her shoulders and raised her up, not stopping when she was on her feet. Instead, he reached underneath her and lifted her, Officer and a Gentleman-style, over to the floor-to-ceiling glass doors that led out onto the balcony.

With the doors still locked, the lights of the iconic Ferris wheel on the end of the pier were visible in the distance. Zander reached over and flicked one of the switches that controlled the lights in the room to off. They could now see out over one of the most beautiful landscapes in the world but those on the outside couldn't see in.

A more poetic man would consider it a metaphor for his life.

He dipped his head and kissed her hard on her perfect pillow lips, then gently placed her down so that she stood in front of him.

She reached for him, but he blocked her hands.

'My turn,' he whispered, before taking a step back. Their sex was always hard, passionate, frantic, forceful... But not this time.

Eyes flaring with fury, she opened her mouth to speak, but he placed his fingers to her lips, shushing her.

First, he pulled off his T-shirt, revealing shoulders that looked like they had been carved from stone, each inflection and curve expertly crafted. His pecs crowned a torso that rose in a perfect V, each abdominal muscle clearly defined. In the land of the Perfect Body, Zander Leith was king, and although she'd seen him, touched him, tasted every inch of him, Adrianna still emitted an involuntary gasp. He bent, pushed his jeans down further, then stepped out of them, making clear he'd been in the commando squad today. Another gasp from his lady. He could see this was excruciating for her. No movement, no sound, just the electrifying torture of anticipation.

Gently, Zander turned her round so that she was facing out of the window only a few inches in front of her. He lifted her hair, making her shiver as he traced a line across the back of her neck with his tongue, moving to her ear, his hot breath making her tremble again. He placed her jet mane over her shoulder to the front, then, still standing behind her, slipped the jacket from her shoulders, let it fall, revealing the black lace cami top. Silently, using only his two index fingers in slow, synchronized movements, he ran lines down each side of her neck and along the tops of her shoulders, down her back until they reached the bottom of her delicate top. He raised it up, her arms lifting so he could pull it over her head. Using feather-light strokes, he ran his fingertips down her spine, then slowly walked round her, stopping when they were face to face, only inches apart, repeating the exploration of every inch of her stomach and breasts using only the tips of his fingers. His gaze was locked on hers for every second, their breathing hard, the electricity between them crackling with desire.

Only when he was sure that there wasn't an inch of her naked skin that he hadn't caressed did he open her trousers, let them drop to join her other discarded clothes on the floor. She took one step forward, leaving them behind; her only adornments now were a black lace thong and the black leather Louboutin ankle boots. The thong broke with one sharp tug. Just the boots left. They could stay.

Her eyes were blazing now, with passion, excitement, fury.

'I want you,' she whispered, her breath coming in short bursts now.

'Not yet.'

Pulling away from her, he moved around behind her again, this time lifting her hands and placing them on the window, so she was bent forward. Still behind her, he placed his hands over hers, his chest on her back, his hips on her ass, his feet between her wide-open legs, he found her, entered her, made love to her until they were both drenched in sweat, legs weak, and his final, ferocious, explosive thrusts made her shout his name as she came... And came... And came...

The lights of the Ferris wheel on the end of Santa Monica Pier were basking the room in a kaleidoscope of colour when he woke and realised he must have dozed for a few minutes. Adrianna was already up and dressing, her breasts barely contained by the lace cami, her taut buttocks clearly visible in the curves of her trousers.

He pushed himself up on one arm. 'Hey. Somewhere to be?' Leaning over, she ran one blood-red nail down the side of his perfect face. 'I'm on the 10.55 p.m. flight to London. I've got a meeting there tomorrow.'

'With your husband?'

She flinched. 'No. He's in New York. But I can't change the London schedule so I need to leave tonight.'

It wasn't long enough. He'd come here tonight expecting, almost hoping, that she would break whatever thing this was that they had, but instead, he just wanted her more, couldn't bear the thought of letting her go. Resisting physical cravings had never been his strong point. Like a true addict, his mind was already forming a plan to get more.

'I have a better idea.'

He pushed himself up, his body groaning, his muscles aching with pleasure and pain as he reached for his phone.

He called a number he'd used a few times before, a personal concierge service that could get him anything he wanted, anytime, anywhere.

The first request was for a limo to take them to another LA destination, with a quick stop at his apartment so he could run in to pick up a few essentials. The car would be on the way before he disconnected the call.

The second request was for a different mode of transport altogether.

Two hours later, he sat next to Adrianna in the chariot he'd arranged for her. They were just about to depart when he realised his actions required one final communication. The press of one button connected him to Hollie.

She bypassed 'Hello' and went straight to 'If you're heart-broken and unemployed, I have three episodes of Scandal and a box of cronuts and I'm happy to share while giving you a lecture on the perils of dating a married woman.'

'Erm, thanks, Holls, but it turns out I'm neither of those first two options.'

'Oh God. You are to self-discipline what I am to the Atkins,' she told him, and from the muffled sound he took it that there would soon be one cronut less in the box.

'Look, I need to go in a minute, but can you cancel the training for tomorrow and block out my schedule for a couple of days?'

'Oh shit, not again. Zander, where are—'

'Mr Leith, Ms Guilloti, if I could just ask you to fasten your seatbelts, as we're about to take off.' The flaxen-haired flight attendant sashayed off down the aisle and through the privacy curtain at the front of the Gulfstream G200.

'Zander, what was...? Zander, are you on a plane? Oh, for the love of God, you're a nightmare. Where are you going?'

'I'll be back in a couple of days, Holls. Seems I've got some stuff to take care of in London.'

19

SARAH

'Fix You' – Coldplay

Spike Hollywood, a luscious den of music and debauchery, was the most popular club in LA right now and the hang-out where anyone who was someone wanted to be. And Sarah. From her vantage point on the staircase between the upper and lower floors, she had eyes on every corner of the club and a full view of the ground-floor bar.

It was all research for her book on the dark side of Hollywood, on the vices that chewed up and spat out the young people who came here with big dreams, and on the demise of wealthy LA kids who felt a compulsion to dance with danger. She'd been coming here a couple of nights a week for the last month and she'd learned some interesting stuff. She knew that every one of the bar staff was skimming the till, the biggest culprit being the male-model-good-looking head barman, who only rang up every second drink, then balanced out any potential stock deficit by overcharging by 50 per cent in the last two hours of the night, figuring that the clubbers would be too wasted to notice. Most of the time he was right, and when he wasn't, he just claimed genuine error and corrected it. The guy could win an Emmy for his performance of the innocent mistake.

Sarah also knew that the pretty blonde waitress was shagging both the bearded dude behind the bar and his goth girlfriend, neither of whom was in on the other's secret.

She knew that two of the door staff were dealing coke and amphetamines for a 300 per cent mark-up, which increased by 20 per cent every hour. It was a natty sales strategy that encouraged the buyers to come early.

She knew that two of the bus girls, whose job it was to keep the tables clean and return empty glasses to the bar, offered the additional service of blow jobs in the store cupboard for thirty dollars per ejaculation.

She also knew that she had to get entry to the VIP room, because that's where the real action took place. Of course, she could just come back with Davie and the doors to the exclusive lounge would open to welcome him, but that wasn't the way to play this. She wasn't going to use him to further her career and then drag him into the ensuing and inevitable fallout. She had to do this on her own. She just hadn't quite figured out how yet.

Her mobile phone buzzed with an incoming text. Davie.

Come home. Require house call. Refusal not an option.

I'm working. Later?

Nope, now. Don't make me come down there…

He added two laughing-face emojis to let her know he was kidding. Maybe. Over the last couple of months he'd shown up here on three occasions, totally buggering up her surveillance, because the moment Davie Johnston appeared, it became all about him.

There was a temptation to refuse, but the truth was, she wanted to see him. It felt like lately they'd had little time for each other because they'd slipped into completely conflicting schedules.

She was out most nights and then rose late, before jumping straight into writing or researching something or someone she'd encountered the night before.

Davie, meanwhile, was juggling the demands of two shows, so he worked until midnight, then headed straight into the office the following morning, meaning that if she wanted to see him, she had to go hang out at the studio and hope that he could spare her a few minutes. Not her idea of quality time with her boyfriend. He regularly reminded her that it was only for a few more months; then this season of *American Stars* would be over and his workload would dramatically decrease. The timescale suited her fine. By that time, she hoped to have the first draft of her book written, and then they could both take their feet off the gas a little and chill out. Not that she wanted them to live in each other's pockets. Absolutely not. Her independence was important to her, and she wasn't going to lose that or surrender it to a guy. Love and devotion were definite pluses, but co-dependency absolutely wasn't.

On the pretence of sending a text, she held her mobile phone up in front of her and slowly scanned the room, videoing the action. It was a method she'd used many times over the years on dozens of investigations and stories. Later, she'd fast-forward the footage and sometimes it caught something she'd missed. A famous face using a disguise in a corner. A drug deal she hadn't spotted first time around. Illicit activity between a couple who'd arrived with other people.

Tonight, she couldn't see much going on. The only notable people in the room so far – other than a few TV minor celebrities, who didn't get up to anything more blatant than taking an obscene number of selfies – were an heiress, a former child actress turned toxic mess and a current pop star who delighted in shocking the world by refusing to keep her clothes on and crossing the explicit lines of sexual decency at every opportunity.

They'd all eschewed the VIP room and were hanging out in a cordoned area in the body of the club. It was attention-seeking at its most obvious, but it also made it unlikely that they'd be up to anything illicit or illegal.

Video over, she noticed the time on her phone. Midnight. Suddenly Davie's invitation seemed pretty appealing. She could do with a few hours off and it gave her an opportunity to make a call she'd been delaying for days.

Outside, the valet took a few minutes to bring up her car from the underground car park, giving her time to run through the call in her head.

Only when she'd cleared Sunset did she dial the international number. Ed McCallum would have just got into the office and would therefore be busy dealing with all the news that would have come in overnight. More than any other time of day, this was when he hated interruptions, so it was no surprise when he picked up on the second ring and barked, 'Yes?'

'You really need to work on your telephone skills,' she replied, laughing.

'According to my wife, there are many skills I need to work on,' he groaned, before dissolving into yet another fit of coughing, which lasted so long it added at least a couple of dollars to her phone bill.

'Ed, please give up the cigs.'

'And what would be my motivation to do that, then?'

She thought for a moment. 'I'll sleep with you. Twice,' she joked.

'I'd take you up on it if I didn't think the exertion would kill me before the cigs did.'

Another coughing fit.

'Listen, before you croak it, I just wanted to let you know I don't have anything on Mirren McLean's mother yet.'

'I thought you were big chums with her mate, that Davie Johnston bloke? Tell me you're not sleeping with him. You could do a lot better. Always thought he was a smug bastard.'

Sarah kept her voice perfectly even. 'Not now that I've promised myself to you. Anyway, I did ask Davie and he reckons Mirren's mother moved to Spain or France, so I don't think the stories about that woman in Liverpool being Marilyn McLean are authentic.'

'Had a feeling it was too good to be true,' he mused. 'Got a Liverpool reporter doing some sniffing around and turns out this broad was a real piece of work. More active in the operation than we thought. Razor Ritchie has been in and out of prison for the last twenty years, and according to whispers, she looks after the shop when he's not around. Regular Bonnie and Clyde.' Sarah thought about this for a moment. If Marilyn had made the move from piece of decorative fluff to conspirator, that made her an even bigger potential threat. Sarah knew what she was capable of. If her brand of single-minded loyalty had been expanded to encompass her lover's business, there was no limit to what she'd do. Marilyn McLean was a danger. Marilyn McLean with experience and contacts on the dark side of the crime line was an even bigger one.

'What kind of stuff was Ritchie's operation into?' Sarah asked casually.

Ed coughed again before answering. 'Christ, there wasn't much they weren't into. Drugs. Guns. Protection. Extortion. Blackmail. The guy cast a warm and cuddly blanket of sheer fucking terror everywhere he went. That's why we're finding it tough to get anything here. Everyone's bloody terrified to go on record. And they were pretty savvy with their technology too. A lot of hidden cameras, stuff like that. According to one fine, upstanding psychopath, the woman was behind a lot of the personal stuff. Apparently she ordered a rival's family to be filmed for three weeks, then sent him a video of his kid's birthday party. It was a pretty sophisticated set-up. Another rumour said they used a drone – a fucking drone – to drop a human finger onto the table at a mole's garden barbeque. Sounds like a peach. I preferred the good old days when the criminals just stormed the room and battered everyone in sight.'

Sarah was struggling now to keep her tone light-hearted.

This wasn't good. Personal attacks? Targeting families? This was starting to sound a bit familiar. Still, she wasn't going to give Ed any clue that she was rattled. 'Now don't go getting all nostalgic on me, Ed. You'll be re-reading *No Mean City* and watching old reruns of *Taggart* next,' she quipped.

'That was last night's entertainment,' Ed retorted with a throaty laugh. 'It's a bugger being too old for porn. Anyway, look, I'll dig a bit more at this end, but I'm not hopeful. We've got no photos, no footage, no one willing to go on record, so no story. Can't run with a bunch of half-arsed fairy tales and urban legends. Would love to get something, though. If this female really does exist, if she really is as dangerous as I'm hearing, and if she's also Mirren McLean's mother...' He tailed off and Sarah knew he was picturing the front pages, day after day, in his mind. Meanwhile, all Sarah could picture was the carnage Marilyn could cause if she turned the spotlight on Mirren, Davie and Zander.

'That would be some story,' Sarah agreed, because she knew he expected her to. 'Look, I'll stay on it. I'll be seeing Mirren next week, so I'll see what I can get from her and let you know.'

'No worries, love. I knew it was a long shot, but it's worth following it up.'

Hanging up, she felt a weird mix of anxiety and relief. Ed was the best editor in the business, but he wouldn't run a story without concrete facts and it seemed like they were proving hard to come by here. On the plus side, that bought her breathing space to track down Marilyn, especially if Mirren was right and she was on this side of the pond. On the down side, it proved just how dangerous she was. If she was scaring the crap out of the criminal fraternity, then she obviously wielded power and posed a genuine threat to them. If that threat had crossed the Atlantic, they were all in trouble.

Slowing the car down as she reached Davie's gates, she pulled to a stop next to the keypad that facilitated entry and quickly pressed in the six-digit code, checking first to ensure there was no one around who could be watching. Actually, there was absolutely no one around. That in itself was unusual. No matter what time of the night, there were usually one or two paps, leaning on their motorbikes or SUVs, hoping to catch some kind of action. Not tonight. The street was deserted. Which made it less embarrassing that the gates weren't opening. Prodding the numbers sharply this time, she re-entered the code.

Still nothing.

Third time. Nothing. She had picked up her mobile to call Davie when they finally began to open, but then stopped when there was a gap just wide enough for the exceptionally large man who was emerging from the driveway to squeeze through. Bloody hell, this guy looked like a tank.

Flicking the phone into her left hand, she quickly pressed '911' but didn't connect the call – that would be the next plan of action if she didn't like what this guy had to say. Who was he? And what was he doing in her boyfriend's house?

'Sorry, ma'am, the code has been changed. Mr Johnston told us to expect you. If you'd like to make your way up to the house, he'll explain the situation.'

Situation? What situation? And why was life with Davie one big drama? This was probably his latest whim. Like the time he put an eighty-inch TV in every room. Or had a skateboard park installed on the back lawn for

Bray. He'd probably read somewhere that Puff Daddy or Céline Dion had upgraded their security measures and decided to do the same.

As usual, he was waiting for her at the door, this time holding two bottles of beer. This was why she loved this man. He'd waited up; he had beer. Sold to the journalist with the simple tastes.

'Bad day?'

To her surprise, instead of answering her, he folded his arms around her and held her tight and close for a few moments. This was new. Oh god, something terrible had happened. She could sense it. He was holding on to her like he never wanted to let her go. In her experience, there were only three things that incited that reaction in a man – relief, fear and guilt.

She hoped it was the first, was afraid it could be the second and prayed it wasn't the third. His woeful track record on fidelity had never been a secret between them, but she absolutely believed him when he said that he only wanted her and was fully committed to monogamy. She trusted him. She did. Absolutely. At least, as much as she trusted anyone who was surrounded by beautiful women desperate to snare him all day. Oh shit, it was definitely guilt.

'So what's with the guy the size of a Portakabin down at the gates and the new security codes? Wait, is this because of that whole 'blood-chucking' thing a couple of weeks ago? I thought that hadn't bothered you?'

He sighed and finally released her from his grip, handing over one of the beer bottles. 'No, not that. We had a bit of a situation today.' Despite his grave tone, Sarah's spirits rose. A situation? That didn't sound like something for him to be guilty about. OK, scratch guilt. That left fear and relief. Either of which were preferable options.

'What kind of situation?' she asked, taking a long slug of the beer and then sliding down the door jamb until she was in her favourite place, sitting on the front step, the lights of Los Angeles twinkling in the distance below them.

'Someone shot at the house.'

'They what?' she spluttered, choking on the bitter liquid.

Davie sat next to her. 'Shot at the house. Then they put a video of it on YouTube. They could have got the kids, Sarah. Bella and Bray had just left in the car and I passed just afterwards. He watched us go. Then a few minutes later, he shot at the gate.'

Sarah's analytical brain, comprehensively experienced in criminal activity and the actions of the seriously mad or bad, did a quick re-examination of the facts. So they'd had a clear shot of the kids' car but didn't take it. Then Davie was in the cross hairs, but again, no shot was taken. So that meant that for now, the desired effect was to completely scare the crap out of Davie. But why? Why would anyone want to freak him out and stress him like that?

What was to be gained?

'Do the cops think there's any relation to the blood thing?'

Davie nodded. 'Apparently both videos were uploaded from the same IP address. Came from a cafe in the Valley. No CCTV, so they've hit a dead end.

'The thing is, what possible motivation would anyone have to threaten me like that? I honestly can't think of anyone who would pull this kind of stunt.'

A deep, sickening feeling sank to her lower gut as she recalled her conversation with Ed only an hour before and her recent discussion with Mirren.

Sure, he had plenty of enemies, people he'd pissed off, but still – this was a whole other level. Who could have the motivation or inclination to threaten Davie's life?

Sarah could think of someone out there who had both.

20

DAVIE

'Life With You' – The Proclaimers

Sarah was already sitting out on the terrace when he staggered downstairs, bleary-eyed and desperate for coffee. Alina didn't even speak as she handed over his mug and then a plate with his usual morning fare – a three-egg-white and spinach omelette, and a small pot containing twenty-six different vitamins and minerals that were – according to his very expensive nutritionist – vital for optimum health. That was the thing about LA. They had vitamins for any deficit, ailment or imaginary affliction. If you had it, or thought you had it, they had a natural remedy that someone claimed would cure it.

He watched Sarah smile as he pushed open the door with his elbow and headed out to join her. This was when he thought she was at her most beautiful. Her deep auburn hair was tied up on top of her head in a messy bun, freckles scattered across her nose and cheeks and her pale skin was covered only by one of his old football tops, leaving her perfect legs bare. 'Cute' didn't even begin to describe it. For the first time in the history of Scottish football, a Partick Thistle strip looked sexy.

Looking at her now, it would be easy to assume she was a student or a young intern on a teen mag. It would take a pretty wild imagination to guess the truth, that she was a twenty-six-year-old journalist who'd spent five years working as a Glasgow crime reporter, one of the toughest jobs in UK newspapers.

She was also hard as nails and fiercely independent – qualities Davie loved.

Most of the time.

In the distance, he could see Drago, his Ukrainian jack of all trades – gardener, driver, handyman – hosing down the terrace around the pool. The garden was simple but spectacular. Sitting above the city, the infinity pool gave the illusion that it was pouring water down on all of Los Angeles. Three cabanas lined one side of the water, each of them equipped with a queen-size bed, a fridge and television. Lush, thick sunloungers, each of them with an adjustable hood, lined the other three sides. The whole area was completely private, with no other house in view. And every square foot of exclusive outdoor luxury was completely wasted on Davie because he never used any of it. With the craziness of his schedule, breakfast on the terrace was as close as he got to outdoor living.

Leaning down to meet Sarah's upturned head, he kissed her, lingering for a few seconds to taste the blend of fresh coffee and pineapple on her lips.

'There was nearly a moment of feverish excitement this morning,' she said, her grin making her look even younger.

Davie sat down across from her, putting his feet up on her lap. 'Oh yeah? Did it involve a guy with a gun shooting at my gates?'

'Nope. It's more unusual than that. Alina almost smiled at me. Think I should be worried? Is it a last token of kindness before she bumps me off? You know, like a last meal for a prisoner on death row?'

Laughing, Davie nodded. 'Very possibly.' Alina's general distaste for any and every woman Davie brought home was legendary. The only woman in his life that the housekeeper was remotely civil to was his mother, and even then it had taken several visits to raise the temperature from icy cold to remotely warm.

'That's why you should move in here. Establish your territory. She'd get used to you eventually. I reckon it will only take a decade or so, so we should really get started.'

Sarah's expression told him she wasn't buying it. 'I have a perfectly lovely apartment.' She took a sip of her coffee. 'And it's working out pretty well living in separate homes, isn't it? We've both got our independence and the crazy hours I keep don't get in the way of your routine.'

She wasn't getting it and he didn't want to press the point in case it set off a red flag. How could he tell her that his subconscious was screaming at him to reveal a dangerous truth to her?

Princess got naked and propositioned me yesterday. Princess got naked and propositioned me yesterday. Princess got...

The gods of full disclosure had activated the mantra on a repetitive loop in his head. Oh, dear God, what was happening to him? What was this, a conscience? 'Keep infidelities and indiscretions secret' had been the mainstay of his marriage to Jenny. They'd both done their own thing; they'd both pretended they didn't. It worked perfectly. Or at least, it did until Darcy Jay turned up with bollocks that were bigger than his and persuaded Jenny to live in a partnership based on openness and honesty. How ridiculously overrated was that?

The truth was, he really didn't want to cheat on Sarah, despite the fact that she clearly wasn't as into him as he was her. That thought hung around for a while and tugged on a loose thread of insecurity.

'But if you lived here, I could do those things I did to you last night all the time,' he teased, using his toe to lift up the bottom of her shirt.

Giggling, she swatted him away. 'Much as that thought is very attractive, I'll put a pin in it for now.'

'Ouch.'

OK, so he'd tried. And he'd try again in a few weeks. In the meantime, he'd do his best not to be in a situation that would allow Princess to be naked and in personal contact with his groin area.

Sarah's expression changed to a more serious one. 'So tell me. What do you reckon to the stuff that's been happening? The blood, the gunshots, the threats? God, that sounds like I'm describing some hardcore computer game.'

'Welcome to my life,' he retorted.

'Davie, I'm serious. What's your take on it?'

'I love the way you wrinkle your nose.'

'Stop changing the subject.'

He watched as her gaze went off into the middle distance and realised that he had to put her mind at ease. He didn't want her looking over her shoulder, being scared. Not that he imagined there was much that would intimidate this girl.

'Look, I'm not worried. I'm really not. There are any number of wackos out there and I think this has to be some idiot messing around trying to get himself some YouTube notoriety. I was furious when I saw my kids on that video, but obviously if the guy was going to take a shot, he'd have done so. He didn't. That tells me it's all hype and nonsense. I've upped the security to keep everyone happy, but I promise there's nothing to worry about.'

Silence. He nudged her with his foot again. Damn, it seemed like she was taking this pretty seriously.

'Davie, I think we should talk about another possibility —' she started, then stopped as the glass door slid open and Alina appeared, looking typically unimpressed at the vision in front of her.

'People at gate,' she announced, her thick Russian accent clipping the words. 'The tall chick who lived with old man for money. Man die.'

It took Davie a few seconds. 'Carmella Cass?'

'That's what I said.' Pursing her lips, she flounced back into the kitchen. Damn, that woman had issues. He liked to think she'd been an assassin in a past life and that her brusque exterior disguised a fierce loyalty that would compel her to defend his life, should that be required. Or perhaps she just hated the whole world. Either way, she was the best damn housekeeper in California, so she was staying.

'What were you going to say?'

Sarah returned his gaze. 'What?'

'You were going to say something before Alina interrupted us. You said we needed to talk...'

Sarah shook it off. 'No, it was nothing.' Rising up, she leaned over and kissed his forehead, giving him the opportunity to pull her onto his knee and kiss her properly.

'Davie, I need to get to work,' she groaned, pulling away. 'I'll call you later. Then if you're lucky, I might come back tonight and let you do some of that stuff to me again.'

'See, I'm irresistible,' he shouted, as she retreated back into the house.

'Oh, baby, you sure are,' came the reply. But not from Sarah, who'd already disappeared, no doubt keen to avoid the inevitable circus that was about to ensue.

Carmella Cass had appeared in the doorway, arms wide open, looking like something from a cola ad in the 1970s. She was wearing cut-off jeans shorts, a hippy fringed T-shirt and a garland of flowers in her hair, all of which was accessorized by a body that was made by God for billboards.

It was, apparently, also made for relationships with men way, way older than she was, Davie realised, as Jack Gore walked out behind her.

Oh crap. He'd never had any time for scruples or principles in business, but some kind of weird loyalty to Mirren surfaced and he felt his $30k porcelain veneers begin to grind as her ex-husband walked towards him.

It was hard to picture this guy and Mirren together. He used to have the respect of the industry, thanks to a back catalogue of movies that made serious money and were mostly critically acclaimed, but in the last couple of years, his standing had nosedived. His last two movies had bombed at the box office – never a good thing in an industry in which you're only as hot as your last $100-million at the box office. On top of that, the well-publicized affair with Mercedes Dance, a twenty-two-year-old actress and star of his last film, had not only cost him his marriage to Mirren, but had also damaged his personal image. And on the subject of image, what was with the physical overhaul? He'd always been a pretty cool, good-looking guy, ageing into a Kevin Costner style of craggy attraction. But now?

Davie bit down on his bottom lip to stop himself from saying something wildly offensive. The guy was a walking cliché. Sure, he'd clearly been working out, but those half-melons in his upper arms had to be bicep implants. And just in case the eyes weren't drawn to that area, there was some serious ink to catch the attention. He was wearing a beanie hat in 75-degree heat, which meant one of two things – either he was auditioning for a boy band or he was covering up a new hair transplant.

'Davie, my man,' he said, holding out his hand in greeting.

My man? Davie bristled again. He wasn't 'his man'. A wave of hatred came all the way from somewhere around 1994. Davie and Mirren had split a few months after they came to LA and it wasn't long afterwards that he'd heard she was seeing Jack Gore. Next thing he knew, they were married and Mirren was gone from Davie's life.

It was hard now to understand what Mirren had ever seen in this guy, but hey, hadn't they all made their fair share of shit choices?

By the look of Jack Gore, he was still making them.

'Sit, sit,' Davie beckoned, and then watched as Gore held out a seat for Carmella, letting his hand sit proprietorially on her shoulder for a few moments before sitting next to her. The moment was only broken by Alina thudding a tray of coffee, water and fruit onto the middle of the table. Davie winked at her, for once on the same insolent page, before turning back to Carmella.

'So how are you holding up?' he asked gently. It seemed like the right thing to say. It was only a couple of weeks since the funeral and it had to hurt.

'Yeah, I'm like, still really bummed out.' She somehow made it sound like she had a flat tyre. Or had missed a flight. Or had bought a pair of shoes only to discover that they were 50 per cent off the next day.

'But y'know, as Jack has been teaching me,' she fired a sweet smile in Gore's direction, prompting Bicep-Man to put his hand on hers, 'Jizzo would have wanted me to, like, move on, y'know? He was all about life. All about my happiness. So I gotta honour that.'

Not for the first time, Davie realised that the contrast between the way she looked and the way she spoke and acted was bizarre. Carmella Cass was one of the most beautiful women in a town stacked with beautiful women. She was a goddess of physical perfection. Long-limbed, breathtaking curves, flowing blonde hair and a face that was so exquisitely contoured it looked like it had been carved by an artist. This was the Christie Brinkley of the post-millennium world. Somehow that gave the impression that she should be smart and focused, yet she was, undoubtedly, wired to an orbiting planet. And right now, he was pretty sure she'd also been indulging in chemical or alcoholic enhancements before her morning cereal.

He recognized this was no time for honesty or sense.

'Of course you have,' he agreed. 'It's what he would have wanted.'

Carmella's eyes filled with unshed tears. 'And he would have wanted the show to continue. You know my baby wanted me to be a star.'

'Yep, he did,' Davie agreed, wondering when she was going to get to the point. When he'd agreed to meet her here this morning, he'd been sure she was going to ask him to divert Jizzo's share of future royalties from re-runs of the show. He'd already had his people look into it and there was a clause in the contract that could make that happen. Jizzo had no family, no dependants, so the unlikelihood of it being legally contested was another win.

She nodded solemnly. 'So I think the show has to go on.'

'What?' Davie had heard her. He was just stalling for time while he ran this one through in his head. How would that work? A show riding on one person? He'd done that before with a car-crash ex-movie star, Lana Delasso, and it had been a disaster when she'd bailed out. Show over. Ensemble casts had the benefit that if one person left, the show still went on. *The Real Housewives* franchise was testimony to that. But Carmella on her own? She wasn't big enough, wild enough or stable enough to carry a solo show.

'We should do another season,' she pitched in again.

This had to be hard for her. She'd just lost her boyfriend and therefore her career. She must be heartbroken. Devastated. No wonder she was making desperate suggestions and clutching at unwatchable straws.

He went back in with a sympathetic tone. 'But, honey, the show wouldn't be the same without Jizzo...'

Her downcast devastation seemed to dissipate in a split second. 'Replace him.'

For the second time, 'What?'

That's when Davie realised that her hand was tracing a line up Jack Gore's thigh.

'Me and Jack are, like, together now and he can take Jizzo's place.'

Jack took the cue to join the pitch. 'Man, it makes sense. Look, I've always been behind the camera but it's time I stepped forward, let people see who I really am. Let people know the real me. I mean, how incredible would it be for your viewers to get inside the mind of a movie legend? You can give that to them, Davie. You can be the man.'

Davie's internal response was summarized with a silent 'Oh Christ.'

Steven Spielberg was a legend. Grazer, Lucas and Bruckheimer too. But Jack Gore? Successful, noted, perhaps even – in his day – brilliant. But the guy was no legend. No denying he scored big on self-esteem and ego, though.

He wondered if repeatedly thudding his head off the table would convey his reaction to Jack's delusion and narcissism. He should have seen this one coming. Jack's aspiration wasn't unusual.

Guys who'd spent years in the industry behind the scenes or on the back end of the camera frequently secretly longed to be in the limelight. The musical director who wanted to step out from behind the piano and be the star. The fashion designer who'd tired of dressing the A-list and decided he wanted to join it.

Singers wanted to be actors. Actors wanted to be singers. Actors wanted to be directors. Directors wanted to be actors. No wonder no one in this town was ever happy.

Again, Davie's mind went on to fast forward. That was his talent, the thing that had brought him his millions. He was a hustler, always looking for opportunities, seeing ten different ways to make a show and deliver a package that viewers would love. He'd done that with *American Stars* and *Here's Davie Johnston*, and he'd done that with the other shows he produced, *The Dream Machine* and yep, *Beauty and the Beats*.

He saw potential where others didn't, saw disaster where others saw a sure thing. And – unlike life – when it came to the shows, he was always right.

So how would this show look?

Carmella Cass was the messed-up poster girl with a daddy complex.

Jack Gore? The guy was a walking ego. Vain. Deluded. Clearly thought of himself as far more important than he was. The extreme grooming pointed to narcissism. The extreme idiocy pointed to a midlife crisis. The fact that he'd had an affair with Mercedes Dance and was now shagging Carmella Cass pointed to a weird thing for women way too young for him. There had to be thirty years between them. Maybe even thirty-five.

The two of them together was bordering on creepy.

There were so many things wrong with this – the biggest of them all being that it would, by default, draw attention to Mirren and Logan. That was the last thing they needed. Especially after Chloe... but Jack didn't seem to be having the same hesitations.

'We wanna call it Beauty and the Best,' Jack added.

Beauty and the Best.

It was ridiculous. Completely inane. And it made him feel a little queasy.

And that's how he knew it would be a hit.

21

MIRREN

'A Good Heart' – Fergal Sharkey

Six p.m. A ringing phone. Mirren was tempted to ignore it, but buckled after four rings, mainly to stop the flutter of anxiety that rose inside her.

For years, she'd panicked every time the phone went, because she was terrified it would bring her bad news about Chloe. It usually did.

Her daughter was wasted in a club. She'd been arrested. She'd escaped from rehab. She owed money to a dealer. She was just calling her mother to tell her she was a fucking bitch for cutting off her allowance. She was sorry. She loved her mom. She was gonna change. Could she have some cash?

Now the apprehension was there for a different reason. Now, it was pure anxiety, flecked with hope that it was Brad Bernson calling to tell her it was all a false alarm and that her mother was currently lying on a sunlounger in the Costa del Sol with some wealthy but brutally cruel hard man. After all, that was Marilyn's type.

The thought caused her to shudder and say a silent prayer that she was right. Losing Chloe had broken her heart. Jack being unfaithful after nearly two decades of marriage had made her mad as hell. But the thought of Marilyn coming back into her life sparked off an emotion that encompassed rage and hatred, but also topped those with fear for the carnage she could cause. To use Logan's vernacular, the story Marilyn could tell about what happened before they left Scotland would do so much damage to Mirren, Zander and Davie that she 'owned' them.

And that wasn't a position that Mirren was going to tolerate. Not now.

'Hello?' she said calmly, hoping to hear Brad's low, assured voice answer.

'Hi, Mirren. It's Perry.'

Mirren tried to disguise her disappointment as she heard her lawyer's greeting. 'Hi, Perry. How are you?'

'I have a massive pain in my ass,' Perry answered truthfully. 'Permission to speak frankly?'

'Granted.' Mirren wondered when Perry had ever done otherwise. It was all part of her steel-balled charm.

'Excellent. I just wanted to give you an update. Pictor are still refusing to budge and their new lawyer is an arrogant prick.'

'They're not moving at all?'

'Nope. I think we need to sit down with Mike Feechan and fire some shots. And on the other side of the fence, Wes Lomax practically had an orgasm when I called him. I've sent the meeting date over to you.'

'OK, leave it with me. I'd like to see if we can resolve this on good terms, with as little fallout as possible. I'll get back to you. And thanks, Perry.'

'No problem. Wish I had better news.'

So did Mirren. Sighing, she hung up. This was the last thing she needed right now, but hey, at least it was a distraction.

A glutton for punishment, she pulled up the document she'd been working on. The next *Clansman* was already in the can. It had been a tough three-month shoot, beginning only a couple of weeks after Chloe had passed away, but she'd welcomed the escape. Now, they were in the editing stage and the launch date was set for six months ahead, which meant entirely different departments of her company were ramping up the activity. Marketing were finalizing strategies and timescales. Distribution were making plans. International rights were working on contracts. Finance were fretting over budgets. And there were lots of those guys. Sometimes it seemed like the bean counters were running the business now.

Mirren was overseeing every department, checking, double-checking, moving things along. Not that she didn't trust her team. Like Perry, most of them had been with her since the start, and they were all, in her opinion, the best in their fields.

Mirren was so engrossed in the spreadsheet in front of her that the knock on the office door made her jump.

Lex Callaghan popped his head inside. 'Hey, just thought I'd come say hello.'

Mirren's smile was instant and genuine. 'Come on in.'

'I'm not interrupting anything?'

'Nope, you're not.'

'Great, because I brought beer.' He swept his hand, carrying two bottles of Bud, in front of him to prove the point.

'You know that office rules strictly prohibit drinking on the premises?' she said, as she took one and screwed off the top. It was a standing joke between them, a variation on the reprimand she doled out every time he pitched up at her office with a very welcome beer.

'Absolutely. I'm hoping you'll fire me and I can go live a life of obscurity in the mountains.'

One of the many attractions of the man that was Lex Callaghan was that there was a good chance he meant that. There were very few stars who sauntered to the beat of Lex's drum. Ten years ago, she'd been casting the first *Clansman* movie and coming up blank day after day. The Clansman had been her creation, a sixteenth-century Scotsman who lived and would die for his land, his family and his honour. He was rough, and he could be brutal, but he had an inherent strength that inspired both loyalty and love. In hindsight, she could see that he was her fairy tale. The man she created to encompass everything she had ever wanted. Millions of readers felt the same connection.

Casting had proven to be a nightmare. Actor after actor tried out for the part, but none of them was right. No, the Clansman's nails were not buffed.

He didn't do yoga. Or take steroids to pump his pecs. He didn't live in the Hollywood Hills or drive a Lamborghini. Yet every man who tried out for the part made her think of one or more of those things.

Until Lex walked in.

There was dirt under his fingernails because a horse on his ranch had broken loose that morning. He wore jeans that had never seen an iron or the inside of a designer boutique. His jet-black hair fell over the searing blue of his eyes; his shoulders were so broad Mirren knew instantly he could carry the weight of the world. He could swim across frozen lochs, scale mountains and run through valleys. This guy was a warrior. Authentic, hard, with a soul that scorned anything fake or superficial.

And best of all, his Scottish grandmother had taught him how to adopt a Highland burr that could make the hairs on the back of Mirren's neck stand on end. He was the Clansman. He could also have been a Bond. She'd heard the rumours that the Bond team were after him at the same time. He'd passed the stringent background checks they inflicted on their 007s, succeeding where a famous Aussie action man, an English West end star and Zander Leith had failed.

For Mirren, their connection had been instant. Lex shunned the celebrity circuit, hated anything that involved a tie and just wanted to do a good job, then go home to his wife, who was, quite literally, back on the ranch.

A couple of hours away on a Santa Barbara plain, Cara's equine therapy centre for addicts was the kind of work that really mattered. Mirren had even sent Chloe there, but she wasn't ready. She'd spent one night in the stables and then called her dealer to come collect her. Too much money, too many demons, not enough sense to see it would kill her.

Lex stretched out on the leather sofa that sat under the window in her office. A low, one-storey building, it was tucked away in the corner of the Pictor lot, right next to a park setting that had been used in a dozen movies.

'Just thought I'd see how you were doing,' Lex said, straight to the point, as ever. He had absolutely no time for small talk or the inane niceties that came with the business.

'I'm OK.'

He looked at her sceptically as she got up and joined him on the sofa.

'No, really, I am. Some days are crap; some days are good. Today is OK.'

She gestured to the piles of paperwork on her desk. 'It helps that we're just about to kick off again and I'm drowning in work. If I ever disappear, I'll have suffocated behind that lot.'

'I'll come rescue you,' he said, his square jaw widening into a smile.

'Excellent. Bring beer that time too.'

There was a comfortable pause for a few seconds. 'Cara was asking if you wanted to come up to the ranch for a few days. You know she'd love to have you there.'

'I know. Thank you. Maybe I'll take you up on that.'

Even as she was saying it, Mirren wasn't sure that she would. The peace. The solitude. The calm. Those were all the things that let her mind go back, to think about Chloe. If she kept busy, then she couldn't hear her heart weep.

'I'm starting pre-production now, though, so it might not be for a while. Tell her I said thanks. I do love your wife.'

'That would be two of us, then,' Lex agreed, without a hint of macho embarrassment. The thought entered Mirren's mind that although he'd never dream of endorsing an aftershave or fragrance line, if he ever did, it would simply be called 'True Man'.

'What's funny?' he asked, spotting her smile.

'Nothing. Sorry. Was just thinking about how nice that would be to come up and chill out for a couple of days.'

'Anytime,' he offered again.

'Thanks. So were you in for the meeting with the marketing guys today?'

'Yep. And you know how much I like those. Congrats on the Oscar nominations. You deserve it.'

Mirren had barely thought about it since she got the news back in January. Three nominations. Best Director. Best Movie. Best Original Screenplay. The latter was the same category that had given her the first Oscar when she originally came to LA and winning it twice would be a real achievement. Yet somehow, something that should be the height of her professional career had been covered by a curtain of sadness and the realization that gold statues and acclaim meant absolutely nothing compared to real life. Perhaps she'd feel differently next month, when the ceremony came around, but for now, it wasn't even making its way onto her radar.

'Thanks. I'm thinking it was a sympathy vote.'

'No, ma'am. I'm thinking it was the star performance by yours truly that took the movie to stellar heights.'

They were both laughing now. 'Yep, that must have been it,' she agreed. 'Your talent is carrying us all.'

'Now that's a line I should've given the marketing guys. "My talent carries us all." Maybe that would get me out of the At Home special they're trying to make me agree to next month.'

This was so typical of Lex. Other stars would love the exposure; he hated it. Other stars begged for column inches; he begged for a quiet life. Not that she was letting him off the hook. This was a business, and while she respected his wishes, they had a movie to sell.

Feigning gravity, she shook her head wearily. 'Lex, sometimes you've got to take one for the team.'

'Yes, ma'am, you sure do. Remind me of that when they're making me pose like a dickhead.'

'I will indeed.'

He stood up and tossed his empty beer bottle into the trash. It went in first time. 'Anyway, I'd better hit the road.'

Standing, Mirren hugged him. 'Thank, Lex. For the beer and the chat.'

'No problem.'

Before he could bail, the door opened again, bringing another of her favourite men into her day.

'Hey, what's this? Is this the kinda stuff that goes on in here?' Logan had one eyebrow raised in question, hands on hips, acting out mock outrage, which he couldn't hold for long because Lex had switched his hug to Logan now, thumping him on the back.

'Logan. Good to see you, bud. All good?'

Logan coughed under the crushing enthusiasm of the embrace. 'Apart from the fact that I now need a new spine, all's great. And good to see you too. Been a while.'

He turned to Mirren. 'So, do I pass inspection?' he asked, gesturing to his clothes.

Mirren did a top-to-toe evaluation. Denim-coloured T-shirt, blue jeans, Onitsuka Tiger trainers, his short blond hair cut over his ears, longer on the top to give him a killer 1940s movie-star look.

Mirren had never been more grateful that his fame post-dated the days of grunge.

She reached down behind her desk and pulled up her purse, then grabbed her black tailored jacket from the coat stand. 'You look great.'

'You two off somewhere cool?' Lex asked.

'Dinner with Mike Feechan. And his daughter. Apparently, she's a fan of South City.'

'Yep, my mother is pimping me out.'

'Hey!' Mirren punched his arm playfully. 'I am not pimping you out. I'm just being friendly.'

Lex nodded. 'Yeah, like a python just before it bites.'

'You two are ganging up on me. Logan, get in the car before I ground you.'

The three of them headed out, still laughing. God, it felt so... *normal*. And that wasn't something she'd felt for a long, long time.

As soon as the thought crossed her mind, a wave of guilt followed right behind it. How could she even start to feel normal in a world in which Chloe didn't live?

Pleasure. Pain. Pleasure. Pain.

Enough. Without either man noticing, she pulled up her shoulders and forced her mood back up. She had to. Logan needed a mother who was strong enough to show him how to move on from sadness and devastation. She'd spent her entire childhood at the mercy of her mother's emotions and she'd be dammed if her children – no, *child* – would do the same. She owed him this. And that meant returning to the old Mirren who could laugh and joke and let happiness into their lives.

At the car park, she hugged Lex again, then slid into the front of her Mercedes and waited for Logan to climb in beside her.

'Thank for doing this,' she told him, while scrunching up his perfect hair. 'And I'm not pimping you out. I'm merely consolidating a business relationship while making one of your fans very happy.'

Logan leaned over and kissed her on the cheek.

'OK, Mama, let's go. But if this guy's a douche, we're bailing after half an hour. Deal?'

'Deal.'

22

ZANDER

'Stay with Me' – Sam Smith

When he woke, Zander had absolutely no idea what time it was. He thought about switching on his phone to check, but he knew he'd be bombarded with messages, most of them from Hollie, all of them furious, so he got up and staggered to the bathroom to find his watch instead.

Four p.m. He groaned inside. Four p.m. meant he'd been in London for sixteen hours and it meant that it was only three hours until they had to be at the airport to fly back to the US. He stepped into the shower and let the jets of water pound his body. Man, Adrianna was a tougher workout than any amount of stunt training. Not that he was complaining. It may have been sixteen hours, but it ranked up there with the best.

In ten hours on the Gulf Stream, they'd only been clothed for take-off and landing. For the rest of the journey, they'd locked themselves in the bedroom, a room so opulent it belonged in one of the leading hotels of the world. Crisp white Pratesi sheets, marble side tables and a bathroom carved from walnut with gold-plated hardware. Not that Zander cared. Overblown luxury was nice, but it had never been his thing.

When they'd landed at Luton, a car was waiting to take them to the Mandarin Oriental Hyde Park in Knightsbridge. The hotel was the ultimate in discretion. They didn't pull up at the front door, risking stray pap shots or overzealous tourists with camera phones. Instead, Sarah Cairns, the head of communications, greeted their limo as it arrived and whisked them through the entrance of One Hyde Park – The Residences. The iconic tower block adjoined the hotel, cost £1.15 billion to build and contained flats that sold for upwards of £20 million.

The building was connected to the main hotel by an underground tunnel, allowing them to enter via the new spa and swimming pool area.

Adrianna had already made the booking, but Zander had called ahead and upgraded them to a suite.

It was a good call. The Park Suite, named for the stunning view over Hyde Park, was sheer luxury, exquisitely furnished, but most importantly of all, utterly private.

The moment they stepped over the threshold, he picked her up, took her to the bedroom. Eat. Touch. Love. That had been enough for both of them, until sometime around four hours ago, he'd finally fallen asleep. Now he'd woken to find her gone and he realised his body was actually craving her, all his senses screaming for her to return, to touch her, to be inside her.

Hell, he had it bad.

So bad he was even developing amnesia about the fact that she was married. This was a first for him. Dating other men's wives had been strictly off limits all his life. He'd seen the damage infidelity could do and he'd wanted no part of it.

His dad, Jono, had regularly come home with a sore face thanks to putting his dick where it didn't belong. He had the same glib retort every time. 'Och, you should see the other guy,' he'd boast, while Zander's mother pretended not to know what had caused the fight. Jono had broken Zander's mother. Years of abuse, years of affairs, years of pain. Zander had decided that he wouldn't travel down any of the branches of his father's path. But then Adrianna had come along and he was lost. Sure, there had been that old cliché that he hadn't known at first that she was married. And yep, when he'd found out, he'd called a halt, said goodbye, broken off contact... But he'd lost all morality points this time around, because he was in full possession of the facts.

Now it was time they faced the inevitable. She had a husband. When he'd met them together he'd been struck by the formality between them. There didn't seem to be any intimacy or physical contract but maybe that was just Carlton Farnsworth's way. You didn't get his kind of ferocious reputation by going round town snogging your wife at parties. Maybe their relationship worked that way, maybe it didn't, but regardless, something in this situation had to change.

'Hello, my darling,' she purred from the doorway and he opened his eyes to see her standing there, looking nothing like a woman who had barely slept in twenty-four hours. Her cream suit was, as always, from her menswear line, but tailored to perfection to fit and flatter her shape. Underneath, a black silk blouse. Her hair was tied back in a chignon, her eyes smoky, her lips blood red. Zander's erection was instant.

'Pleased to see me,' she said. It was a statement, not a question.

'I was wondering where you'd gone to,' he replied, watching as she crossed the room to turn on the bath taps and slowly begin to undress. He was so tempted to reach for her, bring her to him, but the view was just as tantalizing and he wanted to enjoy it for a little longer.

She slipped the jacket from her shoulders as the water gushed from the taps. 'I had a meeting with my buyers here. The reason I came to London, remember?' she answered, her amusement making his hard-on start to throb.

One by one, she opened the buttons on her shirt, before letting it fall onto the cream tiles of the floor. Underneath it, she was naked, her breasts swollen, her nipples hard.

'Keep going,' he told her.

Obliging, she undid the button and zip of her trousers and elegantly kicked them off. Completely naked now, except for her heels. That was her thing, he'd realised. Shoes and diamonds. She liked to have sex wearing both. He was about to respond to the invitation when she stepped out of them and into the bath.

'Come. I'll be lonely in here.'

He flicked off the shower and joined her, sitting at the opposite end, then gasped as she slid along his legs and mounted him. His hands went to her buttocks as he pulled her tighter, his mouth finding one of her nipples, then the other. The water sloshed out of the tub as she rose and fell, her deep red finger-nails piercing the skin on the back of his ripped shoulders.

Moments later, there was very little water left to bathe in when they both collapsed, spent.

Adrianna twisted the taps on to replenish the water. When she relaxed back at the opposite end, Zander picked up her foot and blew the bubbles from it, then massaged it gently.

'So are we going to talk?' he asked.

One of her eyebrows rose in a perfect arch. 'About?'

'Damn, this is going to be a completely messed-up role reversal here,' he admitted sheepishly, before going on, 'About us.'

Adrianna lay her head back against the curve of the bath rim. 'Ah, us.'

Zander playfully bit the end of her toe. 'Just making sure I have your attention.'

Adrianna used the other foot to flick water in his face, but he didn't rise to the bait. He was usually a man of relatively few words, so if he had something to say, he had to get it out before he blew it.

'Look, what we've got is pretty special. I've never felt like this before, never had this need for someone before. But the thing is, I don't share.'

'Then we have a problem,' Adrianna challenged him.

'We do. I'm not going to give you an ultimatum...'

'Good. I don't respond well to those.'

'I guessed that.' It didn't take a genius. 'But I want you with me. Not sharing. Just you. And me.'

'I can't do that.'

'Why?'

'Zander, I've told you before. My husband...' She tailed off, pensive. 'My husband is a very straightforward man. We understand each other. He knows that occasionally I have "special friends", but he indulges me, as long as it means nothing.'

Suddenly the water felt like it had turned icy cold.

She saw the reaction on his face and added, 'This is more than that, but still... I cannot leave him.'

'Why?' he asked again.

'Because he is not a man to leave,' she said simply.

'Even if you want to be with me?'

She sighed wearily. 'Zander, please don't do this. My husband and I fit. We work. On all levels.'

Zander exhaled, feeling his gut twist as he understood what she was saying. It was difficult to argue. What they had was physical, sexual, but not emotional or based on compatibility or hours of conversation. They hadn't hung out. They didn't have the same sense of humour. She didn't know his history or understand what drove him. And he didn't want her to see inside his head. This was why he didn't do relationships. This was why he preferred to stay alone, detached. It didn't take an expensive therapist, and God knows, he'd met many in rehab over the years, to explain to him that something in his psyche put up a barrier that said, 'no emotional attachments, no pain.'

Clearly, he should have stuck to that in this case too.

Adrianna rose from the water, leaned over and kissed him, tenderly this time. 'I think our time together is incredible. Can't it just be that?'

Her pout was irresistibly sexy, her body glorious, her voice intoxicating. Fuck, this one hurt.

'Now we must go, as I have to be back in New York by morning.'

He knew this already. They'd agreed he would drop her in NYC and then head on to LA.

They dressed in silence, and on the way back to Luton, Adrianna put her head on his shoulder and slept. Traffic was light, so the journey took barely over an hour, but from setting off to destination, he changed his mind a dozen times about where he should go from here. Did he want to see her again? Of course. No other woman had ever inspired this level of desire in him. And if he was honest, there was a bit of irony there. Over the years, he'd met hundreds of women, slept with many, dated some. But the one woman he'd actually fallen for was choosing a better option.

She murmured as his shoulders clenched, causing her head to move slightly.

But back to the point. He didn't share. Couldn't stand the thought of her with someone else. And what kind of man was her husband that he seemed to be cool with her seeing other guys? What a freak.

As the car pulled up to the terminal building, Zander gently shook her awake. The buzz was gone now. This was like the comedown after a bottle of Jack Daniel's and a mountain of coke. Yet he wasn't ready to say goodbye, was glad of another few hours together on the plane.

The VIP rep at the airport was waiting for them and rushed them through a side door to a private corridor that took them directly to a waiting area for private jets. At the door, a customs official checked their passports and ushered them through to—

'Hello, my dear. And Mr Leith.'

Zander stopped dead. In front of him, looking up from the newspaper he was reading, was Carlton Farnsworth, eyeing them with fairly ill-concealed amusement.

Adrianna reacted instantly. 'Darling, what are you doing here? Not that it isn't a lovely surprise.'

Zander didn't trust himself to speak as he watched her cross the room and kiss him. 'Zander and I had a very successful trip to London. He absolutely wooed our buyers there.'

It wasn't a success. He hadn't met buyers. No one was wooed. Yet every single word that came out of her beautiful mouth sounded like the absolute truth.

'I brought the jet so that we can head back to New York without taking Mr Leith out of his way,' Carlton Farnsworth replied. 'I was just saying to Sergei here that you'd been working far too hard lately. Time I took care of you and recharged your batteries.'

For the first time, Zander noticed the guy in the impeccably tailored, undoubtedly Adrianna Guilloti, black suit, standing in the corner of the room, his face completely impassive.

He may have been an actor for twenty years, with a string of awards and a billion-dollar franchise, but right then, Zander had no idea how to react to either the husband or the close-protection guy, who had clearly forgotten to pack his friendly disposition.

Adrianna stepped straight in. 'That's wonderful, darling,' she told her husband, her voice warm and engaging. 'Wonderful.' She strutted back across the room and held her hand out to shake Zander's in a purely professional manner. 'Thank you, Zander. For the use of the jet and for being the perfect gentleman.'

Zander had never felt further from perfect.

This was so wrong. So, so wrong. And yet what else could he do? Refuse to let her go? Cause a scene? Berate her husband? But then, what had Farnsworth done to deserve that? Zander was the one in the wrong, and right now that guilt was strangling his feelings for Adrianna in a chokehold.

Farnsworth shook his hand, his grip tight, his expression giving no hint of jealousy or malice.

'We're ready to take you through now, Mr Farnsworth,' the attendant waiting behind the desk informed them. 'And, Mr Leith, we'll be ready to take you through in ten minutes.'

Zander nodded, barely able to digest the words as he watched Adrianna being ushered towards the door by her husband. This wasn't how he rolled. This was wrong in so many ways. He couldn't let it happen, didn't have the patience to let it play out. He had to make it clear how he felt, put all the cards on the table, make a case for giving their relationship a chance to develop into something more than just the best sex he'd ever known. And if she wasn't prepared to give them that chance, it was time to walk away.

He stepped forward. Time to be honest. Time for some uncomfortable truths. 'Adrianna?'

23

SARAH

'Boulevard of Broken Dreams' – Green Day

The breeze from the ocean was doing nothing to clear her head, and neither was the high-grade caffeine from the store at the end of her street. Marina del Rey had been Sarah's third choice of location in which to unpack her suitcase when she'd moved here from Glasgow the previous autumn. Santa Monica was number one, but it was way out of her price bracket. Venice was next, but the combination of bad parking and tourists made it just a little unpredictable for a female living on her own. So in the end, she'd found a gorgeous but small one-bedroom apartment in Marina del Rey – a man-made harbour with six peninsulas, around which 6,000 boats were docked. Her home halfway down Tahiti Way gave her a view out onto a basin packed with yachts and, beyond that, the next strip of apartments on Marquesas Way. The area was largely home to couples and professionals, with families attracted by the still waters of Mother's Beach. Sarah rarely went to the sands. Instead, she liked to sit on the balcony once the morning haze had burnt off, shaded by the balcony above, and write. The lifestyle pieces she was doing for several magazines paid some of the bills, reporting on any major LA stories for the *Daily Scot* paid some others. But every month, her savings went down just a little bit more, making the urgency to get a book deal increase by the week. And no, saving cash by moving in with Davie wasn't an option.

She'd almost told him about the possibility that Marilyn McLean was in LA this morning. Almost.

Although she'd promised Mirren that she wouldn't, it somehow felt disloyal to keep things from him. But what purpose would telling him serve?

There was nothing he could do for now, until Mirren's PI established if Marilyn was even in the country, so all telling him would do was freak him out.

And Sarah was freaking out enough for both of them.

She'd be stupid not to wonder if Marilyn was behind the attacks on Davie, either out of some twenty-year-old grudge or as a precursor to some kind of twisted extortion attempt. But even to her ultra-suspicious, crime reporter's brain, it was unlikely. Marilyn hadn't been seen for two decades, as far as Sarah was aware, Marilyn knew no one in LA, and there was no actual evidence that she was here now. The stuff that was happening here seemed to be the work of more than one person. Sure, anyone with a bit of cash could buy any kind of services in this town, and if Marilyn had criminal connections in the UK, then it wouldn't be much of a stretch to expand them to the US. But still, the chances that it was her who was wreaking havoc on Davie's life were slim.

Sarah finished her apple fritter, knocked back the rest of her coffee and then took the cup and plate inside. Writing out on the balcony was tough. There was too much temptation to watch the yachts go by, peering inside them, looking for a famous face or inventing an imaginary life for a stranger. Whole days could pass and her word count would barely budge, so she'd rationed herself to breakfast and lunch outside, coming back after meals and working at the laptop that was set up on a gorgeous old console table she'd picked up at the Fairfax and Melrose Flea Market for fifty dollars. It was the only place where you could peruse five-dollar sunglasses while mingling with a crowd that included stars like Courtney Cox, Victoria Beckham and Kate Hudson.

Relocating to LA was the best decision she'd ever made. There were many things about Glasgow she missed. The humour. The office full of unpredictable characters. The buzz of putting a newspaper out every morning. The drive to make sure that the best breaking stories had her byline on them.

Other than that, she didn't miss anyone special from home. It would be lovely to have the occasional Sunday lunch with her parents, but their twice-weekly phone calls filled that void. She'd been in a three-year relationship with a lawyer, but that was gone, ended when she caught him indulging in a spot of mutual masturbation with his best friend's girlfriend over Skype.

Relationship over, and no, it hadn't broken her heart. By that time she'd already met Davie and sensed a connection.

It hadn't been a tough choice to make the move. It was late February now. If she were back in Glasgow, she'd be in thermal clothes, freezing her ass off in torrential rain while door-stepping some piece of criminal crap. Or on the tail of a bent cop who was tipping off a crime family about their surveillance.

Here, she was basking in the heat of another glorious day, wearing a vest and denim shorts to go to her day job. True, she was still on the trail of criminal crap, but at least the beverages beat the insipid dishwater spat out by the vending machine at the *Daily Scot*. She poured another coffee, this time an espresso from the chrome masterpiece that sat on the caramel granite counter in the kitchen. The LA Marzocco GS/3 had been a gift from Davie when she moved in, and it perfectly illustrated the differences in her lives – the piece of machinery that made her coffee cost more than two months' rent.

After turning on her MacBook, she pulled up her 'Work in progress' and checked the word count: 40,000 words, with twelve chapters already written. So far she'd covered the subjects of Hollywood deaths, the ageing process, drugs and alcohol, the club scene and the rise of talentless fame. That was her favourite topic. A look at the stars who had no extraordinary skill other than to make money. It was the modern-day Pied Piper situation and she was at a loss to explain it. Were people's lives really so empty that they worshipped at the temple of a nobody because they wore great clothes, or had a sex tape, or had a great ass?

Loose leaves fell out of her notebook when she turned to the page of scribbles she'd jotted down after last night's visit to the club. The current chapter was 'Behind the Fame', a look at the reality behind the lives the young stars in the town were leading. The image of perfection and gilded privilege masked the fact that half were in therapy, and the main reason the others weren't on a psychiatrist's couch was because they were too arrogant and wasted to agree to seek help.

Over the years there had been so many high-profile examples of teen-star meltdowns, breakdowns, therapy or behaviour that ended with the slamming of a cell door. Britney. Lindsay. Paris. Justin. Sky.

They were the poster stars for a generation who no longer needed a talent in their quest for fame. No actors, no footballers, no singers. Now they just wanted to be famous. Didn't matter how they got there.

In the club last night, there had been several faces she'd recognized in the crowd, a couple of rising actresses on a hit vampire gorefest. The stars of a reality show based around the boutiques on Melrose. A rapper and his entourage of six stunning models had passed her on the way to the VIP room. But there was nothing new, nothing that was going to give her a real edge on this subject – and if she was going to get the kind of book deal she needed, she was going to have to pull in something sensational.

Closing the notebook and switching back to the laptop, she stared at the screen for a few seconds, hoping for inspiration. Nothing. No matter what angle she took, it had been done before. What she needed was fresh information, a new scandal, something she got to first, so she was going to have to up her game and get back out into the clubs tonight. There was plenty of material out there. She just had to find it.

Sighing, she opened the camera function on her laptop. Last night's phone footage had automatically downloaded from her iCloud and it was much easier to watch on the bigger screen.

She turned down the volume, having no wish to permeate her calm with the thudding assault of a deafening techno beat. The camera started to slowly pan from the left of the screen. As it passed a recess in the far wall, a glimpse of flesh made her press 'pause' and zoom in. She hadn't noticed that the night before. A guy in a fluorescent orange T-shirt, his red jeans pushed down his thighs, had the legs of a girl in a short yellow and green striped dress wrapped round his waist and they were in full-blown sexual motion. Sarah didn't recognize either of them, so they were obviously just clubbers out for a good time. Although, if she did encounter them in the future, she might suggest that if they wanted to have that good a time, they should probably wear clothes in a colour that didn't make them look like they were starring in a flick called Rainbow Porn.

Moving across the room now, the camera dipped down onto the lower floor, taking in the entrance to the room and the two security staff standing there, one of them in conversation with a clubber, the other eyeing the revellers for trouble and potential business for their two-man drug ring. The bar came into shot, populated by the extraordinarily attractive staff who were robbing it blind. Nothing of note there. That was the bar in any club in LA.

Over to the far corner of the room now, the wild crowd, Jordan Lang and his buddies, all of them coked up and partying, grabbing at the girls in their group. As the son of Kent Lang, one of the most famous producers in the history of film, you'd think he'd have a little more discretion. But no. Sarah had heard through the club-scene gossip that his father had cut him off a long time ago, seeing him for the wasted asshole that he undeniably was. It was no secret that he and Mirren's daughter, Chloe Gore, had been an item for a while. What had she seen in him? Good-looking, yes, but so clearly a grade-A sleazebag. Or douchebag, as they said here.

The image on the screen stopped as it reached the end of the footage. Nothing of use there so far. Shame. Time to get back to the job of actually putting words onto a page, then. Moving the cursor across the screen, intending to shut down the video function, she inadvertently nudged the 'play' button and it started over again. Couple in doorway having sex. Security guys on door, one scanning the room, the other talking to...

Her finger hit the 'pause' button like it was a buzzer on a quiz show and she'd suddenly realised she had the right answer to the jackpot question.

She stared. Stared harder. Zoomed in. Stared some more. Changed the angle. Increased the brightness. Panned back out.

And stared again.

Neither man was looking in the direction of the camera.

The security guard, six foot of pure muscle, was leaning over, listening to what the other guy had to say, but their hunched postures didn't conceal a sleight of hand that was passing something from one man to the other.

The stranger was wearing a black T-shirt, jeans, leather jacket, a beanie hat pulled down low on his forehead, but it was his face that Sarah was fixated on now.

There was something in his profile that she recognized. The angle of his jaw, the curve of his cheekbones, the contours of a face that she had seen many times before.

Sarah sat back and let the contradictory emotions pull her gut in two different directions.

This was it. This was the story. The one that would make her name.

It was also a story she didn't ever want to write.

She stared again, hoping to reach a different conclusion. But no.

Standing there, taking a small package from a prolific drug dealer, was a guy who made the hearts of teenage girls across the globe beat faster.

Standing there was Logan Gore.

24

DAVIE

'Crazy World' – Aslan

'For fuck's sake, can you call those two off? I feel like I'm in some kind of messed-up movie called Honey, I Shrunk the Guy From TV.' Davie flounced into the room like a petulant child, slamming the door on the two close-protection officers assigned by security chief Mark Bock. They'd been stuck to him like glue since the moment he left home, came to the studio for a run-through, rehearsal and soundcheck, headed back out and hit the gym, stopped off at the *Family Three* studio to see the kids, had an awkward conversation with his ex-wife, Jenny, and her partner, Darcy, who just happened to be there at the same time, then returned to his production offices. If those guys really wanted to save his skin, they could start by taking out Darcy fucking Jay every time she sneered about his paternal competency.

He slumped onto the leather chair at the head of the board-room table. Mellie was sitting with a coffee and her feet on the desk, taking five minutes off from being producer, director and show runner of the whole fucking world. She acted like he'd just strolled in with a cheery 'good afternoon.'

'You're late,' she told him, like a schoolteacher irritated by an insolent child. It wasn't far from the truth. 'You missed Mark Bock.'

'Good.'

'Davie, don't be such a brat. You need him. Some psycho out there has something twisted on you and you need to start taking it seriously. It totally pisses me off.'

'Why?'

'Because I always thought that if anyone was going to butcher you while you slept, it would be me,' she said dreamily.

Davie's laughter snapped him out of his fugue. 'OK, so where are we?'

Mellie checked her watch. 'An hour until showtime. Don Michael Domas is in dressing room one,' she said, in a tone that was as close as she ever got to sounding impressed. Domas was one of the five-star ensemble cast on *Call Me*, the sitcom that was the *Friends* of this generation. 'Lauren Finney is in dressing room two. Carmella is in dressing room three, and on a scale of wasted she's probably a six.'

'She came to the house this morning with Jack Gore. Wants him to replace Jizzo on the show.'

Mellie looked up, nodded slowly, thinking about it. 'I used to think he was a pretty impressive guy, but he's seriously off the rails. Midlife-crisis city. That whole thing with Mercedes Dance last year was a train wreck,' she mused, citing the on-set affair with the young actress that had destroyed Jack's marriage to Mirren. 'And since the DNA test proved he wasn't daddy dearest and his movie tanked, he's just a fucked-up, inappropriately dressed has-been who is desperately trying to reclaim his youth and career.'

She paused, before concluding, 'So I think he'd be perfect.'

'See! That's why I love you. Set up a meeting with the network and we'll run it by them, but I'm in. And they'll go for it if we push it. Done deal,' he said confidently, shoving his reservations about Mirren's opinion on this to one side. He'd already rationalised it in his head. She'd understand. She knew this business. If he didn't do this, they'd take the idea somewhere else and it would get made by someone with even less scruples than him. At least this way he could keep an eye on it and make sure nothing – other than Jack's very existence – caused any more damage to Mirren and Logan.

'Will do. OK, we need you on set in thirty minutes, so if you want to go schmooze the talent – or Carmella – then go now.'

Davie jumped back out of his chair, re-energized. Nothing kept his mood down for long. He'd been this way since he was a kid, always on the go, a million things to say, every bit of him restless. He was like a bag of snakes on a caffeine rush.

'Don't dare move,' he warned the black-suited lumps of muscle at the door as he passed them. He wasn't going to come to danger in his own frigging studio. Unless Princess was in the building. The thought gave him a minor shudder. That had been a close one. Must avoid at all costs.

Thank God *American Stars* was a weekly show and he didn't have to face her again for another few days.

Tonight, it was all about *Here's Davie Johnston*. Domas would ensure great ratings, but he was too smart on media to say or do anything that would have the office workers of America chatting at the water cooler tomorrow morning. That was Carmella's job. And music from Lauren Finney would give him another iTunes boost among the kids. It was all good.

Davie headed for the corridor that housed the dressing rooms. He was old school. He didn't send production staff to do his research or set up links to conversation items. Too impersonal. He genuinely wanted to get to know them, probe a little deeper, find angles to make the interviews meaningful and insightful. He'd already spent an hour on Facetime with Domas this week and by the end of it they had a pretty good rapport going and had already established a baseline of trust.

In the Domas dressing room, the man himself was remarkably chilled. Most stars came with an entourage in double figures, all of them bowing to his every whim. Not Domas. He was lying on the sofa, completely relaxed, necking a beer while watching an old Bond movie on the TV. In the corner, one assistant, immersed in a book. Who even did that in LA any more?

Domas leaned up on one elbow and shook Davie's hand. 'Good to meet you,' he said casually. 'Thanks for having me on the show.'

Davie hoped his surprise wasn't obvious. The majority of the guests expected him to thank them; then they'd spend at least ten minutes blowing mutual smoke up each other's ass, declaring eternal admiration and a history of worship.

The expression 'Big fan of your work' was exchanged in LA as often as an STD.

By the time they were finished, they'd have done everything but promise the other an internal organ should a transplant ever be required. Then they'd part and have forgotten the conversation by the following week.

'Saw you at the Globes. Congrats. You deserved it,' Davie told him truthfully. Domas had won the award for Best Actor in a Television Series, Musical or Comedy.

His reaction to Davie's praise was so laid-back he was pretty sure the gold statue was already gathering dust in the back of a cupboard. Either that or he'd had a large spliff within the last hour. 'Yeah, made my mother proud,' he shrugged, before his expression changed, signalling a relevant thought had entered his head. 'I hear you're an old friend of one of my buddies.'

Davie looked at him quizzically, before Domas went on, 'Zander Leith.'

Davie paused, stuttered, recovered. 'Yeah, we kinda grew up together. He's a good guy.'

'He is,' Domas agreed.

Davie made a show of checking his watch. 'Listen, bud, good to talk to you. I gotta go get organized, but I'll see you on set. And thanks for being here.'

He was back. Full-on schmaltz and superficiality. And just a few beads of sweat on his palms left as evidence of the conversation.

Outside, he exhaled as he headed to the next room. Zander. Every room he was in contained a big fucking elephant and it was called Zander Leith.

They'd re-established contact the previous year, when Sarah's investigation into their past had brought them all together again. But that's where it had stalled. He still wasn't sure how to address his relationship with Zander now. Childhood best friends. A major trauma killed their relationship. Didn't speak for twenty years. Reunited last year when their past threatened to bite them on the ass. Oh, and in the process of that, they'd discovered, as forty-something year old men, that they actually shared a father, a man they'd both despised. Hallmark didn't make greeting cards for that relationship. He was glad the wall of separation had come down but he just wasn't sure how to step across the rubble.

It was on his list of things to get sorted. Or he could just avoid it like he'd been doing for the last six months.

Outside Carmella's dressing room, he put his hand on the doorknob and then hesitated as he heard the unmistakable sound of a female approaching orgasm. He kept on walking.

In dressing room two, Lauren Finney was sitting on the sofa, looking like some kind of ethereal creature from a mural depicting a Greek tragedy. Her long waves of red hair flowed from a middle parting, sweeping past huge blue eyes and over skin the colour of alabaster.

She wore a simple white flowing top over tight grey jeans and black leather boots, with the hint of pale silver nails showing through the peep-toes.

No jewellery, no crazy costume and very little make-up. Just a girl and a guitar.

'Davie, hi,' she greeted him warmly, raising up her arms to hug him.

What a find she'd been. If he fucked up the rest of his life, at least his Wikipedia obituary would honour him for discovering the exquisite talent of Lauren Finney and making her a star. He hated the pretentious nonsense when two-bit singers with delusions of talent called themselves 'Artists', but that's what this girl was. She wrote her own songs, performed them exactly the way she wanted to, and all the fame and money bullshit came a long way below the music. And the best thing of all was that there were no pushy parents, no manipulative agent or manager, no controlling love interest. Her mum and dad were both liberal academics with no desire to live out their failed dreams vicariously through their offspring. Instead, they were quietly supportive and happy to let their little girl make her way in the world. On the representation side, he'd ensured that she signed to Cal's agency, making their mutual success the best for all parties. And on the boyfriend side... Davie struggled to remember. There had been a childhood sweetheart when she'd first auditioned for *American Stars*. They'd been together for years and the boyfriend had featured in one of the early VT's for the heats. Davie had made sure that hadn't happened a second time. A romance was sweet, but he wanted the audience to fall in love with Lauren and that wouldn't happen if she seemed unavailable. Davie vaguely remembered him being at the shows, but by the end of the series, when Lauren lifted first prize, they'd split and he'd hot-tailed it back to Tennessee.

'Hey, sweetheart. Thanks for coming in on your night off,' he said, hugging her.

Lauren's appearance on *Here's Davie Johnston* was not just another handy stunt of cross-pollination for his shows, but it also helped to expose her to a different audience. As host of *American Stars*, she spent all week in rehearsals and doing press, making sure the show ran perfectly while maximizing every opportunity to persuade even one more viewer to tune in. It was exhausting, all-consuming and it could wear on the soul, but Lauren had never complained. It was just one more reason to love her.

'No problem. Can't believe I'm here, to be honest.' Genuine humility. Another reason to love her.

'I mean, Don Michael Domas and Carmella Cass. And, er, me.' Her scepticism was authentically self-deprecating.

'I swear to God you're my favourite out of all three,' he told her, hugging her again. He wasn't lying.

She was also his favourite contestant of all time – no ego, no pretensions and never once had she believed the hype. Nothing churned his stomach quite like the ones who were nobodies on episode one and by the time they were in the third week were referring to 'their fans'. Get real. They were just viewers who'd have forgotten their names by the beginning of the next season.

'See you in an hour or so. You're closing, so they'll come get you when they're ready for you.'

He headed into wardrobe and make-up, and thirty minutes later, after a routine that he had down to a fine art, he was on set, running through the final prep. The studio audience were already in their places, the atmosphere crackling with excitement thanks to the energetic and enthusiastic performance by Dan, the warm-up guy.

Davie reckoned that half of them were tourists who had feverishly bought the tickets online before their big holiday to LA, and the other half were probably here to see Don Michael Domas. But for the next hour, they were in his hands, and that was all he cared about.

He spotted Carmella waiting in the wings, looking utterly gorgeous in a white skirt that barely covered her arse, but showed off her long, tanned limbs to perfection. Her blonde hair was a shaggy mass of post-coital waves. She looked like sex on legs, like the ultimate wet dream, like every teenager's fantasy. She did not, however, look like a woman in mourning for the love of her life who went to the big rock palace in the sky less than a month before. Oh yes, this would be tomorrow morning's water-cooler conversation for sure.

'You OK, sweetie?'

'Davie! I'm fine!' It was somewhere between confident reassurance and a spaced-out slur. For a split second, he contemplated canning her slot. This was supposed to be a solemn, heart-tugging interview about the loss of Jizzo, with a subtle reminder that the entire season was now available on Netflix. Gotta keep the publicity wheels turning.

From the gallery, Mellie had visuals on him and a direct line into his ear. 'Holy shit, she looks like she's spent the afternoon upside down being screwed around a room.'

Davie didn't argue with her.

'Why don't I look like that after sex?' Mellie asked, her tone a mix of bitterness and sadness. 'I look more like I've been through a car wash.'

Davie fought to keep the laughter under control. He had absolutely and unequivocally never been sexually attracted to Mellie Santos. Women who scared the crap out of him rarely turned him on. However, when it came to caustic wit and sharp professionalism, they didn't come any better.

'Is she ready?' Mellie added wearily.

Davie leaned in close to Carmella and lowered his voice so that only she could hear him. 'OK, now remember. You're sad. Lonely. Can't believe he's gone. Don't know how you'll ever replace him. That's how you're feeling, Carmella?'

'I am, Davie,' she said, pouting.

She had to nail this. If she fucked it up, one outcome would be that he could be accused of exploiting her grief. Or manipulating her for ratings. Or worse, if she came off as insincere, she'd lose public sympathy, and if that went, popularity would be next. Whether the series with Jack Gore got the green-light or not, Carmella was still under contract to him and she was a valuable commodity. However, didn't he know how quickly that could crash and burn? One wrong move, one misjudged comment, one act of stupidity and a career could be over. In this case, that would leave him paying a huge salary to damaged goods while losing the number-three show in the ratings. Carmella was a loose cannon and there was always a risk she'd hit the wall of car-crash TV. But she wasn't going to do it on his watch.

'Right, then let's go. And you look gorgeous,' he added. Always good to boost the ego just before they took their seat on his couch.

'OK, let's go, people. Ten. Nine...'

Davie made his way to his entrance point as tonight's band, Space Tragic, launched into the first few notes of their latest track. They were a Coldplay-style band, all melancholy and ripped-out souls. Davie wasn't sure whether their music made him want to kill himself or them.

Thankfully, tonight's song, while lyrically intense, had a relatively upbeat rhythm, so it didn't bring down the mood in the room.

When the voiceover announced him, Davie burst onto the set, full of energy, thanking them for an incredible performance, while internally hoping he'd never hear anything they'd written ever again.

He then thanked the audience, told them who'd be on the show, waited for the ecstatic frenzy that greeted Don Michael Domas's name to die down and went straight into the introduction of the first guest.

Up until now, he'd kept the preamble positive and jocular, but it was time for an emotional twist, a tug on the heartstrings that would, he knew, make compelling viewing and lock arses to seats across the country.

'Tonight, we're joined by a long-time friend of the show, a woman who only last month lost her whole world right here in the studio...' His voice was thick with sorrow until he paused, keeping the audience spellbound as they watched the poignant moment play out. 'Ladies and gentlemen, Carmella Cass.'

Instead of waiting at his desk for her, he walked to the wings, hand outstretched, and guided her on, a beautiful moment of chivalry that gave no hint that his motivation was worry that she would stagger on and then fall off her Jimmy Choos on live TV.

Davie led her to her chair, where she sat down and waved to the audience, expression sad but grateful. It spurred their response on and their ovation got louder and lasted longer. Meanwhile, in ear, he could hear Mellie screaming, 'Camera five, get the fuck out of there – she isn't wearing any fucking panties. I can't hear what she's saying, but, Jesus, I can read her lips. Switch to three. Switch to three!'

Davie fought the urge to look, but saw the camera to his right retreat like it was being pursued by a line of moving fire. Breaking her in gently, Davie kicked off by expressing his condolences and asking her how the last few weeks had been.

She launched into a monologue about support from the fans soothing her heartbreak and only rambled slightly.

Good start. Suitable tone. Tick. Appropriate heartbreak. Tick.

Covering up of undoubtedly wasted state. Tick.

He could even see that what he and Mellie knew to be after-sex dishevelment would appear to the audience as a woman broken, consumed by heartache, no longer able to care as much about the superficial things in life like perfect grooming.

So far, so 'Widow in Mourning'. Only a few more minutes to keep it up, then a plug for the box set and they were good to go. Happy days.

'And tell me, Carmella, what do you miss most about Jizzo?' Oh, he was really going for it now, cranking the heartstrings to breaking point.

Before she answered, she leaned over, picked up the glass that sat by the side of her chair and took several sips. That was OK. Give her time to gather her thoughts. Keep the tension building.

'Oh, you know, stuff,' she finally told him, her voice cracking this time. 'The way he would tell me I was beautiful in the morning. The way he took care of me. I like someone to take care of me. Makes me feel real good. Safe. Kinda like nothing can go wrong. But... But it did.'

Davie had survived longer than most in this industry and he knew it was down to three things: the ability to spot an opportunity and capitalize on it, his willingness to cross lines to get the best shows and pure instinct when something was off.

She was staring into the middle distance now, still sipping on her drink, but there was something going on. He was losing her for some reason.

'Jizzo always said he'd never leave me. Never go away. He lied.' Oh fuck, she was getting antagonistic now but it wasn't coming from a place of anger. She seemed almost defiant, proud. Davie half expected her to stand up and break into the first verse of 'I Will Survive'.

'Davie, what the fuck is going on with her?' Mellie bellowed in his ear. 'Is she starting to trip out? This is some weird shit right here.'

Davie didn't disagree. It was definitely coming off the rails and he wasn't sure why. Unless...

'Oh shit, who put that drink there?'

As Mellie vocalized the question, Davie had exactly the same thought at the same time.

The glass sitting by Carmella's side wasn't the usual style of water glass laid out for the guests, which meant it had been put there by someone else. Maybe Carmella? Maybe one of her lackeys? Maybe Jack Gore? But definitely, absolutely not – he could see now – containing water. He'd put his money on pure vodka. Maybe gin.

She knocked back another slug and swayed to the side a little before righting herself.

Davie's brain screamed unspoken instructions at her. Come on now, sweetheart. Stick to the script. Remember, you're sad. Lonely. Can't believe he's gone. Don't know how you'll ever replace him. That's how you're feeling, Carmella.

Apparently, Carmella was reading from another script altogether.

'Jizzo lied,' she repeated, more of a wail this time.

Davie's teeth began to grind. This was the kind of performance you acted out in front of your mates while you were sat on the floor eating ice cream in your pyjamas. Or at the reading of a bad soap opera. That's what this was. A bad soap opera. A really tragic daytime debacle for people who sat in their living rooms on brown stained sofas in the middle of the day eating chicken from a bucket.

Mellie's voice had shot up the urgency scale. 'For the love of God, close her down, Davie. Right now. Wrap it up.'

'But I don't care,' Carmella warbled in the sing-song voice of the drunk and deranged. 'I don't care at all. Because I've got my little Jacko now. And my Jack is gonna take care of me and never ever, ever, ever leave.'

25

MIRREN

'Love The One You're With' – Luther Vandross

The patio deck at Moonshadows was quiet, the calm before the storm of the evening diners. Mirren had been counting on that. Taking Logan to any restaurant, even in LA, where stars were on every street corner, could rapidly turn into a crowd-control situation. While adults were happy to take covert snaps of Tom Hanks or Jennifer Aniston in a restaurant but leave the big names to enjoy their meals, teenagers had no such restraint or discretion.

Moonshadows had always been one of her favourite restaurants. Situated on the PCH in Malibu, it had a laid-back vibe that she loved, a mixed clientele and, most importantly, great food.

Mirren and Logan slipped into either side of a white booth on the sundeck, overlooking the Pacific. Her newly amplified anxiety made her look around, scanning the other faces within view, looking for one she never wanted to see again. Nothing. All clear. If only Brad Bernson would call her to say this was all a messed-up figment of her imagination. So far, she'd heard nothing. That was Brad's style. He would only call when he had something to report. No news was good news, so she had to let it go. Inhale. Exhale.

She turned to look at the breathtaking view, the sun low on the horizon, the waves rolling in from the ocean and crashing below them. It was calm. Uplifting. It was just what she needed right now.

And sure, so her motivations for being here might not come from the most spiritual place, but she was damn well going to enjoy this time with her boy.

'You OK?' he asked her, picking up the menu and flicking straight to the desserts. He always did that. Chloe had too. It was their thing. Now it was just his thing.

She felt the familiar grasp of grief around her gut and made a forceful effort to snap it off. Later. Later, she could go home and cry until she was hoarse, but not now.

Smiling, she leaned over and squeezed his hand. 'I'm fine, honey. Thanks for doing this.'

'No probs. I remember when I used to drag you into school to talk about movies because the other kids thought you were a big-shot producer—'

'I *am* a big-shot producer,' she feigned outrage.

'Absolutely. Anyway, I kinda dug that. Gives me a kick that it's working the other way round now. And I'll stop telling people you're pimping me out. Eventually.'

They were still laughing when a startled gasp interrupted them, followed by a staccato burst of 'OMG. OMG. OMG.'

Mirren looked round to see Mike Feechan, his arm loosely over the shoulder of his eleven-year-old daughter, Jade, who looked to be entering a state of shock. Mike leaned over and kissed Mirren on each cheek, then shook Logan's hand.

'As you can see, Jade is slightly surprised,' he said with a smile. 'I hadn't told her you'd be here in case anything cropped up and you couldn't make it. I fear it would have taken a lifetime to recover from that blow.'

'OMG. OMG.'

When Logan gave her a casual wave and a 'Hi. Good to meet you, Jade', she almost passed out.

Mirren reached out and beckoned to her son's number-one fan. 'Why don't you come and sit here?' she offered warmly, pointing to the seat next to her.

'I am, like, going to die right now,' she gasped.

'Can you at least wait until after we've eaten because I'm starving?' Mike asked, deadpan.

She shot him a look that Mirren recognized so well. Hadn't Chloe had that same expression on a thousand occasions? That look that said, 'You are so uncool. I can't believe you said that. I can't believe you are my parent. Please stop embarrassing me.'

Mike winked at Mirren. 'As you can see, my leverage for arranging this has already expired.'

'It certainly has,' she agreed. He looked completely different out of the office, she decided. In the boardroom at Pictor, he was the corporate big shot who didn't even look casual when he dressed down in a black polo and matching chinos on a Friday. Logan had stood up to shake his hand and then let him pass into the booth first, so he was sitting directly across from Mirren. He was as tall as Logan, and his shoulders every bit as broad, the physique of a man who worked out daily. Boxing, Mirren guessed. Maybe triathlon. Not yoga. She couldn't see him chilling out long enough to get in touch with his inner chi.

This was a guy who oozed strength and who chose activities that required power. The fact that he was the head of a studio at forty-five said he was a workaholic – probably why his marriage to Jade's mother had failed. Mirren wracked her memory for any information stored on his past history. Married to a lawyer, divorced a few years ago, mutual decision, no one else involved. That was it.

It struck her she should probably have done a bit of research, purely for professional purposes, of course.

Beside her, Jade was refusing to look at Logan now, clearly so overwhelmed it was easier to bury her head in the menu. Mirren's heart melted a little. When she was that age, she'd been obsessed with Spandau Ballet. She could still sing every word of every one of their songs. If Martin Kemp had ever ambled into her local cafe in Glasgow while she was eating a bacon roll and drinking a can of Tizer, they'd have had to resuscitate her.

Apart from the chronic blushing, Jade's face bore a strong resemblance to her father's. It was obvious that her wide mouth, sallow skin and piercing blue eyes came from him, as did the deep brown hair, although the natural curls must have been her mother's contribution. Mike wore his hair straight, short at the sides and back, longer on the top so that it flopped slightly over his forehead. From the neck up, there was a bit of David Duchovny going on there. From the neck down, it was more Hugh Jackman.

Focus, Mirren. Back in the game. What was going on with her? This was business. OK, so it was dressed up as personal, but as far as she was concerned, this was just breaking the ice with the new guy, getting to know him a little better, improving relationships so that they could gain a mutual respect that would pay off in the day job.

Logan took control of the conversation, asking Jade about her school and the cheerleading squad and her position on the soccer team. How brilliant was he at this? Years of meet-and-greets had obviously taught him how to handle the situation perfectly, and somewhere between the food order being taken and their dishes being placed in front of them, Logan had prised Jade out of her shell and they were chatting away comfortably. Sometimes she couldn't believe this amazing kid was hers.

Mike's gaze caught hers and she could see he was both amused and delighted.

'She hasn't talked this much to me since she was five,' he joked, earning another glance of total disdain from his daughter. The conversation flowed happily throughout dinner, neutral subjects that were inclusive for everyone. It was only when the dessert plates had been cleared and Logan and Jade were compiling lists of their favourite songs 'ever in the whole wide world' that he leaned over towards Mirren, allowing them to strike up their own conversation. 'I don't want to make you sad, but I was so sorry to hear about your daughter.'

The sympathy caught her by surprise and her reply stuck in the back of her throat. It did that sometimes. All would be fine and then a thought or a kind word would collapse her windpipe, making it impossible to breathe. She saw Logan check on her out of the corner of his eye and it was enough to kick-start her body into action again.

'Thank you.'

'How are you doing?'

'I'm OK. Some good days, some bad. But mostly bearable,' she said, knowing that if he had any people-reading skills at all, he'd realise she was lying. None of it was bearable. She doubted it ever would be.

'We're opening a centre in her name next month. It's called Chloe's Care and it will operate a drop-in centre for young people with substance issues. Somewhere to go. Not a rehab. Or a therapy centre. Just somewhere that a kid can go and talk if they want to, or just be in an environment where they know they're safe, with professional help on hand when they're ready for it.'

'Wow, that's incredible.' It wasn't a glib retort – she could see that he meant it. 'How is it going to be funded?'

'Twenty per cent of the profits from McLean Productions and the rest will come from fundraising. I have a feeling Logan will be recruited to help with that.'

'Are you pimping me out again?' he asked, teasing.

'For a good cause, son.'

'Ah, that's fine, then.'

Mike's gaze went to the patio entrance, where a woman had arrived and was clearly scanning the tables.

'Nicole,' he said, waving, as Logan read the situation and stood up to let Mike out of the booth. Jade's face fell. 'Noooooo.'

The woman was at the table now. 'I think you're about to take over my title of least favourite parent,' Mike joked.

'Nicole, Mirren McLean and Logan Gore. This is Jade's mum, Nicole. It's a school night, so she's come to collect her.'

'Not leaving,' Jade said sullenly.

'Look,' Logan nudged her, 'I'm going on tour in a few days, but how about I come visit your school when I get back?'

Jade's face could have functioned as a beacon to warn incoming ships of danger. 'Really?'

'Absolutely. Hang on, take a pic with me.' He picked up his phone and took a double selfie. 'What's your number?'

Jade told him and then screamed with glee as she watched him send the pic to her with a text saying;

I hereby promise to visit Jade when I get back from tour. Love, Logan.

It was enough to get her to leave happily, if still slightly reluctantly.

Nicole's smile was wide. 'Thanks. And good to meet you.'

With that, mother and daughter were gone and Mirren noticed there had been very little dialogue between the parents. Amicable for the sake of Jade, but not friends, then. Interesting. She made a mental note to press Lou for information later. If there was a story to tell here, Lou would know about it.

In his hand, Logan's phone buzzed and he checked the screen before returning his attention to Mirren. 'Do you mind if I shoot off now? It's just, er, some of the guys are meeting tonight and I fancy hanging out.'

Mirren grinned, realizing he wasn't quite telling the truth. She had given birth to him, watched over him almost every day of his life and it was so easy to see when he wasn't being entirely honest. His eyes would dart to the side, his jaw would tighten, and he'd have exactly the same expression as the time when he was five and she found three candy bars under his bed and he denied knowing how they got there. 'Something you're not telling me?'

Her voice was teasing, light-hearted. 'There's been a few of those texts over the last few weeks. I'm thinking my son has found a girlfriend and he's reluctant to tell his mother in case I disapprove. Life was so much easier when I could hack into my children's phones and computers and spy on their every move.'

'You did that?' Logan feigned horror. In truth, it had always been part of the deal. Full access to all devices until they turned sixteen. Mirren thought it would help her keep them safe. How foolish she had been. Chloe had two secret cell phones by the time she was fourteen and used them to order her next high to be delivered to school.

Bloody hell. It crept into every thought, every sentence, got so far under her skin that sometimes she felt it was all there was to her. Regret. Despair. Sadness.

'Can I take the car?' Logan asked, standing up and reaching for the keys with a cheeky wink.

'Sure. I'll get a cab home.'

'I'll drop you,' Mike offered immediately, then to Logan, 'It's the least I can do for your mom after you made me Parent of the Year.'

'Mike will drop me,' she corrected herself.

Logan shook Mike's hand, kissed Mirren on the cheek and headed off.

'Nightcap?'

'Nightcap would be good,' she agreed. 'Brandy. On ice. I'll be right back.'

She headed to the washroom, leaving him to order. She'd missed this. God knows, this wasn't a date, but she'd missed male company, conversations with someone she didn't know, learning new things, talking to a guy who knew little about her past and nothing about her mistakes. There was something escapist about it, something that allowed her to just be. Not to be Chloe's mom, or Jack Gore's ex-wife. Just to be.

In her purse, her phone started to ring as she pushed open the door to the washrooms. Lou.

'Hey, honey. Are you checking up on me?' she asked, laughing.

'Have you dangled Mike Feechan over the balcony of Moonshadows by his ankles yet?'

'I was just about to do that when you called and interrupted me.'

'Ah, sorry. I'll let you get back to it. I just wanted to let you know that your ex-husband is a feckless, no-good piece of crap...'

'I knew that already.'

'Who continues to astonish and delight with his levels of stupidity.'

'Oh god, what's he done now?'

'I've sent you a clip. Gotta go. I'm having dinner with Jackie Collins. I frigging love her.'

'More than me?'

'Ooooh, it's close,' Lou confessed.

Mirren was still chuckling when she hung up.

Checking out the room, she made sure she was alone before pressing 'play' on Lou's incoming text. A video filled the screen, one that Mirren didn't quite understand.

That girl, the model whose boyfriend died. On Davie's show.

Carmella – was that her name?

On the screen, she started to speak, and Mirren could see immediately that she was altered. Drunk? Stoned? Definitely not sober.

Carmella practically trilled, 'I don't care at all. Because I've got my little Jacko now. And my Jack is gonna take care of me and never ever, ever, ever leave.'

Mirren's stomach lurched; her legs trembled. This was too close. That girl couldn't be much older than Chloe, she clearly had some of the same issues and yet Jack was sleeping with her?

Rage. Pure rage.

What was wrong with people? Didn't anyone have a decent bone in their body, or were they all so bloody self-absorbed that they just did whatever the fuck they liked whether it was the right thing to do or not?

For nineteen years she'd been married to that man, and she'd loved him for every day of that, even though he was largely absent from their lives. He'd spent more than half of every year out on location and many of the months at home locked in the editing suite. Mirren wondered now how long they would have lasted if they'd actually lived together. Judging by the man she knew him to be now, it wouldn't have been long. But back then, she was just desperate to have her family, desperate to make it work and desperate to have the kind of stability she'd craved since she was that child sitting outside because she wasn't wanted inside.

Leaning on the vanity unit, she stared at the woman in front of her for a few seconds before she realised it was her own reflection. Her skin looked pale. Her eyes tired. There were lines on her face that hadn't been there this time last year. The face belonging to that woman was the face of exhaustion. Of a broken soul. The whole world was moving on and yet she couldn't, still stuck in a quagmire of regret and devastation.

She couldn't stand to look at it for a single minute longer. Leaving the washroom, she headed back to the table. Mike was signing the check, two large brandies already on the table. 'Do you mind if we just head off?' she asked. 'I don't think I'm in the mood for brandy after all.'

He covered the surprise well. 'Not at all. Of course. Let's go.'

Outside, he guided her to a black Range Rover. Predictable. After telling him her address, not another word was spoken in the ten minutes it took to reach the Colony. When security saw her, they were waved through, and Mirren directed him to her driveway.

Only when they'd stopped did he turn to speak to her. 'Look, are you OK? Only, and maybe I've got this completely wrong, you seemed fine and then you seemed really pissed off and I'm not sure what happened.'

A sigh escaped her.

She reached over and opened the door. By the time she got round to his side of the car, he'd stopped the engine and jumped out too. Wordlessly, she put her key in the door, opened it, deactivated the alarm and took one step inside, only turning then to see him standing there, bewildered.

It took a moment for her brain to transmit her thoughts to her vocal chords.

'Right now, I really don't give a damn that you're the head of the studio. I don't care what you think of me or whether you had a good time tonight. Right now, I just want someone to come in here, and lie with me, and make love to me, so I can forget, for just one night, how much my life hurts. If that's you, please come in. If not, then thank you for dinner.'

Mirren turned and walked into the house without looking to see if he followed.

26

ZANDER

'Fire and Rain' – James Taylor

Adrianna didn't even look back when he called her name. It was as if she knew what he was going to say and didn't want to hear it, so she completely ignored him, acted as if he hadn't spoken, like he wasn't even there. She just strutted forward, head held high, her arm wrapped around the crook of her husband's elbow. From the floor-to-ceiling windows, Zander watched as they crossed the rain-swept tarmac and stepped onto the gleaming Challenger 300 that was parked directly beside the Gulfstream G200 that had brought them here.

His hands had shaped themselves into fists, and his jaw was clenched so hard it was making his teeth ache. His gut was twisting so tightly it felt like it was ripping his insides apart. This was like the worst comedown ever. Worse than the after-effects of a three-day coke binge. Worse than waking up to the sound of a cellmate pissing in a steel toilet.

Fuck, he really, really needed a drink.

Every day that thought crossed his mind, and every day he pushed it away, but right now he'd never felt more like locking himself in a confined space with a bottle of Jack Daniel's and a whole lot of self-reproach.

'Mr Leith, we're ready to take you through now,' the smiley ground-control attendant told him.

His head was buzzing. When he boarded the plane, he couldn't remember the walk from the terminal, his whole brain still consumed by the sight of her walking away, not turning back.

Again, fuck, he really needed a drink.

On board, it was the same hostess who had been there on the way over, and if she looked surprised to see him alone, she didn't show it. Over the years Zander had had many wild times on private jets. There was the time he flew from New York to Paris with eight models, three bags of coke and a legendary guitarist, renowned for debauchery and excess. Only when he woke up back in the Big Apple did they realise they'd been too messed up to remember to get off the plane in France.

On another occasion, flying from LA to Miami for a location shoot, he'd played Wild Turkey strip poker with an actress famous for playing the ditsy lead role in chick flicks. Every time one of them lost a hand, they had to down two fingers of Turkey and remove an item of clothing. By the time they were an hour east of California, they were doing stuff that was undoubtedly illegal in several of the states below them.

'Can I get you anything, Mr Leith?' Fuck, he really needed a drink.

He could have one. Who would know? He could take a bottle right now to the bedroom and drink himself into a stupor, then sleep it off until he reached LA. Job done. Oblivion achieved.

Chloe would know. He wasn't sure he believed in the afterlife, and he definitely didn't believe in heaven or hell, but if they did exist, he was pretty sure she'd be above him, calling him all the fuckers under the sun for even considering getting wasted.

He'd promised her. Just a few weeks after they'd met for the first time in the salubrious surroundings of a rehab clinic, he'd promised her that they could both do this, swore he'd get her through it and they'd come out the other side sober and clean.

He did. Chloe didn't.

If he fell off the wagon now, he'd never forgive himself, not for being weak and capitulating, but for letting her down. 'No, I'm fine, thanks. I'm just going to go next door and sleep. Can you wake me when we're twenty minutes out from LA, please?'

Wendy from Nebraska didn't even try to hide her disappointment. She'd only been in this job for two months and Zander Leith was the biggest star she'd flown with. What was the point of fame, fortune and a private jet if you were just going to sleep your way through it? Going by all the scandals and court cases over the years, she thought he'd have been a wild ride. In all respects.

Zander closed the door behind him and stripped off his jacket and shirt, then his jeans, leaving on the boxer shorts with the Guilloti label. The irony almost made him laugh. The same woman who had just walked away from him was still all over his ass.

A knock on the door and then it opened without waiting for a response. The flight attendant had removed her neck scarf and opened the top buttons on her blouse, revealing a cleavage that a lover could get lost in.

'Mr Leith, are you sure there's nothing I can do for you?'

She couldn't have made the suggestion any more salacious if she'd written it on a thong and delivered it with her teeth. Now she was blatantly staring at him, showing absolutely no acknowledgement or embarrassment that he was as close to naked as it got without a full frontal. Her gaze lingered on the wide, carved shoulders, the beautifully defined pecs, then paused in the groove between every single bump of his perfectly formed abs, stopping to linger on the point on his lower torso where a deep V-shape from one side his pelvis to the other disappeared at the middle point under the waistband of his shorts.

'Thanks, but I'm good. I'm just going to catch some sleep.'

'No problem,' she replied, the tightness of her mouth suggesting that it was indeed a problem.

She backed out of the door and Zander stood for a moment, head facing upwards, eyes closed. That old feeling was making every synapse in his brain, every nerve in his body scream for something to numb the pain.

Endless therapists and addiction experts had probed him for details of how and when this started. He'd never told them. What was he going to say? That when he was a kid, he'd sneak booze into his bedroom and drink until he couldn't hear his pissed-up father shouting that he was going to kill his fucker of a son? Or his mother, crying as she said another decade of the rosary and prayed to Our Lady for the husband she adored, her tears running over the latest set of bruises he'd just delivered? Or that he drank in the good times back then too? When he and Davie and Mirren would spend night after night sitting on a bedroom floor with a bottle of cider, Simple Minds blaring in the background, smoking cigarettes they'd pilfered from a parent's fag packet?

He'd drunk when he was terrified, when he was down, when he was up. But after the night his father was killed, he drank to forget. Because no one should have to remember what happened in the hours before Jono Leith was murdered, or the hours after his rancid soul had left his body.

Only six people knew the truth. Zander. Mirren. Marilyn. Davie. Davie's mother, Ena. Sarah.

Sarah had only discovered the truth the year before, after some serious journalistic digging, but the others had lived with it for a lifetime and they'd managed to do that without using anything to block it out.

Zander couldn't. Hadn't.

But now there was no choice, because the alternative was a dark road that he would have to walk alone. His life was better than it had ever been. He'd reconnected with Mirren. His relationship with Davie hadn't settled yet, but it would. His career was riding high and materially he had everything he could possibly want. He couldn't fuck this up. Adrianna Guilloti and her messed-up mind games were not going to take this away from him.

Fuck, he really needed a drink.

But his last thought, as he climbed into bed and fell into a welcome sleep, was that he wasn't going to have one.

It was still dark when he woke and for a moment he was disorientated. His senses kicked in. Noise. Movement. A plane. Horizontal. A cover. Bed. A body next to his. Adrianna.

No, back.

He squinted open his eyes and was met with darkness. Groping around with his free hand, the one that wasn't trapped under the person sleeping beside him, he located the button on the headboard that switched on the bedside lamp, then turned to see the stirring form of the flight attendant, her shoulders naked, and from what he could feel in the places where their bodies touched, she was wearing underwear but not much more.

He pulled his arm away and sat up, the fear rising as he recognized the repetition of a thousand other mornings when he'd woken up in bed with someone he didn't remember going to sleep with. Hang on. No. He hadn't had a drink. There had been no drugs. He'd gone to bed alone. Which means she must have slipped in here during the night. He didn't know whether it was cute or a violation of his human rights.

He watched as the movement woke her and she opened her eyes, squinting against the light.

'Ah, Mr Leith. I think we'll be landing soon,' she said with a cheeky grin. Reaching over to where he'd left his cigarettes and lighter, she took two out of the packet, lit them at the same time and then handed one over to him. He was pretty sure they were now breaking a federal law, but he decided that was the least of his worries.

'I hope you don't mind,' she said, gesturing to her form under the bed sheet. 'I was bored, and you looked so comfortable.' As excuses went, it wouldn't win any awards, but she had a glint in her eye and a cheeky grin that made him smile.

'Look, if you want to report me to my bosses, go ahead. I wouldn't blame you.'

She took a puff on her cigarette and then flicked the ash into a water glass on the bedside table.

Zander put his head back and closed his eyes again for a few seconds. Why did things like this happen to him? Why? Was a normal life really too much to ask for?

'So,' she checked her watch, 'it's half an hour until landing and I can get up, bring you some breakfast and look suitably repentant about my boldness...'

It was impossible not to look at her when she spoke, and even harder not to laugh.

'Or I can stay here and give you the in-flight safety briefing you missed at the start.'

Again, the cheeky smile made it perfectly clear which option she would prefer. The choice wasn't too difficult. In his head, the image of Adrianna walking away with her husband, leaving him a free man. A free man with a gorgeous woman lying next to him in bed.

No debate. He leaned towards her, kissed her, and within seconds his Adrianna Guilotti's were, like his relationship, tossed to the side.

The in-flight cardio workout was intense, highly pleasurable and mostly silent until a thump announced their arrival on the ground at Van Nuys airport.

Wendy from Nebraska popped her head up from under the cover. 'Welcome to LA,' she said, with a grin. 'I hope you've had a pleasant flight.'

When the door opened, Zander turned to say goodbye, his hair still wet from the rapid shower he'd taken while the jet taxied to the gate.

She'd put her number into his phone under the name 'Wendy'. He'd said he would call.

Maybe he would, he decided. An uncomplicated relationship. Wasn't it about time he gave one of those a try?

Hollie was standing leaning against her Durango on the tarmac, chewing gum and looking about as impressed as she should be after her boss had gone missing. She'd had to pull every trick in the PA's book to track down where he was, cited a national emergency to get details of his homeward flight and skipped out on a long-awaited date to come and collect him.

'You look like crap and you'd better have bought me a present,' she told him, bypassing niceties. 'But hey, you look sober, so there is indeed a God.'

Zander turned to wave goodbye to Wendy.

'Oh, you didn't,' Hollie murmured, making it clear that she knew he most certainly did.

As soon as they got in the car, before her foot hit the gas, she started with the interrogation, the one born of security, not curiosity.

'OK, so did she have a phone, and could you have been filmed at any time?'

Zander rolled his eyes, totally familiar with the questions which had come straight from the security chief at Lomax Films, designed to protect all stars from blackmail, scandal and media shit-storms.

He cast his mind back. When he woke, he'd been under the covers and still had his shorts on – all good. After that, he'd certainly have noticed if she broke off to take a selfie.

'No, and no.'

That was enough for Hollie to get the car moving, but there were still more questions to answer as she drove.

'Was there anyone else involved or present other than yourself and Miss Shag Air?'

'Nope.'

'Did you notice any electrical items or suspicious devices that could have been used to film your… Performance?'

'Apart from the CNN live-broadcast crew in the corner, no.'

'Don't get smart or I swear to God I'll hit Rodeo Drive with your credit card tomorrow.'

'Feel free. You deserve it.'

'And did you take any substances or alcohol prohibited by your current contract with Lomax Films? Incidentally, if you say, "yes," I'll beat you around the head.'

'No.'

'Excellent. Last question. Given that you've just renewed your membership to the mile-high club, do I take it things with your very married fashion boss are over?'

Zander stared straight ahead, the word 'Over' touching a raw nerve. 'I told her I wanted her to leave her husband.'

'Oh dear Christ, you didn't,' Hollie exclaimed, taking her eyes off the road to look at his stony face. 'Oh dear Christ, you did. And she turned you down.'

Hollie's eyes were wide as he nodded ruefully. 'Yep. And now's the time you tell me what a dick I've been,' he said, resigned to the truth.

'Zander, I've been with you for ten years. You've made so many fuck-ups that on your scale of dickdom, this barely makes a spike.'

He appreciated the effort to make him laugh, especially as it worked.

'Look,' she continued, 'having an affair with a married woman wasn't smart. Having an affair with the wife of a highly shady, multi-millionaire property mogul, even less smart. But hey, things happen. You felt something for someone; they didn't feel it back. So the inflight entertainment was, what, revenge?'

He shook his head. 'A distraction that was offered – I didn't ask.'

She knew him well enough to believe that was true. Zander rarely instigated new encounters, but as with all his vices, he just had a hard time saying no.

'Fair enough, but maybe you don't need any more distractions. The suits have just given the all clear to resume filming. You're in a good place with your sobriety. The only dark cloud is this relationship and the fact that her husband could have you taken out with one phone call…'

That was framed as a joke, but it was a bit too close to the truth to make him laugh.

'Maybe…' she paused for a second, then continued, 'Maybe it's time to move on.'

As they drove the rest of the way to Venice in comfortable silence, her decisive manner sparked a tiny seed of resolve in him.

Time to move on. Everything else was good.

For once, he wasn't fucking up and wasted. He could handle normal life like a normal person. And normal people made mistakes and moved on.

No drama.

'OK, I'm just going to come in and pick up your mail and erase the death threat I left on your answering machine when you ran off last week,' Hollie informed him, laughing.

Not for the first time, he wondered what he would do without this girl. Crumble, was the obvious answer.

Thirty minutes later, they turned off the Speedway to his home.

It wasn't the most obvious place for one of the most successful actors in the world to live. Most of the A-list pitched their heated swimming pools in the Hills, Bel Air or maybe Santa Monica or Malibu. Those areas held no appeal to Zander. He still lived in the same green wooden apartment block he'd moved into when he first arrived in LA. The back of the block overlooked the car park, but it was the front that had him sold. There was only a walkway between his apartment and the Venice sands, allowing him to open the balcony doors of his third-floor home and let the sound of the ocean be the back-drop to his time there. His only concession to fame and money had been to buy the other apartment on the same floor and knock them into one, giving him a loft-style arrangement with a glass wall and a balcony spanning the whole of the sea-front view.

He gestured 'hi' to the two homeless guys who lived in the car park outside his home. They'd have missed the food parcel he left for them every couple of days. He'd make it up to them tomorrow.

He waved again to the building caretaker who sat in the glass-partitioned office on the ground floor, then headed up the stairs behind Hollie, his travel bag thrown casually over his shoulder.

'So can we make a deal?' she asked as they reached his landing.

'Shoot,' he replied, as she used her key to open the door.

'Oh, don't tempt me,' she joked. 'If only that time in juvy didn't stop me getting a gun licence. Anyway, the deal is, no more disapp—' She stopped mid-sentence, froze, causing him to almost walk into the back of her.

For once, she said nothing, just stood there, her mouth open with shock.

'Holls, are you—' Zander's words went the same way as his assistant's – lost in a sea of incomprehension.

He scanned the room once, twice, trying desperately to force the sight in front of him to make some kind of logical sense.

It didn't.

Every piece of furniture was upside down, every fabric was sliced, every dish broken, every glass smashed. It looked like a scene depicting the aftermath of an apocalyptic tornado.

He stepped forward, dazed, but Hollie darted her arm out to stop him.

'Don't touch anything until the cops get here.' Her voice cracked. 'Zander, who the fuck would do this to you?'

27

SARAH

'Something Inside So Strong' – Labi Siffre

The roof garden in West Hollywood's Soho House was busy, as it always was on a Thursday lunchtime. It wasn't Sarah's favourite place to dine in LA – too full of Brits with mockney accents using clichéd tripe. *'I'm in a weird headspace.' 'I'm percolating ideas.'*

It was almost like there was some kind of competition to see how many wanky clichés they could fit in one sentence.

However, it did have a few compensations. The roof garden was a stunning work of topiary bliss. Wooden slatted floors, hanging triffids and meandering plants on terracotta pots were scattered throughout a terrace that came with incredible views of the Hills.

There was also an emotional connection. This was where she'd first met Davie last year. He'd been wasted after celebrating his tenth wedding anniversary to a woman who hated his guts and was only stringing the marriage out so that she could get a better financial settlement after ten years together. Davie realised it the night of the party, and filed for divorce the next morning, less than seventy-two hours before the actual day of their anniversary.

Was it really only last year? It felt so much longer. It amused her that she wasn't sure if that was a good thing or a bad thing.

Back then, she'd been over here on a week-long holiday from the *Daily Scot*, after a conversation with a dying Glasgow crime lord, Manny Murphy, had thrown up the possibility of a connection between the actor, Zander Leith and Jono Leith, one of his crew in their younger days. 'A mad bastard' he'd called Jono, before going on to say how he'd just disappeared off the face of the earth one day.

It was the name that struck her as unusual. Leith.

'Don't suppose he was any relation to Zander Leith?' she'd asked, feeling totally ridiculous for even vocalizing such a ludicrous question. Of course he wasn't related. Zander Leith was one of Glasgow's most famous exports, the guy who'd gone off to Hollywood with his buddies Mirren McLean and Davie Johnston, where they'd won Oscars and were now three of the most powerful players in the industry. Surely she'd have heard if Zander's dad was a lowlife criminal?

'Zander...' Manny's tongue had rolled the name around for a few moments, while a red rash of embarrassment crept up her neck. 'You mean the bloke in the films?'

Sarah hadn't even filled the pause with an answer.

'Aye, hen, that's him. Back then he was just wee Sandy. And aye, Jono was his old man.'

His answer had astounded her. And she'd been even more intrigued after she did some research and discovered that Jono Leith had gone to ground back in 1989 and never resurfaced. Her interest had been piqued again when she'd realised that the three friends who had gone to Hollywood hadn't appeared together in a show, interview or event for the last two decades. Obviously there had been a falling-out, but why?

It had been enough for her to beg Ed McCallum for a week off and head for LA. It had taken longer than a week, but eventually she'd discovered the truth and realised that, like Jono, it should stay buried. His remains were still deep in the garden of Davie's old house in Glasgow, steeped in cement hurriedly procured from a local DIY store by traumatised teenagers Davie and Zander, because Mirren—

'Hi!'

Sarah's attention was snapped back to the present by Mirren's voice beside her.

'Mirren, hi! Thanks for coming.' She stood up to kiss the woman on both cheeks before Mirren took the seat across the table.

Not that she was being critical, but Sarah couldn't help but notice that Mirren looked tired and pale. It wasn't a surprise, really. The woman had been through so much in the last year and yet she was still standing. Sarah felt an inkling of sorrow that she could potentially add to those woes. Not today, though. She'd thought long and hard about how to play this and she just hoped she could pull it off. It would all depend on whether Mirren bought in to her story.

The waiter was at their side in seconds with menus and water. Sarah waited until he was gone before opening with. 'How are you?'

'I'm great, thanks.' Her smile didn't reach her eyes, but Sarah didn't take her lie personally. The two women barely knew each other, and although they did share a couple of mighty large secrets, they hadn't yet established the kind of friendship that led to shared confidences and authentic feelings.

To any other diners they'd have looked like two friends out for a casual lunch. They swapped small talk before ordering, then carried on exchanging stories, mostly amusing ones about Davie, until Sarah's chestnut ravioli and Mirren's Jidori chicken arrived. Only when the first morsel had been speared did Sarah move the conversation on to the reason they were here.

'Any word from Brad Bernson?'

Mirren's face didn't even flicker with surprise. 'No, nothing. He's come up blank in LA, and I've asked him to contact a former colleague who now operates in the UK to do some subtle digging there. I'm hoping he'll come up with something soon. Preferably a death certificate.'

The venom in her words took Sarah aback. Not that it wasn't warranted, because it most certainly was, but it still evoked a jolt when Mirren said it out loud.

Mirren put her fork down on her plate. 'Have you come up with anything?'

'Nothing yet. She was in a relationship with the guy in Liverpool – we both knew that. What I didn't realise is that apparently she played an active role in his organisation. Turns out she was quite the criminal, a nasty piece of work, especially to people who crossed her. It was all behind the scenes, though, and no one in the know is prepared to talk so far for fear of reprisals.'

Mirren nodded thoughtfully. 'So she was more than just a whore this time. S'pose it makes sense. We both know she had no limits. What about her boyfriend?'

'He is definitely still in custody, but there's been no mention of Marilyn's name in any of the press or online reports, and certainly no connection to you. While that's a good thing, it also means that there's also no mention of where she is now.'

Mirren listened intently to every word and Sarah realised this was why she was arguably the most successful woman in Hollywood today. Nothing got past her. She listened, absorbed, analysed.

Sarah hoped it wasn't noticeable that she took a deep breath before her next entry into the conversation. She'd thought this through a dozen times in the last few days and she knew that she had to put her proposal forward carefully. This was like a game of chess. One move. Then another. Repeat until check-mate.

'I think you should know that Davie is being targeted by someone.'

Mirren looked up, aghast. 'What do you mean, targeted?'

'There was the whole "splattered with blood outside the studio" thing.'

'But I thought that was just a crazy prank. To be honest, I thought he'd probably set it up himself.'

Sarah nodded, nonplussed. 'Yep, I can see why you'd think that. But it came with a death threat. And there have been other incidents. Someone shot at his gates just a few minutes after his children had passed through them.'

'Oh god.' Already pale, it now appeared that Mirren had no blood left under her facial skin at all. 'Do you think it's my mother?'

Sarah shook her head slowly. 'I really don't think so. If the rumours from the UK are true, she would probably know how to set something like this up, and she'd have the money and maybe even the contacts here. Not that help would be hard to find. It takes a day in LA to rustle up someone prepared to do anything for cash. But why would she only target Davie?'

'Never underestimate how much she hates all of us, or how much she will have twisted the truth in her own mind to make herself blameless. Or how evil she truly is,' Mirren replied, her voice low.

'I don't,' Sarah replied. OK, here goes. Knight makes a move on pawn. 'However, I think this bears the hallmarks of someone younger. Someone internet-savvy and looking to make a name for themselves. You're right in what you said earlier – it seems like a stunt. And besides, nothing has happened to Zander, has it?'

'Not as far as I know...' Mirren answered calmly. 'But I haven't spoken to him in a while.'

'I'm sure he'd have let you know if anything had.'

'You're probably right. Did you tell Davie about Marilyn?'

Sarah's temperature rose a couple of degrees. This was where it was going to get tricky. Rook moves three squares, takes bishop.

'I haven't. That's probably why he hasn't mentioned the attacks to you. He's got no idea they could be connected to you in any way. I'll be honest, I thought about telling him, but as we discussed before, it would only add to his worries, and God knows, he's stressed out enough.'

Mirren thought about this for a few moments. 'I still think it's probably a good idea to keep it that way. At least until we know more.'

Sarah nodded. 'His head of security has got a full-scale operation on it. I think he's the most protected man in LA right now.'

'I bet that's pleasing him,' Mirren said, smiling, her sarcasm lifting the mood a little.

Sarah was back on the chessboard. Queen takes bishop.

'But I wanted to ask you a favour. One that serves both of us, actually.'

'Go on,' Mirren prompted.

'You know I'm writing a book about fame and the vagaries of Hollywood. One of the areas I'm covering is teen stars, youngsters who have made it big and are facing the kind of pressures no one outside their world can understand.'

Mirren didn't reply, just listened.

'Logan falls into that category.'

Sarah spotted the suspicious raise of a lioness's eyebrows as she prepared to protect her cub and rushed to clarify. 'Of course, I don't want to write about Logan...' That was true, although semantics might be in play there. She didn't say she wouldn't, only that she didn't want to. 'But I would much appreciate experiencing the world that he lives in. I know he's about to go on tour with South City...'

'Tomorrow,' Mirren confirmed.

'Yes. And I'd like to go with them. I'd like you to arrange that.' It was a long shot, but she had to play it. After seeing Logan buying drugs in the club the other night, she was hugely conflicted. Just like the Jono Leith story, this would be another one that could make her career, yet she wasn't sure it would ever make the light of day. She was sure of her plan, just not of what it would achieve. A cracking chapter in her book? Access to the dealers? A scandal that could take down one of the biggest pop phenomena since the Beatles? All true. But even as she thought those things, she knew she wouldn't trash Mirren McLean's kid. That family had been through enough. However, if it led her to a bigger story, one that she could run while protecting Logan, that would work for her. She had to try.

'You said it would help me too?' Mirren asked. *Queen has opportunity to face off against queen.*

'I'm one of the few people who knows of Marilyn McLean's existence, knows what she looks like and the threat that she poses. If that threat is against you, it could also be against your son. I know he's got a security team protecting him, but they're not likely to be on their guard against an elderly woman. I can keep an eye on him. Look out for any signs that something could be amiss.'

Queen makes aggressive move on opponent's queen. Now the wait to see if the game was hers.

It was a few moments before Mirren replied, her words thoughtful.

'I agree. I'll make it happen. I'll have my assistant contact you with the details. And thank you.'

Sarah had won, yet she now felt crap. Should she have told her the whole truth? *All of the above stands, but hey, I also saw your son buying drugs and I want to get the inside story?* Economics of truth were in play once again. Both women had agreed not to tell Davie so as not to panic him over a situation that may not exist, and now Sarah was doing the same to Mirren. And yet this didn't feel like an act of magnanimity.

'Is it wrong that this scene is making me freak out a little? Should I be worried?'

Neither woman had noticed Davie approaching, and now he slid into one of the other two chairs at the table. Sarah had asked him to join them for coffee, saying that she was having a 'get to know you' lunch with Mirren.

Across the table, Mirren's throaty laugh sounded utterly authentic.

'Absolutely. Your ex-girlfriend and your current girlfriend deep in conversation. We just need Jenny here to compare notes.'

Sarah watched in awe and admiration as Mirren transformed from the worry and gravity of their conversation to the carefree chat of now. If Mirren hadn't made it as a writer and movie-maker, she'd definitely have had a career in acting.

'Listen, I need to shoot back to the office,' Mirren was saying now and Sarah realised it was because she couldn't keep the pretence up any longer.

'OK, but tell me first what you two were talking about,' Davie said, clearly enjoying the company.

Sarah decided it was time to execute the final move in the plan. 'Actually, we were talking about my book and Mirren has had a brilliant idea that will really help me,' she said, transmitting her thoughts to Mirren via their locked gaze.

Mirren took the hint. 'I did. And don't hate me, Davie, but you're going to have to live without your lady for a couple of weeks. I suggested she go on tour with the boys. It'll be great material for her and I'll feel so much better if Logan has another friendly face with him. Can't have my baby getting lonely.'

Davie's stages of reaction were so transparent it was almost funny. The knee-jerk frown said he didn't want Sarah to be away from him, the subtle shift to pensive said he realised it would help her, the smile and glance at Mirren said he'd do anything for his old friend, and finally the nod of the head said that he'd decided it was a great idea.

'Absolutely! You know, I'm so glad you two are meeting up. Not to sound like an emotional adolescent...'

'You were always an emotional adolescent,' Mirren teased.

Davie winked at her. 'OK, I was. But anyway, I knew you'd get on and that makes me happy. Although,' he reached out and put his hand over Sarah's, 'you'd better behave yourself on that tour. I don't want you getting into any dodgy situations,' he said, his tone jocular but making a point.

'Oh, I will,' she reassured him. 'Anyway, it's a tour with young guys in a boy band. What could go wrong?'

Checkmate.

28

DAVIE

'Shine' – Take That

'Have you been eating right? You looked far too skinny last time I saw you. It's not normal.'

Davie's eye roll was so protracted that he almost crashed the Bugatti into a Stars' Homes bus tour heading down North Beverly Drive. That would have been a story for the tourists to take home.

'Yes, Ma, I'm eating right. And I'm not skinny,' he said, realizing he was once again back being the petulant twelve-year-old. Skinny? Did she have any idea of the work that it took to keep his body looking like this? This wasn't skinny; this was 9 per cent body fat over muscle that had been built, pumped and honed by a personal trainer to anyone who could afford his extortionate fees. Davie could and did. And he wasn't skinny.

'How are the kids?' Ena asked, speaking loudly because she was still of the opinion that transatlantic calls required you to raise your voice and speak more slowly than normal.

His mother was of a generation that hadn't quite caught up with modern life. She still lived in the house in Glasgow where Davie had grown up. She had retired from her three different cleaning jobs now, so spent her nights volunteering on the soup bus in Glasgow's city centre, a mobile refuge for the homeless and street workers who needed a meal, a warm blanket or just someone to talk to.

The trappings of his life did not impress her in the least. Others saw a $40-million Baroque mansion. She saw a huge house that was far too big and 'Who would want to rattle about in there?'

Others saw a career that epitomized the very pinnacle of success. She wondered when he was going to get a real job and actually build something because 'All you do is talk for a living. It's not proper work, is it?'

When he'd married Jenny Rico, a successful someone who was regarded as one of the great beauties of her time? 'Far too concerned about herself, that girl. Doesn't lack confidence, does she?'

All of which was said in the dry, caustic tone of the Glasgow mother who is determined not to let her offspring, or her spouse, get too big for their Gucci boots. 'Five hundred dollars for a pair of boots? You two need your heads examined.'

'They're great, Mum,' he said now. 'I saw them last night. They were asking when you'll be back over.' He wasn't lying to her. For some inexplicable reason, the kids loved their grandmother, probably because she was the only person in their world who actually treated them like kids. She told them off and insisted on manners and good behaviour, while being happy to spend all day with them, not entertaining them with elaborate days out and expensive shopping trips, but just talking. Hanging out. Last time he'd left them alone, he'd come home to find them on their hands and knees, scrubbing the kitchen floor, all three of them laughing at a joke he wasn't in on. It was one of the best things he'd ever seen, despite the fact that Alina had taken it as a personal slight on her cleaning standards and sulked for a week.

'Och, I'll be back over soon, son. Maybe Easter.'

'I'll book you a ticket,' he told her, delighted.

'Aye, OK. But not one of those first-class ones. Shocking waste. All that money just to lie down in a room next to folk you've never met.'

They said goodbye and he hung up, still laughing. She was some woman. Brutal. Honest. And utterly unimpressed by him. Actually, he realised, a lot of the same qualities as Sarah. Maybe that was why she was so damn infuriating. He wanted her to be fulfilled and happy, but damn it, there was no denying the truth. If he was totally honest with himself, he wanted her at his side, not working, just being together, having fun, being there when he needed her.

Yes, he was a selfish prick. That wasn't a newsflash. And yes, he knew he was coming off like a relic from *The Good Husband Guide, 1940*.

But it was more than that. She kept him off balance, always feeling a little insecure, and for a guy who was self-aware enough to realise that his inherent personality sat on a seesaw of insecurity and arrogance, that wasn't a good thing. Falling in love? Good. Falling in love with a woman who wanted to live life on her own terms? A one-way street to instability.

Shaking off the irritation, he pulled the Bugatti into a reserved space outside the network's HQ, then jumped out, aware of the glances of the people walking by on the sidewalk. It felt pretty good to be him right now. His mother might think he was too skinny, but he knew that by LA standards he was looking killer, especially today. Navy trousers from the new Tom Ford line, a pale blue shirt, his trademark colour ever since a stylist told him that it emphasized the colour of his eyes, and on his wrist, a vintage Panerai Kampfschwimmer, this one bought for $1.5 million at auction in New York when the network had commissioned *Here's Davie Johnston*.

The receptionist beamed at his arrival and took him personally to the executive lift, punching in a code that would take him to the top-floor boardroom.

When the door slid open, he saw that the board, Mellie and his agent, Cal Wolfe, were already seated.

'Good of you to get here,' Cal said breezily.

The suits smiled at the predictable joke. Of course they smiled. Davie was riding high in the ratings at the moment, therefore he could do no wrong. He could be late. He could fuck up. He could screw their wives. But as long as he was pulling in record viewers and avoiding public scandal, they'd indulge his every whim and late arrival. Besides, now he had The Oscars preparations and rehearsals to use as an excuse too. He was only co-presenting, so the full weight didn't ride on him, but even so, he'd been working with the writing team for a couple of months now, perfecting his links. The jokes were written, the 'impromptu' comments rehearsed until he could recite them in his sleep. His suit was ordered – custom Armani. They'd done a few run throughs on a mock up of the stage in a theatre downtown. He was feeling confident about it, buzzed up and ready to get to the full-scale rehearsals in the days before the ceremony.

'Sorry guys, Oscars stuff,' Davie quipped, with a nonchalant wave of the hand. Good to remind them who they were dealing with here.

At the head of the table was Hank Wilson, one of the few old-school TV guys who hadn't being replaced by a young, flash bastard who spent all day talking about his work as 'Art' while ruthlessly cutting corners to save budget. Hank didn't get the whole reality-TV thing at all, but he was six months off retirement, so he'd defer to his right-hand woman, Jacqueline Cosh. Davie gave it ten minutes until she mentioned her 'Art'.

Hank launched straight into business. 'Good to see you, Davie. Jacqueline, can we have a ratings summary?' he asked. Jacqueline tripped off a whole swathe of figures – domestic, East Coast, West Coast, syndication, international and online numbers – but Davie waited for the summary.

'*The Dream Machine* is at number two in entertainment. In reality, *Beauty and the Beats* is sitting at number three. *American Stars* is number one. And in talk shows, *Here's Davie Johnston* was number one this week, and we're only four weeks in.'

The whole room burst into a round of applause. Davie didn't stop them. Number one. Thank you, Jizzo Stacks. You just bought me another Panerai.

'Congratulations, Davie. Great job.'

Davie didn't need to be told. Even Cal Wolfe's pointed face beamed with happiness, and Davie knew it was because there was a clause in the contract that added 25 per cent to Davie's fee if they reached number one in the first six months. Cal would, of course, inherit 10 per cent of that. Not bad for just turning up to work in the morning.

Jacqueline Cosh stepped in again, obviously keen to establish her presence by taking control. 'OK, so tell us about the proposal for the new show. Obviously, *Beauty and the Beats* has reached the end of its... lifespan,' she finished with a slight hesitation, suddenly aware that her rush to assert her authority had prompted an unfortunate use of words.

Taking the heat off, Davie stood up, always happier to stand while he was pitching. He found the ability to pull the room in and the dynamic edge were stronger if he was on his feet, moving.

He launched into the pitch, summarizing the backstory of *Beauty and the Beats* and repeating the ratings figures from a few moments before.

He then expressed brief condolences for Jizzo Stacks, before like Carmella – moving swiftly on to his replacement. Jack Gore. He felt a twinge of guilt that he hadn't mentioned the possibility of Jack replacing Jizzo to Mirren, but he told himself that there was no point broaching it until it was a real possibility. And he wouldn't know that for sure until after this meeting.

As he outlined the concept, there were a few surprised faces in the room. The older ones knew Jack as a respected producer of decent films, married to Mirren McLean, a power couple in the industry. The younger ones knew him for the scandal of the affair with Mercedes Dance the previous year, the huge flop of his last film and the fact that Carmella had mentioned him on *Here's Davie Johnston* only a few nights before.

Davie made a convincing argument, outlining Jack's image, his style, the human interest in the relationship with Carmella, the idiosyncrasies of a man who was desperately trying to reclaim his youth, while using his money and fame to attract a young woman who clearly had some kind of sugar-daddy thing going on.

It was TV gold, he told them. Genius. A top ratings hit. He'd bet his Panerai Kampfschwimmer on it.

When he finished, he took questions. There were enquiries on cost increases or reductions, locations, shoot schedules and a discussion with marketing on image, demographics and appeal. They'd lose the rock viewers, the ones who had genuinely respected Jizzo for his body of work, as opposed to Carmella's body of hotness. Davie was confident that those were minimal, and besides, Gore brought other things to the party.

He paused, preparing to play the trump card. Logan Gore.

Son.

Member of South City.

Sold a million copies of their last album in the first weekend of release.

No, Logan wouldn't take a role in the series, but Gore's association and the prospect of his son possibly appearing on camera would have the teenagers of this nation tuning in long enough to get them hooked.

A few more questions were bandied about, but Davie, in his element, batted every one of them right back. This was his wheelhouse. Pitching, hustling. Making things happen.

And they did. It took Davie forty-four minutes from walking into that room to get an agreement. A green light.

In the lift going back down, Cal Wolfe shook his hand. 'Davie, my man, that was stellar.'

'You taught me everything I know, Cal,' Davie replied with a wink. They both knew it wasn't true, but mutual gratification was the basis on which most relationships worked around here. Mellie audibly tutted. 'OK, after you two boys have finished with your simultaneous ego orgasm, we have some stuff to sort out. I'll look at the figures before we talk to Jack Gore on cash. Be good to get him for less than we paid Jizzo.'

Both men expressed agreement as the lift doors opened and they stepped into the foyer of the building.

'I'll also scout locations, check out his house, his office, see what we can work with. Would he be open to switching to another house?'

Davie shrugged. 'Not sure. I do know he's living in a rented pad because Mirren got the house in the divorce.'

Crossing the reception area, he pulled his sunglasses back down onto his face, ready to head outside.

'Which brings me to my last point...' Mellie went on.

'You love me?' Davie fished, grinning.

'I do,' Mellie said sweetly. 'Like I love my bulldog. Who also spends an inordinate amount of time licking his own dick.'

Cal Wolfe eyed her with open admiration.

Mellie got back on track. 'But my point is, how will Mirren McLean feel about you putting her major dick of a husband on TV and opening their lives up to a shitload of scrutiny and a lack of privacy that only the truly narcissistic psycho would ever want?'

Davie stopped mid-step. Shit. This was all real now. It was happening and he was going to have to face the challenges this could bring to his newly repaired bond with one of his oldest friends. He'd convinced himself he could spin enough positives to combat the 'notoriety by association' storm this would undoubtedly unleash for Mirren and Logan.

'Leave it with me,' he replied, following Mellie and Cal out of the door. 'I'll smooth it over with Mirren.'

Mellie stopped dead. Davie followed her gaze and realised it was trained on the Bugatti. The one that sat in the space where he left it. The one that now had four slashed tyres and side panels that looked like a figure-skating team had been ice-skating on them.

Mellie whistled, low and stunned. 'Well, I hope she handles it better than the person who did that.'

29

ZANDER

'Demons' – Imagine Dragons

Zander tossed a Marlboro up and caught it between his teeth. As always, he didn't light it within the confines of Hollie's car. He was far too attached to his balls to risk losing them.

'I don't get it,' Hollie said for the third time, brow furrowed, her fingers massaging her temples. 'Are you sure?'

Zander shrugged. 'Pretty much. I've been through the whole place with the police and the Lomax team and I can't see anything missing. And can you please put your hands back on the wheel? You make me nervous when you drive with your knees.'

She shot him an irritated look. 'It makes no sense. It really doesn't. Why would anyone ransack the place and leave with nothing?'

Zander was nonplussed. 'Maybe they were disappointed with what was there. I should have left a note giving them Davie's address.'

The disparity between the lives the two men had chosen to live in LA said everything about who they were. Davie chose a $40-million mansion in Bel Air that said 'power and wealth'. Zander had chosen an apartment in Venice that said 'non-materialistic and couldn't really give a toss'.

'Did the security team check for bugs and cameras?'

'Yep, nothing planted. And I can't tell you how weird I think it is that that could even be a possibility.'

A couple of moments passed, the void filled by the Tim McGraw track coming from Hollie's sound system. Zander could almost hear Hollie's brain working overtime and knew that in that 180-second pause, she'd have considered twenty-five different scenarios, and at least half of them would have a fatal outcome for him. Apparently, worrying – she'd informed him many times – came as part of the job.

'Still think you should move into a hotel until they find the freak who did this.'

'Nah, it's fine.'

'It's really not fine. Nothing about this is frigging fine. Jesus, I can feel extra wrinkles popping up with the stress. You're making me old, Zander Leith. I'm going to be a haggard, dried-up old crow who is so unattractive she never has sex again, and it'll be all your fault. You're ruining my life.'

'If it gets that bad, I'll have sex with you,' he consoled her, taking the bait and running with it. 'You can keep your eyes shut and pretend it's someone you're attracted to.'

The sucker punch she doled out only slightly bruised his bicep.

'So what's the story with this meeting, then?' he asked her, stretching out and putting his feet on the dash and realizing he could still smell salt water in his hair. He'd had a clear schedule today, so he'd spent it hanging up at Zuma with Don Michael Domas and a couple of other surfers. They'd been out on the boards for hours, just them, the waves and a few carloads of paparazzi back on the beach. A couple of years ago, he was the most famous of their group. Now they were probably all there for Don Michael, and that suited him just fine.

'I have absolutely no idea. And get your feet off my dashboard. Wes's assistant called me an hour ago, said he wanted to see you in his office and asked if you could head over any time after 8 p.m. I'm guessing he has an update from the security team or another nomination has come in. Either that or you're in trouble. Anything I should know about?'

'I thought you knew everything already?' he teased.

Hollie nodded confidently. 'Correct. I'm like an oracle. And I foresee major problems in your future if you put your penis anywhere near Adrianna Guilloti again. Please tell me it's over.'

Zander had another, almost uncontrollable, urge to light the cigarette.

Was it over? He hadn't heard from her since she'd walked away that night at the airport. Nothing. Not even a phone call the next day to explain, resolve, recriminate, argue... Nothing. He'd got that one so, so wrong.

'It's over.' It was. His days of bad decisions were done. From here on in, he was going to be going with the flow. Karmic calm. Only things that were good for the soul.

Hollie was definitely good for the soul – even if not always great for the ego.

'I need to say this. Your apartment? Could that have been her disgruntled husband trying to piss you off?'

Zander shook his head. 'Can't see it. He won, didn't he? He's already pissed me off.'

'Fair point. OK. Now that you're no longer thinking with your privates, please return to being an emotional vacuum, a dark, brooding soul who couldn't form an attachment with two tubes of glue and a roll of tape. I liked you better that way.'

The car slid to a stop at the barrier that was blocking their entrance to the Lomax lot. Lomax Films had been built from scratch. It had fought off all challengers, and while it wasn't on the scale of Sony or Time Warner, it could whip Miramax and Lionsgate in a fair fight.

Security at the studio was tight. Too many crazies out there. One of them walking around with personal knowledge of the interior of his home.

'Hi, Denny. How's the wife?' Hollie asked the rotund officer who'd been a constant presence on the gate since the beginning of time. Hollie asked him the same question and got the same answer every time she drove through.

'Still hates me,' he chuckled. 'But since Denzel Washington ain't coming for her, I'm all she's got.'

The gate rose and he waved them through. The lot, so busy during the day, was eerily quiet at night, despite the fact that there would undoubtedly be filming taking place right now in at least a couple of the sound stages. Lomax Films put out around a dozen movies a year and their TV division currently had nine syndicated shows in production, all crime, para-normal and drama. Wes Lomax didn't do comedy. He didn't do reality. And yes, his professional and personal values did have synergy.

Wes Lomax had been a top-deal player in this town for over forty years for one simple reason. The guy made great screen. He could spot a winner while wearing a mask and having a four-way with three high-class hookers but he'd never lost control because he loved film more.

According to Hollywood folklore, the only person who had ever refused to work with him again was Mirren McLean. Zander was fairly sure that twenty years down the line, that one still stuck in his throat.

The first time Zander had met the mogul, he'd been nineteen years old. He, Mirren and Davie had been working in bars and hotels in St Andrews, forced to flee Glasgow after Jono had the misfortune to end up very dead.

The road out of there started with Mirren. When they were kids, they'd laughed when Mirren said she wanted to be a writer, but she didn't give a fuck what they thought.

She'd written their story and Davie had served it up to Wes Lomax. Not only Mirren's story. Their story. A story of brutality, abuse and murder that seemed too horrific to be real. They were counting on it.

The Brutal Circle.

Wes Lomax bought it. With Mirren as writer and Davie and a reluctant Zander in starring roles. It killed him that they were making money from his father's death. Not that the old bastard didn't deserve it.

That wasn't the point.

No one ever suspected that it was all based on truth. Jono Leith died because Marilyn McLean had gored the fucker to death, not because she hated him, but because she loved him way too much. When she'd caught Jono raping Mirren, she'd killed him. And if she hadn't, then Zander would have stepped up and finished it. So would Davie. So would Mirren. Mirren had begged Davie and Zander to cover it up so the boys had hidden the body. It hadn't taken long for Marilyn to twist reality and blame Mirren for seducing Jono, a nauseating interpretation that was far from the truth.

Mirren's way of dealing with the trauma had been to write about it and that story had led to stardom for them all.

That's what had been too hard to bear. It felt like he owed Jono something because his cold, rotting corpse had given them Hollywood lives. It ate at him. So he drank. It made him bitter. So he drank. He cut off all ties with Mirren and Davie, the two people who reminded him of it every day. So he drank.

Mirren and Davie couldn't handle the memories either so it had been easier for them to part ways too. They'd all found their own ways to deal with it. Mirren built a new family. Davie went after power and money.

And Zander drank some more.

But Wes Lomax stuck with him because he'd spotted a rain-maker. Zander's performance in *The Brutal Circle* had caused the kind of phenomenon rarely seen. Zander Leith became Seb Dunhill, the spy who could outsmart Bourne and kick Bond's ass, while looking even better in a suit.

The first Dunhill movie cracked $100 million at the box office and every one of the five since then had broken its predecessor's record. Sure, Zander was a fucked-up addict off screen, but on screen, he was the man who saved the world.

While he owed his first movie to the grave of Jono Leith, he owed everything else to Wes Lomax.

Over the years, their relationship had found a mutually agreeable equilibrium that sat somewhere between boss-employee, mentor-protégé and father-son. The latter connection was responsible for Wes metaphorically kicking his ass every time he screwed up, then dragging him back out of the gutter.

It was never established who Wes loved more, Zander or Seb Dunhill. Zander hoped he never had to find out.

Outside his office, Wes's assistant, Monica, was still sitting there, even though it was after 8 p.m.

There was loyalty, there was commitment, and then there was Monica.

Groomed to perfection, she was in her sixties but looked forty-five, thanks to Wes's twice-yearly bonus of a $50k voucher for the best cosmetic surgeon his money had already bought. The generosity probably explained why she'd never taken advantage of the fact that she'd been hired in the days before confidentiality clauses had existed, by telling Wes to shove his job and then writing an exposé that would undoubtedly sell by the millions.

Nothing went on in this office that Monica didn't know about. Every email was routed through her system, every call taped and logged. She knew who he saw, who he liked, who he screwed, and this morning she'd pressed 'record' on the camera that had filmed Wes going down on an award-winning actress who'd come to see him wearing nothing but Dior's Poison under her coat. She also knew that Wes would watch it later while relaxing with a cigar at his $10,000 desk.

'Hi, Hollie. Go on in, Zander. He's waiting for you.'

The veins on the side of Zander's neck began to pulse. It was nothing obvious. A vibe. An inflection in her tone. Hi, Paranoia, it's been a while. He shook off the feeling of unease and headed on in.

Wes didn't rise to the occasion. He sat behind his sleek black marble desk, his face a stony mask of fury. Zander knew there were only two things that made Wes Lomax really, really fucked off. Losing money and the prospect of losing money.

He had no idea why he'd be connected to either option. The last Seb Dunhill had killed at the box office and Hollie had said the suits had okay'd the return to work on the next one.

'I'm just going to get straight to it, son,' he said, in the manner of a father who'd just found out that his son was peddling crack on a street corner.

Hollie glanced at Zander, clearly picking up on the vibe too. Something was very off with this conversation and it was just getting started.

'Your drug test came back positive for coke.'

Zander smiled. Ah, it was a wind-up. Wes was famous for his pranks, liked his twisted games of power. There was the time he'd had Zander's DB7 towed. The time he'd rerouted his private jet to the middle of some Midwestern desert.

Zander wasn't biting. 'Sure it did. OK, so why are we really here?'

Wes's expression didn't change. He was really playing this one out. 'It came back positive for coke,' he repeated. 'How could you have been so fucking stupid?'

Hang on, this was getting way too real now.

Zander sat forward in his chair. 'This has to be a joke, and you're pushing it too far, Wes. Let's move on.' His voice was low and controlled.

Wes may be his boss, but he was fucking with the one area in which Zander didn't see the funny side. He'd survived drugs. Chloe hadn't. Sense of humour? Fail.

Wes slid a cigar along his desk, used a small Samurai dagger he kept on an ornamental stand to slice off the tip, then lit it with a gold lighter before replying. 'No joke. But you know that. So you're back on the stuff.' It was a statement, not a question. 'You're back on it because you're a fucking idiot who can't keep his fucking life together!' Pushing up onto his feet, he was roaring now.

'Oh shit,' Hollie said under her breath, but loud enough for Zander to pick up on. He glanced over at her, saw her eyes wide, jaw dropped. None of this made sense. So it was a mistake. A false positive. Shit like that happened. They just needed to repeat the test and it would all be cleared up.

However, he wasn't going to get into a screaming match with Lomax, so he kept his voice calm and even. Ironically, not something he'd be able to carry off if he was using.

'Wes, this is messed up. I'm clean, have been since Mirren's girl died.'

'You are not fucking clean!' he shouted. Hollie found her voice. 'Wes, I promise—'

Wes turned on her. 'Don't fucking defend him.'

Line crossed. 'Don't dare raise your voice to her, Wes,' Zander warned. 'Don't fucking dare. Not ever. I'm clean. Repeat the test.' This time the words were coming out staccato and through gritted teeth.

If he'd had so much as a hint of coke in his system, he'd have been across that desk and Wes Lomax would be making an appointment for the replacement of his $100,000 veneers.

'Too late. It was a one-time deal with the insurance company. One strike on drugs. And, son, you just struck out.'

Fury and disbelief wrestled for superiority in Zander's reaction. Disbelief won. Just.

'Come on, Wes, don't give me bullshit. I'm clean. It's a mistake. And you fucking know it.'

Wes's rage calmed to a steely fury. 'Save it, son. I've heard it all before. You're done.'

'I'm done?' Zander said, with a laugh of utter incomprehension.

'You're done,' Wes repeated. 'They won't let us go back into production with you.'

'So you're what? Going to replace me?'

A sudden flicker to the right in Wes's eyes told him that was exactly what was about to happen. Bond had been through many incarnations. Seb Dunhill was about to follow suit.

Zander could have argued, stated his case, begged, but fuck that. He'd learned a long time ago that there were only two options when dealing with someone who thought they had more power. Walk away or take them out.

He got up from his seat, turned, headed for the door.

This time, unlike last, he was walking away.

30

MIRREN

'I Don't Want a Lover' – Texas

On the scale of things she wanted to be doing today, this was pretty near the bottom. Despite her reticence, Mirren forced her face into a smile and pushed open the office door. 'Good afternoon, everyone.'

She slipped into the first empty seat, having absolutely no time for the politics of who-sat-where. Only then did she scan the assembled faces. Perry. Euan Stoker, chief suit for Pictor. And of course...

'Good afternoon,' Mike Feechan said casually. 'Good to see you.'

Only Mirren detected that it was a somewhat loaded statement. A few nights ago, they'd had sex. Yes, another man had actually seen her naked. However, since then, living up to the cliché, Mirren hadn't called, hadn't written...

She had, however, completely avoided all of his attempts to contact her.

A shudder made her shoulders tremble at the memory. It wasn't that the sex had been bad. Actually, it had been good. Really good. There wasn't the heart-thudding innocence of first love that she'd had with Davie, or the familiarity she'd had with Jack. But Mike had been hot and sexy, and it had reached an orgasmic climax they'd both enjoyed. The problem wasn't physical. There had been no connection, no words and when he did try to speak, she shushed him by putting her finger to his lips. He got the message. No talk. No whispers. This wasn't making love; it was sex. Pure, aggressive, grasping, intensely energetic sex that left no room for thinking or tenderness.

Only when their heartbeats were returning to post-coital normal did Mirren speak.

'I don't usually do that,' she'd said, embarrassed.

'Neither do I,' he'd answered, smiling. She believed him.

'I don't want to be rude, but you should go before Logan gets back. I wouldn't like him to see you here.' She'd tried to make it sound as gentle as possible, but there was no getting away from the fact that it looked like he was being dismissed. Duty over. Job done. Thank you and goodnight.

Mike's face had flinched with surprise, but he didn't argue, and she didn't give him time to make other suggestions. She'd headed to the bathroom, returned when he was already gone.

The thought of climbing into a bed in which she'd just had sex with a virtual stranger didn't appeal, so she'd wandered through to Chloe's old room, slipped under the covers and nodded off there, before waking in the morning and realizing that for the first time in months, she'd slept through the whole night.

The next morning, when she'd reached the office, there had been a dozen roses waiting on her desk, no card, next to an assistant with an inquisitive expression.

'Someone is popular this morning,' Devlin had sing-songed cheerfully.

'I helped an old lady across the road,' Mirren had replied, so coolly that she could see Devlin was actually wondering whether to believe her.

At lunchtime, Devlin had called through to her, 'Mike Feechan is on the line for you.'

The wave of cold dread was instant. She wasn't ready for that. Couldn't do it. Her emotions were still locked in a place that left her utterly numb. The thought of opening up to someone, embarking on a new relationship, filled her with a level of discomfort that she knew probably bordered on irrational.

'Tell him I'm unavailable. And if he calls back, tell him the same thing.'

That had been it. Contact severed. He'd taken the hint. There was, however, no getting away from the uncomfortable reality that they had to work together.

This meeting in Feechan's office had been set up prior to the night of the Malibu dinner and she couldn't pull out. The deadline for contract negotiations to be settled was fast approaching and the standoff had to be broken, thus this tête-à-tête – just Mirren, Mike, and the lawyers, Euan and Perry.

Performance time. Mirren conjured up another smile. 'Good to see you too. OK, let's get started, shall we?'

There was a flicker of something she couldn't read in Mike's eyes, but he took her lead. Not for the first time this week, she realised, toes curling with embarrassment.

'Euan, can you outline the situation?'

Stoker cleared his throat and kicked off with a run-down of the main contract points already agreed. They were all on the same page on shooting schedules and timescales. The script had already been agreed, as had the casting. Distribution was in place. Every team in both Pictor and McLean Productions had submitted their plans and strategies, and all had been rubber-stamped. Which brought them to…

'Merchandise,' Euan finally announced. 'We need to move it to 25 per cent. The deal should never have been done at 10 per cent in the first place.'

'But it was,' Mirren said calmly.

Mike casually adjusted the sleeves on his white shirt and then sat forward, hands clasped on the table in front of him. As he moved, Mirren immediately recognized the faint scent of Amouage Dia Pour Homme. She'd once bought it as a gift for Jack and loved the blend of woody tones, herbs and leathers.

'Mirren, we want to work this out, but we can't stick at 10 per cent. No other franchise out there works on that basis.'

He was reasonable. Likable. Came over as genuinely sincere. But to Mirren, the choice was simple – the money went into her company's bank account or Pictor's bank account. She'd made the studio millions over the years, so she saw absolutely no reason to concede on this. If they wanted her loyalty, they were going to have to honour the terms of their original deal, because the fact was that Mirren hadn't got to where she was today by allowing big studios to push her around.

Perry took a breath, ready to step in and Mirren could see that she had a page of figures in front of her: projections, costs, profit. Mirren immediately realised that she didn't have the patience to carry on with this. She wasn't going to budge.

Arguments were futile, so what was the point in wasting everyone's time? She subtly put her hand on Perry's arm to stop her. 'I have worked with Pictor for a decade and it's been mutually beneficial. I don't appreciate your actions, or agree with them on any basis. Our terms remain the same.'

'Mirren, we appreciate the history, and trust me, we do not want to damage what has been an extremely profitable relationship. But the terms are unreasonable. You have to give something here.'

'I really don't,' she answered calmly, before rising to her feet. 'Please have the contracts drafted, original terms, before the end of the month. Otherwise I'll take the *Clansman* franchise elsewhere. Thank you for your time.'

No one said a word as she left Feechan's office. Twenty minutes later, she was back behind her own desk when Perry knocked and entered, her face a mask of amusement. 'Anytime I need someone's ass kicked, remind me to call you.'

Mirren smiled wearily. 'Sorry if I stole your thunder this morning. I know you were prepared to make the arguments, but I just preferred to cut to the chase.'

Perry leaned on the back of the chintz-covered seat on her side of the desk. 'You certainly did that. I thought Mike Feechan was gonna bust his gut when you left. He didn't look happy at all. Dismissed the two of us and then there was a loud banging sound. I think he kicked the desk.'

'I'm sure he didn't,' Mirren replied, laughing at Perry's flair for the dramatic.

'Anyway, I think there will be hell to pay over at Pictor this afternoon,' Perry concluded.

'I can imagine.' Actually, Mirren wasn't sure that she could. Her entire experience of him in the few hours she'd spent with him fully clothed were of a pretty straightforward guy. 'Did you set up the meeting with Lomax?'

'Monday. The patio at The Ivy.'

'Great.' Her gaze went to the clock on the wall next to the door. 'Damn, look at the time. I have to go. Let me know when they come back to you.'

'Oh, I will.' Perry headed out, clearly satisfied with her working day.

An hour later, Mirren was sitting across from her best friend and editor of the *Hollywood Post*, Lou Cole, for their weekly dinner date.

'Oh, girl. Rookie mistake number one: do not have alcohol with an attractive man when you're feeling vulnerable. Rookie mistake number two: do not ever sleep with studio head while in negotiation over terms of contract.'

Mirren gave Lou her best deadpan expression. 'I bought the first one but you made the second one up.'

Lou let out her glorious cackle, turning the heads of the other diners at Giorgio Baldi on West Channel Road in Santa Monica. The couple having a romantic dinner at the next table didn't look entirely impressed. Thankfully, no one could overhear the conversation, because Lou was always given the same round table in the corner of one of the most intimate restaurants in the city. It was perfect for watching the action, but offered privacy for passing on salacious gossip to her dinner companions.

The dining area was dimly lit, small, almost like a beautiful room in a welcoming home. One that Paul McCartney, Rihanna, George Clooney and Gary Barlow liked to visit when they were in town.

But in this restaurant it was all about the food. When Pulcione, the main man, described the specials, it was almost lyrical. Succulent. Enticing. Exquisite temptation. And it all lived up to the promise. The dover sole was to die for. The Maine lobster with warm sorano beans was sensational. The agnolotti with white truffle sauce was cooked somewhere close to heaven.

Mirren held up her hands. 'Look, you have to cut me some slack. Until Mike, I'd slept with two men in my life: Davie and Jack. My experience is limited, and my understanding of the niceties of sexual politics needs some work.'

She groaned out loud and covered her face with her hands, finally opening them when Lou's laughter became contagious enough to make her shoulders shake.

'Don't mock. Take pity. Rescue me.'

'Honey, you don't need rescuing; you need a twelve-step plan to get you back in the game.'

Mirren speared the olive in her Martini and bit into it. 'I have no game.'

'Exactly. You have no game. This is why you need me. So how was it?'

'What are we, fifteen?'

'I'm serious. How was it?'

'Lou, it was a mistake. A one-off, not to be repeated, definite mistake. My head was just in a really messed up place.'

'Uh-huh. But what about from the neck down?'

The romantic couple at the next table shot them synchronized evil glares as laughter cut into their doe-eyed moment for a second time.

'So what happens now?' Lou asked, mischief written all over her face.

'Nothing! We're locked over the merchandise negotiations so this couldn't have happened at a worse time.'

Lou nodded, feigning seriousness. 'You're right – probably thinks you screwed him to get some leverage on the deal.'

Mirren groaned. 'Thanks, chum. Just when I thought I had already reached an all-time low...'

Her smile said differently. Where would she have been without Lou for the last few years? No matter how much crap had been thrown at her, the one constant in her life was the woman with whom she could talk, cry and laugh until her jaw hurt, and often all three, alternated in the course of one evening. The truth was that sleeping with Mike had been a ridiculous error of judgement that she'd been beating herself up about all week. It was the first time she'd had a one-night stand, and it would be the last. And yet, in Lou's utterly incorrigible hands, it had been reduced from a major fuck-up to a tiny blip. 'Play up the good stuff, cope with the bad, ignore everything else' was Lou's motto. And she was right. So she'd had a one-night stand? So what? In the grand scheme of things, did it really matter?

'Look who it is!' Lou's exclamation interrupted her thoughts. She turned, expecting to see Davie Johnston. He'd asked to meet her and she'd suggested he join them tonight for an early dinner before he went to the studio for tonight's *Here's Davie Johnston*. He was probably feeling lonely without Sarah around. Mirren turned and saw, to her surprise, Lex Callaghan and his wife, Cara, were about to pass their table. They spotted her at exactly the same time.

'Mirren! So good to see you,' Cara exclaimed, her arms wide. The two women locked in a tight hug, while Lex greeted Lou with an affectionate kiss. 'All my favourite women in the same place,' he joked.

'Yep, so you can run along and leave us to have a girls' night,' Lou quipped, then turned to Cara. 'We have sex revelations and a large splash of scandal.'

'Oooh, I'm in,' Cara giggled.

Lex feigned sorrow. 'I know when I'm beat,' he said mournfully.

'You look incredible,' Mirren told Cara. It wasn't an empty compliment. Cara's long black hair, a throwback to her Native American heritage, hung in one long, glossy ebony sheet. Her dark skin and wide brown eyes gave her an exotic beauty; the simple white shift dress added a timeless elegance. She might spend most of her life in jeans and riding boots, with the wind in her hair and dirt under her nails, but she definitely knew how to pull off the formal look too.

Mirren realised this was an unusual place to meet them. They rarely came into the city and they definitely didn't do upmarket restaurants.

'Special occasion?' she asked.

Cara shook her head. 'Nope. I had to come into town for a couple of appointments, and Lex has an early call in the morning, so we just decided to make a night of it and stay up at the shack.'

'The shack?' Lou asked, horrified. Lou didn't do 'shacks'. She did five-star hotels with a concierge who could tend to her every whim.

'It's not actually a shack,' Mirren said, calming her down. 'It's a little bit less rustic than it sounds.'

The shack was where Lex stayed when he was in the city.

Not for him the glitzy opulence of the grand West Hollywood chain hotels or the bijou boutiques. Instead, he'd bought a cabin in the hills of Topanga, half a mile from civilization. He'd made some concessions to modern life. There was electricity, hot and cold running water, comfortable furniture and a fifty-inch plasma TV on the wall, but that was about the extent of his modernizations.

'Would you like to join us?' Mirren asked automatically.

Cara grinned. 'Thank you, but we'll leave you to it. Much as I'd love to hear those sexual revelations, I only get this man out a couple of times a year and I want to have a long chat to him to see if I still like him.'

Another flurry of hugs and they were off to the table waiting for them on the other side of the room.

'God, I love them,' Mirren said as she sat back down.

'They're one of the elusive few,' Lou added.

'Few what?'

'Few couples who've never had a single rumour of infidelity.' Lou's job on the *Hollywood Post* gave her an encyclopaedic knowledge of every failing, flirt and fuck in town. There was very little she didn't know. Whether she chose to publish or not was a different story. It was Lou who'd uncovered Jack's affair with Mercedes Dance the previous year. It was Lou who'd told Mirren that Mercedes was pregnant. And it was Lou who'd discovered that the DNA test showed the baby wasn't Jack's. Not that it mattered to Mirren. The point was that he'd broken their marriage and no piece of paper with a negative DNA result could patch that wound.

'Sorry, sorry, sorry!' Davie announced as he burst in on her in a restaurant for the second time in just a few days.

'No worries. We were just talking nonsense until you got here. You can take over doing that now,' Mirren teased, between double kisses and hugs all round. Lou knew Davie from moving in the same circles over the last twenty years, but they hadn't been friends until he and Mirren had rekindled their relationship.

Mirren knew that Lou loved his cheek, his balls and his energy.

They immediately launched into a flurry of orders and chat that took them well into their main courses. 'So tell me, are you missing Sarah?' Mirren asked.

Davie nodded. 'Look, I know I'm supposed to be all cool and macho, but man, I hate that she's away. I'm not designed to be on my own,' he admitted.

'You never were,' Mirren told him. 'Remember when your mum was working nights? You practically moved in with Zander, and then when we were older, we had to come stay with you.' Her words sparked a memory for both of them. The first time they'd slept together was when she'd been hanging out in his bedroom on a freezing winter night while his mum was at work. They were sixteen. It was no different to a hundred other nights, until the moment they had a cuddle to warm up and Mirren asked him to kiss her. She discovered later that he'd been in love with her for years, but at that moment, she'd been terrified. He was too. They kissed, made love and stayed together for years, convinced they were soulmates.

They were – until Jono Leith's death destroyed them all. In that single moment, their futures were jacked onto a different track. Not only by the scars of what they did and what they saw, but because they'd always know just how close love and hate really were. Marilyn had been Jono's lover for years and adored him, was obsessed by him, lived her life for the moment he walked into a room and extinguished her spirit the moment he left. He was her king, until he committed the ultimate sin, and Marilyn snapped, plunged a knife into his chest, pulled it back out and then left him to die on her kitchen floor.

Love. Hate. Love. Hate. Madness. Death.

Jono Leith was gone. Her mother had never been there for her in the first place, but right then, that didn't matter. Because the reason she plunged a knife into Jono Leith's heart broke Mirren's.

'Hey, you OK? You've totally slipped into a dwam.'

The sound of the old Scottish word made her smile as she remembered Davie's mum using it regularly. *That boy of mine. I swear to the Mother of God he spends his whole blessed life wandering about in a dwam.*

The memory jolted her back to the guy in front of her. Forget the past. It's done. All that really matters is what's happening right here and now.

The rest of the meal was filled with indiscreet rumours and salacious chat, and Mirren realised this was the most she'd smiled in a long time. It felt good. Gave her hope. She didn't believe for a minute that time healed, but perhaps if she could occupy it with tranquillity, peace and laughter-filled nights like this one, then it would become bearable. At least, bearable enough to prevent her from having sex with men she barely knew.

'So listen, I need to shoot off soon, but there's something I have to talk to you about,' Davie announced after the waiter had cleared their plates.

Mirren eyed him with a smile and a raised eyebrow. 'Ah, here it comes. And there was me thinking that you wanted to join us for my sparkling wit and personality.'

'That too,' Davie admitted.

Was it Mirren's imagination, or was his left eye twitching slightly, that telltale sign he'd had as a kid in times of stress, lies or trouble? Mirren's stomach clenched with anxiety, her mind already going to the worst-case scenario. He'd found out about Marilyn potentially resurfacing. Damn, she should have told him. She should have been honest. He deserved that. Or maybe he was just going to tell her that some wacko had shot at his gates. Sarah had told her that in confidence, so she hadn't even told Lou. Yeah, that must be it.

Yet, the way he was looking at Mirren, almost apologetically, made a shiver of fear run up her spine. Oh no. What was this?

His eye twitched again as he continued, 'But other than that, there's something else I really need to tell you...'

31

DAVIE

'Love Runs Out' – One Republic

In the busy dining room at Giorgio Baldi, Lou decided to make a diplomatic exit and rose from her seat. 'Jennifer Garner is over there. Love that girl. I'm just gonna go for a quick chat.'

Davie stood up while Lou left the table. It was a habit bred into him in childhood. His mother, Ena Johnston, didn't have much, but she had high standards of what was acceptable when it came to manners, and she made sure her son lived up to them.

'OK, then, go for it. What's up?' Mirren asked, one eyebrow raised in curiosity.

Why did he suddenly have the feeling that what he was about to do was the equivalent of kicking her when she was down? Why hadn't he considered a bit more seriously that Jack Gore's presence on a show that Davie produced might be an issue for Mirren?

The reality was, he'd never known Mirren and Jack Gore as a couple. They'd already been apart when Davie and Mirren reconnected, so he just hadn't thought it through properly at all. Wing and a prayer, that's what he'd done. And now it was time to face up to the consequences.

OK, preparing arguments for the defence. First up, it had been a lot of years since he'd had to consider anyone else's feelings and he was out of practice. Hopefully, that one would both bring her round and even elicit a tiny tug of sympathy. Win. Win.

Second argument: he hadn't wanted to bother her because he knew she had so much on her mind right now. Didn't think it mattered. He had a hunch she might not see it that way. Lose. Lose.

Third argument and killer close: his previous thought that if he didn't make the show, someone else would. *Beauty and the Beats* had killed in the ratings, and any other network would give their right ball to pick it up. At least this way, he could treat it sensitively, make sure that Mirren and Logan were protected, that Jack was portrayed as an island: a middle-aged, midlife crisis, tattooed island. In an AC/DC T-shirt. Knob.

However, now, looking at Mirren, so unsuspecting and curious, he could see the holes in every argument. It all came back down to the same thing. He should have thought about this more seriously and told her sooner, got her thoughts before he even pitched it to the network. Who was the asshole now?

'Look, this is really difficult, and I really hope we can work it out. The series I produce, *Beauty and the Beats*...' he started. 'You know it used to star Carmella Cass and Jizzo Stacks, but sadly Jizzo died...?'

Mirren's frown of confusion suddenly turned to something that looked like relief or understanding.

'Ah, honey, are you going to tell me that Carmella is seeing Jack? Thank you, but don't worry – I already heard about it and I saw the tabloid coverage of the funeral.' She put her napkin on the table and exhaled, and for a second Davie felt the unfamiliar feeling of goosebumps prickling up his arm. God, he'd loved this woman. Loved her so much it had taken him years to recover from the hole inside him when she left. His break-up with Mirren had shaped him, changed him. Hustling and determination to make something of himself had always been part of his nature, but back then, ambition had been secondary to how he felt about Mirren. She had been all that really mattered to him. If she'd wanted to stay in Glasgow and live a completely different life, he'd have gone with it.

Jono Leith's death took away that option.

Then, when they'd got to LA, it was different. They were changed. Too much pain, too much horror. They were drowning in the memory of what had happened and it sucked away everything that was right about them being together.

So they'd agreed to walk away from the only person they'd ever loved.

That's when he'd changed. It was like she was his balance, the good part of him, and when she was gone, what else was there?

It became all about Davie Johnston.

Twenty years, and every one of them lived on his own terms, doing exactly what he wanted, when he wanted and considering no one else. It had occasionally backfired. The three-way with Jenny and Darcy was a case in point. A wild night with two of the most beautiful women he'd ever seen had turned out to be a one-way ticket to divorce. In truth, it was for the best, though. His marriage to Jenny had never come even close to what he'd had with this woman sitting in front of him right now.

He realised she was waiting for a response to whatever it was she'd just said. Not that he had any idea what it was. Blind panic was proving to be the ultimate amnesiac.

Fuck it, he wasn't telling her.

Bail out, bail out now! His brain, the part that was responsible for self-preservation and the aversion to rocking bloody huge, unstable boats screamed.

'Yeah. But see, erm, the thing is...'

What the fuck was the thing? This was ridiculous. He was Davie Johnston. Scared of no one. He had a $40-million house and a homicidal housekeeper. He'd made it in this town. He could do this. He had to take responsibility.

'Carmella would like Jack to replace Jizzo on *Beauty and the Beats*.'

OK, so maybe not quite taking full responsibility, but that was just semantics, wasn't it? As long as the salient points were shared, what was the difference?

Mirren paused, her glass midway to her mouth, then quickly knocked back a large gulp of Pinot noir, before replying, 'Jack. On a reality show. God, that's ridiculous. The man's lost the plot.'

Another sip of wine and a weary sigh. 'Davie, I know it's probably a bit weird saying this to you, but when I look back now, I honestly don't know how Jack and I ever made it work for all those years. The man is a fool.'

Oh shit, her sadness. It was so real he could almost touch it. And she was still talking.

'I just think that after you and I split up, I needed an anchor, you know? Somewhere to belong. I wanted a family so badly and he was my opportunity to make it happen. He was away on location so much, and when he was at home, he worked such long hours that we weren't actually together long enough for me to realise what a dick he was.' Another pensive moment, another sip of wine, another sigh of sadness. 'I just got carried along with how happy the kids made me, how relieved I was to have a unit. A real family unit.'

She paused again for a moment and Davie wasn't sure where she'd gone to in her head. He wanted to reach over and take her in his arms and hug her until she didn't have that haunted expression in her eyes any more. But more than that, he realised that he just wanted to sit here and listen to her talk. He knew what it took for Mirren McLean to open up to anyone, and here she was, sharing stuff that probably really hurt to reveal. 'I'm glad I'm out of it now.' She smiled sadly and he absolutely believed her. 'I just want peace from here on in.' A rueful laugh. 'Does that make me sound melodramatic?'

No. It really didn't, but unfortunately, he couldn't say that, because the functioning of his mouth and vocal chords appeared to have been battered to death by dread and panic.

Mirren obviously mistook his silence for sympathetic listening skills, as she carried on, 'I can't tell you how horrible last year was with...' as she let the words trail off, Davie realised her eyes had filled up. Her jaw clenched shut, obviously unable to say the words. She didn't have to. Chloe's death had been a horrific event and he'd watched how hard Mirren had fought to get through it.

When she spoke again, she'd slightly changed tack. 'With Chloe. But what made it even worse was Jack being such a prick. To be honest, I really couldn't give a fuck about the affair from a loyalty perspective. I exorcized my anger over that when I put his Maserati over a cliff at Trancas Canyon...'

The confession sparked Davie's memory of that event. It had been all over the news, and for a time, no one was sure if Mirren was in the car when it rolled. He had the sudden thought that in the next few minutes, she was probably going to wish that Davie had followed the path of the Maserati.

'But it was the scrutiny that made everything even tougher to bear. Seeing headlines in the tabloids. People discussing our lives on entertainment shows. Fuck-up comedians making jokes at our expense. Everyone had an opinion, relished the gossip, loved the drama, but we were living it.'

Davie finally found a voice, searching for a glimmer of hope. 'I can't even imagine how much of a nightmare that was. How are things now with Jack? Is it amicable?' Perhaps if they were still mutually supportive, she'd be happy for him and support his new career opportunity.

Mirren nodded. 'You know, it's OK. As long as I can stop Lou from taking out a contract on him, it'll be fine.'

OK, she'd lightened the mood. That was a good sign.

'I just wish he'd fade back into the background. Go off on location again. Stop living like a publicity-seeking, walking midlife crisis. Logan has to be in the public glare because that's his job, and he handles it brilliantly. But every time Jack does something that's totally ridiculous or laughable, we're back on the covers of the magazines at the supermarket checkouts. They dredge up our history. Print pictures of Chloe. Tarnish her name even further. I can't stand it, Davie. I just want to go back to living a life that isn't a talking point for strangers. And Jack needs to stop being a tit to make that happen.'

Hope eradicated. Fuck. He couldn't tell her. He could feel his heart pick up a pace that came close to palpitation, and he was fairly sure that not even the combined efforts of trimmed armpit hair, deodorant and a couple of injections of underarm Botox could stop damp patches appearing in the oxters of his pale blue Balmain shirt. This was the deepest conversation they'd had in decades, she was being so open with him, and he could now see that he was about to deliver the emotional equivalent of a bullet to the heart.

Nothing in the busy room had changed, yet suddenly he felt claustrophobic, unable to breathe, like the walls were closing in.

Bugger. Bastard. Fuck. Help.

Mirren refilled her glass from the bottle on the table and shook off her seriousness, as if she was suddenly embarrassed about revealing her feelings. That was so typically Mirren that Davie curled up just a little more inside as she spoke, clearly trying to be light-hearted.

'Christ, listen to me. What do I sound like? Sorry, Davie, I don't know where that all came from. Must be getting melodramatic. I blame my age. Or this very nice wine. Anyway, how did they take the rejection?'

Davie wasn't following. 'Who?'

'Carmel. Carmen. Sorry, what's her name?'

'Carmella.'

'That's it. How did she take it when you pointed out it was ridiculous?'

Silence. Long silence.

Excruciating silence.

And prayer. Dear God, if a meteor is ever going to hit earth and blow it apart, annihilating the human race, please make it right now. Out of the corner of his eye he saw Lou head back towards the table, spot the awkward moment, pivot on the spot and go join a table headed by a guy who might just be Pierce Brosnan. It was hard to tell. They kept the lights low to enhance the mystery.

Mirren's eyes had narrowed now, focused on his face, the optic equivalents of laser beams that could fry human matter in seconds.

'Davie?'

'I didn't reject the idea. The thing is, Mirren...'

What? What was the thing? Arguments. One. Two. Three.

He closed his eyes and picked one.

'The thing is, if I don't make the show, then someone else will. The first series killed in the ratings and at least three other networks want it. At least if I'm producing it, I can handle it properly, make sure you're protected.'

'Protected? How does having Jack Gore acting like a dick on TV every week protect us?' Her voice was low and deadly, in the manner of a movie mob guy right before he orders a hit to wipe out everyone who has ever crossed him. 'Close it down, Davie. Make sure this doesn't go ahead.'

Davie's eyes darted left, right, his brain trying and failing to form cognitive thought. 'I can't.'

'Yes, you can, Davie. Because if you don't, you and I are done. So you'll do it.'

It was almost a whisper. A threatening, furious whisper. 'I can't stop it, Mirren, because...'

His brain screamed, *'Say it. Say it. Just fucking say it!'* He was a man on death row, thirty seconds until they pressed the button that would switch on the current, and he knew he had to make his confession, tell the truth, own his mistakes.

'The contracts were signed this morning.'

The next day, he would be entirely grateful that, other than Lou, there were no journalists in Giorgio Baldi that night. He would give thanks that no other diners were covertly filming their meeting. Because if either of those scenarios had played out, then the world would have seen or heard about the dinner conversation between Mirren McLean and Davie Johnston that ended with her standing up, smoothing down her skirt, flicking back her long Titian mane and strutting to the door – but only after she punched him square in the face.

32

SARAH

'Live While We're Young' – One Direction

It was still hard for her to believe she was actually here.

This might just be the most intoxicating environment Sarah had ever experienced. The atmosphere was thick with hot, throbbing lust and raw sexuality. The stench of bodies, the noise, the heaving, breathless energy. It was utterly mesmerizing.

'Hey, how's Lois Lane doing?'

Deeko, the South City manager, had been calling her that since she'd joined the tour. He thought the journalistic reference was cute. It was, the first time. Now, it was starting to wear a bit thin, but she wasn't going to chastise him. Bite. Hand. Feed. As he came into her peripheral vision, she didn't turn to face him, strangely unwilling and unable to take her eyes off the action.

From her position just off stage left, she had a panoramic view of over 66,000 spectators screaming for the five boys in front of them, singing, fainting, pleading with them not to leave.

'Lois Lane is thinking that if she could put in a request to come back as a specific person in the next life, she'd like to return as a member of South City.'

She wasn't entirely joking. The lives these guys lived were seriously outrageous.

They'd flown on a private jet out of LA, headed to New York to do a couple of TV-show appearances – *Good Morning America* and *Letterman* – then headed north to Toronto to kick off the next leg of their North America tour. Sarah had done her research: all tickets had sold out in minutes when they'd gone on sale eight months before, and were already swapping hands for over $1,000 on ticketing websites. It was a phenomenon that was repeated for every date they were booked to play. She was twenty-six. This was making her feel forty-six. It suddenly struck her that forty-six was only a few years older than Davie. She was dating a guy who was – technically – old enough to be her dad. Was that what was behind her reticence to settle down and play happy families?

That was for worrying about when she got back. Right now, she was on tour with the biggest band in the world, and she wasn't going to lie, this was pretty exhilarating stuff. Suffocating too, sometimes. The boys were never alone, and they rarely rested.

Toronto had been a screamfest, Ottawa two days later had been off the chain, and now they were... Where? Bugger, three dates in and she was losing it already. Montreal. Of course! But she could now understand the old 'every town looks the same' road-tour cliché, because every day did follow the same pattern. When they'd landed this morning, they'd headed straight to the hotel for four hours of back-to-back interviews with press, entertainment shows and influential celebrity websites. As soon as they were done, they were shepherded into a convoy of black SUVs and whisked to the stadium for a soundcheck. When that was over, they went back to the hotel for a couple of hours' intensive training with their fitness team. A quick break to eat and then back to the stadium for meet-and-greets, where they smiled, shook hands and hugged a line of fans that felt like it would never end. After the concert, it was either back to the hotel for a few hours' sleep before flying out or straight to the airport to head to the next city, where they would land, the familiar convoy of black SUVs would pull onto the tarmac, and they'd do it all again.

And of course, almost every single moment of every single day was played out to the soundtrack of screams. Crowds of girls waiting for them at airports, outside hotels, at TV studios, at the stadiums.

The bodyguards certainly earned their money. Now she was here, she could see that there was no way Marilyn McLean, or anyone else for that matter, was getting anywhere near these boys.

The security team was twenty-strong, all former Navy Seals. Sarah knew they were trained to kill. She just wasn't sure how those skills translated to pulling twelve screaming, overwrought teenage girls off the lead singer in a boy band.

The team worked as a collective but each of the boys had their personal guard. Logan's was one of the oldest in the crew, a thirty-eight-year-old called Eli, who watched everything and said little. Occupational hazard, she supposed.

In the days she'd been with Logan, she'd seen and learned a lot. He came over as the rock of the group, the one who liaised most with the management, kept an eye on everyone and made sure things ran smoothly.

A few days of research and first-hand experience had given her an insight into the dynamics of the rest of the group. Jonell, the lead singer, was undoubtedly the diva. He was a typical frontman, all ego and demands, and under no doubt that he mattered most. There was no question he'd begin to irritate her soon. There was only so much leverage being five foot six and incredibly cute could buy a guy.

Ringo, on drums, was the geek, the one who risked repetitive strain injury of the thumbs by spending every non-drumming moment on his Xbox. Everywhere he went, it got set up first, the headphones went on, and he zoned out of the world. She'd yet to have much time with the lead guitarist, Lincoln, or keyboard player, D'Arby.

It didn't matter. Logan was the focus. It was all about him. She just hadn't decided yet if that's because she was looking out for Mirren or because he was another chapter in her book. A collective roar snapped her out of her contemplation and saved her from answering her own question. From her position on the side of stage left, she watched the boys break off on the last note of their hit 'Not Taking You Back', then throw their hands up in thanks and bid farewell to a heaving, throbbing mass of hormones and hysterics.

A new night, same deal. They'd now take a bow one by one, then step forward and face different angles of the stadium and blow out love and thanks to every corner and curve in the room.

It all looked so effortless and slick, but Sarah had already sussed that Deeko had every single minute of this organized and choreographed to perfection. It wasn't quite a dictatorship, but it was close. The man wasn't the manager of the biggest band in the world because he left anything to chance. Although, for someone so sharp, he still hadn't realised that the backwards-baseball-cap thing just wasn't working for him. She hoped he assumed that she was smiling at the action on stage. The boys had just taken their final bow, and a crowd of 66,308 were screaming for more, begging them for a second encore.

They bowed again, last time, then ran towards where Sarah and Deeko were standing. Sarah was confused. That wasn't the plan. Jonell and Ringo were supposed to exit stage right, Logan, D'Arby and Lincoln stage left.

Only when they got right up close could Sarah see that it was more of a chase situation. She flattened against the wall as Ringo ran between her and Deeko, then D'Arby followed. Logan paused as he reached her, only for Jonell to slam into him, repeatedly, knocking him five feet forward until Ringo's arms flew from the back round his waist and tried to restrain him. Deeko jumped into the mix, his arms out, acting as a barrier, Jonell trying to fight his way over him to get to Logan.

'You fucking threw me shade, man. You fucking know it.'

Logan had his hand up. 'Hey, calm down. Jonell! Take it down, man!'

He didn't get the option to take it down. Eli, Logan's personal protection officer and another guy Sarah knew to be Jonell's man appeared out of nowhere and dragged them ten feet apart. Sarah, still pressed against the wall, tried to make herself invisible so she could see how this played out. On the other side of the wall, the crowd were now chanting, 'South City, South City, South City,' like brainwashed cult members worshipping in the temple of their gods, with absolutely no idea that right at this moment two of the chosen leaders were being ripped apart, one still desperately fighting to get to the other.

Soaked with sweat, arms wide, Logan took a step forward, Eli's arm held loosely in front of him, ready to push back if necessary. It wasn't.

'Let it go, Jonell.' His voice was low, strong, but ignored. Jonell lunged again, and it took the combined efforts of Deeko and the Navy's finest to hold him back.

'Fuck you, man. These dogs don't know about you, but I do.' Sarah's investigative mind was racking up the questions.

What did they not know? And how could she find out?

'And what, Jo? Huh? What about it?' Logan challenged him.

Jonell still had fury oozing out of every pore in his twisted face. 'We're over. D'ya hear me?'

Logan almost smiled. Sarah had absolutely no idea what was going on, what was behind this or what was going to happen next, but she couldn't help admire Logan's style so far. He had this. Whatever it was, he had it.

'You mean that, Jo? Because that might just be the best news I've heard all year.'

With that he turned and walked away to a loud scream behind him of, 'You're a dead man. D'ya hear? Dead man walking!'

Logan kept on going. At least a dozen people now stood within earshot, no one quite sure what to say or do.

'Get him to the car,' Deeko ordered security, not making eye contact with Jonell.

South City, South City, South City.

The chants hadn't diminished in the moment it had taken for two-fifths of South City to come to blows. Sarah slipped past the others, running to catch up with Logan and Eli. They were jumping into the car as she got to them and she took a chance. Up until now, she'd ridden with the staff: the PR team, record-label guys, hair team or the back-up security.

As she stepped up beside the door of the GMC, Eli moved to stop her climbing aboard but Logan waved her in. "S'OK, Eli, let her ride.'

Eli did as requested, climbing into the front, leaving Sarah with Logan in the back, his face obscured by the towel he was now breathing into as he dried his face and hair of his post-concert sweat. If only she had an eBay account, she could have paid this month's rent with what she'd get for that small rectangle of absorbent fabric.

Or maybe she'd get more for the tight white T-shirt that was so wet it had gone almost transparent, outlining every single groove of his toast-rack abs and the hard curves of his biceps, triceps and delts.

Bugger, this was strange. To her, he'd always been Mirren Gore's eighteen-year-old son. But right now, she was seeing him as rock and pop star Logan Gore, member of South City.

The chant started again in her head. South City, South City, South City.

This time, Sarah wasn't sure if it was the voice of the crowd or her own.

The flashing blue lights of the police escort on either side of them added a disco effect to the interior of the vehicle as they sped through the streets towards the airport.

'So that was intense. I take it he didn't get the memo that it was "Don't Beat Up Logan Day"?'

Logan dropped the towel from his face and smiled. 'I guess not.'

'So what was...' She struggled for the right terminology to use. What did teenagers say these days? Oh, for god's sake. She was only seven or eight years older than this guy and she struggled to talk the same language.

'... his beef?' she finished weakly, unsure as to whether she'd just used the language of *The Wire*, circa 2007.

If she was ludicrously out of touch with the modern vernacular, Logan chose not to notice or mock.

Instead, he shrugged. 'Who knows? It could be any one of ninety-nine things on any day of the week.'

Her instinct was to probe more, dig deeper, but she didn't want to push. As far as Logan knew, she was here as a favour to his mum, in a purely observatory role, gaining some insight for a book she was writing about Hollywood. He had no inkling of his mother's agenda in protecting him, or of Sarah's agenda in finding out what the hell he was up to that night in the club.

He rested his head back on the top of the leather seat. 'So how's it been so far? Crazy ride, huh?'

'Insane. It's a lot to deal with. Do you ever find it hard to keep going?'

Not exactly subtle, but sometimes the direct approach was the best one.

'Nah, not really. You just need to keep it in perspective, you know? How many other guys get to do this? All I really care about is singing, and I get to do it every night.'

It was a press line that she recognized from at least two of the interviews he'd given in the last couple of days. OK, so that's how he saw her. Someone to spin lines to. Deliver sound bites.

Ironically, that's when the journalist in her started to call the shots. Time to change the subject, make it personal and build up some trust. This guy intrigued her. His story read like a TV drama. Son of Mirren McLean and Jack Gore, both successful film-makers. OK, right now that might be stretching it a bit where Jack was concerned, but no one could deny he'd made a few great movies over the years. But back to the point. Son of success, brother to a dead sister claimed by drug abuse, grandson to a psychotic woman who may well be on the hunt, pop star, absolute hunk and all-round good guy – who just happened to be on her camera buying drugs in a Hollywood nightclub. That was a whole lot of baggage and a whole lot of stuff that wasn't adding up.

That meant there was a story here.

Softly-softly. 'I haven't had a chance to thank you yet for letting me come on tour. I appreciate it. It was so good of your mum to set it up. She's a great lady.'

Too much? She didn't want to come over as insincere or patronizing.

'Yep, she is.' He agreed without a hint of annoyance. Great. He was buying the friends act so far.

'You from the same city as her? Glasgow?'

'I am. You've never been?'

He shook his head. 'Mom never wanted to go. She's got no family left there. Both her parents are dead, so she always said it would be too hard. I get that.'

Sarah nodded. 'Me too.' His story backed up what Mirren had told her over lunch – Jack and Logan thought her parents were dead. That was going to take some explaining if Marilyn McLean waltzed back into their lives.

'I feel bad for her, y'know?' he said. 'She's had it about as crap as anyone could have it this last year and she doesn't deserve it. I know she's got Aunt Lou, but sometimes I feel bad she's got no other family to look out for her.'

There was a steely sadness in his eyes and Sarah suddenly realised that he saw this as his responsibility. Was it too much for him? Was that what the drugs were about? Were they an escape from the pressure?

'She's got Davie and Zander now too,' Sarah offered.

'Yeah, I guess. So are you gonna tell me what it was about?' Sarah had a horrible feeling this was about to go deep.

'What?' she asked breezily.

'Come on,' he flashed his poster grin, the one that made the screams notch up a few decibels every time. 'The whole "those guys growing up together and then not talking for twenty years" thing?'

Shit. She was the only one with no connection to the entertainment industry and yet she was the one who was having to put on a performance.

'Just drifted apart, I guess.'

'Nah, I'm not buying it.'

'Why?'

He thought about it for a moment. 'They're too connected to each other. It's not a casual thing. Something deep there. Just a vibe I'm feeling.'

She tried to deflect him with humour. 'Maybe you should be in my line of work, then. Investigative journalist. You know, if this gig you've got going on just now doesn't work out for you…'

She took advantage of his laughter to change the subject. 'Anyway, tell me more about you. Sorry, that sounded like a middle-aged sleazeball hitting on a chick who's way out of his league.'

'Thanks. Is it the fact I shave my legs?' he teased her, making her blush. Blush! Bloody hell. Sarah hadn't blushed since… since… Probably ever.

'And yet, despite the fact that I've just mortified myself, I'm going to keep on talking. So. You. Are you seeing anyone? I promise I'm not hitting on you! I was just thinking it might be tough to maintain a relationship with all this craziness.'

Logan rolled his shoulders one by one, easing out the stress. 'Kinda. Been seeing someone for a few weeks. Keeping it on the down-low, though, until we see where it's going.'

He hadn't said who it was, so he clearly didn't want her to know. No point in pushing – might put his defences up. Chill. Take it slow. Go sympathetic, empathetic.

'Must be hard with all the scrutiny. I don't envy you.'

He shrugged. 'She doesn't want the heat but I'm realistic about it. When we're selling this many records, people are going to be curious, want to make money off us in any way they can. If that means some dick is surfing in a dumpster looking for my trash, then hey, good for him. He's the one in the dumpster. Anyway, it won't last forever, and when it's gone, I'll probably miss it. Look at my dad...' He let that one trail off, but the implication was clear. Jack Gore, searching for any kind of profile or exposure he could get.

Sarah didn't respond, let the silence hang. It was a technique she'd used a thousand times over the years, on everyone from politicians to drug pushers. Eventually, they'd fill the silence, just like Logan was doing now.

'So you don't get shit from the paps when you're out with Davie?'

Sarah shook her head. 'I'm strictly an off-camera, under-the-radar kind of girl. We enter and leave everywhere separately, we don't do the gossip mags, and he knows if he mentions me in an interview, he'll incur a wrath that includes the words "idiotic" and "dick". I just don't want to be defined by him. Does that make sense? Damn, I sound like Gwyneth Paltrow. If I start talking about my inner power, point it out and I'll shoot myself.'

The car banked sharply to the left, then stopped suddenly. Outside, Sarah could see the tarmac at Montreal-Pierre Elliott Trudeau International Airport and the jet waiting, door open, stairs in position, bags being loaded into the hold.

Eli jumped out first, opened Logan's door and then accompanied him to the bottom of the steps. Sarah got herself out and trailed behind them. Obviously, in Eli's world, security trumped chivalry.

Only a few feet in front of her, she saw Logan speak closely into Eli's ear, then gesture towards the trailer containing the luggage. Eli nodded and peeled off.

The noise of banging doors disturbed the night as each car in the convoy slid to a stop and discharged its cargo. Sarah hoped Jonell was in one way at the back.

She followed Logan up the steps, watching from the corner of her eye as Eli spoke to the crew loading the luggage, then stepped forward to look closer at the cases as if searching for something.

On board, Logan walked to the table and chair set nearest the cockpit and slid into one of four caramel-coloured leather seats. Sarah had watched him do this every night so far. He would then open his laptop, pull on his Bose headphones and lose himself in the screen until he fell asleep.

Movies? Games? Conversations online? She made a mental note to establish what kept his attention for the hours in the air.

'Come sit with me,' he suggested, smiling. 'I'm not great company at night, but if you're there to protect me, I won't have to sleep with one eye open,' he joked.

Result.

'Are you sure?'

'Absolutely.'

Sarah almost felt bad that he seemed so open and trusting. With all this subterfuge and duplicity, she was never going to heaven.

Sliding into the bank of two seats across the table from Logan, she pulled her cross-body messenger bag over her head and dumped it on the seat beside her, then shrugged off her black leather bomber jacket. There was no squad of lackeys waiting on her hand and foot, so she'd quickly learned that it was best to carry everything she needed with her, allowing her main bag to travel with the rest of the crew's stuff. The Prada bag had been a gift from Davie – another month's rent – but Sarah cared less about the label and more about the fact that it was just big enough for her passport, purse, MacBook, notebook and phone. The outfit had become standard too. Black skinny jeans, a white, black or grey tank, leather jacket. Hopefully she was pulling off the balance between just enough rock chick and not so much that she looked desperately clichéd.

Right on cue, Logan reached up into the overhead locker and brought down a laptop and headphones, then booted up the laptop and slipped the headphones round his neck while it was loading.

One of the four flight attendants passed through the cabin with a tray of food and snacks, all of which were pre-arranged according to the band members' preferences. The South City rider could be a book chapter on its own, and no detail was overlooked. What these guys wanted, the universe duly delivered.

'Good evening,' the flight attendant greeted her, before her gaze went straight to the most important person at the table. 'Hi, Logan. Can I get you anything?'

'Just water and a couple of bananas, thanks.'

Only when she'd passed them over did she almost grudgingly turn to Sarah, making a half-hearted effort to make her smile look genuine.

'Anything for you?'

'Coke, please. And one of those muffins.'

'Here you go. Full dinner service will commence as soon as soon as we're in the air, Logan.'

'Yeah, thanks,' he said, as she moved further down the aisle. At the same moment, there was a burst of activity at the back of the plane and Sarah looked to see Jonell, his bodyguard, his assistant and Deeko come on board. Despite Jonell's obvious resistance, Deeko directed him into the back booth and wasn't taking no for an answer.

Sarah turned back and caught Logan's eye and a flicker of what? Sadness? Annoyance?

'Everything OK?' she asked, while her inner voice screamed, *What the hell is all that about?*

Logan smiled casually. 'Don't worry about it. It's nothing.'

It most certainly didn't look like nothing from where she was sitting.

They were heading back down the East Coast, so they'd be in the air for a couple of hours. That had to be enough time to get some kind of insight.

The head of security moved through the plane checking everyone was accounted for and there were no unexpected guests. When he returned to the front, he nodded to the head flight attendant, differentiated by the smart jacket over the standard blouse and neck scarf, who then disappeared into the cockpit.

They'd be taking off soon and this was looking good. Logan on one side of the table, Sarah on the other, a couple of hours in a confined space. She saw Logan's eyes dart to the side, a question written on his face, until Eli slid in beside her, pushed a red wash bag across the table.

'Your toiletries, Logan.'

There was no mistaking the subtle but definite exhalation of relief. Sarah's story senses began to tingle. He was having that reaction over shower gel and shampoo? Seemed highly unlikely. Eli got back up and headed to the rear of the jet, while Logan pulled the bag down onto the seat next to him.

Sarah just had to be patient. He was bound to nod off at some point. And as soon as his eyes were closed, all she had to do was find out what kind of baggage he was actually carrying.

33

Sometimes it's like an actual physical pain.

Loss. Hurt. Alone. Forgotten.

People hit you with fucked-up clichés. Time heals. Life goes on.

I want to take them, holding them by the back of the neck, and slam their faces into a wall until there's only pulp and bone, and then ask them if time fucking heals. Move on, you faceless cunt, move on. And stop bleeding on my fucking floor.

Today I'm OK.

Today I'm on track.

Knowing what's ahead helps. Gives me something to hang on to.

Time doesn't heal – you have to heal yourself. And if someone takes something away from you, the only person who can right the wrong is you, no matter how long it takes.

I'm patient.

I've waited.

I'll wait longer.

Because I know. Time will heal.

The faceless cunt will bleed on the floor.

And I'll move on.

34

MIRREN

'Trouble' – Ray LaMontagne

On the outside, her appearance said, 'Cosmopolitan, wealthy, successful businesswoman.' On the inside, her feelings said, 'I'd rather have my internal organs removed with a blunt scalpel than go through with this today.'

The Mercedes-AMG's computer told her it was a balmy 75 degrees as she signalled left, steering off Wilshire and onto North Robertson Boulevard. She was driving more slowly than necessary, reluctant to reach the destination and conscious of the pounding pain in her right temple. It had been there for days now. In fact, she could pinpoint the rough time it flared – somewhere between punching Davie and getting home a few nights ago.

Just thinking about that conversation made her gut twist. What the hell was wrong with him? How could he do that to her? She wanted to cut the shadow of Jack Gore from her life and move on, and yet now, thanks to her former love, she was going to have to see bloody billboards of her ex-husband when she was driving down Sunset. What a fricking farce.

Davie had always been impulsive, thoughtless, short-sighted when it came to other people's feelings, but it came from a place of innocence and immaturity. Well, not now. The man was forty-bloody-two – those excuses no longer stood.

Yet, somehow, looking back on that conversation, what really hurt her wasn't that Jack wanted to do a show, that he'd shacked up with some twenty-five-year-old model, that he didn't have the decency to let his son know... Nope, none of that. What hurt her most was that Davie had kept it from her. She didn't believe for a second that he hadn't considered her thoughts on this – he'd just chosen not to let anything get in the way of making this show. The profit was more important to him than she was. And that – after everything they'd been through – stung more than anything else.

The flash and ring of her in-car communications system flagged up an incoming call. She checked the screen on the dash. Mike Feechan. Oh sweet joy, this day was just getting better and better.

Since their night together and subsequent meeting, he'd called and he'd texted. She'd ignored both. If her life was a movie, sleeping with Mike would be a scene that was left on the cutting-room floor. Mistake. Physically enjoyable at the time, but an error nonetheless. And if he thought the fact that they'd hooked up would make her roll over and surrender on the deal, he was very much mistaken. Wasn't gonna happen.

As she pulled into the kerb outside The Ivy, she could already see that the restaurant had delivered on the request she'd made when she'd asked Perry to book the table. Behind the kerbside white picket fence, at the most prominent table, sat Wes Lomax, in full view of the paparazzi parked on the opposite side of the street. Mirren knew they'd be itching to find out who he was meeting. She was also aware, without a doubt, that Wes would know exactly what she was up to. He was a master at playing this game.

The valet opened her car door, handed over a ticket and then stood to the side before taking her place in the driver's seat and driving the car off to park it. Across the road, the back doors of three black SUVs suddenly opened, and the vehicles vomited out a collective flash mob of paparazzi, who'd spotted her through the blacked-out windows and put two and two together. This was an unexpected couple. Wes Lomax. Mirren McLean. She could see how the speculation would play out, could predict the chain of thoughts on the grapevine. Wes and Mirren? Definitely not a romance. Wes Lomax liked them younger, subservient and double-jointed – which was why two twenty-three-year-old former members of an Eastern European Olympic gymnastic squad were right now happily ensconced in his home, lying partially naked on his sofa, practising English by watching *Friends* reruns and porn. Could that *be* any more wrong?

Besides, rumour had it that Mirren and Zander Leith had a thing going. In fact, there were many stories and rumours, some with no basis in fact.

They grew up together back in Glasgow and had been friends, like, forever.

Nope, I don't think so. I heard they split and she was seeing Davie Johnston.

The guy off American Stars?

Yep. My friend's cousin is married to a publicist who knows an actress who's sleeping with a guy who was having dinner in some flash Beverly Hills restaurant last week and he, like, totally, was eating her face and then they had a fight and she emptied a glass of wine over his head. That totally happened.

Mmmm. OK. So if they're not a couple, then it must be work.

Oh my God, did you, like, ever see The Brutal Circle? *She wrote that movie and it was, like, epic. Best movie ever. I saw it sixteen times in college.*

Yeah, and that was a Lomax movie. OMG, that's it! They're going to make another movie together. Bet it's one of those ones with the Scottish guy. You know, in the skirt. The Clansman? *Yeah, that's it!*

It so is.... National Enquirer? I've heard first-hand that Mirren McLean and Wes Lomax are gonna make a new movie together. It's about a guy in a skirt... No, not a cross-dresser.

Yep, that's how it would undoubtedly play out. She was counting on it.

Shoulders back, posture impeccable thanks to years of Pilates, Mirren widened her smile as she reached the table.

'Wes! So great to see you.'

'Mirren McLean, it's been too long. Darling, you look terrific,' he said, loud enough to be heard in neighbouring zip codes.

Hugs over, she slid into the seat nearest him, so that they were sitting at right angles. It made it much more likely that the paps would get them both in the frame if they were huddled close together. Sitting across from each other ran the risk that one or the other could be cut out of the shot.

As Mirren placed her phone and Aspinal Manhattan clutch on the table, a waiter appeared to take their drinks orders. It was on the tip of her tongue to request her usual still water, room temperature, no ice, when she suddenly changed her mind.

'Wes, after twenty years, I think this little get-together should be celebrated.'

Of course, he sussed that out immediately, and his cheeky grin told her he liked her style. 'Champagne, darling?'

'Absolutely.'

The waiter retreated to the bar, leaving menus for their perusal. They both ignored them, having no need to check what was available. This was Hollywood. Everyone had a lunchtime dish that their nutritionist, dietician, personal trainer, shrink or life coach approved of, and they didn't vary from that choice. Ordering off menu wasn't so much a regular occurrence as a national sport.

Wes leaned forward, hands clasped on the table. He was looking good, Mirren decided. Obviously whatever he was doing with the Olympic gymnasts was working for him. At sixty-something, he had the physique of a man who still trained on a daily basis. He hadn't succumbed to cosmetic tweaks or obvious hair dye, so he had that slightly older, natural, George Clooney-esque thing going on. And of course, he still had that twinkle of raucous mischief in his eye.

'So. Twenty-odd years. You don't write, you don't call...' he chided her.

Mirren laughed, maintaining a façade that bore no relation to how she was actually feeling. Outside, carefree and jovial. Inside, head pounding a little harder. 'I know. You're right. I'm sorry. I got sidetracked along the way,' she answered with mock apology. 'Forgive me?'

Wes cracked another grin, this one a slight leer. 'Forgiven. But only because you're beautiful.'

Mirren gave him a look of reproach. 'Wes, add up your girlfriends' ages and you might get into my ballpark. I'm way too old for you, and you're way too old for me.'

His roar of laughter could be heard across the street. More fodder for the grapevine.

'OK, so what are they holding back on?'

Mirren knew exactly what he was asking, but she decided to string it along. 'Who and what?'

The waiter appeared with their drinks and they paused the conversation until he'd departed.

'Cheers,' Wes toasted, clinking his glass against hers. The click of the paps' shutters was frantic. Champagne at lunchtime. That very rarely happened outside of Charlie Sheen's house. The rumour that she and Wes both had alcohol issues would be a footnote on the *Enquirer* piece.

Wes cut back to the conversation. 'OK, here's how I see it, and tell me if I'm close.'

Mirren would bet her AMG that he'd read the situation pretty much perfectly.

'Despite many attempts on my part, you haven't sat down with me in over twenty years. So I'm guessing that means Pictor are holding back or attempting to change the terms of your deal. It wouldn't be at your instigation, because you're too loyal for that.'

So far, so perceptive. Mirren took a sip of champagne and continued to listen.

'I'm thinking it's either production budget or merchandise.' He pondered that for a few seconds before making his choice. 'Production budget. They're hurting and they want to take 5 per cent off the last movie's costs.'

'Merchandise,' Mirren said with a grin.

'Damn! Must be losing my touch.'

'Never,' Mirren countered.

'OK, so they want to up their cut of the merch profit and you're resisting. They won't budge, so you decide to go for a high-profile lunch with the rival that will scare the shit out of them on two counts: one, they'll know I want *Clansman* at Lomax, and two, we have history, so you're more likely to move to me. They'll think I'm attempting to poach you and capitulate on the terms.'

Mirren realised that she'd been absolutely right to do this. He got it. He was actually enjoying it. The champagne bubbles soothed her pounding head just a little.

'Doing good so far,' Mirren cajoled.

'But the truth is that you have absolutely no intention of coming to Lomax at all.'

'None,' Mirren agreed.

'And you knew that I'd already have this sussed before we sat down.'

'I did.'

Wes roared with laughter again. 'I'd swap my girlfriends for you anytime. Just say the word.'

'I won't,' Mirren told him, going for somewhere between charming and amusing. 'But now that I'm here and we both know where we stand, I wouldn't mind having lunch with an old mentor, if that's OK with you?'

Wes raised his glass in toast once again. 'That's fine with me, honey. But let me tell you, I do want you back at Lomax and I want the future *Clansman* movies there. I've waited a long time for it, and I've been patient because I know that loyalty is important to you. But if you ever genuinely want to think about leaving that crowd of incompetents at Pictor, I'll be waiting at the bank.'

'Thanks, Wes. I appreciate that.'

The waiter returned to take their order – two ten-ounce Kobe New York strip steaks, both medium rare, broccoli, spinach and sauce on the side.

They passed the next hour with industry gossip and Wes's recklessly indiscreet insider stories about things that were going on in the town. The action star who still hadn't left his wife despite the fact that he'd been having an affair with his male manager for over five years now. The ageing actress who was currently in a Beverly Hills clinic having the butt implants she'd had inserted in the Dominican Republic removed because one had exploded. The British ex-soccer player who was screwing at least six of the moms on his kid's little league team bench.

Outrageous, but in Wes's twisted hands, utterly hilarious.

They'd switched from champagne to coffees when Wes's face had a glimmer of sadness. 'You know, I'm sure glad I was mostly right about why you wanted to see me today. It did cross my mind that you might want to plead Zander's case.'

'Plead Zander's case for what?' she asked, puzzled.

Before he could answer, her phone buzzed to signal an incoming text. Her hand moved to switch it off when she noticed the name of the sender.

Brad Bernson.
'Excuse me a second, Wes. I need to check this.'
'No worries. I'm just heading to the washroom.'
As soon as he'd left the table, she held up her phone, opened the text.

Confirmed. Marilyn McLean entered the US on 10 January 2014. Flew London Heathrow to LAX. Hired black GMC at airport. Present whereabouts unknown. Request permission to recruit additional investigators to track.

Her stomach threatened to collapse and her hands automatically began to shake.
Breathe. She had to breathe. Had to make her fingers work.

Do what you need to do. Any cost. Find her now.

Her trembling thumb pressed 'send'. Her instincts had been spot on. The woman on the beach when they were commemorating Chloe's birthday. The wave of utter dread that came upon her when Sarah mentioned her name. A sick, niggling feeling that was there every time she pictured her mother's face. It wasn't the face of now. It was Marilyn's face from twenty years ago. Now? Mirren had no idea what she looked like. She could be sitting at a nearby table on The Ivy's patio and Mirren would be entirely oblivious. Instinctively, she scanned the other diners, then exhaled. All too young, too male or too famous. Thank God. But that didn't mean she wasn't out there somewhere, across the street perhaps, just watching, waiting. Oh fuck, Logan!
Mirren immediately forwarded the text to Sarah with a supplementary;

Watch over my boy – alert the band's security.

She'd call her as soon as she got out of here too. In fact, she wanted to get out of here now. The job was done. Mission accomplished. The news would undoubtedly already have reached Pictor that Mirren was being courted by Wes Lomax. Wes was taking his time getting back to the table and she could see him stopping to shake hands with half the diners at the inside tables. She summoned the waiter and hurriedly paid the bill. There was no way she was letting him pick up the check. This was her deal, and there was every chance the cash benefit of today's lunch was going to have many more zeros than the cost of two steaks. Although in truth, she couldn't give a rat's ass about percentages and profit right now. All she cared about was getting the hell out of there so she could think.

He finally slid back into his chair and she summoned every ounce of self-discipline she had to cover up the fear and act like nothing was wrong. Just another five minutes, then she could switch her full focus to the Marilyn situation.

'Wes, thank you for today. I have to get back to the office.'

'No worries, m'darlin'. Mirren, I was serious when I said I want you at Lomax. I'll beat your deal. When you're ready. Anytime.'

'Thanks, Wes.' Lifting her purse and phone from the table, she was about to stand when his last comment sprang back into her mind.

'Wes, what did you say before about Zander?'

'About pleading his case?'

'Yeah, that's it. Why would I want to plead his case? Something happened?'

Wes leaned forward to ensure confidentiality for the first time in the last hour. Mirren immediately realised that didn't bode well. If the most indiscreet alpha male in Hollywood wanted to keep something secret, it must be seriously bad.

'Listen, this is between you and me. Wanna keep it quiet. Although, it won't stay that way for long,' he said pragmatically.

That sick, queasy feeling was gripping Mirren's stomach for a second time.

'He failed his drug test. Cocaine.'

If he'd announced that Zander had just walked bollock naked down Beverly Drive and announced his candidacy for president, she couldn't have been more shocked. No. It just couldn't be. He wouldn't.

'Wes, that's got to be a mistake.'

Wes shook his head. 'Honey, that's what I've said every time I've pulled him out of a clinic or a cell. Look, it breaks my heart. We've been together for a long time. But sometimes you just have to face facts. The guy's an addict. He's always been an addict, he will always be one, and we ain't gonna change that.'

No. No. No. No. She struggled to process.

'Wes, he's not now. I know how bad it was, but you don't get it. He promised Chloe, and he'd never break that. He can't be using again.'

It was the pity in his eyes that caused her heart to crack. 'Mirren, I know it's hard, and I know what you've been through, but I had the sample tested twice. This isn't a mistake. Ask yourself how many times you've seen this before.'

The crash just became a full-scale breakage. He was right. Time after time after time Chloe made promises, swore she was clean, vowed that she'd never touch the stuff again. And every single time she lied. Every time. That's what addicts did.

She'd believed Zander, she truly had. But medical drug tests didn't lie. If he was using again, she didn't want him anywhere near her for two reasons: she would despise him for betraying his promise to Chloe, and she couldn't love him in case she lost him to an overdose of poison. She couldn't lose another piece of her heart or grieve for another soul.

Zander Leith and Davie Johnston, the two guys – after Logan – that she'd loved more than any others, had only just come back into her life.

Now she knew that she couldn't let either of them stay.

35

ZANDER

'Don't Give Up' – Kate Bush & Peter Gabriel

The Santa Monica cliffs rose high over Bungalow 1 at the Fairmont Miramar Hotel on the corner of Ocean Avenue. It was a paradoxical view. Turn one way and glance over the calm blue seas of the Pacific Ocean; glance in the other direction and your eyes met the towering force of nature that was the mountains.

Right now, Zander was neither looking nor impressed with either. Instead, he was sitting on the whitewashed steps outside the bungalow, smoking a cigarette and nursing a double espresso purchased from a drive-through Starbucks on the way here.

Living the dream.

Hollie, sitting shoulder to shoulder with him, leaned over, removed the cigarette from his hands, took a long, satisfying puff on it, then handed it back.

'You don't smoke,' Zander pointed out.

'I'm starting,' Hollie replied. 'I've come to the conclusion that the only way to deal with this life and you is to imbibe as many chemical substances and cocktails as possible. Excuse the irony in that statement.'

Despite himself, he smiled, then leaned over and nudged her. 'Thanks for believing me. I can't decide whether that makes you loyal or deranged.'

'I think definitely both. But you know if I had any doubt at all, I'd kick your ass.'

He didn't doubt it for a second. In the car home after the meeting with Wes, he'd had one priority – making Hollie believe him.

As soon as the doors were closed, he'd turned to her and spoken slowly and calmly. 'I didn't use.'

At first, she didn't reply.

He repeated, 'I. Didn't. Use.'

Her gaze had locked on his. 'I know. I believe you.'

The strange thing was, he knew that this time she did. She had no reason to trust anything he said. God knows, he'd lied to her before, usually right before she found him lying upside down in a pool of his own vomit beside a dumpster in a strip club's alley.

'Why?'

'Because if you were using, then right now you'd be ranting and raging and you'd probably have punched at least one wall on your way out. You get crazy defensive when you're guilty. But more than that, I've watched you every day since Chloe died and I know that even when you want to get completely wasted, she stops you. I think she always will.'

The uncharacteristic lump in his throat had prevented him from answering. All he'd wanted to do was reach over and hug her. He had no idea what he'd done in life to deserve Hollie Callan being a part of it, but he was so, so grateful. His anxiety level plummeted. She was there; she believed him; he didn't need to say another word. Instead, he'd started up the car and pulled out of the lot, completely silent. Eventually, Hollie cracked.

'Zander, we need to do something about this. Obviously it's a mistake. A huge, great, freaking big mistake. We need to get people on it, question it, get it sorted out.'

'No.'

'What?'

'Forget it.'

'Forget it?'

Hollie had looked at him like he'd gone completely crazy. It might have been close to the truth. It was more than that, though. He was seething at the injustice of it and the fact that Wes hadn't even given him the benefit of the doubt. Fuck that. They didn't want him? Fine. He'd move on. He had enough money to last him ten lifetimes, and let's face it, the twenty years he'd spent in this business hadn't exactly brought him happiness and fulfilment. All that mattered was that the people he cared about knew the truth. But as for the movie bullshit?

Enough.

He was done.

And suddenly, that didn't feel like such a bad thing.

'Oh, here we go,' Hollie had exclaimed, throwing her hands up in the air.

Zander wasn't following. 'What?'

Hollie was the one who switched straight to rant-and-rage mode. 'You and your strong, silent, pride bullshit. I know what you're thinking. You're thinking that if they don't believe you, they can go fuck themselves.'

When no argument was forthcoming, she'd ploughed on. 'But it's not that simple, Zander. If they cancel you, the word will go out that you're using again and your career won't survive the backlash.'

'I don't care. I'm done,' he'd replied calmly.

'Oh, cut the big, butch nonsense. I believe you're clean, Zander, but after this, the rest of the world won't. You think anyone will give Downey Jr another chance if he fucks up again? Mel Gibson? Come on, you know how it works. If this gets out, there's no coming back for you. And if you want to walk away from this life, then fine. No problems. But do it on your own terms, not because of some lie or fuck-up that we can't explain.'

It made sense. He knew it did. But weariness had consumed him. Nothing was where it should be. Nothing was bringing him happiness. At that moment, he'd just wanted to keep on driving, see where he ended up. Just keep going until this cloud lifted from his shoulders and he felt he was somewhere he wanted to be.

Mirren.

Why had he thought of her at that moment?

He had to tell her about this, but how could he? Didn't she have enough going on right now? For no other reason than for her, he needed to prove that he hadn't taken drugs, hadn't let down her daughter.

'OK, I'm buying it, but, Hollie, whatever way this rolls out, I'm done with this. I'm over this business. I hear you on the drug test, though – we need to find out why it's messed up.'

'Hallelujah.' Hollie had immediately snatched her phone and dialled the number of Zander's lawyer, routing it through the Bluetooth system on the DB7 so that it was on hands-free. For his sins, Bernard Edwards had been on Zander's payroll for a decade, the different divisions of his company handling everything from assault charges, past and present, to false paternity accusations, contracts and negotiations.

'Hollie Callan,' Bernard had stated the obvious. 'What can I do for you?'

'It's not good when your number is pre-programmed into a lawyer's phone,' Hollie had observed, laughing, 'Sorry to call you so late – and no, he's not in jail.'

'So you just pre-empted my next question,' Bernard had replied.

'Is this a bad time to tell you you're on speaker and Zander is here?'

'There goes my Christmas bonus. Hi, Zander. Sorry about that, but I'm guessing you're not calling me at this late hour because all's going well in your life.'

He had a point.

'If only. Listen, Bernie, here's what's happened.'

He'd outlined the situation, Wes's reaction and his own response.

Bernard listened in silence, except for the rustling of paper as he flicked over a page in his notebook. He famously took handwritten notes of every meeting and phone call.

'Leave it with me. I'll get the guys on it now. We'll have a writ on Lomax within the hour demanding complete confidentiality on the test results and on your contract termination, and we'll also secure the test results, clinic details and analysis so our own people can look into it. Do you want to use your own investigators, or shall we use ours?'

'Go with your guys – keep it all in-house,' Zander had told him.

'We don't want any of this getting anywhere near the press,' Hollie had added.

'If it does, it won't be from our end. However, the confidentiality writ doesn't guarantee there won't be a leak at Lomax – just means they can't publicly announce it. Look, we'll come down heavy, lay it on thick, protest innocence, wrongful accusations et cetera. Hopefully, that'll be enough to keep a lid on it until we find out what's going on. I'll keep you posted.'

'Thanks. Appreciate it.'

Hollie had cut the call. 'OK, I'm feeling like we're being productive here. Argh, I'm fricking furious. How can this happen, Zander? I don't get it. How can a negative test somehow turn into a positive one?'

Zander had pulled up and stopped at a red light on Pico. 'Mistake. Wrong label. Contamination. Could be any one of loads of reasons, I guess.'

'And you don't think the timing is strange?'

'What timing? Oh, here we go. You have a conspiracy theory. I'm a grassy knoll.'

'Come on. Your apartment gets trashed one day, positive drug test another? It's like we're in the middle of a really bad movie and you're next to die.'

'Shit happens.'

'Not like that it doesn't. I don't know. Just feels off. I want to get to the bottom of it. I'm gonna talk to Bernard about that too. Get his guys to dig around.'

'Right, then, Nancy Drew.' He'd turned right onto Ocean Drive and headed towards the Fairmont Miramar. Hollie had offered to let him stay with her until they got his place straightened out, and while his first instinct had been to accept, his second was to refuse on the grounds that he infringed on her life enough. Hadn't she already said she was dating? Going out? The last thing she needed was Zander sitting on the couch when she came home with some dude.

Easiest thing had been to check into a bungalow at the Fairmont, where he had the mountains behind him, the ocean in front of him, and he could be on a board up at Zuma in fifteen minutes. He'd only been there a couple of nights, but so far, so bearable.

At the hotel, he and Hollie had jumped out of the car, then she'd walked round and took his place in the driver's seat. Sometimes it was easier for her to take the DB7 home and collect him in the morning. If she left it up to him, they were invariably late. Not that they had anywhere to go now.

Unemployed. Disgraced. Wrongfully accused.

As he'd crashed out to sleep that night, his last thought was that he really didn't give a fuck.

Now, in the morning light a couple of days later, his feelings hadn't changed. For the first time in decades, he'd had a couple of sober, work-free, interruption-free days to really think about his life, and much as deep introspection wasn't his thing, he knew he should care that it had all gone to hell. But fuck that. Look at his life: what did he have to show for it? No kids, no marriage – the longest relationship he'd had would be considered a short-term romance in anyone else's relationship book. He'd never travelled – unless it was to a location shoot or to the premiere of a Dunhill movie. Even then, he'd fly in a couple of days before the premiere for press junkets and straight back out after the screening. He'd been to Tokyo, Sydney, London, Johannesburg, Shanghai, Rio, Paris and Rome, and he'd never seen anything other than the inside of a hotel or limo.

As promised, Bernard Edwards had filed a wrongful termination case against Lomax, and Zander saw Hollie's point about leaving on his own terms, but the truth was, it still didn't matter. Would it bring Adrianna to him? She'd made it perfectly clear that she wanted him only when it was convenient for her and he was a bit too old and too wise to be someone's bitch. Had his movie career brought him any other long-term happiness or fulfilment? No. It was a job.

Beside him on the step, Hollie took his cigarette off him for the second time and inhaled deeply. 'No word yet on the tests. Bernard's people are on it, though.'

'Cool.'

'Cool? Is that it?' she replied, her irritation obvious.

'What's up with "cool"?'

'Because it's not fricking cool. None of it is. I don't get this, Zander – I just don't get why you don't care. Is it because of her?'

He knew she meant Adrianna but was being bloody-minded by not saying her name.

'I don't know,' he answered honestly. 'I just know that I'm finally sober, after all these years and now that I'm seeing things with a clear head, I'm not sure it's what I want. Fuck, I sound like a spoilt brat.'

'You do,' she agreed. 'But you're—' Her words were interrupted by the ringing of a cell phone. Hollie checked the two phones sitting on the side table. 'It's yours.'

She looked at the screen, then immediately adopted an expression of concern. 'It's Mirren. Have you told her yet? You need to tell her.'

'I will.'

He pressed 'Accept'. 'Hey, Mirren.'

She didn't even open with a 'hello'. 'You failed a drug test.'

A statement, not a question. 'Yeah, but—'

'Don't fucking dare give me an excuse, Zander. You promised.'

He could hear she was crying the kind of tears that came from rage and anger, and the realization that he had made her feel like that confirmed his suspicions that he was the biggest prick on the planet.

'Mirren, it was a mistake. An error. We've got people investigating it.'

Her laugh was thick with scorn. 'Really, Zander? That's all you could come up with? It was a mistake? How many times have I heard that? A mistake.'

Now she just sounded weary and devastated and stressed. Really, really stressed.

'I believed you. I really did.'

'Mirr—'

'Oh fuck off, Zander. Stay away from me. I've had enough of liars to last a lifetime.'

Snap.

Hollie came out of the bungalow carrying two glasses of soda and saw his face. 'Shit, what happened? What did she say?'

Snap.

The synapses in his brain couldn't connect to formulate an answer. He was too focused on the two glasses...

Snap.
On the cravings that had suddenly overtaken his mind and body.
Snap.
And he knew. He absolutely, definitely knew that he needed to top up the soda with Jack Daniel's.

36

SARAH

'Somebody's Watching Me' – Rockwell

Another day, another city. And much as she was reluctant to admit it, Sarah's enthusiasm for the road was beginning to wear thin. How pathetic was that? The glimmer of her rock-star life was tarnishing faster than a Stratocaster in a storm.

There had been New York, Toronto, Ottawa, Montreal, back to New York and now they were working their way down the eastern Seaboard. New Jersey. Philadelphia. Baltimore. Washington DC.

One upside was that the rest of the crew had stopped treating her like a stranger and started to treat her like she was just another one of the team. It was a positive move, made them less wary around her, made them drop their inhibitions. She knew now that Ringo was having a full-blown affair with one of the dancers, whose boyfriend worked on the crew as a light technician. Unlike Ringo and the dancer, Sarah also knew that the lighting technician had been aware of the affair from the start and was hoping it would burn itself out. She really wanted to advise Ringo to avoid standing directly under a rig.

She'd also learned that Jonell was the prima donna of the group, the irrational, quick-tempered, aggressive pain in the ass who found fault with everything and let everyone know he wasn't happy.

She'd discovered that Lincoln and D'Arby had been a couple for years and were already planning to move to Europe when the band was over. They reckoned they had another five years at the top, max, before the next big thing shuffled in wearing matching outfits and moving in choreographed synchronicity. But it was the stuff she'd discovered about Logan that had puzzled her most. That red bag never left his side, other than when he was at a stadium or on stage, when he'd give it to Eli, who'd then plant it somewhere until after the show. It was driving her crazy and she needed to know what was in it. She'd considered everything from stealing it to setting it on fire. The enigmatic Eli was puzzling her too. Most afternoons at some point, he'd disappear, and when he returned, a look would pass between him and Logan, a question asked, answered, an exhalation of relief.

There was a knock before Deeko's assistant, Ashika, popped her head round the dressing-room door. 'Half an hour, Logan. You all good?'

'All good,' Logan replied, spitting the words out in time to the bicep curls he was doing in front of the mirror. Sarah had realised it wasn't through vanity. He was a switched-on cookie, this guy. He understood that the way he looked was part of his job and he worked at it. A five-mile run every day. Weights in the morning. A top-up session to pump him up before he went on stage.

On the sofa, Sarah lay tapping on her MacBook. Since that night on the plane, Logan had been happy for her to hang with him before and after the shows. In truth, Sarah could see the irony of fame. The bigger you got, and they didn't get much bigger than South City, the more you were given. The boys each had their own dressing rooms at every arena; they travelled separately in their own cars; they had their own assistants and bodyguards. But the flip side of that was that they didn't spend much off-stage time with the only other people who understood the lives they were leading.

A text pinged in on her phone. Mirren.

All OK? No sign?

None. Don't worry.

In the first couple of days, she'd sent long, chatty texts back, but she'd soon realised that all Mirren really needed to know was that Logan was safe, especially now they'd established that Marilyn was in the country.

Thank God tonight was the last night before a week-long break that would take them back to LA. With every day that passed without the investigators locating Marilyn, Sarah felt more uneasy about Davie not knowing she'd come back from obscurity. She was going to speak to Mirren when they landed back in California. It was time to tell Davie, and if Mirren didn't do it, then Sarah would. In the meantime, Mark Bock, Davie's head of security, had been updating her daily on the situation and there had been no more security breaches. Somehow that felt like the calm before the storm. Or maybe she'd just been watching too many episodes of 24 to pass the time she spent hanging out in dressing rooms.

'Looking forward to getting back to LA?' she asked Logan as he finished his reps.

'I can't even tell you how much,' he whistled, dropping the 10-kilogram barbells to the floor. 'I'll miss ya, though,' he said with a wink.

'Understandable. I'm the best dressing-room ornament ever.'

A dressing-room ornament that still hadn't found anything out. Nearly two weeks of her life wasted. For what? Nothing. Sure, it was another chapter in the book, but it wasn't anything that would set the world on fire. She'd tried to dig into the beef between Logan and Jonell, but everyone had just glossed over it. Put it down to tempers fraying on the road. She'd grilled Deeko, Ashika, the sound guys, the roadies, but if there was a long-standing problem between the guys, no-one was talking. There had been no more signs of Logan getting up to anything untoward. And she was no expert, but he never seemed high and she'd never seen even a physical tell that he was using. Did he only do drugs when he wasn't on the road? Is that why he was buying gear in the club. Was it only for recreational use? This wasn't making sense. There had to be more going on here, but if she didn't find out what it was tonight, she was done. Epic fail.

'I'm just gonna hit the shower and get suited,' Logan told her. It was her cue to go. Usually she'd head out to the side of the stage, find a good position to watch from, chat to the wardrobe staff, who were already up there, setting up the costume changes.

A thought struck her. She knew what she did for the next half-hour, but what did Logan do? The decision was made before she even got to her feet.

It was risky. Stupid. If he found out, it would destroy every shred of trust between them, but she never got a story by considering the 'what if?'s.

As soon as she heard the shower go on, she flicked her phone to silent, clicked through to the video function, pressed 'record', then slipped it behind a cushion on the sofa, so that only the tiny pinhole of the camera peeked out.

Heart thudding, she got up and left the room. Fifty yards down the corridor, though, she changed her mind, turned, started running. Almost there. He'd still be in the shower. He'd never know. Ten yards. Just about there. Bugger, why did Logan's dressing room need to be the very last one in the corridor? Five yards. Four. She was aware of someone coming round the corner in front of her from the other direction, moving towards her.

Three. Two.

But it didn't matter. Because the person in front of her was Eli, and he now had his hand on the door of Logan's dressing room and was looking at her quizzically. 'You OK?' he asked.

No. Just no. Really not OK.

'Sure,' she said breezily. 'I'm just...' Just what? OK, choices. She could say she'd left something in the dressing room, but there was a risk he'd attempt to help her find it. Not good.

She could... She could... Oh crap. She tried to remember where the exit at this side of the corridor took her. Maintenance? Front exit? He wouldn't believe she had a reason to go there.

'Running. I'm feeling like a slob with all the craft services and room service, so I'm just running some of it off. See you later.'

With that, she turned and jogged back the way she'd come. Halfway down the corridor, she briefly turned round, to see he was still there. And by the look on his face, it was obvious that he didn't believe a word she'd just said.

Stomach clenching with panic, she headed up to the side of the stage and waited. And waited. Half an hour had never seemed so long. A lifetime later, the lights changed, the crowd roared, and the band appeared, ran past her, down the steps to the hydraulic lift under the stage. They all stepped in. The crowd roared louder. The anticipation escalated. The atmosphere in the Verizon Centre crackled with a tornado of hormones and excitement as South City rose through the floor, culminating in a scream that was high on the noise-pollution scale.

It had to be now. It was going to be the only chance she had. After the concert, they'd head straight from the stage to the car. Shit, she hadn't thought this through.

Surreptitiously checking around her, she saw Eli standing twenty feet away in deep conversation with Jonell's bodyguard. Now. It had to be now.

Keeping close to the shadows of the wall, she slipped away, left the side stage area, took the stairs down to the lower floor two at a time, retraced her steps, ran along the corridor, got to Logan's dressing room and—

'Jogging again?'

Eli had appeared from the other side of the corridor for the second time. How the fuck did he do that? And oh crap. Oh fucking crap.

This wasn't good. Bluff or fess up? Bluff or fess up? Bluff or...? Bluff.

'Ah, no, not this time,' she said with too much forced jollity. 'I think I left my phone in Logan's dressing room. Just came back to check.'

'I'll help you look,' he responded dryly. Bluff called.

He opened the door and waved her in. As she passed, she wondered if he could see that the hairs on the back of her neck were standing on end.

OK, play this properly. She immediately headed for the sofa, but played it cool, scanning the room as if searching, while positioning herself so that he couldn't get to the phone first. 'Nope, I can't see it.'

She really couldn't. It wasn't there. Fuck! Where was it? Eli had already found it. Right now, he was staring at her like that because he knew exactly where her phone was, exactly what she'd tried to do and exactly how he was going to dispose of her body.

But then... 'Oh, here it is!' The level of relief was way disproportional, more on a level of saving a child from a burning building or pushing someone out of the path of a speeding car. She snatched it up, the motion making the screen come alive, so she quickly turned it, pressed it towards her body, then stepped to the door. Eli didn't move.

He was still in the doorway, eyes still trained on her. 'You're sure that's it?' he asked, obviously expecting her to do the normal thing and look at it again to check. From the angle he was standing at, he'd have full view of the screen.

'Positive,' she said breezily. He still didn't move.

He was blocking her path. He had no intention of moving, and his face was a mask of cool suspicion.

The time for bluffs was over.

He knew she was up to something she shouldn't be.

If he asked to check the phone, he'd soon discover she'd been filming Logan, which, as well as being wrong on every level, was probably illegal.

He just needed to ask and it was over. The question was, would he?

37

DAVIE

'Eight Letters' – Gary Barlow

Davie was on his way to do something he really didn't want to do.

It sparked a flashback to when he was a little kid and his mother would bribe him to do things he didn't like doing. The dentist. The doctor. Working hard at school. The reward was always the same. They'd get the bus into Glasgow and they'd go to the cinema to see the movie of his choice. Twice a year, maybe three times if he was lucky. They didn't have the cash for that kind of thing, but sometimes if Ena had picked up a bit of extra casual work, or got a bonus from one of her three cleaning jobs, the multiplex was his oyster. And he loved it.

Now his movie-viewing experience was slightly different. He watched them on his home cinema, a $200k exercise in indulgence, with a bar, a permanently stocked popcorn maker, reclining leather chairs and sofas, and any title he wanted to see, whether they'd been released yet or not.

That was the kind of pull Davie Johnston had in this town. And that's exactly where he wanted to be now. Lying in the dark, escapism on the screen, his mind anywhere but here.

The truth was, he couldn't put it off any longer.

He'd been avoiding it for months. Stalling. Deferring. Until now.

The pool at the Fairmont Miramar had a gaggle of twenty-somethings with perfect teeth, hard bodies and high-grade ambition lying on the sunloungers that spanned each side.

It hadn't been hard to track down Zander. It never was if you knew how to find someone. A call to a publicist, who'd call another publicist, who'd call a friend, who'd call a bit actor who worked as a personal trainer to a star who had a chef who knew a waitress who had slept with the chauffeur who'd driven him home.

Or some variation of the above.

Davie had simply asked his agent, Cal Wolfe, to find out where Zander was living, and thirty minutes later, he'd called back with an address that surprised him. He'd been sure Zander lived in Venice Beach, but this was in Santa Monica.

Odd.

Now he was approaching Bungalow 1, and even though he was the one who needed to meet, there was a huge part of him that was hoping Zander was out. Busy. Sleeping. Anywhere but here.

'Davie?'

None of the above. He was sitting on the steps outside the bungalow, white T-shirt, jeans, smoking a cigarette. This could have been any one of a thousand nights in their youth.

Zander sitting on some kind of concrete structure, a cig dangling from his mouth.

Only difference was, back then, he wasn't staying in a hotel room that cost the same for a week as it would now cost to buy the houses they'd grown up in.

'Hey.' He considered offering to shake hands and then decided against it. Too formal. Too weird.

Davie kicked off the conversation. 'Hope you don't mind me coming out here.'

Zander shrugged. 'Not at all. Good to see you.' Davie wasn't sure if that was a lie. If it was, it was a convincing one. He sat down on a small brick wall that bordered the steps.

'Good to see you too. This your new digs? Thought you lived in Venice?'

'Long story.' Zander answered with a shrug. 'Change of scene felt like the right move.'

That was it and Davie knew better then to push. Zander would tell him the details if he wanted him to know. Given his mate's lifelong tendency to keep things close to his chest, Davie didn't expect that to be any time soon.

Zander's dismissal of the question created a lull in the discussion.

The great thing about old friends was that they could have a comfortable pause in a conversation without feeling the need to fill it. Unfortunately, this wasn't one of those moments.

Davie cracked first. 'I've fucked up with Mirren.'

Zander squinted against the sun as he looked up. 'What happened?'

Davie launched into the story, leaving nothing out. Zander barely commented, and yet, somehow, about halfway into the story, Davie realised it was OK.

It was yet another flashback to their childhood relationship. Zander would sit there, smoking, the strong, silent, brooding type, while Davie gave a long-winded, dramatic but funny account of some situation he found either shocking or moving. A feeling of comfort descended, and Davie could see by the lowering of Zander's shoulders, the loosening of his jaw that he felt it too.

'Oh, man, you are so fucked,' Zander said, when Davie got to the bit in the restaurant when he finally told Mirren the truth.

'What the fuck were you thinking? Why didn't you give her a heads up before it was a done deal?'

'Because...' Davie let that hang.

'Because you bricked it?' Zander answered for him, correctly as it turned out.

'Yeah, that pretty much sums it up.'

'So what did she say when you told her?'

'Nothing.'

'Nothing?'

Davie shook his head. 'Nothing. She just got up and punched me in the face.'

'Christ, I love her.' That was all he had to say for it to become one of those bizarre moments in life. Zander started a chain reaction that began with him laughing, and before long, Davie succumbed to the hilarity until they were both wiping away tears of amusement.

'I feel for you, pal. I do. Do you remember she did that to me once?' Zander asked.

It took Davie a moment, but he got there. 'You took a bottle of whisky from your maw and da's cupboard,' he said, his Scottish accent becoming thicker. 'And when your maw found out, you said it was Mirren. Your maw asked her about it and Mirren took the blame then gave you...'

'A black eye that lasted a fortnight,' Zander confirmed, with a rueful grin, before going into the bungalow and returning with a bottle of water for him and a beer for Davie. They drank in silence for a few minutes before Davie spoke again, this time from the heart, the crazy moment of surreal amusement gone.

'I don't know what to do, Zander. I just got her back in my life. Can't lose her again.'

He realised as he was saying it that it was just as relevant to this guy here.

He hadn't wanted to come, but now that he was here, he didn't want to be anywhere else.

Zander swallowed a mouthful of water.

'You know what you have to do. You have to cancel the show.'

Davie nodded, his body language screaming 'reluctance'. 'The contracts are signed. No cooling-off period. Bastard Gore knew what he was doing.'

'So pay him,' Zander said. 'If it's the money...'

'It's not the money.'

Actually, it was partly the cash: $2 million, up front, for doing nothing. That thought made Davie's teeth grind. It was more than that, though. He could handle losing the money. He just didn't know if he could handle losing the show. If the figures continued to grow on their current trajectory, it could easily bring him $10 million over the next three years. That was a whole lot of visits to the cinema with Ena Johnston.

But... It was the only way. He already knew it. He'd just had a vague hope that Zander could see another way out.

The sun was beating onto Davie's back, so he pulled off his blue Armani

T-shirt, then immediately wished he hadn't. There was no doubt he was in great shape – he was lean, muscular, and last weekend's spray tan was still giving a glow. With his black curly hair swept back with hair wax that cost $200 a tub, he was definitely an attractive specimen of manhood – unless he sat, as he did right now, next to Zander Leith. Six inches taller, eight or more inches bigger in the shoulders, the biceps, the chest. Zander was a powerhouse of raw masculinity. But hey, as everyone would say when they were kids, Zander got the looks, but Davie was the funny one.

'If it's not the money, then buy him out. Cancel it. Take satisfaction in the fact that you might be out of pocket, but that guy is officially a wanker.'

'I'll suggest that description for his obituary in the *Post*.'

'I think Mirren probably has a few more names to add to that.' Davie spotted Zander's downcast expression when he said Mirren's name this time and wondered what that was about. Was there trouble between them too? He knew better than to ask. Zander would tell him if he wanted him to know. Besides, right now there was something else that was preoccupying his mind.

Unable to hold it any longer, Davie shattered the peace like a grenade. 'So are we going to talk about us?'

Zander's shrug told Davie that he knew exactly what he was talking about. His response was classic underplayed Zander. He thought about it for a few moments, before asking, 'Do you feel like you need to?'

Good question. Davie wasn't sure. As kids, living in the same street of terraced houses, they'd been best friends through choice, through mutual affection and a joint dissatisfaction with their lives. And all those years of hustling and grafting and achieving the impossible paled into insignificance when he'd found out last year that Jono Leith was not only Zander's father but Davie's too. His mum, Ena, had had a brief affair with him over four decades ago. That's why she and Davie had lived in that terrace. So his dad, that arrogant, deluded, cruel, megalomaniac prick could see his lad growing up.

The bottom line was that Davie loved Zander like a brother, before he knew he actually was.

Davie shrugged. 'Guess not. Didn't matter for all those years. Doesn't need to matter now.'

'Good. Case closed.'

Davie grinned. 'Glad to see you've discovered a new level of emotional depth and spirituality.' Amused sarcasm dripped from every word.

Zander countered, 'West of Scotland DNA. Can't argue with genetics.' The stereotype of the West of Scotland male who couldn't find his emotions with a search team and a Sherpa was one they were both familiar with. Growing up, they'd been surrounded by men like that. Suppressed feelings. Brusque exteriors. Boys don't cry.

Zander stubbed out his cigarette on the wall, then tossed it into his empty bottle. 'If it makes you feel any better, Mirren is fucked off with me too.'

So he'd been right. And Zander was actually going to open up about it. Maybe they could do the brother thing after all. He tried not to seem too eager to dig in case it shut Zander down.

'What have you done?'

'She thinks I failed a drug test.'

'Did you?'

'Yep. But I'm clean. Was when I took the test too. Must have been messed up, so we've got people looking into it. In the meantime, they won't insure me, Wes is being a dick and I've been fired.'

'So it's all going well?'

'Great. Never better. Every day above the ground is a good one.'

'Excellent.'

The two of them were grinning again. Ridiculous. The guy's life was falling apart and yet, somehow, there was black humour there.

'What about you?' Zander asked. 'All good? Apart from the whole "Mirren decking you" thing?'

Davie nodded. 'Sarah is on tour with the South City guys, so I haven't had sex for weeks. My ex-wife is a lesbian and her partner hates my guts. My kids think I prefer Justin Bieber. And I've got some mad stalker who's trying to freak me the fuck out. So yeah, all good.'

Davie's phone rang and he was about to flick it to voicemail when he spotted Mark Bock's name on the caller id.

He knew better than to ignore it. If Mark couldn't find him there was every chance he'd round up a SWAT team and come looking.

'Davie?'

'Yeah.'

'We have a situation.'

'Are the kids OK? Sarah?' He felt his heart ramp up to palpitation mode.

'They're OK. Everyone is OK.'

Davie didn't get it. 'So what's the problem?'

'It's your house, Davie. Fire crews are there now. It's not looking good.'

38

MIRREN

'Love Me Again' – John Newman

The blinds in Mirren's office were closed, which was a necessary discretion as she was standing in the middle of the room, on a white sheet, wearing a black balconette bra and a matching lace thong. Janet Reger. Her red waves were twisted up on top of her head and secured with a pen, chopsticks fashion, and her stylist, Maddie, was hollow-eyed, anxious and showing every stressed-out symptom of 'Oscars' madness month'.

'OK, we're down to the blush Dior sheath or the gold Chanel,' confirmed Maddie, a blonde, bespectacled lesbian who had the face and body of a model and the creative brain of a true fashionista.

Mirren looked at the two dresses hanging from hooks on the back of the office door. Over the years she'd had dozens of fittings here. She was so constrained on time it was far quicker for the stylist to bring the options to her, rather than visiting each fashion house in turn. This year, Chanel, Dior and every other major label had sent dresses over, because she was nominated. She couldn't help thinking that she'd got the sympathy votes. Would her name be up there if the establishment weren't making a show of support over her daughter's death? Maybe. But maybe not.

She'd get a better sense of it at the ceremony on the big night. In the meantime, she just had to get dressed and get out of here. None of this mattered. All that she cared about today was heading for the one event that did really matter to her: the opening of Chloe's Care, the drop-in centre she'd funded to support troubled youths.

'OK, let me try the blush one again. I think that was my favourite.'

'I think so too,' Maddie agreed. 'Since the year that Charlize Theron won in gold, anyone else pales by comparison. No offence.'

That's why Mirren loved Maddie. Brutal honesty was refreshing. The fact that she had the balls to say what she thought reassured Mirren that she'd never go to an event looking like crap on Maddie's watch.

Maddie had just brought the dress over to the protective white floor sheet when the door burst open.

'Really? Lunch with Lomax? That's how we're going to do this?' Mike Feechan stormed in, paying absolutely no regard to the fact that she was standing there wearing less than a lingerie-store mannequin.

Devlin, her assistant, ran in after him. 'Sorry, Mirren, I couldn't—'

Mirren spoke with absolute calm and authority. 'It's fine, Devlin. Maddie, can you excuse us? If you leave both dresses, I'll make my decision and let you know in the morning.'

Maddie eyed the furious and pacing form of Mike Feechan. 'You sure you want me to go?' she asked.

Mirren smiled. 'Positive. And thank you.'

Reluctantly, both Maddie and Devlin left the room and Mirren turned to face Mike, who was standing leaning on the front of her desk, arms folded, face furious, dressed appropriately for the occasion in a black open-neck shirt and black trousers.

'Something you wanted to discuss?' she asked, determined to show no embarrassment whatsoever about the fact that she was near to naked. She would not defer to him, nor would she let him intimidate her.

In fact, he would have no effect on her at all. Other than... Oh wow. The tingles of attraction were unavoidable, as was the fact that just looking at his shoulders, his blazing eyes, his narrow hips, was causing a distinct reaction in every one of her erogenous zones.

'Lomax? And of course it was as public as it could be, so you're sending a message. Is that really the kind of game we're playing here?'

'I don't play games,' Mirren countered calmly. They both knew she was lying. 'But you seem to forget – I'm not the one who wants to change terms. I'm not the one jeopardizing the relationship between our companies. That's all on you. But if I decide to react to that, then I'll damn well do it, and I'll damn well do it in any way I please.'

She should stop there. She knew she should. But she was just weary, totally pissed off. Zander. Davie. Mike. Jack. What was it with everyone letting her down and acting like assholes? No more. No bloody more. 'If you have a problem with that, I really don't care. Now get out of my office and next time you want to see me, call and make an appointment. I have better things to do with my time than this.'

Now it was her blue eyes that were blazing, as she stood, arms folded, chin high, daring him to disobey her.

He pushed himself off the desk. 'I won't be blackmailed – directly or indirectly,' he said, quietly this time.

'And neither will I.' she retorted, words strong, definite.

He headed towards the door, stopped halfway, turned to face her, stopped, stared.

Several seconds passed. Neither moved; neither spoke, the challenge clear.

His eyes lowered, took in the curves of her breasts, only half covered by the fine lace of her bra, the pale, beautiful contours of her body. Mirren let him look, didn't say a word, until his eyes returned to hers.

This was her game. Her play.

She walked forward, reached up, curled her hands into his hair, pulled his head down until his lips pressed hard against hers.

All bets were off. From defiance to urgency, from fury to frantic, it was suddenly a frenzy of lust and passion.

Her hips were against his now, his hard-on pushing back against her stomach, making a ripple of sexual excitement run up her spine.

Releasing his hair, and with impressive speed and dexterity, she flipped open the buttons on his shirt one by one and then pulled down each shoulder, exposing his hard, dark chest. The thick batch of hair proved that there was no male grooming here.

'God, Mirren. I. Can't. Get. Enough of you,' he murmured huskily, setting off yet another wave of exquisite pleasure.

Stretching round her, he cleared the desk behind her with one sweep of his hand, then back to her, kissing her, murmuring her name. They took turns to pleasure each other, to lick, to bite, to tease, hands in hair, lips pressed hard against each other, until they both came in a sweating, frantic, trembling crescendo.

It took what felt like minutes but was probably only seconds until the tremors stopped, until he pulled her up, held her against his chest, both of them silent until eventually he spoke. 'I don't know how to do this,' he told her. 'I'm usually a dinner-and-a-movie kinda guy.'

Mirren pulled back so she could look up at him. 'I like dinner. And movies. But I don't have room for them right now,' she said honestly, perhaps a little sharply.

Inside, she was groaning. And not in a good way. Multi-million-dollar deals and presentations to thousands? Not a problem. Intimacy with someone she hadn't known for at least ten years? Might take her a while to catch up with that. She'd never had casual sex before. What was she supposed to do after it? To say?

Damn, why couldn't she pause this to go call Lou, find out what was normal? She resisted a sudden urge to laugh. My god, this was ridiculous. She was a forty-one-year-old woman and she ran the world, yet she didn't have a clue what to say or do in this situation. It didn't help that she was naked.

Another thought. What if he thought she was having sex with him to manipulate him on the deal? She'd never slept with anyone in this town to get anything, and she wasn't going to let him think otherwise.

'Mike, I don't want you to think this is about the deal, because it's not.'

A flicker of confusion, before he pulled back. 'Seriously?' Oh crap, she'd offended him. He bent down, picked up his trousers, his shirt, pulled both of them on, followed by his shoes, all of it in sharp, angry movements.

She should say something, but everything that formulated in her head came out wrong.

She hadn't meant that to happen. It didn't mean anything.

Could they just forget it? She'd just been horny.

Right place, right time.

Everything sounded like a cliché, could be taken any one of several different ways, so instead of speaking, she grabbed a robe from the pile of clothes left by Maddie, pulled it on, said nothing.

For a moment, she thought he was going to leave without another word, but as soon as he was dressed, he stepped towards her. 'I don't know what's going on with you. If this is just a fuck-buddy thing, then fine. I can do that. But don't blow me off like that. I'm not yours to dismiss. And I didn't for a moment think it was about the deal. I actually thought it was because you were into me.'

With that, he turned, walked out, and whether or not the slam of the door was intentional, it still made her jump.

Well, that went great.

The clock over the door chimed and she realised she'd have to worry about it later. Nipping into her en-suite washroom, she had a quick shower, threw on the jeans and navy sweater she'd left there this morning and pulled her hair back, tying it with a band. No make-up necessary. On the way out, she ignored a loaded glance from Devlin. Oh, the sweet mortification. Ten years and she'd finally given him something to be shocked about.

Later, as she pulled into an empty space on Sunset, directly outside Chloe's Care, she decided it had been the right decision to avoid a high-profile opening. That wasn't what the centre was about. If there were celebrities and press and a whole fanfare of attention, it would alienate the very people who wanted to use it. Instead, Mirren had been working with the other charities, foundations and street crews that looked out for the teenage homeless, addicts and club casualties, spreading the word that the centre would be opening. Chloe's fame would do the rest. By the time she died, she was a regular in the tabloids and on the entertainment shows for all the wrong reasons. Everyone knew who she was. Everyone knew she was a druggie. Now everyone knew she was dead.

Mirren just hoped that message struck home with some of the young people out there, and if it did, they now had somewhere to go for help. She'd been counting on Zander and Davie to come and support her, but that was a blowout now. Logan and Sarah were on tour. And Jack was being an arse. So that left Mirren and Lou. Right now, that felt like the story of her life.

Mirren pulled up outside and took her phone from her bag. A text from Lou.

Hi, babe. Running few mins late. Blame Brad Pitt. Go in without me. Be there soon.

Leaving the car and crossing the sidewalk, Mirren's stomach churned with nerves. It looked quiet. There didn't seem to be many people milling around. Had she made a bad call building this? Would the kids she was trying to reach trust her? If not, they'd just have to work harder. Reach out. Her daughter deserved that. And nothing, no one was going to stop her making this the place it had to be. This was Chloe's legacy. It was all she had left.

Mirren pushed open the door and entered; the sight in front of her and the wall of sound made her stop dead in her tracks. In the main hall there were seats for fifty, and from here it looked like every one was taken, with another thirty or forty standing around the room in pairs and groups.

There were young, old, every race, both male and female.

It was a sea of people, some talking, some crying, some staring into space, some with their heads on the table, eyes closed. It didn't matter what they were doing. All that mattered was that they were here.

Mirren scanned the room, happy, relieved, moved, sad – but most importantly of all, completely unaware that one pair of eyes was watching her every move.

39

ZANDER

'Make It Rain' – Ed Sheeran

The sweat was dripping down his back, his heart was thudding, his legs weak. He needed this to stop. Really, desperately needed this to stop. Slamming his hand on the button in front of him, Zander jumped off before the treadmill came to a standstill and placed two hands on the nearest wall, leaning forward, letting his lungs recover and his forehead be soothed by the cool surface.

How many miles had he run in the last twelve hours? Too many to count. He couldn't sleep. He couldn't think. The cravings were taking over and he couldn't block them out. He just knew he had to keep busy, keep moving, not crack. He'd wanted to go with Davie to his house, some kind of fire the call had said, but Davie had blown him off. Didn't want it turning into a media circus, he'd said. Zander got it. In this town, one celebrity was a story. Two together, especially at the scene of a drama, was a conspiracy tale that stayed in the headlines for months.

Telling Davie about Mirren, opening the history of their friendships, picking the scars of their genetic connection, all of it combined had thrown

Zander seriously off balance. As soon as his mind went back there, the anxiety welled, the fear made him tremble, the anger made him want to roar. And all of it made him want to be numb.

The old Zander would be sitting in a bar right now, necking Jack Daniel's and nipping to the toilets every half-hour to do a line. The old Zander would figure, *Fuck it – they think I'm guilty, so I may as well be fucking guilty*. The old Zander would wake up tomorrow in a hospital or a cell. Right now, all he could think about, all he wanted to be was the old Zander. He headed for the shower, then pulled on jeans and a black T-shirt. Maybe he'd head out on the board. See who was around. Man, he was going stir-crazy in here.

This had to get better. Had to.

'Zander?'

Hollie had entered the bungalow without knocking, and as soon as he saw her face, he realised that things getting better wasn't on the cards anytime soon.

'Holls?'

She stopped, stared at him, eyes wide with something that didn't look good. Fear? Horror?

'Holls, you're freaking me out. What's up?'

'I... I...'

'Aw, shit, the test?' He finished towel-drying his hair, then chucked the towel back into the bathroom. 'Look, Holls, I was clean. I don't care what it says. I was clean. I'm still clean. I'll do any other test they want me to do, and if they don't believe it, we'll sue. Either way, we'll deal with it.'

'It's not the test.'

For the first time, he stood still. Had he heard that right?

'Not the test? So what is it?'

Now he could see her face was pale, drained of colour, her brown hair still wet, her jeans and vest crushed as if she'd pulled them on quickly. This wasn't how Hollie rolled. This couldn't be good.

'The flight,' she stammered.

'What flight?'

'Back from London. The girl.'

None of this was making sense. What girl?

'Oh, for god's sake, Zander!' she exploded. 'The flight attendant on the plane back from London. Bernard Edwards phoned. He's had a call from the *LA Headline*,' she said, naming the most notorious tabloid on the supermarket checkout rack. 'She's selling a story on you. She's claiming you exposed yourself to her, sexually harassed her, groped her. She's portraying you as the worst kind of lecherous sex pest and she's signed an affidavit saying it's all true. Zander, what the hell happened? What's happening to you? What's going on?'

The questions she was firing at him didn't even register because his thought processes were still stuck at the accusations, the part of his brain that dealt with incoming threats screaming in outrage. Groped her? Sex pest? What the fuck...?

'Hollie, I swear—'

She put her hand up. 'Zander, don't. Don't say it.'

His ab muscles clenched. Did she think...?

'I know she's lying. I saw her waving you off. Big grin. Thank you for flying Shag Air.'

Her tone held no humour, just weariness and sadness. As if her legs couldn't take the weight any longer, she flopped down onto the couch, her stricken face turned towards him.

'Still think my conspiracy theories are crazy? Zander, none of this is making sense. We've had the wackos and the lawsuits before...'

Over the years, there had been many. The assault claims when he hadn't even been in the same state. So many paternity claims he could have populated a kindergarten if they'd been true. There was one specimen of insanity who regularly called the FBI claiming Zander had stolen his spaceship. It came with the territory. But the outrageous lies were easy to spot and even easier to disapprove. This was something else.

One weird incident was understandable, but this was starting to feel very different. Raymo Cash and his assault charges. The false drug-test results. His apartment getting ransacked. And now this. This was starting to play out like he was being punked by a sadist.

Hollie was still venting. 'But this is more than bad luck. It's like you're under siege. Under attack.'

Zander sat down next to her, rubbed his temples, trying to stop the anxiety that was building inside him from exploding. He needed to be on a board. He needed to be in a bar. He needed to be anywhere else but here.

He was Zander Leith – he'd spent his whole life using alcohol and drugs to block out his issues and take away his problems. And now – oh, the fucked-up irony – life was hitting him with all this shit when he couldn't even go get wasted to get through it. This really wasn't working for him.

'Look, I'm heading over to see Bernie at the office now. Come with me, we'll see what he says, get a better handle on it. Hopefully, he can shut it down until we can get to grips with it. This is becoming a way too familiar pattern.'

Zander didn't move. Couldn't. His head hurt; his stomach ached; every single sense and nerve in his body was crawling with cravings.

'You go, Holls. I've got some stuff to deal with. Something I need to do.'

Decision made, he was propelled into action. He sprang off the couch, grabbed his boots, pulled them on, picked up his car keys.

Hollie jumped up, her anxiety matching his. 'Zander, don't. Come with me. Don't go anywhere else. Zander! Zander! Fuck!' He was out of the door, running towards the car park, breathing laboured, sweat already forming on his forehead despite the cool of the early evening.

Had to get out of there. No more. He'd tried. He'd done everything they'd wanted him to. Nothing worked. He might have been wasted before, but at least there had been good times. Crazy fun. Somewhere to go, things to do, people to do it with. Now? Nothing but shit. He'd always been a loner, but one that needed the flip side of crazy to balance it out. Now? He couldn't stand to be alone for a single night longer. It wasn't psychological; it was a physical need. A desperation to feel differently. Feel like he was alive.

He pulled the car out of the car park and headed along Ocean Avenue towards the I-10 freeway. The streets were packed with tourists, students, families heading back from the beach as dusk began to fall. Over to his right, the pier, the Ferris wheel giving off a kaleidoscope of colour, taking him back to that night in Shutters, with Adrianna, holding her, touching her...

He put his foot on the gas, anxious to get there, needing to be there now.

The miles passed; the minutes stacked up; his mind went to automatic. He knew the way to his old stomping ground with his eyes closed. How many times had he driven there completely wasted and yet still made it to his favourite bar or club intact, clutching a fistful of money, a stoned model and a death wish?

He cut off the freeway onto La Cienega, headed north, then hung a right onto Sunset. Almost there. Traffic was heavy, the tail end of rush hour. Most of the clubs not open yet, but the bars already teeming with people. This was the world in which he belonged. Not the sanitized normality of five-star hotels and manufactured perfection. This was where he should be.

It took another fifteen minutes, tension twisting his gut until he got there, pulled into a parking space, cut the engine. He wanted to run in, burst through the door, but he forced himself to stop, breathe. Did he really want to do this?

He put both hands on the steering wheel, then placed his forehead on top, not giving a damn who saw him or how it would look. He was done caring, done worrying. He had to start living his own life, and he had to start now.

Unable to hold back any longer, he jumped out of the car, senses assaulted by the familiar sights and smells.

Over to his right, the bar he'd played poker in every week, even though it had cost him cash, jewellery and, once, the car that had sat outside on the kerb. He never did know when to fold and walk away.

On the left, a strip joint that was home to Destiny, Carmen and Sugar, ladies who knew their way to his apartment and who had shared many nights that were just clouds in his memory now. Next to that, the club in which he'd punched out Raymo Cash the first time, earning him a huge fine and a stint in rehab. That was where he'd met Chloe. The thought made his gut twist a little more. Nope, don't go there. She'd understand. She was an addict. There was nothing about how he was feeling now that she wouldn't recognize.

He paused at the door, took a breath, steeled himself. No going back.

Pulling open the door, he stepped inside. No one gave him a second glance, but why would they? No one was here for him.

He headed for a table in the corner, sat down, willing his breathing to return to normal.

Eventually, a woman approached him, smiling. She was tall, black, beautiful.

'Hi. I'm glad you're here,' she said warmly.

He tried to return the smile but the tension in his face made it tough.

Undeterred, like she dealt with this kind of reaction every day, she carried on. 'Welcome to Chloe's Care. I'm Pauline.'

With each word, his tension came down a tiny notch.

'I'm Zander. I'm an addict, but I'm clean. And I just need to be here,' he replied.

40

SARAH

'Dirty Little Secret' – The All-American Rejects

If she died right now, her tombstone would read as follows:

Here lies Sarah Mckenzie, who died of a heart attack brought on from being a duplicitous spy who almost got caught.

The jet was more subdued than it had been after the earlier legs on the tour. The lights had been dimmed since take-off, and most of the band and crew were either sleeping or plugged into headphones, watching stuff on laptops and tablets. At least the war between Logan and Jonell seemed to have calmed down. They'd been hanging out earlier and it all seemed amicable. Obviously, their fight had been just another little blip on the landscape of life on the road.

Across from her, Logan was now fast asleep, mouth open, a tiny dribble of drool coming from the left-hand side of his lower lip. His fans called themselves the Logangstas. She had a hunch that if the Logangstas could see their hero now, he might slip down their devotion scale just a little.

Her watch told her they still had two hours until they touched down in LA. Home. Kind of. Was it weird that she was beginning to think of that city as home? She associated it with Davie now and damn, she'd missed him – far more than she'd expected to. She decided with a smile that she could admit that to herself, but never to him – he was cocky enough. She'd tried to call him earlier but his phone went straight to voicemail. He was the busiest guy she knew, so it wasn't a surprise.

It wasn't just Davie that was making her bond with California grow, though. She adored her little flat in Marina Del Rey and the laid-back life there. This time last year, she'd never have believed she'd live anywhere but Glasgow, and yet here she was, on a jet with a band, headed for her apartment overlooking the sea.

That's if she got there in one piece. At the moment, it was looking debatable. She turned her head to look a few rows back on the other side of the plane, and yep, Eli was still staring at her.

She'd called his bluff back at the stadium and he'd backed down. Hadn't asked to check her phone. His demeanour made it damn clear he was suspicious, though, and since that moment he hadn't taken his eyes off her. He'd joined her and Logan in the limo after the gig. Sat within her eye line on the plane. And now, there he was, still staring. If he ever chose a different line of work, he'd make someone a great stalker.

Unable to resist, she gave him a sweet smile and a wave. He didn't reciprocate and she was fairly sure he was visualizing flying daggers entering her spinal area.

At least it would put her out of her misery. The suspense of not knowing what was caught on her phone was killing her, but there had been no opportunity to check it. If she'd disappeared to the washroom for the length of time it would take to watch half an hour of footage, she'd arouse suspicion. Now everyone was sleeping, except Eli the Stalker, it was still too risky. He could walk by at any moment, see what she was watching and there would be a cop car waiting for her on landing.

Making a decision, she stood up and headed over to where he was sitting. His expression didn't change as his eyes watched her approach. Leaning down, careful not to waken anyone else, she whispered, 'Think I might have eaten something that doesn't agree with me. If I'm not back out in ten minutes, can you call the medical team?'

He didn't even make a pretence of going along with the joke, just followed her with his eyes as she headed for the loo.

OK, so that bought her ten minutes. Not long enough to watch the whole thing, but at least it gave her time to fast-forward through it quickly and check if anything was untoward. In the luxurious, black gloss bathroom – nope, they bore no resemblance to the tuna-can toilets on commercial flights, and yes, she was now ruined for any other mode of transport for life – she sat on the lid of the toilet and plugged her in-ear headphones into her phone. A ton of messages popped up on the screen. Dammit! She'd flipped the phone to silent when she was busy playing Bond. No time to check them now.

Messages later, video first.

Sarah pressed 'play'.

Nothing to see. An empty room. She fast-forwarded until she spotted the door from the dressing-room shower opening. 'Play.' An image of a naked Logan filled the screen. Oh holy shit! And great – she was probably now breaking at least half a dozen federal laws, despite the fact that she'd snapped her eyes shut. Prising them slightly open again, she was relieved to see he'd pulled on a pair of Calvins. Relief. And incidentally, whatever training regime he was following was totally working for him. He was, quite possibly, the fittest almost twenty-year-old she'd ever seen.

On camera, she watched as he picked up his laptop and brought it over to the sofa where she'd been sitting. Closer. Closer. Oh no, no, no, no, stop!

He plumped down, missing the cushion that had been concealing the phone by inches. The evidence of how close she'd come to being caught made sweat beads pop out right across her forehead.

Logan had his laptop open now, and the angle of her hidden phone had given her a perfect view of the screen. His cursor moved to the Facetime icon and he clicked.

The ringing only lasted a few seconds before it was answered and a familiar face filled the screen. Pale skin. Huge blue eyes. Long, deep red hair.

Lauren Finney's smile showed perfect teeth and true affection.

'Hello, baby,' she greeted Logan.

Sarah's eyes widened. Well, blow me with a boy-band member – she hadn't seen that coming. What kind of crap investigative reporter was she that she had let that one totally get by her? Logan and Lauren?

Although, of course, it made perfect sense. He was a teenage star, member of South City, lived a crazy life of fame and adulation.

Lauren was only a couple of years older, a girl discovered by Davie on *American Stars*, an artist who'd become a household name, a phenomenal success as a singer and presenter, who now also lived a crazy life of fame and adulation.

They were made for each other.

'God, you're beautiful. I miss you, babe,' Logan groaned. Sarah's heart melted just a little more towards this kid. Whatever Mirren had done with him, she'd done it well.

'I miss you too. Wish you were here,' she said, then gave a rueful smile. 'Not that you'd fit in at the moment, though.' Sweeping her hand around the room behind her, Lauren was obviously making a point. Sarah squinted to see what it was and eventually realised it was flowers. Dozens and dozens of flowers. 'Honey, look at this. It's out of control.'

'I wish I could say they were from me,' Logan told her, sighing. 'They all from your ex?'

Lauren nodded, her beautiful face now a frown of weariness. 'Yep. He's refusing to give up. Trust me, the day you send me flowers is the day we're done. Even the smell of them gives me the creeps. I've asked house-keeping to have them gone by the time I get back from the show.'

An arm became visible on the screen, and Sarah realised that Lauren was checking her watch. 'Honey, I have to go. I can't wait to see you later. Will you come straight from the airport? I'll be home by then.'

Logan nodded. 'I will, and Lauren?'

That incredible Julia Roberts smile again. Sarah decided if she were a less secure human being, she'd be excruciatingly jealous. Sod security, she was turning a mild shade of green.

'Yeah, baby?'

'You have no idea how great tonight is gonna be when I see you.'

Lauren giggled. 'I love a man who makes promises he can keep. Bye, baby.'

On the scale of instant feelings of crap, Sarah suddenly ricocheted right to the top. Brilliant. She'd planted a camera, risked a horrific breach of trust, almost had herself taken out by a lethal close-protection agent, inadvertently broken a dozen different laws, seen Logan naked, totally invaded his privacy, and all to end up with a bird's-eye view of a cute scene that belonged in a romcom.

OK, enough for now. Eli was probably lining storm troopers up outside the door this very minute. Her thumb went to move to the 'stop' button when the image on the screen jiggled and she saw that Logan had turned to greet a new arrival.

Eli's profile came into view. Great. He was bugging her in real life and on screen now too.

Her thumb moved again and—

Stopped.

Froze.

Eli wordlessly paused in front of where Logan was sitting, pulled something out of his pocket. Shit, she should switch off. She suddenly didn't want to see anything that could incriminate Logan. He was such a sweet kid, and everyone made mistakes, and what business of hers was it, anyway? It was different when he was just the catalyst for a chapter in her book, but over the last couple of weeks she'd really grown to like him. And then there was Mirren too. How could Sarah possibly be complicit in anything that would hurt that woman? Hadn't she been through enough?

She should stop. Definitely. Yet... She couldn't, because she had to know. It was like watching a car crash in front of her and she couldn't walk away until she knew exactly what the body count was going to be.

Using her thumb and forefinger, she enlarged the image, zooming in on Eli's hand. A small, clear bag with what looked like white power inside. Another bag. Little blue pills.

Bollocks. Total bollocks.

Don't take them, Logan. Don't take them!

Logan wasn't listening. He got off the couch, took them from Eli's hand, headed over to a large holdall on the other side of the room, opened it.

Sarah knew what was going to happen, but she still couldn't switch it off. From the holdall, he pulled out that bloody red bag, the one that had bugged her the whole tour, and dropped the little packets inside.

There was absolutely no pleasure in the fact that she was right.

Damn it.

She fast-forwarded to make sure she missed nothing else. Logan getting dressed. Logan fixing his hair. The runner coming for him. Logan handing Eli the holdall. Everyone leaving and then nothing until her own face appeared, making a pretence of searching for her phone.

Then it faded to black. So now she knew.

The question was, what was she going to do with the information? Obviously she had to tell someone. There was no way she was going to let Logan go down the same road as his sister. Right now, he was handling it well, still functioning, lucid. So well that she'd never once spotted that he was stoned. But how long would that last? She knew how it worked. The time would come when he needed a little more to get high. Then a little more. And more.

Before long, he would be just another addict, and the fact that he was in a band that was heading for global domination wouldn't matter a damn, because all he would care about was the next fix.

If anything, his position was more dangerous than that of the run-of-the-mill junkie, because he had unlimited funds and a long line of people desperate to get him anything he wanted. Including that fucker, Eli. Sarah was suddenly furious. How dare he? How fucking dare he? And no, she couldn't exactly claim the moral high ground, given her little recording stunt, but a professional on the payroll supplying a young guy with drugs? Military training or not, she wanted to go out there right now and kick his arse up and down the length of the plane.

Ladies and gentlemen, this is your captain speaking. Please ignore the crazed young woman in the aisle, kicking the crap out of a South City protection officer. Thank you, and have a pleasant flight.

A knock on the door interrupted her thoughts.

'Two minutes,' she said brightly. No doubt it was Eli. He probably had some kind of Jedi ESP and realised she was coming for him, so he was trying to get in there first. The important thing was that despite every instinct telling her to go out there, guns of indignation and fury blazing, she couldn't and shouldn't react until she'd worked out a plan for the best way to handle this.

Sighing, she was just about to switch her phone off when she remembered... She clicked into the text function. Seventeen new messages. What? She didn't even know seventeen people in LA.

Scanning the list, she realised every single one was from Davie.

Just in case you see the news... Don't worry – I'm OK.

The news? Why would he be on the news? And why was he saying he was OK?

Next text:

Been a fire at house. Not sure how bad.

Next text:

Heading there now.

Fuck, I'm here.

Smoke everywhere.

Can see flames.

Fire service here.

Kitchen gone.

Christ, it's a mess.

Can't find Alina.

Where are you, Sarah?

They won't let me go in.

Can't stand here doing nothing.

This is a nightmare.

Fuck it, I'm going in.

Don't worry. I'll be fine.

Love you.

41

It's almost time. Almost.

The watching and the waiting have been intolerable, but I did it because I had to make sure I got this right.

There will only be one shot. One chance. Because once people know about me, then they'll come for me.

You think I don't know that?

You think I've spent all this time planning and watching and making it right and that I'm so deluded I believe I'll just walk away when I'm done?

I know that won't happen. But I don't care.

That's the thing about having all that matters taken away from you.

Once it's gone, you have nothing to lose. And the gain?

That's easy. There's only ever been one upside on this. I'll take away from you what you took from me.

And I'll look you in the eyes and I'll make sure you know.

You'll know it was me who did this to you.

42

DAVIE

'Burn' – Ellie Goulding

Karma. Was that what this was? Was this retribution for every fucked-up asshole thing he'd ever done in his life?

Sitting on the terrace, in an all-weather lounger, Davie pulled the blanket tighter around his shoulders and scanned the chaos that surrounded him. The fire crews were mostly gone now, just a couple of guys with clipboards, still walking around the premises. Mark Bock and a dozen security guys were here too. Mark was in the security room, running through CCTV footage from around the property. The rest of the team were patrolling and securing the grounds. Horse bolted. Stable door shut.

'I bring you tea. You should not try to go to fire. You crazy ass.'

Alina pointed out the obvious as she handed him a mug. It was the only one he used. His mum, Ena, had brought it for him on her last visit, from the Starbucks shop at Glasgow airport. He had no idea why it meant something to him, but somehow it did.

It had only been saved from the carnage because he'd had a coffee out on the terrace before he'd headed off to see Zander, and he'd left the mug outside on the table. Alina had switched her operation HQ to the fully stocked kitchen in the pool house. 'Pool house' was perhaps an understatement. It was a three bedroom guest house, larger than the entire row of homes he, Zander and Mirren had grown up in, that sat on the opposite side of the pool terrace to the main house.

All he could think when Alina gave him the mug was *Thank God Ena hadn't been here when this happened*. Look how he'd reacted when he thought Alina was inside. Dozens of LAFD's finest and he decides to play hero and run into a burning building to look for a housekeeper who spent her whole life conveying the impression that she thought he was a knob.

Meanwhile, he, it would seem, thought he was Bruce Willis in *Die Hard*, charging in, trying to be the hero. Although, he didn't remember a scene in *Die Hard* in which two firefighters blocked Bruce at the door, pushed him back, at which point he tripped over a sprinkler that protruded from the grass, twisted his ankle and ended up sprawled on the ground, with the sprinkler rain soaking him.

Pathetic.

Utterly pathetic.

Especially when Alina had turned up half an hour later after her daily trip to Whole Foods.

He'd almost risked his life for an empty house. Karma.

'Hey, Davie. Can you come take a look at this?' Mark Bock shouted to him from the security office. Located in the back of the pool house, it was an impenetrable room that monitored everything that happened in the grounds and around the perimeter of the property.

Groaning, he pushed himself up and headed over, getting a better look at the house as he passed. The main body of the property looked OK, but the kitchen was destroyed. One exterior wall of the room had completely crumbled; the others were black with smoke, water still running out of the open doors.

The damage didn't faze him. That's what insurance was for. But it was the potential devastation this could have caused that was twisting his gut right now. His kids could have been here. Sarah. His ex-wife. Although, if

Jenny and Darcy were inside, he wasn't sure he'd have been quite so gung-ho in charging to the rescue. He may have toddled real slow.

In the security room, Mark was sitting at a bank of monitors. 'Come look at this, Davie.'

Shuffling under the weight of his wet clothes and blanket, Davie did as he was instructed. Mark pressed 'play' on an aerial shot of the house, taken from the top of the roof and programmed to capture everything within 200 yards, 360 degrees. That just about covered the grounds and drive.

Davie stared at the screen, saw nothing. Stared some more. Still nothing. Then he saw it. A black dot in the distance, increasing in size as it got closer, hovering above the house, static, then swooping down to a spot right outside the French doors that led to the kitchen.

'What the fuck...?'

'It's a drone. Remote-controlled. Battery-operated. We're seeing them all over the place at the moment, flying low over celebrity houses to capture images for the paps or unscrupulous investigators using them to gather evidence in divorce cases. Almost impossible to track. The person who sent that here could be sitting ten miles away.'

'Christ...' Davie whistled in disbelief, his eyes going back to the screen.

There was no sound on the footage, which made it even more surprising when the machine, or gizmo, or whatever the fuck it was called, exploded into flames. It was strangely hypnotic. The flames went high, blue at the tips...

Mark noticed that too. 'Some kind of accelerant was on there. That's the reason for the blue flames.'

Davie nodded, back to watching as the flames appeared to diminish. Then he noticed a new flicker. The flame from the drone was now encompassing a tiny area of the door to the kitchen. Then a bigger area. Then bigger.

Mark pressed 'fast forward', and in less than a minute, the flames had enveloped the whole door.

'That's how it started and you can clearly see it was deliberate. It's time we had that conversation, Davie. You need to face up to the fact that this isn't some harmless weirdo. Someone has a serious wish to cause you harm.

And until we find out who it is, you need to get clear of here and go somewhere you can be protected.'

'Fuck that. I'm not leaving my home. We can stay in the pool house until the main house is habitable again.'

'Then I can't guarantee your safety.'

'Davie! Davie!' The edge of desperation in Sarah's voice made him drop the blanket and dash outside, sore ankle forgotten. As soon as she saw him, she ran to him, like a scene in an action movie in which the heroine runs to thank the hero who just saved her life.

Only Sarah wasn't that heroine.

As soon as she was in front of him, her expression of pure relief turned to something else altogether.

'What the fuck did you think you were doing? "I'm going in"?' she quoted his text to him. '"I'm going in"? Are you crazy?' She was yelling now, top of her voice.

'I've been worried out of my mind! It's all over the news – the images of the smoke, and the fire, and they didn't know if you were OK...' She was babbling, crying, ranting, furious, relieved, and Davie smiled because he didn't think he could love her more.

'Don't bloody smile at me. You're an arsehole!'

'I think that may already have been mentioned today,' he informed her.

'That's because you are!' Still shouting, mascara tears streaming down her face. 'Why didn't you text me back? Why? Why would you do that?'

Davie shrugged sheepishly. 'Sprinkler soaked my phone.'

Sarah looked stunned.

Incredulous.

Then suddenly burst into a weird, surreal laugh. 'Are you telling me you live in a $40-million house...?'

He knew what was coming, but he couldn't help pointing out the obvious. 'Might be less now. Fire damage.'

She ignored him. 'And you only have one phone – *one phone* – with my number in it?'

'I'm a crap boyfriend.'

She slumped down onto the wet grass. 'And I'm a crap girlfriend.'

Davie sat down beside her, put his arm around her, pulled her head onto his shoulder, melting at the sight of her crushed, disconsolate face. 'Honey, you're not. I'm glad you weren't here. I really am.'

She popped her head back up. 'What?'

'I don't think you're a crap girlfriend for leaving me here,' he explained.

The lines between her eyebrows puckered into a frown. 'Neither do I.'

'Oh.' This was one of those situations when he felt like he should know what she was talking about but really didn't. 'Then why are you a crap girlfriend?'

He watched her inhale deeply. Oh shit, she'd cheated on him. She'd shagged someone on tour. Fucked someone on the tour bus. She was leaving him for a boy-band member. Ouch, even that thought hurt. How could he have lost her in such a short space of time? He should have called more. Paid her more attention. Showed her that—

'Marilyn McLean is in LA.'

The words were like a mallet to the mind. Total knockout, possible concussion. 'What?'

A tear ran down her face and she wiped it away with the grubby palm of one hand.

'Marilyn McLean. She's in LA.'

'Why?'

'We don't know.'

'We?'

She sighed wearily. 'Mirren and me.'

He didn't know what to say to that. Even after twenty years, the name 'Marilyn McLean' still took him back there, still made him want to vomit.

'Sarah, I'm not getting this, so you're going to have to explain it to me.'

She took a deep breath. 'A few weeks ago, Ed at the *Daily Scot* called me, said some crook in Liverpool had been arrested and everything he owned confiscated under the Proceeds of Crime Act. There was a rumour going round that his wife claimed to be Mirren McLean's mother. Basically, she lost her man and her access to money – then she disappeared.'

'And you didn't tell me this?'

'Davie, you were busy. It was at the same time as you were launching the show and Jizzo died. I went to Mirren. Told her. She hired a PI, asked me not to worry you until we had proof that she was here. We found out this week that she definitely is.'

Unconsciously, Davie ran both hands through his hair, his standard reaction in times of pressure and stress. 'What the fuck would Marilyn be doing here? She hated all of us.'

Sarah gestured to the chaos around her. 'I think she might already be doing it.'

Davie turned his head away from her and threw up on the grass.

When he turned back, she reached for his hand. 'I think we need to get out of here. Go somewhere safe until they find her.'

Mark Bock had just come within earshot. 'I was just telling him the same thing.'

'Mark, there's some additional information you should know. Mirren McLean has a PI called Brad Bernson,' Sarah told him.

'I know Brad. He's a good guy. Ex-FBI.'

'That's him. Can you give him a call? He'll fill you in. But this goes no further. No LAPD. It's about as confidential as it gets.'

Mark didn't ask questions. Davie knew he wouldn't. He'd once told him that he'd spent his life working for people with secrets and when police became involved, the chance of a leak multiplied. It was why Davie felt safe with Mark Bock looking after him. Present situation excluded.

Sarah turned back to Davie. 'But, Davie, you have to listen to me. We can't stay here. If you stay, I stay, and that puts us both in danger.'

'That's the worst emotional blackmail ever.'

'Indeed it is.'

He thought about the angles for a few moments. The fire would be all over the news, so there would be sympathy out there for him right now. The story naturally spun out in his head. If he had to take a week off after inhaling smoke when he ran into the burning building to save his housekeeper, a poor, frail woman who lived to cook and loved nothing more than country music, America and her boss, Davie Johnston, then the nation would understand and support him.

Genius. Actually genius.

He was getting carried away with the prospect of TV appearances, press interviews and maybe a campaign for the fire service when he realised he had another priority, a task that had to be carried out before he could move on.

He had to fix his karma.

'Look, I'll come with you – we can go wherever you want – but there's something else I have to do first.'

43

MIRREN

'I Would Die 4 U' – Prince

Mirren hung up the phone feeling exhausted after another call from Brad Bernson. They'd discovered that Marilyn had been staying in a motel in Santa Monica, but she'd checked out the day before. No location on her now, but they were working on it. Wearily, she slid out of the cream leather booth in the corner of her kitchen and made a cup of tea. As she drank it, she stood looking out of the window at the ocean, too anxious to sit.

The calendar on her wall had a thick red circle around a date that was creeping up fast. The Oscars. She was pretty sure that none of the other nominees were currently sitting in their kitchen, dreading the event, too wrapped in anxiety and fear to even feel a shred of joy that they were about to be part of Academy Award history. This was Mirren's second nomination. She'd won the last one twenty years ago. She had no expectations of winning another, but still she had to be part of the circus.

She was so deep in thought that she didn't realise Logan was behind her until he wrapped his arms around her shoulders and kissed the top of her head. 'Morning, Ma.'

Just two words but so, so good for the soul. Having her boy back was bitter-sweet, though. She wanted him there, needed to be able to see for her own eyes that he was OK, but was this putting him in danger? At least on the road he was surrounded by security and there was virtually no chance that anyone could get to him. Here at home was different. He liked to try to live a normal life. He'd stick on a baseball cap and head to a restaurant. Stop in at a store.

How could she stop him?

She had to let him know that there was a risk, but how did she do that without confessing that she'd lied to him for years? How could she suddenly introduce a grandmother to him, with a 'By the way, I think she might be a psychotic maniac'?

Yet she had to keep him safe.

There was a buzz at the front door and she checked the monitor in the corner of the room to see her friend waving at the screen. Despite her woes, she smiled. If there was one person she wanted to see today, it was Lou.

Logan let her in and returned to the kitchen with his arm slung around her shoulder. 'Aunt Lou pined for me every moment I was gone,' Logan told Mirren, with Lou grinning beside him.

'It's true,' Lou agreed.

'Says life hasn't been worth living without me.'

'Also true,' Lou confirmed breezily, before coming over to hug Mirren. 'Figured the boy needed an ego boost. Must be hard being him,' she said in a stage whisper. Logan was still laughing when he grabbed a soda from the fridge and headed out to the back yard. Mirren looked out of the window and saw that he'd lain down on a lounger, headphones on, eyes closed.

He was always like this for the first couple of days when he came off tour. Needed to recharge the batteries.

She made Lou a cup of coffee and they slid into the semi-circular dining booth. How many days and nights had they sat here over the last twenty years, discussing every issue, solving problems, making plans, and especially over the last year, crying into their coffee cups over the shit-storm life had served up for them.

'OK, honey, you're going to have to get your Oscar's glow going soon, because you can't go looking like this,' Lou said, typically blunt.

Mirren gestured to her sweats. 'I was considering a different outfit.'

Everyone in Hollywood knew that the prep started months before the big day. Zero carbs. Nips and tucks. Punishing workout regimes. Laser peels. Chemical peels. Hair treatments. Liposuction. Fillers. Make-up rehearsals. The only thing she'd done so far was select her dress, and even that had been half-hearted.

Lou wasn't deterred by Mirren's deflection. 'Girl, you look awful. You OK?'

'Just tired,' Mirren told her. 'Bit stressed.'

'Did you agree terms with Pictor?'

'Nope.'

Pause. Lou eyed her curiously.

'Why are you looking at me like that?'

Lou's eyes twinkled as they narrowed. 'Oh, you did.'

'Did what?'

A cackle from her friend now. 'Oh, you so did,' she repeated. 'You had sex with Mike Feechan again.'

Mirren had no idea why she was blushing. 'Yeah, well. Moment of weakness,' she confirmed.

'And, sweet baby, you like him.'

'Lou, I have no idea who or what I like right now. I really don't.'

'Why? Look, honey, I know Chloe has gone, but you still need to live some kind of life.'

Lou's misdirected sympathy made her groan inside. She so wanted to tell her about Marilyn. Keeping this huge weight of worry from Lou was only making it heavier.

'I know, but it just seems like whenever I get on a steady footing with someone, the rug gets pulled from under me. I'm just not ready.'

Lou was quiet for a moment, and Mirren couldn't help thinking she was building up to something.

'You talking about Zander?' she eventually asked.

Mirren shrugged. 'He failed a drug test.'

'I heard,' Lou said softly.

Of course Lou knew. She was the editor of the *Hollywood Post*. No one farted in this town without her knowing about it.

'I can't believe he'd do that. I trusted him. He promised...' Her words tailed off as she felt a huge lump form in her throat.

Lou sighed. 'Honey, I wasn't planning on saying this today, but it's just gonna get worse.'

Mirren put her mug down on the table. 'What do you mean?'

'The *LA Headline* is about to do a story on him. A flight attendant on a private jet back from London is saying he exposed himself to her, groped her, harassed her. They're doing the whole sex-pest angle. It's not going to be pretty, hon.'

Mirren tried to speak but nothing would come out. Her chin dropped, her throat closed, and suddenly, she couldn't breathe.

Mirren was shaking her head, desperate to get the words out. Lou put her hands on hers. 'Honey, I'm sorry, but it's better I tell you than you hear it from someone else.'

Mirren shook her head, gasping for breath until her oesophagus finally opened wide enough for her to speak. 'He didn't do that.'

'Baby, I know he's your friend, but the girl has signed an affidavit to say he did. It's a pretty compelling case.'

'He didn't do it,' Mirren repeated forcefully.

Lou exhaled. 'You can't be sure.'

'I can,' Mirren blurted.

Suddenly, it was enough. No more. Enough lying, enough secrets. Lou would never betray her, never breach her trust. It was time she knew.

'I can, Lou. Because a long time ago, someone attacked me, violated me, and if Zander reached him first, he'd have killed him for it. It changed our lives. All of us. He would never, ever touch a woman that way.'

Now it was Lou who responded with utter incredulity. 'And you've never told me this? Mirren, I'm so sorry. But – oh my god, I can't take this in – what happened?'

Mirren sighed, every ounce of resistance leaving her. It was time.

'The man who did it was Zander's father, Jono Leith. He was a criminal, a piece of scum, the most evil man who ever walked the face of the earth.' Self-preservation slowed down her heart, made her nerve endings numb and she slipped into an almost trance like state as she began to relive the past. 'He beat Zander's mum every chance he had. And Zander too.'

'That explains a lot,' Lou murmured, voice oozing sympathy as a new understanding of Zander's infamous demons dawned.

'He and my mother were lovers my whole life. She was obsessed with him. No matter what he did, how many other women he screwed, how many times he humiliated her, despite years of broken promises to leave his wife. She worshipped him. Was addicted to his arrogance, to the danger, to the life he promised her year after year, to the money he threw at her after he'd fucked her. She thought she was someone because she was the girl-friend of Jono Leith. It was all she had. Him and a whole twisted fantasy about their happy ever after. But that changed…'

Lou didn't interject, just listened intently to every word.

'When I was seventeen, he raped me.'

Mirren heard Lou's gasp, but it was almost abstract, surreal. Tears were flowing down her face, but she felt strangely calm. Resolute. Like she had to exorcize the demon.

'Zander and Davie were nearby. Davie was my boyfriend, Zander was like my brother. I told them. Zander ran fastest, wanted to get to his dad first, and he would have killed him, Lou. He really would have.'

'But he didn't?'

Mirren shook her head. 'No, because my mother had already stabbed him to death. Not to protect me.' Mirren's voice was quiet now, a whisper. 'But because she couldn't cope with the fact that Jono Leith, the love of her life, had wanted me instead of her. So she killed him.'

'Oh, Mirren…'

'Mom?'

Mirren's head snapped round and she saw instantly that Logan, standing in the doorway, face pale and trembling, had heard every word.

Another piece of Mirren's heart broke.

'I'm sorry, Logan. I didn't want you to ever know.'

He was shaking his head, fists clenched, jaw tight with fury and pain and devastation for her. 'Don't dare say sorry, Mom. Don't dare. This isn't your fault.'

'*The Brutal Circle*,' Lou suddenly interjected, a realization astounding her. 'This is the storyline of *The Brutal Circle*.'

Mirren nodded. 'All of it true. I wrote about what happened. The rest... Well, you know.'

Lou sat back, flabbergasted, trying to take it all in. 'No cops back then?'

Mirren shook her head as she moved along the booth to let Logan sit. He took her hand in his as she continued, 'I didn't want them involved, didn't want anyone to know what he'd done to me or what my mum had done to him. Zander and Davie buried him...'

'They what?' Lou's eyes widened, no amount of Botox capable of disguising her incredulity.

'They buried him,' Mirren repeated, 'And no-one missed him. Jono was a criminal who lived a pretty dangerous life. Everyone thought he'd done a runner. We came here. End of story.'

'I can't believe I don't know this about you guys,' Lou said, almost to herself. 'How does anyone survive that? Hell, I feel even more sorry for them now.'

Even through the trauma, Mirren realised that was an odd comment. 'Feel sorry for them why?'

Lou looked at her like it was obvious. 'Haven't you heard what's been happening over the last couple of weeks?'

Mirren shook her head. She'd heard nothing. Probably because she'd told both guys she was done with them. In a contest of crap timing, this one was a winner.

'Zander's house got ransacked last week. The drug-test fail. These accusations. And Davie. He had the weirdo stalker with the blood thing, then his car got trashed, and then the fire...'

'What fire?' Mirren's voice had real urgency now.

'There was a fire at his house yesterday. Don't worry – he's OK. But that had to be terrifying.'

She'd known that a couple of odd things had happened to Davie, but not all this.

Fire. Stalker. Housebreaking. Accusations. Why hadn't she known all this? Why hadn't she put all this together before?

'Lou, this isn't random.'

'What do you mean?'

It all made perfect sense now. 'Zander has lost everything. If the fire was worse, Davie could have too. And...' She paused, unable to finish the sentence. 'We need to get out of here. Logan, we need to go somewhere safe.'

'But why? I don't get it.'

Tell them. Tell them now.

'Because my mother is here in LA and I think she's behind all of this. In her twisted mind, I took away the thing she loved more than anything, and then me, Davie, Zander, we made these incredible lives off the story of what happened.

'She thinks we took everything from her back then. Now I think she's trying to do the same to us.'

44

ZANDER

'Ashes to Ashes' – David Bowie

The banging on the door of the hotel bungalow woke him with a start.

If this was housekeeping, they clearly weren't paying attention to the 'Do not disturb' sign.

Zander always slept naked, so he grabbed a towel, wrapped it round his waist and padded over to the door, checking his watch on the way. Two p.m. Probably time he was up anyway.

He opened the door, fully expecting to see the maid. Wrong. Mirren McLean, Lou Cole and Logan.

Taking a step back, so the door was wide open, he let them enter, shaking Logan's hand as he passed. 'All right, bud?'

Logan turned the handshake into a hug. So one out of three was prepared to be cool with him, Zander decided. Not bad odds.

Lou Cole scoped him from head to toe and muttered something about her lucky day. Mirren barely made eye contact. OK, so it was a start.

As soon as he'd closed the door, Mirren spoke.

'Still in bed at two o'clock?' She didn't look annoyed, more concerned.

Zander picked up a plain white cotton T-shirt from the pile that the laundry had delivered the day before and pulled it on, leaving him only semi-naked now.

'I was out last night.'

Her left eyebrow raised. It was one of her mannerisms he'd always thought was hilarious. It was impossible for her to hide irritation or cynicism because it was, quite literally, written all over her eyebrows.

'He's been doing overnight shifts at Chloe's Care,' Lou offered. 'Two of my stringers reported it back last night. Don't worry – I've killed the story.'

Mirren switched from cynical to surprised, then went straight on to apology. 'I'm so sorry, Zander. I didn't know.'

'I asked them not to tell you. Didn't want you getting worried that I was up there trying to score.'

Mirren looked embarrassed, and he registered the weirdness of this situation. Clearly he was missing a chapter here. The last time she spoke to him, she'd told him to fuck off; now she was standing in his hotel suite. Why?

'Zander, I need you to come with us,' she told him.

His heart sank. An intervention. He supposed he should have seen it coming.

'Mirren, I'm not perfect, God knows. But I'm not the fuck-up you think I am, and I'm not buying into any intervention. So thanks, but you can go.'

He turned to head back into the bedroom, where at least he could pull on some jeans and lose the shower-scene chic.

'Zander, this isn't an intervention; it's an apology. I should have believed you. I'm so sorry. I know you didn't fail the drug test. I know it was a false result,' Mirren blurted. 'I think your house being ransacked, the accusations that woman is making, and maybe the whole nightclub fight that night we were together were set up too.'

This caught Zander's attention and it took him a moment to process the relief. 'Thanks,' was all he could manage for a moment, then, 'I don't understand. Why do you think it's all a set up? Apart from the fact that I didn't do coke and I didn't do anything wrong to that woman.'

He watched as a whole spectrum of emotions crossed Mirren's face. Fear, fury, determination.

'Because my mother is in LA. I think she's doing this.'

Zander froze, 'What?'

While his body was somehow suddenly incapable of movement, his brain was exploding.

Marilyn McLean. Fuck.

His eyes darted to Lou and Logan, and Mirren could tell exactly what he was thinking. 'I've told them everything,' she admitted.

Just when Zander thought it was impossible to feel any worse, another layer of anxiety came to settle on top. No one should ever know everything unless they were there, unless they had as much to lose as the others who were involved. Mirren. Zander. Davie.

But then, he trusted Logan. And Lou…

'It will never be repeated, Zander. I swear,' Lou assured him. He believed her.

Sighing, he went into the bedroom, pulled on his jeans, more to buy time to think than out of modesty.

'So what makes you think it's Marilyn?' he asked when he re-joined them.

Mirren relayed the story yet again, every sentence twisting his gut just a little more. He hated Marilyn McLean with a passion that could never be underestimated. Jono was a bastard, and she was the woman who loved a bastard, who allowed him to control everything, who didn't care that he was married and that Zander had to lie in bed night after night listening to his mother weeping because her husband was in the neighbour's bed. Marilyn McLean was the reason his mother died a broken woman, thinking her husband had left her, when really he was in a shallow grave only feet away from her home.

Zander listened, evaluated. Mirren was still relaying the details. 'I think she was the one who set Davie's house on fire too.'

Another half-turn on the twisting gut. But come on, surely this was way out of Marilyn's comfort zone and capabilities?

'Mirr, how could your mother pull this off? Someone was shooting at Davie's house. Managed to set it on fire. Persuaded some chick to lie about me. That's a whole lot of crapola from one person.' Even as he was saying it, he could hear Mirren's answer, and he knew she was right.

'Because Marilyn's a manipulative, clever bitch. And for the last twenty years, she's been shacked up with one of the biggest crooks in the UK and working alongside him. You think she hasn't learned things? Made contacts? I don't think there's anything she isn't capable of.'

Reluctantly, Zander agreed. Mirren was right. Marilyn had always been on the dark side of evil. The way she'd treated Mirren, been obsessed with Jono, manipulated everyone to get what she wanted. She'd killed before. Zander could see why Mirren would absolutely believe she would kill again.

'I think she's out to destroy us, Zander. We can't go to the police in case it leaks, and Davie and I have got a team of people on it, but in the meantime, we have to go somewhere safe. You have to come.'

Zander thought about it, a cascade of mixed emotions pulling him in different directions, but there were two overriding arguments that made his mind up for him. If Marilyn was out there and coming for them, she no doubt had a psycho-bitch plan. And if he was with Mirren, then he could look after her, protect her.

'And what about Davie?' he asked.

'We're going over to meet him now. He's not going to be thrilled at the prospect of coming with us, but it's the only thing that will keep us safe.'

He thought some more, then nodded. 'I'll come.'

There was never any doubt, but the relief on Mirren's face was palpable.

He hadn't protected her last time and his father had almost destroyed her. That wasn't going to happen again. Not ever.

If Marilyn was going to come after any one of them, she was going to have to get through Zander first.

45

SARAH

'Is There Something I Should Know?' – Duran Duran

How many times had she watched the footage? Maybe a dozen? And yet she was still strangely compelled to watch it again, hoping the outcome would be different, hoping that it told a different story. It never did.

Right now, it was on freeze on the huge eighty-inch monitor in the lounge in Davie's guest house. She'd linked her laptop up to it, because it was the only decent-size screen available now that the main house was out of bounds.

Time to wrap it up. Move on.

There were more important things to deal with today. Mirren had called to say she was on the way over, needed to talk to them. Sarah had already guessed what it was about.

Marilyn.

They needed a plan. A strategy. Or perhaps Mirren was calling to tell them she'd found her. Sarah sent up a silent prayer of hope. If they had, it would be game over. They could unpack the suitcases that were sitting in the hallway, ready to go to a house Davie had rented, and return to normal life. They'd spent last night here in the guest house, only because Brad had a whole protection team patrolling the estate. It was time to go somewhere more anonymous. She could finish the book and there would be a storming chapter about a close shave with a lethal stalker. No names mentioned.

In the meantime, the chapter about the boy-band singer's secret drug use was definitely off the table. She couldn't use it, wouldn't do that to Mirren, to Logan. Breaking a story like that would make her career, change her life, but it wasn't worth it. Urgh, twice in two years! Last year, she'd been the first and only journalist to find out the truth about the past lives of Davie, Zander and Mirren, but she'd killed that story when she fell in love with one of the people it would hurt most. Now she was about to kill a second story because she couldn't hurt Mirren. She was obviously getting way too soft for this game. Strangely, that didn't feel like such a bad thing.

She looked back at the image on the screen, finger hovering over the 'delete' button. Logan Gore, clearly buying drugs, in an LA nightclub. Delete it. Cancel. Remove it from memory. Pretend it didn't happen.

'Sarah?'

The voice made her jump and she turned to see Mirren and Logan in the doorway.

'Alina let us in and...' Mirren's eyes travelled to the screen and she froze.

Logan's followed, before he murmured a horrified, 'Fuck.' Sarah considered shutting it down, but the damage was done.

Instead, she got up from her chair. 'Mirren, I'm so sorry...'

Mirren wasn't listening. Uncomprehending, aghast, she was staring at Logan. 'Logan?'

The pain in her voice and face were unbearable to witness. Oh god. She'd done this to her. She should have been more careful. And Logan. Her anger with him for being so reckless was suddenly diluted by an unexpected wave of sympathy. He was such a good kid and he'd been through so much. Losing his sister, his parents' divorce, Mirren's grief, the fame, scrutiny and sheer workload of being in the band.

'Logan, tell me that isn't what it looks like,' Mirren whispered, still staring at the screen. It was hard to imagine that it could be anything else. 'Tell me what he's giving you there. Tell me it's not...'

'Mom, it's not. It's not. It's not what you think, I promise.'

'But it's drugs.'

'No, it's—'

Mirren rounded on him, pure venom spitting out with every word. 'Do not dare lie to me, son. Do not dare!'

'Mom, I'm not—'

'Stop. Stop lying to me. You bought drugs? You use drugs? Do you know what that's cost us? Did you not see your sister lying cold? Did you not see her dead?'

Mirren was screaming now, pure, heart-wrenching, guttural wails.

'Don't, Mom. Don't do that,' he cried. 'Switch it off. Switch it off!' he yelled at Sarah.

It was something in his eyes that made Sarah stop, her words trailing off as she followed his stare and realised that he wasn't looking at himself up there on the big screen. He was looking to the right, at another figure, partially hidden in the shadows.

She saw it now. It triggered a memory. Suddenly, it made sense. Absolutely perfect, complete sense.

'Logan. Logan!' she repeated, trying to get his attention.

'Switch it off!'

Oh fuck, he was hysterical. This was excruciating.

'Logan, you have to tell the truth,' she urged, knowing it was the last thing he would want to do.

He turned round, punched the wall behind him. 'I can't. I can't!'

'Logan?' Mirren repeated, the word dripping with pain.

There was a silence that Sarah was desperate to fill, now that she'd joined the dots she hadn't seen before, but this had to come from Logan.

'No. I'm saying nothing. It was me, Mom, OK. It was me!' Sarah realised he wasn't going there. Wasn't going to do it.

'It's a choice, Logan,' she shouted, desperate for him to do the right thing.

'It's a choice. Him or your mum. Who are you going to hurt, Logan? Jonell or your mum?'

'Noooooo,' he roared. 'Don't.'

Sarah knew then she was right. Her eyes went back to the screen, to the figure standing a few feet away from Logan, partially concealed by his hoodie. It was the bandana peeking out from underneath that had given it away. Red camouflage design. Jonell wore it every night on tour. Everything made sense. The weird friction between Jonell and Logan. The fight early on the tour. The red bag. The fact that Logan carried drugs, yet he was never wasted or high.

'I can't do it. I can't let him down. He needs me. Can't let him die.'

Oh God. Oh dear God.

'Jonell or your mum, Logan,' Sarah repeated, calmer this time. She had to bring this back, make it right.

'What is it, Sarah? What am I missing?' Mirren begged.

'Tell her,' Sarah said to Logan.

'No.'

'Tell her.'

He screamed, an anguished wail, a tortured, trapped scream. 'I buy it for Jonell.'

'What?' Mirren whispered, not understanding this at all.

But Logan wasn't stopping for questions. He was charging on, like a burst dam, pouring out the facts, drowning everything in its path.

'He's using. Smack. Pills. Whatever he can get. I bought it for him. Every time. I had to, Mom. I couldn't let him near the dealers, couldn't let them suck him in. So we made a deal. I'd buy it. Give it to him. A little less each time. Until he was strong enough to make a break.'

'But, Logan, there are professionals—'

Without warning, the teenager exploded again. 'Like the ones who helped Chloe? Like the ones who fed her more drugs, and talked to her, and told her she could kick it, and then let her out to hang with dealers and watched her fucking die! She's dead, Mom. My sister is dead.' He was shouting now, pained, desperate, distraught. 'And I can't lose anyone else!' He slid down the door frame, sobs wracking his shoulders, buried his head in his knees.

Rivers of tears were flowing down Mirren's cheeks as she went to him, wrapped her arms around him, holding him tight to her.

'You won't, Logan, I promise. We'll help him. I'll get him back for you. We'll make it OK,' she murmured, her promises full of conviction.

Sarah watched as Logan's arms came around his mother and they held each other, two tracks of tears mingling together as they fell.

Sarah didn't think she'd ever admired anyone more than Mirren McLean.

She absolutely believed every word she said. She'd fix Jonell.

She'd help her son.

She would protect all of them. Or she'd die trying.

46

DAVIE

'Moves Like Jagger' – Maroon 5 & Christina Aguilera

Mark Bock had already filled Mellie in on the essential details, twisting them slightly to conceal the truth. There was a security risk. They were fairly certain that Davie's stalker had started the fire. Therefore he was being advised to take a few days off until they could track down this creep.

'Hey, what are you doing here? A sniper could take you out in a heartbeat,' Mellie warned Davie the minute he walked into the production office at the studio. She was obviously switching from her producer-director role to detective.

Davie scanned the room. 'Thanks, Rookie Blue, but there are no windows in here.'

'True,' Mellie agreed. 'But you need to go. Mark said you're heading out of town? It's all very mob movie. Hope you're wearing a vest and they've chipped you so they can track you when the freak kidnaps you.'

'Has anyone ever told you that you should work with victim support?'

Mellie shrugged, grinning. 'Nope, but I can see why I would have potential. Now can you get out of here? Lainey Anders is standing in for you on *Here's Davie Johnston* and she's way hotter than you.'

'Man, what's a guy gotta do to get some sympathy around here?' Time to get to the point of the visit. This had to be quick, so he'd already called ahead with instructions.

'I'm going as soon as I've spoken to them. Did you ask them to come in? Where are they?' he asked, knowing she'd have done as he requested.

'Dressing room two. Carmella said she needed a lie-down. Which is Carmella-speak for two lines of coke and a half-bottle of vodka.'

'Thanks. Love ya. See ya later,' Davie crooned as he left to the sound of Mellie feigning retching.

It took thirty seconds at a pace to reach the room, throw the door open and...

Wow. Model porn 101. Carmella, in a short, pleated miniskirt and tank, was bent over the make-up station, while Jack Gore, trousers at his ankles, exposing a large rose tattoo on his right buttock, was taking her from behind.

'Davie...' Carmella sang, and he could see immediately that she was completely wasted.

What the hell kind of world was this that he lived in? No wonder his karma was shot to fuck.

Time to clean it up.

'Hey, man, what the hell—' started Jack, who had pulled out and was now standing there, flaccid and dangling in the breeze. Obviously not a man who liked an audience.

'Don't mind me,' Davie replied, as he pulled a thick wad of paper out of the folder he was carrying. 'Jack, you perverted, pathetic piece of crap, this is your contract for *Beauty and the Beats*,' he announced, at exactly the same moment as he removed a Zippo from his pocket, lit the stack of papers and dropped it in the metal trash can, praying he wouldn't set the studio on fire. To lose his workplace in the same way he'd lost his home would just be careless. 'I've recalled your payment from Escrow. Sue me if you like. It would be career suicide, but do your worst, mate. And, Carmella...'

To his relief, Carmella had attempted to stand and was now being held up by the wall. He always felt it was easier to give his employees constructive criticism and advice when their naked nethers were not in his direct line of sight.

'Carmella, you've still got the show, but there are two conditions. You need to dump this douchebag, and you're going to rehab. Mellie will set it up. Fail on either and I'll replace you. I've always wanted to do a show with Naomi Campbell.'

Carmella's wail illustrated that she may well be a floating chemical soup, but she definitely understood the threat.

'Who the fuck do you think—' Jack Gore started, an offensive that seemed less menacing with the whole dangling penis thing. 'Jack, save it. You're a loser. Mirren McLean was far too good for you. And let me tell you, if you cause her one more moment of pain or embarrassment, I'll bury you.'

'That's intimidation and harassment,' Jack bleated.

'No it's not,' Davie countered. 'It's karma. And a promise.'

As he strutted out of the studio, fire alarms wailing thanks to a smoking litter bin in dressing room two, he just hoped the gods of karma were paying attention.

Because if Marilyn McLean was around, they were going to need all the divine intervention they could get.

47

MIRREN

'Chasing Cars' – Snow Patrol

'This is like the most screwed-up family vacation ever,' Zander said, smiling, as he pulled his suitcase out of the trunk of the Dodge Durango.

Mirren knew he was just trying to keep everyone positive and she appreciated it.

Hollie jumped out of the other side of the Durango, just as Davie and Sarah drew into the space next to them.

All three cars present and accounted for. They'd driven in convoy from LA up to Santa Barbara, after persuading Davie and Sarah to come with them. They hadn't taken much convincing, although, with a week until the Oscars, Davie had stipulated that he needed to get back to town in time for some serious pre-ceremony grooming: fake tan, teeth whitening, haircut, and the preparations for the ceremony itself. He'd explained that he'd been rehearsing for weeks, but there were another two full days of run throughs before the ceremony and he wouldn't miss them.

Lou had bailed out on the trip though. Pre-Oscar's week was her busiest time, with endless features and speculation about winners, losers, movies, futures and box-office receipts. Besides, Lou was under no threat. Marilyn wouldn't be interested in her. Mirren. Zander. Davie. That was who she would blame.

Mirren only blamed herself.

She honestly hadn't thought that her mother was a threat from 5000 miles away.

When Marilyn had sent her that demand for cash a couple of years back, she should have paid more attention. It was a horrible letter, saying Davie, Zander and Mirren had made money from what happened to them back in Glasgow, and she wanted a cut. Wanted her share. Mirren sent the letter back with a 'Return To Sender' across the front. Now she wished she had gone with another strategy. If only she'd sent some cash, bought her off, used it as a way of keeping Marilyn on side, or at least establishing where she was and what she was doing, but at the time, she'd been too busy with Chloe, too busy trying and failing to keep her family together. Now that she knew what had happened to her mother, it made her wonder. Was Marilyn thinking the police were closing in on Razor and she wanted cash to leave? Or maybe she wanted to branch out and needed some seed money to get going. Or was it just greed and some twisted game to add another zero to her bank account?

Davie and Sarah alighted from a white Bugatti Veyron and Mirren couldn't help but laugh. They were escaping danger, keeping a low profile, avoiding harm, and he still came in a million-dollar car with tiny boot space for luggage.

'I know exactly what you're thinking,' Sarah told her. 'His own car got trashed, so they loaned him this one. Very low key and I'll be wearing the same clothes for as long as we're here since there was only boot space for luggage big enough to hold three pairs of knickers.' Sarah then turned to Logan, who was pulling a backpack out of the trunk of Mirren's car. 'Hey. Are we OK? You know, I'm so sorry it went down that way. For what it's worth, I caught you on that video completely by accident when I was filming the club. I was about to delete the recordings, that's why I've never asked you about them or let anyone see them.'

For a moment, Mirren worried that Logan would resist the olive branch, but she should have known better. Her boy was way too decent for that.

'We're cool,' he told her. 'To be honest, I'm glad. Jonell is gonna hate me, but at least it's not all on me now.'

Mirren took a deep breath and said a silent prayer that the intervention worked. She and Logan had spoken to Deeko, the band manager, and told him what was going on. He knew Jonell was getting high, but had no idea where he was getting the supply. In the grand scale of rock and roll band management, this was a minor blip, so he'd been cool about taking control of the situation going forward. Mirren had set him up with a couple of the addiction specialists at Chloe's Care and they were working on a plan. Mirren was just glad it no longer involved her son. Had he been stupid? Sure. But he was nineteen and his heart was in the right place. That, she could live with.

'This place looks incredible,' Zander said, scanning the view. A huge ranch, and several outhouses, in the middle of green land that stretched in every direction, horses roaming free in many of the fields.

At that moment, the door of the main building behind them opened and a stunning woman in jeans, a plaid shirt and cowboy boots walked towards them, arms outstretched.

'You finally came to visit!'

'Cara, thank you so much for letting us come. Sorry it's such short notice. Cara, this is Zander and Hollie, Davie and Sarah, and of course you've met Logan. Everyone, this is Cara Callaghan, who owns this place. Her husband, Lex, is the Clansman.'

'You're the one who should be the movie star,' Davie told her honestly, even if it came off as totally cheesy.

Beside him, Sarah groaned. 'Cara, I'm sorry. He's been in Hollywood too long. He's now coated in smarm.'

Cara's eyes crinkled as she laughed, making her even more attractive. Lex Callaghan was a lucky guy, Mirren thought for the umpteenth time.

'I'll check, but I'm sure we've got a smarm-recovery programme that will help him with that,' Cara carried on the joke.

If Mirren had questioned whether or not this was a good idea, here was her answer. They'd all been through such crap lately, they knew the extent of the threat, and they knew it wasn't over, and yet up here it felt like they could breathe. That was all she wanted – not to feel like every moment was an exercise in fear.

They were here, they were together, and this gave Mark Bock and Brad Bernson and their teams space and time to find Marilyn.

'So how long are you staying? You're very welcome to hang for as long as you want.'

'Thank you, but just a few days. As you know, we've all had some... *issues*... back in LA and we just needed some fresh air.'

Mirren had outlined the situation when she'd called Cara to ask if they could come. A stalker, she'd told her, before filling her in on Davie's house and the whole shooting-at-his-gates incident. She'd also told her about Zander's apartment being ransacked. The intention wasn't to freak her out, but to be open about the fact that there might be some danger.

On the phone, Cara hadn't hesitated. 'Honey, up here, we've had pimps and we've had dealers. We preach serenity and calm, but we know how to handle it if it goes the other way.'

Cara worked with addicts of all ages, many of them referred to her by the more progressive judges, who understood the benefits of equine therapy. It didn't always work. Chloe had been up here once, but no amount of healing could fix a soul that didn't want to be fixed.

Now, Cara was just as understanding, hugging Mirren again. 'This is the place to find it, honey. Stay as long as you want. My next group of clients doesn't arrive for another couple of weeks, so there's just me and a few of the hands here. You'll pretty much have the place to yourselves.'

The fact that there wouldn't be others around reassured Mirren even more, as there was less chance of a sneaky photo of Davie or Zander ending up on Instagram. It gave her privacy to try to sort out the rest of her life too. Pictor were still standing firm on their original offer and refusing to budge. And Wes Lomax must have a mole somewhere, because he knew that and was blowing up her voicemail with suggestions that they talk for real, not just for show, about the *Clansman* coming to Lomax. Mirren's head was aching with it all. She needed this place for safety, but for peace too, for space to re-evaluate her future.

'Why don't you all come on into the house and we'll get you some food and show you your rooms? Davie, you're in the anti-Smarm Suite.'

They were all laughing as they started to cross the front yard, until the sound of another approaching vehicle stopped them.

When it came to a halt and the dust settled, they watched the newcomer climb out of the car. Mirren shielded her eyes from the sun as she walked to greet the new arrival.

She hadn't been sure about this at first, but Logan had told her how important it was to him and she didn't have the heart to refuse him. He needed this, needed some balance to counteract the darkness in which he'd been living. And if her boy needed that, she wasn't going to be the one who stood in his way. The only condition had been that the Marilyn situation wasn't mentioned, that the reason they were here would be described as a holiday.

Mirren held out her hand, making a concerted effort to be as welcoming as possible. It was the least she could do for Logan.

'Hi, I'm Mirren. Logan's mum.'

A hand met hers; a smile mirrored her own.

'So pleased to meet you. I'm Lauren. Logan's girlfriend.'

48

ZANDER

'Better Man' – Paolo Nutini

The early morning sun was beating down on the back of his head. Had been that way for a while, but he wasn't ready to move. Since they'd arrived yesterday he'd craved this – just being out here alone. Maybe solitude was his new addiction. No one else around. No noise. Just him.

And he felt... Nothing. Just nothing.

Numb.

'You OK there?' He looked round to see that Cara was only a few feet away, heading towards him. She climbed up beside him, sitting on the top spar of the wooden fence that surrounded the paddock. In the middle distance, four horses, three of them grazing peacefully, the other one standing to the side, looking out to the other field.

'I'm—' He stopped. What was he? Good? The usual flippant answer? Why? What was the point?

She watched him. 'You don't know, do you?' she told him calmly.

There was a tenderness in her voice, a care. This wasn't a Hollywood conversation. An all-is-fine-an'-yeah-I'm-great. Or a therapist conversation in which they looked for clichés of desperation so that they could spout some psychobabble tosh.

She was listening. Watching.

'I don't,' he admitted. 'I have no idea.' He shrugged it off, embarrassed. 'Look, I'm sorry. It's just been a crazy time. Got a lot on my mind.'

'You know what, it's OK to tell yourself that if you want to,' she said.

His eyes narrowed. 'And what if I don't?' he answered, suddenly weary.

She let that hang there for a moment and he didn't rush to explain. Opening up wasn't what he did, especially to a stranger, a beautiful woman he'd known for five minutes.

Yet she had a serenity, a calm that made him want to tell her everything. This wasn't a flirtation or a physical attraction. It was something else, something he'd never felt before.

Neither spoke, both looking out at the horses in the morning sun, their breathing strangely synchronized.

'I see you,' she said softly.

His eyes went to the horse that was alone, limping now along the perimeter fence. 'Am I that one?' he asked, the words catching in his throat. 'The broken one?'

Her black hair barely moved as she gently shook her head. 'No, Zander. You're that one over there.' He followed her eyes off into the distance, where a solitary Mustang he hadn't noticed before, stood, his graceful silhouette dark against the sun. 'You're lost,' she said quietly.

'So what do I do? How do I find my way?'

Why was he asking her? She didn't know him. Knew nothing about where he'd come from.

'You have to find a home. Not a house, a home. A place to belong. A place of love. And then you can start building a life – one that is for you, not anyone else. One that makes you whole. It's not about career, or fame, or any of that other stuff. It's about you. It's your choices.'

He thought about what she said. What was it about her? What was it about this place? He wanted to hold this, grasp on to this moment of pure peace. It was so far away from the noise of his usual life: the addictions, the issues at work, the dangers and the threats. And Adrianna. So far away from Adrianna. He hadn't heard from her at all. Not a word. The air hostess allegations hadn't been made public yet, so it wasn't down to that – it could only be because she didn't care. And now, being here, he wasn't sure that he did either. What they had wasn't real. It was a movie. A fairy tale. A lyric in a song. But it wasn't real. And he had a feeling that the woman standing next to him now only dealt in reality.

'I met someone else like you once.' Her smile was wide, warm.

'What happened to him?'

'I married him,' she said, her eyes full of love. 'And he found a balance. Found a way to make his life work.'

He paused, thinking. He didn't want this to end. This was what life was about. Peace. Quiet. The only other time he felt like this was when he was out in the middle of the ocean, nothing else for miles, just him and his board.

Now he'd found that on land. And he'd found someone who understood that. In his life, he didn't think he'd met anyone with the peace and wisdom of Cara Callaghan.

'I don't ever want to leave here,' he told her honestly.

'I get that, but you have things to do, things that you need to fix. Running away won't do it, but you don't need me to tell you this. You don't need me to fix you. You just need to find your way back.'

She leaned over, hugged him. 'Come back anytime. Lex and I will always be here for you. When you're ready to heal, we're here.'

Jumping down, she squinted against the sun, staring at the horse in the distance. 'Slow and steady. Your friend over there needs that too. Slow and steady.'

She headed back inside, and as if the lame horse saw that he'd been left alone, she slowly walked over to him and stood silently beside him. He wasn't sure how much later it was when Hollie appeared from the same direction.

'Thought I'd better come rescue you. You've been stroking this horse for the last hour,' Hollie pointed out.

She looked less stressed up here too, even if she hadn't quite got with the whole 'At one with nature' thing – as evidenced by the fact that she still had a cell phone in one hand and an iPad in the other. However, she'd made a concession to the casual environment by pulling her hair into a ponytail and donning a pair of denim cut-offs and a pale blue vest – not an outfit she'd generally wear in the city because, in her words, she was a size fourteen in a sea of size zeros. Zander had no idea why she cared about that shit, but apparently she did.

'She doesn't seem to be complaining. She's lame. Just needs a bit of love.' he said, patting the neck of the mare beside him.

'So you don't want to talk business?' Hollie asked him.

'Nope.'

'Not even if I told you that the *LA Headline* are still stalling the flight attendant story?'

Zander shifted his gaze from the horse to Hollie. 'How come?'

'I think Lou pulled a couple of strings. The *Headline* belongs to the same publisher as the *Hollywood Post*. She just pointed out that she had it on impeccable authority that the story was false and that the *Headline* would lose credibility if they ran it and it was then disproved. Not that they had any credibility in the first place,' she muttered, her disdain obvious.

'Cool.'

'Cool? Is that it? Zander, this buys time to find out what's going on, and it stops your name from being trashed all over town.'

'Cool.'

'Aaaaaargh, you are the most annoying man I have ever met. Seriously. You know, you can be a complete dick. Complete. Matt Damon does not do this. If Matt Damon was the victim of a smear campaign, he'd fight back. Stand his ground.'

She punched his upper arm, clearly determined to evoke a reaction.

'It's not all about you, you know? I've pulled you out of gutters and strippers' beds, I've bailed you out of jail, I've worked with you for ten years, and I've put up with an unholy amount of shit that would have driven a saint to suffocate you in your sleep. You're a nightmare, Zander Leith. A frigging, full-scale, hot-mess, total nightmare.' He could feel her breath in his face as she squared up to him, bold, fearless, furious.

'And if you're not going to go to bat for yourself, I've no fricking idea why I'm bothering. Aaaargh! What? Why are you doing that?' she demanded.

'Doing what?'

'Staring like—'

He stopped her when he leaned down, and slowly, gently, brought his free hand up to the side of her neck and lowered his face to hers, stopping just a heartbeat away from her lips.

'I want to kiss you. Is that OK?' he murmured, his voice thick with emotion that had come out of nowhere.

'No!' she pushed him back. 'Don't you dare. Don't do that, Zander.' Her voice wasn't angry. It was something else.

Something he wasn't understanding. What just happened had taken him completely by surprise. It wasn't planned. And hell, she wasn't happy.

'I'm not some chick for you to play with. If you're going to be an asshole, go do that to someone else.'

She turned on her heel and stormed off, leaving him with a suffocating wave of that feeling. The one he'd had many times before, right after he'd fucked up and right before he'd discovered the price he was going to pay for it.

49

SARAH

'Run The World (Girls)' – Beyoncé

Sarah sat in one of the study areas, a gorgeous, rustic room, with three overstuffed sofas set out round a huge brick fireplace. The walls were lined with old books, the floor made of stone, with a large rug in the centre.

It was cosy, comfortable, a perfect escape, but most importantly, it was the only room in the house with a TV. It was all very well this home-on-the-ranch stuff, but she still needed to work. This wasn't an episode of *Little House on the Prairie*. Davie, Mirren and Zander could afford to take time out, rest up, but she still had rent to pay at the end of the month, and no, she wasn't letting Davie cover it.

Thus, here she was, sitting in the study, her laptop connected to the TV screen in front of her so that she had a better view of the videos and images she needed to scrutinize as part of her research. Today, she was on the 'Celebrity Feuds' chapter. Chelsea Handler, Katy Perry, Mel Gibson and Miley Cyrus weren't coming out of it well.

Footsteps interrupted her flow of thought. 'Save me. Save me from these guys and horses,' Hollie begged as she came into the room and flopped, lengthwise, on the couch, before putting a pillow over her face.

Sarah laughed and waited for the barrier to come back down. After a few seconds, Hollie removed it, but not before thudding it off her head a few times.

'Why? Why do we have these egotistical, famous, nightmare men in our lives? Why?'

Sarah shook her head, chuckling. 'I fell in love with mine. I have no idea what your excuse is.'

'I needed a job and I thought he was hot,' came the reply. 'What can I say? I was young, poor; I needed the money...' The two of them were laughing now. Sarah had only met Hollie a couple of times before they'd come up here, but she could see now that they had a lot in common. Both organizers, both logical thinkers, both smart, both utterly infuriated by A-list stars who were a long way from any of the above.

Her attention was broken by a new face at the door.

'Do you mind if I join you?' Lauren asked, her expression so warm and sweet that no one could possibly refuse. She came in and sat on the free couch, directly across from Hollie.

'Sorry,' Hollie said. 'I'm just having a moan.'

'Ah, I like moans. What's the subject?'

'Having to deal on a daily basis with famous men.'

Lauren let out a delighted giggle. 'Oh, I'm in on this one, sister. Where shall we start?'

Hollie knew that Lauren wasn't aware of the situation with Marilyn, so she kept it general. 'How about with the fact that they don't take enough care of their own safety?'

'Ah, that's not just famous guys. My ex-boyfriend was a cop. Which is ironic because he was completely crazy. Loved the whole danger stuff – the fast cars, the fights, the threats.'

'Why did you split up?' Sarah asked, her journalistic side getting the better of her.

'It was just too hard. We'd been together since I was sixteen, so all my adult life so far. After the show gave me this career, I had no time to keep a relationship going and he wanted more. Still does. Even after all this time he's relentless and refusing to accept it's over. Still wants me to go back to my old life with him. That's why it works with Logan. He knows what the business is like so there's no demands, just support.'

'And I don't suppose it hurts that he's pretty easy on the eye,' Hollie teased.

Lauren was about to answer when Hollie's phone buzzed and she groaned when she checked the screen. 'You have got to be shitting me.'

'What's up?' Sarah asked.

'It's a Google alert. Apparently Adrianna Guilloti has just announced a new celebrity endorsement, Charles Power,' she said, naming a famously handsome fifty-something actor who was still churning out great movies, a couple of them co-starring Mercedes Dance. There had been a whiff of a scandal a few years before when his wife had cited Mercedes in a petition for divorce, but they'd reunited and the rumours had gone away. Charles Power hadn't acted with her since and Hollywood's short memories had fully rehabilitated his reputation.

'Isn't that Zander's role?' Sarah asked. 'So, what, has he been cut?'

Hollie swung round to a sitting position and picked up her iPad, but Sarah's fingers were already flying across her own keyboard.

'There's a video of the press conference on the Guilloti website,' she said, as she clicked through to it and then pressed 'play'.

'Son of a bitch,' Hollie exhaled, as Adrianna Guilloti stood on the steps outside her HQ on Fifth Avenue, her husband on one side of her, Charles Power on the other, a crowd of suits in the background.

Flashbulbs were going off as she stepped forward to the press podium that had been set up for the announcement.

Hollie, Sarah and Lauren watched, transfixed. 'Wow, she is one beautiful lady,' Lauren observed.

'Yep, for a total bitch,' Hollie retorted.

Ouch. There was obviously history there and the journalist in Sarah was desperate to ask. She made a mental note to save that one for later, and a physical note on the pad beside her to consider a chapter on celebrity endorsements.

'Ladies and gentlemen, I'm delighted to announce that the new face of Adrianna Guilloti menswear is the incredibly dashing Charles Power.'

The applause melted into a flurry of questions from the press. 'Adrianna, can you tell us why you have replaced Zander Leith?'

'Has your company cut ties with him?'

'Can you tell us why?'

Sarah realised that Hollie was holding her breath.

On screen, Adrianna appeared utterly unflustered and answered smoothly. 'I'm afraid Mr Leith's schedule no longer allows him to represent our brand, and we felt that the strength, exquisite attraction and – all pun intended – *power* of Guilloti made us the perfect match for Charles Power.'

Hollie let out a strangled moan. 'Lauren, your cop ex-boyfriend might have to lock me up, because I want to kill her. I do.'

Sarah wasn't paying attention, still mesmerized by the screen. Money. Elitism. Glamour. It was all wrapped up right there. Fashion. Another chapter in the book.

The camera panned back as Adrianna took another question and Sarah's hand snapped the 'pause' button.

'Hey, I know that guy,' she said, pointing to one of the faces in the crowd. Her frown had commandeered her facial muscles. 'Who is he?'

'That's Adrianna Guilloti's husband,' Hollie answered.

Sarah shook her head. 'No, not him. The guy standing at the back, over at the edge of the screen. How do I know him?' she mused. 'Or am I going crazy? He just looks so... familiar.'

Hollie and Lauren studied the face she was pointing at, before Lauren shrugged and Hollie said, 'No idea. Never seen him before.'

'Must be mistaken,' Sarah decided. She wound it back, checked again. Definitely something familiar, but nothing more than that.

Obviously she was so wound up about the Marilyn situation that she was imagining things.

How crazy was that?

50

Tempting.
 So very tempting.
 The change of plan, the new location, the surroundings, the other people.
 I thought about changing my own plans, bringing forward the inevitable.
 Tempting.
 But no.
 I've waited so long for this and I won't be rushed. Too much planning, too many hours, too risky to change because of a trifling matter like opportunity.
 After all, wasn't that what changed the course of everything in the first place?
 Opportunity.
 And I'll take mine when the time is right, when I'm ready. I will watch it, savour every second.
 I won't be controlled by other people.
 Because I'm the one who will control them.
 And I'll make them weep. Make them suffer.
 I'm going to rip out their hearts.
 And then I'll laugh while they bleed.

51

DAVIE

'Slippery People' – Talking Heads

'Thanks for coming up here, Mark,' Davie shook his Head of Security's hand, then turned to the man next to him and shook his hand too. 'Brad, pleased to meet you – Mirren has told me good things about you and I'm grateful that you joined forces with my guy here.' Formalities over, Davie gestured to them to take a seat at the long white wooden table in the kitchen. Both in dark suits, the two of them looked exactly like the ex-cops they were.

Zander and Mirren were already there and got up to greet the new arrivals, looking expectant.

In the story of his life, this was going to be one crazy-ass chapter. They'd been up here for three days now and he could see they'd all reacted to it in completely different ways. Mirren was still concerned, stressed, but there was definitely an edge of irritation in there too. Zander? He was broody but seemed to relish the peace. What was wrong with that guy? He got up with the sun every morning, stayed out with the horses until sunset, and no matter what anyone threw at him, he just shrugged it off. Lost a million-dollar endorsement deal? No biggie. Your assistant is pissed with you? It's all smooth, man. Psycho-killer bitch is on your tail? Just roll with the punches. When they were kids, Zander had been the deep one, the strong, silent type. Davie always figured it was because he couldn't be happy, couldn't show emotion. If Zander loved something, whether it was a toy or a cigarette or, later, a bottle of Scotch, Jono took it away just for fun. No surprise, then, that over the years, Zander retreated, showed less emotion, until he was this man of stone on the outside and a fucked-up mass of chaos on the inside.

This time had been good for them, though. They'd reconnected, hung out. He wouldn't put them back in the close friends category yet, but he was beginning to think maybe they'd get there.

Mirren opened it up and got straight to it. 'OK, gentlemen, where do we stand?'

Brad Bernson was the first to pitch in with a reply.

'Here's what we know. Marilyn McLean entered the country on 10th January. She hired a black GMC, stayed in a motel on Robertson, then moved to another hotel in Santa Monica for a week.'

'Past tense?' Mirren asked. Davie felt the optimism rise. Yes! Past tense. She'd done the Hollywood Walk of Fame, the bus tour of the stars' homes and then fucked off back to Liverpool, or Glasgow, or wherever she'd dug her hole now.

'She checked out four days ago,' Mark replied. 'Handed the rental car back, left the motel.'

'So she's gone?' Davie clarified.

Mark shook his head.

Damn.

'To be honest, we're not sure yet. We don't have a record of her on a flight leaving the country, but that doesn't mean she's still here. We've managed to get hold of the manifests for all the American airlines, but we've got nothing on Iceland Air and British Airways. Both had flights departing around the time she handed back the car. And of course, she could have travelled somewhere inland. Also, two cruises left Los Angeles Port that morning, one for Hawaii and one for Mexico.

'So she could be anywhere?' Mirren asked, clearly furious. 'How the fuck can a sixty-year-old woman go on the run and two agencies combined can't find her?'

Both men looked deeply uncomfortable, and Davie felt his own sense of frustration coming into play. He had to get out of there. Needed to get back to the city, back to work. It was only three days until the Oscars, and there were run-throughs booked for tomorrow and the day after. He'd already decided he was leaving tonight no matter what they said, but the fact that Marilyn could still be around was going to make it a harder sell to Sarah. 'What about Raymo and the girl from the plane?' Zander asked. 'If they were involved, Marilyn had to have connected with them.'

Mark nodded. 'Absolutely. We've interviewed Raymo and he's standing by his story that it was a spontaneous attack.'

'He's lying,' Zander replied.

'In fairness, I think you're probably right, but we've got no proof.'

'And the girl? Wendy?' Zander probed.

Brad Bernson sighed, obviously uncomfortable. 'We called the number she put in your phone but it's dead now. She's quit her job and there's no sign of her at her apartment. She's in the wind.' There was a silence as this was processed.

'We have to warn you,' Mark Bock spoke again, 'that it's not advisable for any of you to attend the Oscars.'

Before Zander or Mirren could reply, Davie laughed as if it was the most ridiculous thing he'd ever heard. In truth, it probably was. 'No way am I missing that. I'm co-hosting the show, and I don't care if I have to commando-crawl on my knees carrying an AK47 and a SWAT shield, I'm going.'

'Your own risk, Davie,' Mark answered. 'But I'm saying it's too big a risk to take.'

'And I'm telling you I'll take it.'

52

MIRREN

'Stronger' – Cher

Mirren had been reluctant to leave the ranch, but what choice was there? What were they to do – just hang out up in Santa Barbara until the end of time? It wasn't realistic. The Oscars were crucial to her career, not just because of the nomination, but because they kept her stock high and she needed to keep the dollars coming in to support Chloe's Care. Especially since negotiations had stalled with Pictor.

But her determination to go was more than just for her image. She refused to be a victim. No way. She hadn't let Jono Leith make her a victim back then, and she'd be damned if she'd let Marilyn do that to her now.

Where the fuck was she?

And why hadn't Brad and Mark come up with anything yet? What the hell was she paying them for? They were her hope for putting an end to this and they'd failed.

So what now?

Now they were all back in LA, they'd ramped up security around their houses. None of them were going anywhere without an armed bodyguard – Logan included - and they weren't making any unnecessary journeys.

Mirren didn't mind that bit. Gave her an excuse not to go into the office. The thought of running into Mike Feechan didn't fill her with joy. It had been different this time – no phone calls, no emails, no flowers. It struck her that she should probably be the one to make a move, but frankly, she had other things on her mind.

'You OK, Mom?' Logan asked her, as he wandered in wearing just a pair of board shorts and carried out his normal morning regime – kitchen, fridge open, orange juice, straight from carton until finished.

'Morning, son. I'm good. You?'

He shrugged. 'Deeko called. They took Jonell to rehab this morning. Apparently he's mad as hell and wants to kill me.'

Mirren felt her heart go out to him. 'You're doing the right thing now, Logan. And it will pass. When he kicks it, he'll see that you made the only good choice, for his sake.'

Logan nodded. 'I guess. Feels like crap right now, though.'

'I know, honey,' she said sadly. It was one of the feelings she wished she could forget. Every time she got Chloe to rehab, her daughter would lash out, cut her off. Every time she confiscated her stash, Chloe would scream that she was a fucker and a bitch. Every time she told Chloe she was doing it out of love, her daughter replied that she hated her.

Being an addict was hard. Helping an addict was harder.

Still, she'd still give anything, everything, to be fighting with her daughter right now instead of looking out on the ocean on which they'd scattered her ashes.

On the counter, her cell phone rang. Logan was nearest, so he picked it up and tossed it over to her.

'Hello?'

'Mirren, it's Hollie.' Mirren automatically smiled. She liked Zander's assistant and loved the fact that she took no crap from him. Although, there had definitely been a weird vibe between them up at the ranch. Not surprising, really. These were definitely stressful times.

'Hollie, hi. Is everything OK?'

'Been better.'

'That doesn't sound good.'

She heard Hollie sigh. 'Look, I'm probably way out of line calling you, and Zander would kill me if he knew...'

'But?'

'I need help. Mirren, he's a nightmare. He's so stubborn and unreasonable and proud, and I can't get him to see that he's in danger of screwing things up permanently.'

Mirren almost smiled. Hollie had Zander down pat. 'What's happened?'

'Wes Lomax. He's being a prick and he won't consider that the drug test wasn't authentic. Zander won't tell him what we know now. So it's a stand-off. Zander is saying he doesn't care, that Wes can fuck off. Meanwhile, Wes is lining up a replacement. The thing is, Mirren, you know how this will play out. If it gets out that he failed a drugs test, even if we know that's wrong, Zander's career is over. If the stuff about the air hostess gets out, he's screwed then too. He's refusing to go to the Oscars because he says it's all a load of crap. And if he doesn't fight this, if he just let's Wes sack him, then he's done. No going back. Missing the ceremony tomorrow night will just get the rumour mill going and people will start digging and God knows what they'll come up with. I get that he doesn't care right now, but he will in the future, I know it. If he wants to quit the business, fine, but he can't do it under a cloud of shame that destroys everything he's achieved. I can't let him.'

Mirren inhaled deeply. For someone who was about as low maintenance as it got, that guy could be hard work. He was flawed, troubled, had his demons, but god, she loved him. More than that, she owed him. She should never have believed he was using again.

'Leave it with me. I'll call you back.'

An hour later, she was dressed in a black roll-neck sweater and a white pencil skirt with co-ordinating Jimmy Choo mono-chrome heels. In the car, she put a call in to Wes Lomax's office. 'Monica, this is Mirren McLean. I need to see Wes in half an hour. Where will he be?'

Wes Lomax might be one of most important men in the business, but there was never a question over whether he would see her. It had been a lot of years since anyone stalled or refused Mirren McLean.

Monica came back on the line. 'He'll be here, Mirren. Are you OK to come in?'

'I'll be there.'

Twenty-nine minutes later, she was standing in Wes Lomax's office.

'Go on in, Mirren,' Monica told her warmly.

'Thanks, Monica.' Mirren returned the affection. Twenty years before, when she first arrived in Hollywood, Monica had helped her find an apartment and settle in. The fact that she was still working for Wes said that under that charming exterior there was a core of steel. Or a monumental pay cheque. Or both.

Wes was sitting behind his legendary marble desk when she entered. There was a crack that ran all the way down the centre. Urban legend had it that he attacked it with an axe in a fit of rage after a deal went sour. The truth was, he'd had an energetic four-way with three generously proportioned ladies and it had proven too much for Italy's finest marble.

'Mirren, darling,' Wes roared, greeting her like an old friend. Mirren had a sudden urge to roll her eyes. She was pissed at him, furious that he didn't believe Zander, raging that he was being such a dick, when the truth was, Wes Lomax had way more vices than his leading actor. He just didn't get caught. Ignoring the effusive welcome, Mirren sat down on the black leather chair opposite him. 'I'll get to the point,' she told him.

'We can do that,' he agreed, sitting forward.

'Zander Leith.'

'What about him?'

'You're going to put him back on the next Dunhill movie.'

Wes laughed. 'I don't think so. Failed a drug test. The boy's uninsurable. Toxic.'

Mirren barely let him get the words out. She was busy, no time for this bullshit.

'The test was faked. I'm not going to explain how or why right now, but trust me, it was. So here's what's going to happen: you're going to put him back in the next Dunhill, and I'm going to cover his insurance bond.'

'Are you crazy? It's millions.'

'I have millions, Wes,' she pointed out the obvious.

'But if he fucks up, the money is gone. Mirren, I know you can write this cheque, but you could lose it all.'

'I won't. He's clean. Always will be.'

'Mirren, I can't—'

She cut him off. 'Also, you need to call him and persuade him to come back on board. Don't tell him I'm covering it. Don't tell him I had anything to do with it. Just make it happen.'

'Mirren, you know I'd do anything for you, darlin', but—'

'And I'll bring *Clansman* to you. Two-movie deal. My existing terms. No merchandise. One-time offer.'

He paused, mid-sentence, and she could see the wheels of his mind working like cogs in a cheap, garish, hyped-up watch. He wasn't stupid. Without the merchandise, it wasn't the best deal in the world, but it was a guaranteed rainmaker that would net the studio tens of millions of dollars. More than that, Wes would just get so much satisfaction in taking this from Feechan at Pictor. A twinge of regret surfaced over that, but what was she to do? If Pictor hadn't tried to play hardball, then they wouldn't be in this situation in the first place.

There was no denying that there was something about Mike Feechan she found irresistible. In another time or place, they might have had something. But this came down to a choice between a guy she barely knew and one she loved. No contest.

'Darlin', you got yourself a deal.' Wes leaned over to shake her hand, his grin as smug as it was victorious.

Mirren reciprocated, then stood. 'I'll have my people draw up the contracts in the morning. It all hinges on you making Zander believe this, Wes. He can't know I had anything to do with it.'

'Don't you worry, honey – I got this.'

Mirren didn't doubt that he had.

In the car, she phoned Hollie. 'Expect a call from Wes Lomax any minute,' she told her. 'Zander is back in. Don't tell him I had anything to do with it, but persuade him to swallow his pride and take the offer Wes is about to make him.'

'Mirren, I don't know how you did that, but thank you. I owe you big time.'

'You really don't,' she said softly. Zander had already paid it forward. He'd tried to help Chloe, really tried. One addict to another. He'd almost succeeded, and he was heartbroken when she died. He and Mirren shared that, and he'd been there for her ever since. She owed him. 'Oh, and tell him I called to make sure he's coming to the Oscars tomorrow night. Tell him I said I need him there to look out for me. He'll come.'

She knew he would do that for her, and she wasn't above a bit of emotional coercion.

As she hung up, a tidal wave of weariness swept over her and she realised that she needed a break. Since Chloe died and Jack left, she'd worked non-stop, desperate to stay busy, but she could see now that she was exhausted. As soon as the Oscars were over, she was taking time off. Perhaps Logan could come with her, if he could be prised away from Lauren for long enough.

She'd broach it with him after the ceremony, see what he thought.

One last hurdle. The Oscars. Much as she'd rather do anything other than parade in front of the watching world, she had to show up, put her best smile on and act like she was thrilled to be there. She'd skipped the usual prep and arranged for hair and make-up to come to the house a couple of hours before the ceremony tomorrow. It would be fine. Her team had worked with her long enough to know what she liked. Devlin had the arrangements down, she knew when she was to arrive, where she was to sit, and the spots she was to hit on the red carpet. That bit didn't scare her. There was more security at the Academy Awards than most governments laid on for visiting heads of state. She'd be safe there. It would be fine.

The screen on the AMG signalled an incoming call. Davie.

'Hey, I was just thinking… I'm guessing you're looking forward to tomorrow night like you look forward to a dose of the clap.'

Despite her worries and weariness, Mirren laughed. Davie had always had that effect on her.

'Indeed.'

'So why don't we stick together? Sarah's not up for it – doesn't like watching when I'm hosting, in case it all goes horribly wrong. Think I should be insulted that she's the only chick in town who refuses a ticket to the Oscars?'

'I like her style,' Mirren told him truthfully.

'And I'll need to go early, because I have pre-show rehearsals. How about we tie up there and then head to the after-parties together?'

'Sounds like a plan. I'll see you there, my friend.'

As she hung up, she realised that she hadn't been bullshitting him. If she had to go, put on a smile and spend the night pretending to be a glittering part of the establishment, the only people she wanted to be with were Davie and Zander.

It was only one ceremony. One night. She could do this.

53

SARAH

'Home' – Blake Shelton

Sarah pulled her cup out from under the $7,000 coffee machine, removed a large tub of butter-pecan ice cream from the freezer and headed for the sofa.

She already had her monitor up on the coffee table and the TV on in the background.

This time last year, she'd watched the Oscars in her Glasgow flat at 2 a.m., entranced by the dresses, the glamour, thinking it was all a pretentious but fabulously entertaining piece of nonsense.

Now, she was in Marina del Rey, watching the Oscars at 6 p.m., entranced by the dresses, the glamour and knowing for sure that it was a pretentious but fabulously entertaining piece of nonsense. One that was being co-presented by her boyfriend. Her actual boyfriend. At that very moment, Ryan Seacrest announced on E! that Davie Johnston had just pulled up and the camera at the entrance area zoomed in to catch his arrival. He must be exhausted. He'd been there all day rehearsing, then home for just an hour to change before heading back for the red carpet.

Of course, he had to make an entrance. Every other star arrived in a limo. Davie had the agency send over a driver to chauffeur him in one of his own cars – the Bentley this time.

'If you've got it, flaunt it, honey,' giggled Sarah, raising a butter-pecan spoon to the TV in a toast. This was definitely the best way to experience the Oscars. If she was there, she'd be worried about saying something stupid or fretting about Davie's live performance. Not that she didn't have faith in him to be brilliant, but that didn't stop the nerves on his behalf. She watched as Davie worked the red carpet, worked the press, and worked the crowd, and so he should. He was back on top in this town. His talk show was a massive hit, *American Stars* was number one, and *Beauty and the Beats*, prior to Jizzo's death, had been number three.

Mirren, Zander and Hollie would be arriving on screen in about twenty minutes. Meeting Hollie had been an unexpected and very welcome bonus from last week. The two of them had clicked immediately, bonded by their similar situations. Sarah was in love with a star. Hollie worked for one. Although, Sarah did wonder when Hollie would realise that her feelings were more than professional. Her over-protectiveness made it blindingly obvious she cared about Zander in more than just a PA-boss capacity.

Sarah had a hunch those feelings were reciprocated. Just a hunch. Although it was backed up by the fact that Zander had asked Hollie to walk the red carpet with him. After a long chat with Sarah, she'd eventually agreed, but she was leaving straight afterwards, skipping the after-parties. Like Sarah, she hated all the pretentious stuff. Too many celebrities, too much arse-kissing, too sore on the feet. She'd offered to come, kick off the heels and chill here with Sarah instead.

That's what new friends were for.

When her boyfriend disappeared off the screen, Sarah turned her attention back to the work in front of her. She'd made up a chart, like a police investigation board, with Davie, Mirren and Zander's names at the top. Feeding off each one, a list of the incidents that had occurred in the last month or so – a list that was all the more chilling now that Hollie had filled her in on the shit that had been happening to Zander.

Davie: house fire, shots fired, blood thrown, car wrecked. Someone with a grudge?

Zander: fight with Raymo, drug test, apartment break-in, accusations of sexual impropriety. Why?

Mirren: possible sighting of her mother. No other attacks. Why?

Her eyes went back and forward across it, trying to make connections, find loopholes, see how it all tied up. Nothing. Not a—Hang on.

Raymo. The air hostess. What was her name? She searched her pile of notes. Wendy.

Mark Bock had already spoken to Raymo, who had stuck to his story, while Wendy had disappeared off the face of the earth.

Those were the links to whoever was doing this. The flight attendant she had no knowledge of – she could get on that one in the morning – but Raymo she knew. He was a nightly fixture on the club scene, someone she'd seen dozens of times before.

Sarah closed her eyes, and – as if she was removing files from a filing cabinet, checking them, putting them back – rewound her memory, drawing up mental pictures of as many of the occasions she'd seen Raymo as possible. Eyes still closed, she worked through them one by one: where he was, what he was wearing, who he was with, who he was talking to.

There were over a dozen files in her memory, checked, dismissed, checked, dismissed, when one night in LiX took front and centre in her mind.

That's when it came to her. The face she'd seen before. Out of context, she'd never have made the connection. But now she had. As she searched frantically for her phone, she realised that at least part of the truth had been out there the whole time.

54

'It's a Wonderful Night for Oscar' – Billy Crystal

Live Report from The Academy Awards, Los Angeles

'Here at the Oscars, I'm Myla Rivera, and we at CXY 5 are bringing you live team coverage of Hollywood's biggest night. Right now, let's look back at the Academy Awards themselves, and the most moving moment of the evening.

'Mirren McLean, producer, director and writer of the Clansman series of books and movies, lost out on her nominations for Best Movie and Best Director, but she did pick up Best Original Screenplay for the latest record-breaking hit, Clansman: The Warrior Mist.

'Mirren's speech was incredibly moving, as she paid tribute to her daughter, Chloe, who sadly passed away recently, and also to a couple of friends who you might just recognize. Take a look...'

Shot cuts to VT. On the Oscars stage, Mirren McLean is receiving her award from Robert DeNiro.

Mirren steps forward, unable to speak as she is given the longest ovation of the night.

Eventually, it subsides, she takes a deep breath, smiles...

'I am so, so honoured to receive this award. Thank you to the Academy and to every single person who has supported the Clansman series by going to the movies or buying the books. Thank you, of course, to Lex Callaghan, my Clansman, and his beautiful wife, Cara, my friend.'

Camera cuts to Lex and Cara in the audience, beaming smiles.

Cara blows a kiss to the stage.

'To my other friend, Lou Cole, for being smart, and beautiful, and woefully indiscreet, and always by my side.'

That one gets a huge cheer of approval.

Mirren pauses, another breath, composes herself, steels herself to go on.

'I'd like to dedicate this to my daughter, Chloe. The world was a brighter place when she was in it and I will never stop missing her every moment of every day.'

The camera pans to the audience. Nicole Kidman. Jennifer Garner. Lou Cole. Tears running down their cheeks.

'I'd like to thank my son, Logan, for being just the coolest, best-looking guy on earth.' *Laughter through the tears now.*

'And finally, I'd like to thank my other family. The one I chose for myself. This is also for Davie Johnston and Zander Leith. I love you both.'

55

It's time.
I'm waiting.
Right here.
You have no idea how long I've dreamed of this.
I'm ready.
Are you?
Because it's time.

56

DAVIE

'Everybody Wants to Rule the World' – Tears for Fears
(Back Where We Started)

The Lomax party was a blast.

Everyone who mattered was there, and they all wanted five minutes with the trio at the centre of the room. Davie knew tonight had been special and he was buzzing.

His performance on the show had been flawless and hilarious, and the camera cut to Clooney and Damon at exactly the right moment, just as the two of them were in peals of laughter at one of Davie's lines.

They'd both be getting calls tomorrow morning with invitations to come on *Here's Davie Johnston*.

He was almost disappointed when Mirren said she wanted to go. Almost.

Most of the seriously big players had left, heading home when their publicists dictated, lest they get embroiled in something that could wipe out a carefully planned, beautifully executed publicity strategy. An outfit that *InStyle* claimed was divine, a perfect performance at the ceremony, being snapped mingling with all the right people, making some important connections... All is well and victorious until, oops, photographed on the way out, next to a dishevelled D-lister throwing up her caviar while flashing the fact that she isn't wearing any knickers. Epic fail.

This was why the biggest of the players, including their own little glittering trio, were now on the way home.

The three of them finally reached the door, collecting their cell phones as they left. Wes Lomax had decreed that all phones and camera devices were banned inside to protect the privacy of the stars. Davie would have been happy to sign a disclaimer that said, 'Snap away. Who needs privacy? And look, I'm talking to Cameron Diaz.'

As soon as he switched it on, it beeped to alert him to outstanding messages, but before he could check them, Lex and Cara appeared.

Davie's Bentley slid round the corner and came to a stop in front of him.

Right behind the Bentley, Mirren and Zander's car slid into position.

One of the valets stopped speaking into a walkie-talkie and sighed. 'Mr Callaghan, I'm afraid your limo will be another ten minutes – it's just manoeuvring out of the gridlock at the end of the drive.'

'Told you we should have brought a horse,' Lex quipped to the group.

'Jump in with us and we'll give you a lift,' Mirren immediately offered.

Lex put his hand up to protest, but Cara stopped him. 'Callaghan, don't you dare refuse. You're not standing here in six-inch heels that have left you with no feeling in your feet for the last hour.'

'But we're heading north,' Lex stated. 'Opposite direction from you guys.'

Davie stepped forward with the obvious solution, addressing Mirren and Zander. 'Why don't you two come with me and I'll drop you home? If you behave, we'll get drive-through,' he joked, while actually thinking that it could work out perfectly. They could drop Mirren first, then Zander in Venice and then he could go visit Sarah in Marina del Rey. She was always saying he should come spend the night at her apartment, instead of her travelling to his house. Maybe tonight he would.

Mirren nodded. 'Sounds like a plan.' She turned back to Lex and Cara. 'And then you guys can just take our limo. Wes Lomax is paying for it, so be sure to clock up the miles.'

'I've always wanted to go to Tijuana,' Cara shrugged, laughing. Kisses, hugs and handshakes were exchanged, before Lex and Cara headed to the limo, while Mirren, Zander and Davie stepped towards the Bentley, thanking the valet, who had the doors open and waiting for them. Zander gestured to Mirren to take the front passenger seat.

Lex and Cara entered the limo, and the doors closed. Davie joked about his new career as a chauffeur as he pulled on his seatbelt in the Bentley, then turned to eye them both.

'Well, kids, we made it,' he told the other two. They both knew exactly what he meant. No sign of Marilyn McLean. She'd obviously gone. Maybe she was never anywhere near them in the first place. Perhaps Mark and Brad would find her, perhaps not. He still wasn't convinced that she even existed any more. It was far more likely that he'd just been the victim of a crazy fan. There were many out there.

'We did,' Mirren agreed.

Zander laughed. 'Yeah, but we still have to survive Davie's driving.'

The limo driver behind them restarted his engine.

Davie put his foot on the gas, heard a cry, looked round. A woman running towards him, clutching a bag, pulling something from it.

He froze.

Neither car moved, yet there was an earth-trembling bang. A blinding flash. The ripping of metal. The screams. The world exploded.

Then a deafening silence.

57

'Wrecking Ball' – Miley Cyrus

Live Report Breaking News – Los Angeles

'I'm Myla Rivera, live here on CXY 5, as we bring you the horrific breaking news that there has been an explosion outside the Beverly Hills Heights Hotel. The incident happened as the stars celebrated at the Lomax Oscars after-party. Details are sketchy right now, but I can tell you that there are reports of casualties, and police are looking at the possibility of a terrorist attack, with claims that this could be the work of a suicide bomber.'

Split screen right – camera on a scene of carnage outside the Lomax Oscars after-party. One vehicle destroyed, another badly damaged, detritus scattered across the road. Yellow-tape cordoned-off areas, investigators in white suits already at work, the whole landscape illuminated by the blue lights of emergency vehicles.

Back on split screen left – Myla Rivera, putting in the Oscar performance of her life, eyes moist with tears, oozing sorrow and sympathy.

'Early reports suggest that the vehicles involved were those of Davie Johnston,

Mirren McLean and Zander Leith. It's also thought that actor Lex Callaghan and his wife, Cara, may have been at the scene. Several people have now been taken to Cedars-Sinai Hospital. There is no word on the injuries or the status of the victims, however...' She paused for effect, milking maximum emotional value, absolutely aware that this clip would be re-run for the next twenty-four hours and be syndicated across the country and possibly internationally. This had to be the ultimate, the pinnacle of her career – she broke the news the night there was an explosion at the Oscars. It didn't get much better than that. But back to the update. OK, pause was long enough, time to deliver the sound bite, the climax, the line that would reverberate around the globe.

'Unsubstantiated reports are claiming that there has been at least one fatality, but other reports from the scene suggest that two people may have lost their lives tonight.'

58

'Fear' – Eminem

Good Morning Hollywood
   Special Report by Clark Koban, Film Correspondent
   The Brutal Circle – 1989

Camera 3 on Sam Mendoza, anchor.

'Last night, Mirren McLean picked up the Oscar for Best Original Screenplay. A couple of hours later, she was involved in a tragic incident after celebrating that win at the Lomax after-party. We will bring you further details as soon as we have them, but in the meantime, to honour this great lady, film correspondent Clark Koban takes a look at the movie that launched her career.'

Cut to pre-recorded VT, Clark Koban, against a background screen of a dark Glasgow skyline, talks directly to camera.

'Is it really almost twenty years ago that The Brutal Circle delivered a harrowing sucker punch to millions of American movie fans? Where were you the first time you watched this classic film, a cinematic game-changer that banked over $150 million at the box office and launched the careers of three Scots who were, incredibly, still teenagers when the script was developed by omnipotent producer Wes Lomax?

'Mirren McLean. Zander Leith. Davie Johnston. Their journey from obscurity to Oscar is the stuff of legend.

'The story, penned by McLean, was a dark, uncompromising piece of writing and Lomax famously claims he was sold by the end of the first page. Within a year, the movie was in production, with Davie Johnston and Zander Leith playing the title roles. It was Leith's first acting role and never has a debut performance made a bigger impact. Rack up those movie clichés, because every one of them applied to the brooding maelstrom of talent. Enigmatic. Compelling. Movie gold. Explosive. There wasn't an instant when he was on screen that he didn't demand attention.

'Right off the bat, Zander Leith was a star who had that priceless ability to hijack the viewer's soul. And in that troubled role as a teenager fighting demons, he delivered a strangely prophetic premonition of the life ahead of him. A lifetime later, Leith remains one of Hollywood's biggest names, but off-screen, the years have been a tangled wreck of troubles.

'But back in 1989, the stars moved into alignment for The Brutal Circle. Mirren McLean wrote an incredible script; Davie Johnston and Zander Leith made it the biggest hit of a generation.

'So does the movie live up to the hype? Has it stood the test of time?

'Thirty seconds after the opening titles roll, you'll have your answer.

'Nothing else matters but the screen.

'Glasgow. 1986. A cold, dark night. A young girl, Lizzy, sits smoking outside her home when a guy (Zac, played by Davie Johnston), wracked with the insecurities of teenage angst, approaches her.

'Why is she out there?

'Because her mother is inside with her boyfriend.

'"But I see you here every night," he counters.

'Lizzy's dead eyes lift to face him. "And every night she's in there with him."

'A new arrival, Zander Leith's character, Jay, son of the local hard guy, Sonny Cole – a boy who has grown up to detest his hard-drinking, wife-beating, psychopath of a father.

'Three dysfunctional kids, bonded by poverty, neglect and the need to belong to something that doesn't come with the risk of a slap or the vicious stab of the cruellest of words.

'They form a family, one that balances on a seesaw of hope that they'll escape and acceptance that they probably never will.

'Lizzy and Zac fall in love; they hatch plans; they look beyond the mire of despair life has delivered to them until Sonny Cole delivers a different fate.

'For years, he's been betraying his wife, spending night after night with Lizzy's mother.

'But now he wants more. He wants Lizzy.

'And what Sonny Cole wants, he takes.

'But it's the last thing he ever does. A betrayal too far. A horrific act of violence that is met with lethal retribution.

'And when the screen fades to black, you know.

'You know that you've just watched a creation of cinematic brilliance.

'And you know how three twenty-something Scots ended up standing in front of the entire cast of Hollywood royalty, picking up an Oscar for one of the best movies that was ever made.'

59

MIRREN

'Holding Back the Years' – Simply Red

Someone in the room. Someone there.

A touch. Her hand. Someone

Heart beating faster, can't breathe. Oh god, no. No. No.

'Mom? Mom?'

Logan's voice. Open your eyes. Her boy. Her boy was there. Smiling.

Mirren forced her eyes to focus, to see him. 'Hey,' he said.

Head. She couldn't move her head. Her eyes scanned the room. A hospital room. She was in a hospital bed. Someone there, in the corner. Who? Coming towards her now. Brad Bernson.

'What happened? Tell me what happened.' She didn't recognize the throaty rasp as her own. Her neck hurt, her vocal chords, her head, everything.

Logan's eyes looked searchingly at Brad, on the other side of her bed now.

'Mirren, it was Marilyn. She was in the street outside the hotel.'

Heart racing, blood pumping so hard, excruciating pain in her head. And fear. So much fear.

'Where is she now?'

A shade on Brad's expression.

'She's gone, Mirren. She died in the explosion. It's over.'

Mirren's world went dark again.

60

ZANDER

'Everybody Hurts' – R.E.M.

Hospital waiting rooms. The closest thing to hell on earth. How long had he been here? Hours? Felt like days. Beside him, Lex Callaghan, both of them bloody, dishevelled, both staring straight ahead at the white double doors in front of them.

In his peripheral vision, he saw Lex's hands clench into fists, then flex, then fist, then flex. The actions of a man on the verge of explosion.

Inside those double doors, his wife, Cara, on a table, surrounded by strangers.

Zander reached out, put his hand on Lex's shoulder, said nothing.

They'd been brought here in the same ambulance, the one that rode behind Cara's.

Hers got priority. Female inside, life-threatening injuries, blood loss critical, stopped breathing, cardiac arrest, dead at the scene until paramedics got her back, restarted her heart and intubated her to get air into her lungs.

By the time they'd arrived, she was already in theatre and Lex had refused to go to the ER. His wife was behind those doors. He was waiting until he could be with her.

Zander understood. At the ranch that morning, she'd told him she'd help him heal. Now it was her turn – it was her turn to find her way back.

And until then, Zander was going to stay by both their sides.

61

SARAH

'We Found Love' – Calvin Harris & Rihanna

'I don't give a fuck. The media blackout stays until we know what we're dealing with. I'll speak when I'm ready and they can go screw themselves.'

Sarah had no idea who Davie was speaking to, but whoever it was definitely got the point.

'Davie, you need to stay in bed. The doctor says...'

He stopped, looked at her, eyes challenging. Sarah met the gaze, held it. He buckled first.

He climbed back onto the bed, wincing as he moved. Behind her, Hollie came into the room.

'Any word?' Sarah asked urgently. Hollie shook her head.

'She's still in theatre. Lex and Zander are waiting up there.'

'And Mirren?' Davie asked.

'She's OK. Logan is with her. Lou is on the way. She's going to be fine.'

Sarah felt the tears spring to the back of her eyes and she blinked them away. If she was religious, she'd be thanking God right now.

There was some activity outside the door, voices, and Sarah got up, looked out of the window. Mark Bock was arguing with one of the cops posted outside. Sarah opened the door. 'It's fine, Charlie. He's with us.'

Officer Charlie Souza stood to one side and let Mark pass. Sarah gave him a grateful smile as she closed the door behind him. Hollie and Davie both eyed Mark expectantly.

'Tell me, Mark,' Davie said simply.

Mark stood by the side of the bed, black suit, tie, unflappable. 'Positive id. It was Marilyn McLean.'

'I saw a woman running towards me. Why didn't I recognize her?'

Mark sighed. 'She looked nothing like the photographs we had. Black hair, not blonde.'

'You sure it was her?' Sarah asked.

'Yep. Positive id from her fingerprint scan when she entered the country. We had a contact in the feds rush that one through. Passport in her purse too. She dropped it as she ran towards the car, so it was relatively undamaged.'

Hollie looked at him quizzically. 'I don't get it, Mark. Why? Why would she do this?'

Mark shrugged his shoulders in resignation. 'The CSIs are still at the scene; cops are still reviewing footage. The truth is, we don't know yet. And the only person who can tell us is dead.' His words silenced the room for a few moments. Marilyn McLean. Dead. If it didn't terrify them, it would be laughable.

The woman travels thousands of miles, comes up with some messed-up plan and now she's dead.

Sarah's eyebrows knitted into a frown. 'She didn't do it all. I think she was targeting Mirren, maybe Davie too, but not Zander. I think the stuff that happened to him came from someone else.'

Only when she saw that everyone was staring at her did she realise she'd said that out loud.

'What are you talking about?' Davie asked, irritated, confused. Shit, this wasn't the time. She should have left it, let things settle.

But now she'd started...

She dipped into her bag, pulled out her tablet, fired it up. The others waited in silence until she pulled up an image. A freeze frame. Adrianna Guilloti's press conference the week before. 'This guy here,' she said, pointing at the bodyguard standing behind Adrianna and Carlton Farnsworth.

'You thought you recognized him when you saw that clip up at the ranch,' Hollie exclaimed.

Sarah nodded. 'I did. Couldn't say where from, though. Took me a while to put it together, but now I'm sure I saw him a few weeks ago with Raymo Cash in LiX. The security cameras there will back it up, but I'm positive. If he was with Raymo Cash, I'm guessing he was planning the attack on Zander. If he did that, I think it's logical that the other stuff – ransacking the apartment, the tampered drug test, the air hostess - was connected.'

'I don't get it. Adrianna Guilloti did all this to Zander?' Hollie asked, confused. 'But she wouldn't... I mean, why would she? They were together. They had a... thing.'

'I don't think it was Adrianna,' Sarah said. 'Look at the guy's eyeline in this shot.'

All four of them stared at the image as Sarah magnified it. The bodyguard's gaze wasn't directed at the woman in front of the camera.

'It was Carlton Farnsworth's bodyguard?'

Sarah nodded. 'I think so. Farnsworth has money to burn. He's as shady as they come. He's got the means, the motive... and maybe a seething rage of jealousy too. If he wanted to scare Zander off, or to discredit him so that Adrianna would have to cut ties, then these are the kind of stunts that would achieve that. Mark?'

Mark Bock nodded. 'I'll have my guys get on it.'

'So it was, what? Revenge?' Hollie's voice had stepped up a notch, bordering on shrill. 'He did all that stuff to Zander because he was fucking his wife?'

At that moment Hollie's phone rang. Gasping, she turned it to face Sarah. The name Adrianna Guilloti flashed on the screen.

Hollie answered it on speaker.

'Hello, this is Adrianna Giulloti. I'm trying to contact Zander Leith but his phone is off. I believe you are his assistant?'

Sarah watched as Hollie inhaled, exhaled, steadied herself.

'I'm more than his assistant. I'm his friend. And you, Mrs Farnsworth, can fuck right off.'

62

DAVIE

'Through the Barricades' – Spandau Ballet

Davie was tired. So tired. The morning sun was scorching through the windows, but he wouldn't let Sarah close the curtains. He wanted to see sky. How 'movie of the week' was that? All he wanted to do was to lie here, hold Sarah's hand and look at the daylight.

He must have had a severe knock on the head that the docs had missed.

Mark Bock had gone back to his office to update his team and get them moving in the right direction. They knew what had happened now, but they didn't know all the whys. Adrianna Guilloti's husband looked square in the frame for all those fucked-up things that had happened to Zander. The guy had a reputation for being shady. He was also richer than God. A lethal combination for someone who could have believed he was in danger of losing his wife? It was up to Mark to get the answers on that.

All that mattered now was that Marilyn couldn't do any more.

'Hey?' A voice at the door. Mirren in a chair, Hollie pushing her.

Davie felt a huge lump form in his throat and realised that he was about to cry. Shit, what had happened to him? There was definitely a concussion going on here somewhere.

Sarah moved back to let Hollie push Mirren to his side, put her hand over his, her eyes full of unshed tears too.

'You OK?' he asked, choking on the words.

Mirren nodded. 'Davie, I'm so, so sorry. Marilyn...' She lost the rest as she put her hand to her mouth to stop the sobs. Davie leaned over, wrapped his arms around her, not caring that stretching hurt like fuck.

'She's gone, Mirr. It's done.'

He held her until her shoulders stopped heaving.

'I can't stand that I came from such an evil bitch, Davie. The things she's done...'

'We don't think she did them all,' Sarah said gently.

'You don't?'

Sarah shook her head, then told her everything. The connection between Raymo Cash and Carlton Farnsworth, her assumptions as to why.

'So Marilyn didn't try to hurt Zander?' Mirren said, more thinking out loud than asking a question. 'That makes sense,' she said, before laughing. But it was a twisted laugh, one that was steeped in bitterness and hate.

Davie put his hand on hers, squeezed it tightly, trying to stop the hysteria that was clearly building. 'Mirren, it's OK. It's OK.'

'Of course,' she spat, 'Perfect fucking sense. Marilyn would never hurt Zander, because he was Jono Leith's son. She didn't know that you were Jono's son too. She only ever knew you and I together, knew how much I loved you, how much I wanted to be with you back then. I took away the man she loved. So it makes perfect sense that she would want to do the same to me.'

63

MIRREN

'I Will Always Love You' – Dolly Parton

Mirren couldn't bear to look at the devastation on Lex Callaghan's face. She'd been there, knew how much it hurt to face losing someone who was part of your soul. How long had it been since anyone spoke?

An hour? Two? That's how long she'd been there, sitting beside Lex, holding his hand.

She'd asked Hollie to bring her up here to the waiting room outside the operating theatres after she'd spoken to Davie. He was OK. Zander was too. Lou was here at the hospital now, downstairs, sitting in a chair in her room, fending off press and calling the shots. Beside Lou, Logan had fallen asleep on her bed, and Lauren was on her way in to support him.

To their left, the lift doors opened and Sarah appeared with a tray of coffees, passed them round. 'Davie is sleeping. Thought I'd make myself useful. Any news?'

Mirren shook her head. 'None.'

Sarah handed a coffee to Hollie, then sat down next to her, seeing what Mirren had already spotted. Everyone's gaze was trained on those white double doors. Hollie's eyes flickered between the doors and Zander, the doors and Zander, as if she just had to keep checking he was there, he was safe, he was in one piece.

Mirren saw it and she knew what it meant. Hollie loved him. She wondered if her old friend knew that in the midst of the carnage, the worry, the terror and the prayers, there was a tiny piece of goodness waiting for him.

A tiny piece of hope.

She just needed that goodness, that hope, to be with Lex too.

At that moment, the doors swung open, and a doctor who wore the posture of a weary man, of someone who had been in surgery for twelve hours, who had been the one person between Cara's life or death, walked towards them. Lex was already on his feet, heart breaking in front of them, raw emotion pouring from his soul.

'Mr Callaghan?'

Lex nodded, unable to speak.

'Your wife sustained a life-threatening wound in the explosion. As you know, a piece of metal lodged in her throat, cutting her windpipe. She stopped breathing and was intubated by a doctor at the scene. Mr Callaghan, it was touch and go, but we managed to repair the damage. It's too early to say for sure, but I think she's going to be fine.'

As the tears ran down her face, Mirren gave a silent prayer of thanks.

Maybe, just maybe, goodness and hope would win.

64

ZANDER

'I'll Stand by You' – The Pretenders

Lex held out his hand to Zander. 'Thanks, man. For being here.'

Zander said nothing, just nodded, smiled, hugged him. He didn't know Lex Callaghan well at all, yet right now he felt like there was no one he knew more. They'd barely spoken, just sat there, side by side, for hours. Some things didn't need words.

Lex said goodbye to Mirren, Hollie and Sarah, then followed his wife's bed along the corridor to the recovery room.

Zander, still in the suit he'd worn last night, headed for the women sitting on the chairs behind him.

Hollie stared up at him as he walked towards her, eyes wide, hair ruffled, tear streaks down her face.

He leaned down, hugged Mirren, kissed her cheek, told her he loved her. He did. He had never been more grateful than he felt right now.

Sarah stood up, put her hands on the arms of Mirren's wheelchair. 'Come on, I'll get you back downstairs. Lou will be causing havoc by now.'

Not the most subtle departure, but Zander appreciated it.

And then there were two of them – him and Hollie – in an empty room.

'I learned something tonight,' he said.

For the first time ever, Hollie didn't have a smart-arse retort, so he continued, incredibly calmly, sure of what he needed to say, even if he wasn't sure how to say it.

'When I almost kissed you at the ranch, it was spontaneous. In the moment. A reflex.'

Hollie nodded sadly. 'I know.'

'And I'm sorry. Impulse control has never been my strong point.'

'I know that too. It's OK, Zander – you don't need to say it. It's gone. I knew then what it meant, and I know now too.'

'You don't.'

'What?'

He totally broke the moment by laughing. 'Hollie, I swear you don't know everything.'

'I do,' she retorted automatically.

'I love you.'

'I know that,' she said, softer now, like a friend reassuring another.

'No, Hollie...' He was getting exasperated. 'I actually love you.'

Their eyes were locked now, hers questioning, his hoping. 'Zander, I can't. I know you too well. This will pass, like everything else. Like the booze. Like the pills. Like Adrianna fricking Guilloti. We need to talk about her, by the way, but that's not the point. Things come and go with you, Zander. It's your nature. It's who you are. I can't come and go.' Her voice cracked. 'I just can't.'

He reached over, put his hand on the side of her face, wiped away the tear that was falling there.

'Hollie, tonight with Lex, I watched him suffer because he thought he could lose Cara and I realised the one person I couldn't lose was you. It's not a craving, or an obsession, or the need for a fix. I just love you. And not as a friend. As you.'

He leaned forward, kissed her, and breathed again when he felt her arms go around his neck. Eventually, her mouth left his as she pulled him into an embrace.

'Zander,' she whispered in his ear.

'What?'

'I love you.'

'You do?' he teased.

'I do. But if you fuck this up, I'll kill you.'

A passing nurse couldn't help but glance at the couple on the chairs who were laughing and crying at the same time. He looked like that guy from the movies. Just another day in a hospital.

'Listen, I want to go down and see Davie. Is that OK? I didn't want to leave Lex before, so I haven't looked in on him.'

Hollie stood up, reached for his hand. 'Sure.'

The elevator had gone down three floors by the time she spoke. 'I don't know if I can do this strong, silent stuff all the time, Zander.'

'Sorry. What do you want to talk about?'

'Nothing. Tell me you love me again.'

'I love you.'

'Excellent,' she quipped. 'At least once an hour, please. You don't have to say anything else. I'll get by on that.'

They made their way down the corridor, their broad grins out of place in the tension-loaded atmosphere of a busy ward.

They didn't care.

'That's Davie's room,' Hollie told them as they approached a door on the right. She let Zander go first, pausing to answer her cell phone. 'Hey, Mark. Yeah, he's just here...'

Zander pushed open the door.

Hollie suddenly sounded agitated. 'What? She didn't...? What guy...? Mark, I'm not getting this. So who planted the bomb, then...? Zander, stop!'

Too late. He froze. Unable to comprehend what he was seeing in front of him.

A bed, a figure on it, Davie... Yeah, it was Davie. Standing over him, a cop, staring down, pushing down. Why the fuck was he doing that? A pillow. Over Davie's face. Davie's legs kicking under the sheet, his body twisting, then slowing, then...

Zander was across the room in a split second. He threw himself over the bed, took the cop out in a flying tackle. Hollie screamed. Screamed. Screamed.

The two men hit the floor, Zander on top, wrestling, got to his knees. He was stronger, fitter. He was punching now, punching the cop's face, pummelling it, the adrenalin calling the shots.

Then he was being dragged, kicking, shouting, dragged off a cop by two others.

And he had no idea what the fuck had just happened.

65

'Creep' – Radiohead

Payback.
　Retribution.
　Justice.
　He took her away. My Lauren. My love. My soulmate. She was everything.
　We'd made promises that we'd be together.
　Davie Johnston made her a star. Took her into his galaxy and out of mine. He stole her.
　And then she didn't want me. My Lauren didn't want me.
　Mine.
　She was mine. He took her.
　So he had to pay.

66

'Starting Over' – John Lennon

Every seat around the kitchen table at the Callaghans' ranch was taken: on one side, Davie and Sarah, Zander and Hollie, Lou and Mark Bock; on the other side, Mirren, Brad Bernson, Lex and Cara.

Sarah held a huge mug of coffee in both hands. 'How's Logan doing?' she asked Mirren.

'Great. He's back on tour. Europe. I think he's in Rome today.'

'And Lauren?' Hollie asked.

'She's with him. Poor girl. That's a whole lot of baggage to deal with.'

The others fell silent until Davie turned to face Mark Bock. 'What's happening with the case, Mark?'

'That's why Brad and I came up to see you folks today. We wanted to give you an update. Gary Bitner confessed to everything that happened to you, Davie. As you know, he was a cop, had been Lauren Finney's boyfriend for six years before she went on *American Stars*.

'When she left him, it triggered some kind of psychosis. He stalked both her and Davie. The house fire, the shots, the first attack outside the studio –

all him. He also planted the bomb in the car, but that didn't work out so well. He took a decommissioned device from evidence storage, got some ex-con he'd arrested on arson charges to rebuild it. It failed to detonate the way he planned. Fired backwards, ripped the metal off the trunk of your car and hit the front of the limo Lex and Cara were in. Sorry, Cara.'

Cara dismissed it with a wave of her hand, the other hand automatically going to the dressing that was attached to the front of her neck. 'It's fine. I'm here. I'll get over it.'

The others had no doubt she would.

'Carlton Farnsworth and his bodyguard were arrested this morning. Raymo Cash rolled on him. Zander, we don't have all the answers on that yet, but it looks like it was set up to discredit you.'

'I think he needed Zander out of Adrianna's life,' Hollie offered. 'They were a weird, messed-up couple. She'd had flings before, but I think this time he thought he could lose her to Zander. Thought he couldn't match him.'

'He clearly didn't know me well,' Zander said, injecting some self-deprecation into the mix.

'And Marilyn?' Mirren asked. 'Why was she there? If she didn't plant the bomb, what was she doing there?'

'We searched her hotel room. She had pictures of you, hundreds of them, Logan too. She'd clearly been outside your house, your office. The bag she was carrying that night? After the blast, it ended up being confetti, all over the street. We think it was a manuscript. Impossible to tell, but she had piles of notes in her room too. In her suitcase, we found a contract and looked into it. Marilyn had a book deal. Seven figures. Me, My Daughter, Murder was the title. That's all I can tell you.'

'That's it,' Mirren said sadly. 'She wanted us to know. She wanted to see all our faces when we found out she was writing a book about us. And I'm guessing she dredged up all kinds of stuff from the past in it.' Mirren didn't need to look at Zander, Sarah or Davie to know that they got the deeper meaning in that. Marilyn was going to tell the story of how Jono died. No doubt painting herself in a good light and blaming Mirren, maybe Zander and Davie too. At the very least, she'd say they hid the body. The scandal would have damaged, probably destroyed, their careers and put a whole lot of hurt and scandal out there for the world to feed on. Mirren emitted a hollow laugh. 'She'd have loved that. Could never resist an opportunity to cause pain.'

Brad handed over a briefcase that had been sitting at his feet.

'It's all here. Everything. Laptop. Notes. No one else has seen it or has a copy.'

Mirren took it. Glanced at Davie, Zander, Sarah, then smiled. The two investigators took it as their cue to leave.

'If there's anything else we can do, you know where we are.'

'Thanks, gents,' Davie said, grinning. 'But I think we're done.'

EPILOGUE

'I'm Yours' – Ella Henderson

The sun was setting on the beach outside Mirren's home as she stared out over the sands.

Zander appeared beside her and handed her a glass of wine. 'You OK?'

'I am,' she smiled. And she was. She really was.

Two figures approached the back of the house from the sands, both tall, both broad, only their colouring different. Logan's white-blond hair a complete contrast to Mike Feechan's dark hair and skin.

He hadn't been happy that she'd moved to Lomax. When she'd recovered from the accident, he'd come to remonstrate with her for leaving Pictor. They'd stayed in bed for three days. A month later, he'd just about forgiven her.

'OK, get the party started – I'm here!' Lou bellowed from the doorway, before battling through the room saying hello to everyone as she passed.

'Davie Johnston, you owe me a huge favour!' she shouted to Davie, who was smooching Sarah over at the bar. Mirren had never seen him so happy. There was a peace about him, especially since he'd been spending time with Zander over the last few weeks. She's asked them if they'd ever tell the world that they were brothers, but they'd both said no. That would mean claiming Jono Leith as father to them both and neither of them ever wanted to mention his name again. It was enough that they knew they were brothers. That was all that mattered.

'Oh crap, what's happened?' Davie groaned.

'Carmella Cass. She's eloped with some guy she met in rehab. Says he's the love of her life. Used to be in some band – not sure which one, but apparently they're in the rock-and-roll hall of fame. Anyway, I've sent a camera crew to Vegas. We'll use the footage on our website and in the paper, but you can have it afterwards for the show.'

'Lou Cole, I love you,' he grinned.

'It's understandable, honey,' came the reply.

'So where's Jack?' Zander asked Mirren, taking the volume down a couple of notches.

'He's in India. Left last week. He's gone to find himself. Apparently Mercedes Dance is there helping with the search. She ditched the baby daddy when she realised he wasn't going to be the next Pacino or DeNiro or Leith. I can feel another show coming on.'

'For Christ's sake, don't tell Davie,' Zander joked, before breaking off to shake hands with the new arrivals, Lex and Cara Callaghan. Lex had lost a bit of weight – worry did that to a person. But the important thing was that other than a scar on her neck, Cara had made a full recovery.

'OK, people, hate to be the organizer here, but it's time. Can we all move outside?'

'Ready?' Zander asked.

'Ready,' Mirren replied.

They all moved out, gathered down at the water's edge in a semicircle. Mirren in the middle, Zander and Hollie standing nearby.

Lauren Finney lifted up her guitar and sang a mesmerising, ethereal version of Barbara Streisand's Evergreen. A single tear ran down her cheek as she finished and Mirren reached over and squeezed her hand. She loved this young woman already. The poor girl had been wracked with guilt over the actions of her ex-boyfriend, but Davie had been great with her. He'd sat by her side, held her hand at every interview, controlled the narrative to make sure everyone knew that Lauren had been a victim of this psycho too. And he acted innocent when the resulting publicity added another half a million viewers to the last few episodes of *American Stars*. Gotta love a man that knew how to work this town.

Mirren took a deep breath. She could do this. She could. 'Thank you all for coming tonight,' she said. 'As you know, this is the most special place in the world to me... And to Zander.'

Tears sprang to the eyes of several of the people around her.

Mirren smiled and lifted her chin. Now wasn't the time for looking back. Today was about looking forward.

'And as you also know, I'm new to this, so please bear with me.'

Mirren pulled out a sheet of paper from the pocket of her white trousers. 'Zander, Hollie...' She reached for them, gently pulled them towards her so they were facing each other.

'Zander Leith, with the powers invested in me by an ordination website...'

Laughter.

'Do you take Hollie Callan to be your lawfully wedded wife, to have and to hold her, to love her, adore her and be faithful to her always?'

'*Always*, the lady said,' Hollie repeated for emphasis. 'That means forever.'

'I do,' Zander said, laughing.

'And, Hollie Callan, do you take Zander Leith as your lawfully wedded husband, to have and to hold, to love, to cherish, to keep on the straight and narrow and out of trouble... Always?'

'Yes. Yes, I fricking do.'

'Then I now pronounce you man and wife.'

And the applause thundered on.

ACKNOWLEDGMENTS

From Ross

To my sister Elaine, Jim, Hollie and Euan. You all know how much you mean to me.

Thanks to the brilliant Ross and King Clans and all my best pals... you know who you are!

Thanks to my long-suffering assistant Moriah Hart for not only listening to my crazy ideas, but for patiently listening to me recording the audio versions over many hours.

Finally, thank you to those people who believed in me from back in the day, especially Paul Cooney for giving me that first job in radio at 16, and to YOU reading now for supporting my career in radio, TV, theatre, film and now in print!

From Shari

I got lucky. Thank you to my love, John Low, for doing life with me for the last thirty years. The family we've built is everything. Gemma, Callan, Brad, and now, our gorgeous little Myla, I heart you all.

To the incredible friends who are never far from my kitchen table, thank you for the laughs, the drama and the caramel wafers.

And with heartfelt gratitude to the journalists, booksellers, bloggers and readers who have shown such support for my books over the last two decades.

And from us both...

Thank you to the brilliant team at Boldwood Books. We love our new home and we're so thankful to every single person who plays a part in the process that starts with our words and ends with our books in readers' hands.

And special thanks to the always effervescent Seamus Lyte, for managing us in a way only he can!

Love, Shari & Ross xxxx

MORE FROM SHARI LOW AND ROSS KING

We hope you enjoyed reading *The Catch* If you did, please leave a review.

If you'd like to gift a copy, this book is also available as an ebook, digital audio download and audiobook CD.

Sign up to Shari Low and Ross King's mailing list for news, competitions and updates on future books.

https://bit.ly/ShariLowRossKing

Explore more glamorous, thrilling fiction from Shari Low and Ross King:

Boldwood

Boldwood Books is an award-winning fiction publishing company seeking out the best stories from around the world.

Find out more at www.boldwoodbooks.com

Join our reader community for brilliant books, competitions and offers!

Follow us
@BoldwoodBooks
@BookandTonic

Sign up to our weekly deals newsletter

https://bit.ly/BoldwoodBNewsletter

Lightning Source UK Ltd.
Milton Keynes UK
UKHW041819140223
416957UK00002B/5